Easter
at
The Lakes

Sara Hylton

St. Martin's Press
New York

Library of Congress Cataloging-in-Publication Data

Hylton, Sara.
    Easter at The Lakes / Sara Hylton. – 1st U.S. ed.
      p. cm.
    ISBN 0-312-20535-X
    I. Title.
PR6058.Y63E27   1999
823'.914—dc21

                        99-15492
                            CIP

First published in Great Britain by Judy Piatkus (Publishers) Ltd.

First U.S. Edition: August 1999

10 9 8 7 6 5 4 3 2 1

Chapter One

Cornelius Harvey was the youngest of eight brothers and four sisters and they were a family of sheep farmers on the Cumberland fells. His father and older brothers worked on the fells, his mother and sisters occupied themselves around the farm, cooking, cleaning and caring for a variety of livestock. Cornelius had decided at a very early age that he was not destined to be a sheep farmer.

He attended the village school where the rest of his brothers and sisters received a modest education, but Cornelius was the clever one. He enjoyed all the subjects his brothers scorned to learn but his father obstinately refused to allow him to take his education further. He was a sheep farmer, he was wanted on the land, education was not for such as he.

He left school at twelve and was sent out with his brothers to tend the sheep, but Cornelius was more often to be found sitting on some hill or other with his books, a fact that earned his father's displeasure and the ridicule of the rest of them.

Cornelius was a dreamer. When he looked across the lake to the mountains beyond, he built a castle in his imagination, resplendent with turrets and battlements, a castle with tall mullioned windows surrounded by gardens and which could only be reached by boat from the other side of the lake. He told nobody about his dream but he never forgot it, not even when his father in desperation decided he should go to live in Lancashire with his uncle who had a responsible job in a cotton mill and who had assured him he would be able to find work for Cornelius.

They all saw him off from the country station. He was wearing his Sunday best clothes and carried a small valise in his hand and a package filled with the sandwiches his mother had made that morning. But it was only his mother who shed tears at the sight of her youngest son's small figure climbing up into the train. The only thing Cornelius cried for was the loss of his imaginary castle across the lake.

His aunt and uncle lived in a row of small terraced houses with tidy front gardens and lace-hung bow windows. His aunt was into church bazaars and singing in the church choir. His uncle was the chief clerk in Thomas Masters' cotton mill, the largest and certainly the most lucrative in the small cotton town.

He ruled the small office staff with justice and dedication. Sitting on his high stool at a desk where he could look at the rest of the staff and supervise whatever they were doing, from the girl on the telephone switchboard to the boy who made the tea. Dark-suited and with his iron-grey hair well plastered down, in keeping with his waxed moustache he was an imposing figure, tall and thin; his scrawny neck emerging from his spotless winged collar gave him the look of an inquisitive turkey. Duly impressed, Cornelius believed him to be a man of some importance and one to emulate.

As the chief clerk's nephew he was found work but he was shown no favouritism. He was to start on the factory floor sweeping up and doing any other menial task that could be found, tasks that were many and varied.

He accepted them cheerfully, so cheerfully that the factory owner saw him everywhere. In the loading bays, on the factory floor, sweeping the aisles and knocking in nails, indeed everywhere where he could be seen to be cheerfully employed, and eventually Thomas Masters made enquiries about the lad who was everywhere. When he learned that Cornelius was his chief clerk's nephew he kept him in mind for eventual promotion.

Cornelius learned well. He grew in stature and knowledge and when the Masters occupied their family pew in the church of Saint Mary, Cornelius could be seen singing in the choir alongside his aunt, his musical baritone adding a great deal of lustre to the choir in general.

Thomas Masters was not the only member of his family to be impressed with the cheerful handsome young chorister. Clarissa Masters did not lack for suitors. An only child, she was a prize greatly to be coveted by every wealthy family in the area with up and coming sons. Clarissa was pretty, but more than that, she had a will of her own.

She regarded the young men who courted her with a great deal of indulgence tempered with suspicion. She knew what they were about. Her mother despaired when she treated them with high-handed frivolity. She advised her daughter to be serious, that they were the elite of the county and hardly warranted her light-hearted attitude, but her father was considerably more astute. Oh, they danced well and conversed with easy charm but they preferred the hunting field to the factories that had made money for their families, and he hadn't worked hard all his life to see his daughter hand it on a plate to one of these feckless but charming young followers. What would happen to the mills in the hands of any one of them? He took it upon himself to drop the occasional word about the enterprising young man whom he had promoted into a managerial position at the mill, even suggesting that he be invited to dinner one evening in the company of his aunt and uncle, the chief clerk and his wife.

Mrs Masters did not see the necessity. Men had been promoted before without the need for them to be entertained to dinner, but Clarissa smiled and Thomas Masters departed for his office well satisfied.

The meal did not start well. Mrs Masters was decidedly frosty, Cornelius's aunt and uncle a little overcome with awe at the vast luxurious rooms and the lavishness of the meal provided for them, but as the meal progressed Mrs Masters and Mrs Harvey discovered a mutual interest in the approaching rendering of *The Messiah* by the church choir, Mr Masters and Mr Harvey talked business and across the table, Cornelius and Clarissa smiled into each other's eyes and fell in love.

Mr Masters was well pleased with the results of his machinations, even when his spouse was rather less enthusiastic, but as the summer progressed the young couple were walking out. They were happy in each other's company and they discovered they had a lot in common in spite of their different upbringing.

In the end even Mrs Masters had to agree that they were eminently suited and Clarissa was happy.

There were many who said it couldn't possibly last, and others who thought they were in with a chance. Even on their wedding day the congregation were divided between those who looked at the young couple through rose-coloured glasses and the others who thought she was throwing herself away on a young man who had come from nowhere and besides, who were his family and what sort of money did he have?

Clarissa neither knew nor cared.

Not to be hurried, Mr Masters made sure that his new son-in-law deserved his promotion but he saw for himself that his daughter was happy in the small stone cottage they had bought them for a wedding present at the edge of the town. Cornelius worked hard. He was never late, always willing and eager to learn more and then the children began to arrive, a son Leonard first followed two years later by their daughter Josephine.

Dutifully, every summer Cornelius took his wife and children to see his parents and it was there he introduced them to the view across the lake and told them of his dream that one day he would build a house there and instead of the draughty old farmhouse they would spend the summer holidays there.

Clarissa was indulgent. It was a dream, something a lonely boy had nurtured in place of a life he hated, but when she looked at his earnest dedicated expression she began to realise that he really meant it.

'What will you call your dream house?' she asked gently.

'I haven't found a name for it yet, but I will,' he answered her.

'But how will you get to it, will you have to sail across the lake?'

3

'There's a narrow lane on the other side of the lake, one day I shall turn it into a road, but it's prettier to cross the lake.'

'Then you'll need a boat,' she pointed out.

'That will be no problem, the fishermen have boats.'

For the rest of the year Clarissa forgot about the dream house, but Cornelius never did. He saved every penny he could from overtime he put in at the mill and then unexpectedly his father-in-law suffered a heart attack. He recovered and decided they would retire to Southport which was flat and with a reasonably mild climate and Cornelius became master of the mill.

They moved into the Masters mansion and Josie went to a private school for girls and Leonard was enrolled at Marlborough College. That was the year an army of builders descended upon the Lakeland village, much to the consternation of those who lived there, and particularly Cornelius's family.

Nothing happened quickly. Permission had to be sought from the local landowner who was reluctant to give it, even when Cornelius explained that it would bring employment to the area. His family thought the idea preposterous and even before the first stone was laid it became known as Harvey's Folly.

The builders came and went as one obstacle after another arose, and then miraculously in nineteen-twelve the dream became a reality and work was begun on the house.

Cornelius knew what he wanted. A stone house with turrets and battlements like a castle he had once seen in a storybook, a castle adorned with Virginia creeper and with gardens sweeping down to the lakeside.

The façade was already built to his satisfaction when war started and the entire scheme had to be shelved because the builders were called up for National Service and there were higher things at stake than the building of a dream.

When Clarissa expressed her opinion that the house would never be completed, Cornelius merely smiled, saying all they needed was patience. The war would not last forever and the mill was making so much money the finished product would be more luxurious than they had even dreamed it would be.

Leonard left Marlborough in the summer of nineteen-seventeen and went immediately into the army, six months later he was killed on the Marne and his death lamentably changed Clarissa into a sad and bitter woman who never completely recovered from it. She had no patience with talk of the house, she would never go there even if he went on with it. It was to have been a place for the family and Leonard was dead and Josie was intent on becoming a nurse in some remote part of Africa.

Cornelius went alone to see his parents in the autumn and stood for a long while looking across the lake at the façade of his dream castle. The Virginia creeper covered the stones lovingly in flaming red and it looked achingly

4

beautiful, but instead of the garden the weeds ran riot through the screes and moss covered the winding pathway from the lake to the house. Time passed, the seasons came and went and the Harvey family scattered. The old people died, the young people married and had families of their own and in time the villagers ceased to talk about Harvey's folly and it was no longer an acute embarrassment to the Harveys who continued to live in the vicinity.

Cornelius and his wife in their turn retired to live in Cheshire and the cotton mill was absorbed into a combine as so many other cotton mills met a similar fate.

Cornelius never forgot his dream castle even when his wife never mentioned it. To Clarissa it became a reminder of what might have been, a beautiful idyll for them in their old age surrounded by their children and grandchildren, an idyll that ended on that morning they learned of Leonard's death, and so Cornelius allowed her to forget it as nothing more than a dream.

Neither of them were to know that it would be another war that would bring a young American back to England so that he could introduce his young bride to the things he had learned to love there. So it was that in the mid nineteen-fifties Mr and Mrs Julius Van Hopper were driving back from Scotland through the English Lake District.

They had spent their honeymoon on what had been a journey of nostalgia for Julius, a journey that he had taken alone before returning to America after the war was over.

At that time he had been enraptured with castles, Welsh, English and Scottish, and he had returned to Boston to fill his family's hearts and minds with stories of them, and eventually to encourage his bride that they should return to Europe so that she might see them also. It was early September, the weather had been glorious but now they were on their way back and this was the last stage of their journey. After three days in London they would be on their way back to America.

Less enchanted than her husband, Emily Van Hopper was not sorry to be returning to shops and cocktail lounges, she'd had a surfeit of country living and remote castles however romantic the setting.

Julius stared across the lake in amazement, bringing the car to an immediate stop and unfolding his map of the area. Emily groaned inwardly at the sight of the stone structure across the lake even when she had to admit that the setting was pretty, the building glowing with crimson creeper in the late afternoon sunlight.

'That's funny,' he said at last. 'There's no mention of it here but it's a castle all right. There must be somebody we can ask.'

'Perhaps it isn't important, dear, it's quite a small castle.'

'Well of course it's important, all castles are important. We'll drive on into the next village, somebody will be able to tell us.'

They had not gone far when they saw an old man walking along the road accompanied by his dog and Julius brought the car to a halt and got out.

He smiled affably, bidding the old man good afternoon and bending down to pat the dog. The old man looked up at him curiously and Julius said, 'I'm wondering if you can tell us anything about the castle on the other side of the lake there, I've looked in my guide book but I can't find any mention of it?'

The old man screwed up his eyes in the sunlight, a frown of concentration on his face.

'Castle,' he said. 'What castle?'

'Why, that one there, across the lake, the one with Virginia creeper all over it.'

The old man's face cleared and he chuckled.

'That beain't no castle, soir, that be 'Arvey's Folly.'

'Folly?'

'Ay. It were never finished. There's nobbut a front on it, there be nowt at the back.'

'You mean it's just a façade, that it was never finished, it isn't old?'

'Oh it's old enough. I reckon it were started soon after the first war but it were never finished.'

'Is there a road to it?'

'There be a narrow sort o' road at the other side o' the lake. Oi don't reckon much on it, not fer your car, soir.'

'How do we get to the road?'

'Ye drives back the way ye came and ye'll see a turn off to yer left, that be the lane. Mind you it's bumpy and 'ardly ever used. I wouldn't be botherin' if I were you, there's nowt to see except a lot o' stones and the back o' the buildin'.'

They stared at each other for a few minutes then Julius said, 'Thanks for your information anyway, I'll take a look at it, it might be some time before we're this way again.'

He returned to his car and the old man watched while they reversed into a gateway and drove back along the road.

What did anybody want to look at Harvey's Folly for? But then they were foreigners and foreigners could be guaranteed to do silly things, didn't they fill the shops every weekend and set out in all weathers to climb the fells and mountains. To old Nathanial Glover you were a foreigner if you lived ten miles over the border.

'We should do what the old man said,' Emily grumbled. 'The road looks like a dirt track and if the house has only a frontage there won't be anything to see.'

'I want to see it all the same. The place looked beautiful from across the lake, whoever thought of building it must have thought so too.'

'Why didn't he finish it then?'

'There was probably a very good reason. Perhaps we can find out.'

She had only been his wife for a few days but she'd known him most of her life and she knew when he got an idea into his head he was like a dog with a bone, he'd never let it rest. The shops and the atmosphere of their London hotel became a remote possibility, something he would shelve until he'd exhausted every enquiry about the crumbling castle.

The lane was bumpy and there were places hardly wide enough to accommodate the car but the determination on her husband's face spoke volumes.

Emily sat in the car watching him climbing over the rubble the builders had left behind. It had rained during the night and his feet slid in the mud-soaked weeds before he stood looking up at the building above him. Windows that looked out across the lake but windows that hid no rooms, and doorways that led out from one wilderness into another.

He picked his way carefully to where the building ended and he could make his way to the front where he could gaze across the lake and look up at the empty windows almost hidden by Virginia creeper and in that moment he felt the same sort of elation Cornelius Harvey had felt but for entirely different reasons.

Cornelius had seen it as a home, a place for his family to be happy in. Julius saw it as an investment, a money spinner like all the other hotels his father and grandfather before him had erected in different parts of the world.

Emily did not miss the look of satisfaction on his face as he took his place next to her in the car. He reversed carefully onto the narrow road but his thoughts were miles away, and unable to stand it any longer she cried, 'Well, what are you thinking about that old ruin?'

He smiled. 'It might look like an old ruin now, my girl, but it won't by the time I've finished with it.'

'You surely don't intend to do anything with it?'

'We'll see. First of all I've got to find out where the owner lives and if he'll see me. We'll book in at that hotel in the village for the night, surely somebody around here will be able to tell us more.'

'But we can't stay here,' Emily protested. 'We're booked in in London, we were on our way there. Really, Julius, you can make your enquiries from there, I'm tired and I don't want to spend another night in some poky hotel miles from anywhere.'

'Just one more night, honey, then we'll head south. It could be a very comfortable hotel.'

The Black Bull hotel was unused to American visitors arriving unannounced in the late afternoon and Emily looked around her in some dismay. A few red cinders burned in the dark grate and the room was depressingly dark as they waited for the landlord to attend to them.

'We'd like to stay for just one night,' her husband explained. 'Can you give us a decent room and dinner, then there's one or two questions I'd like to be asking you.'

'I'll get me wife to get a room ready,' the landlord said. American visitors spent well and tipped well and it could be they had relatives in the area. He suggested they sit near the fire and he'd see they had a cup of tea, and before they could agree he hurried over to the fireplace and shovelled coal onto the fire.

Avoiding his wife's eyes, Julius said, 'Well, it's not so bad, love. I'll talk to one or two of the locals later on and hopefully in the morning we can get off to see the chap who owns the land.'

Tea was served with hot buttered muffins by a rosy-cheeked country girl and by this time the fire had come to life and was blazing happily in the grate. Julius poured the tea while his wife sulked, but by the time the landlady had appeared to show them up to their room she felt considerably warmer and less truculent.

In spite of her fears the room was charming. A white-walled room with low oak rafters and with a rich Wilton carpet on the floor and long velvet drapes at the window. A fire had been lit and the landlady said, 'These autumn evenings can get cold, and there's an electric blanket on the bed, The bathroom's next door, I hopes you'll be very comfortable.'

'I'm sure we shall be,' Julius said opening the door for her, and when he returned Emily was sitting on the bed to test its resilience.

'Well,' he said smiling. 'It couldn't have been any better than this in London and we wouldn't have been getting there until midnight at the very least. Here we'll get a good meal and a good night's sleep. You have to admit it's very pleasant.'

Emily agreed that it wasn't too bad.

They were served an excellent meal in the dining room after which Julius stated his intention of joining the locals in the bar so Emily said in some degree of annoyance that she would retire to bed to read her book.

He quickly learned that the landlord and his wife had only occupied the hotel for just over two years so were hardly likely to know much about Harvey's Folly. When he mentioned it however, the landlord said, 'Ask old Joe, he's well on ninety and he's lived in these parts all his life. He knows everybody, what their jobs were, if they had any money or not, and who they married.'

'Is he guaranteed to come in here?' Julius asked.

'Allus round about nine o'clock. 'E usually comes in with his youngest son and his grandson. They allus sits over there near the fireplace, you can't miss 'im. 'E wears a red woolly 'at and usually 'as 'is lurcher dog with him.'

The locals appeared in dribs and drabs and Julius made himself affable by buying drinks and talking about the countryside. Promptly at nine, three men came into the bar, an old man wearing a red woollen cap, two other men with him neither of them in their first youth and a disreputable grey lurcher dog. They went to sit near the fire and the landlord winked knowingly in Julius's direction.

The bar was rapidly filling up with people so Julius sidled round to where the three men were sitting and asked if he might join them. They moved closer together, eyeing him doubtfully, but when he asked if he might buy them a drink they became considerably more affable even to enquiring where he had come from.

'I'm from Boston in the U.S.A.,' he explained smiling. 'I was over here during the war and I've brought my good lady back to see the things I liked looking at, castles and the like.'

'Oh ay, yer'll find plenty o' them i' Scotland and other parts o' the country,' the youngest man said agreeably.

'We've been all over the place, Wales too but not Ireland, we're saving that for another time. I was interested in your castle just along the lane there.'

They looked at each other with the same sort of surprise the old man had exhibited on the road. Old Joe was the first to speak.

'There beain't no castles round 'ere,' he affirmed.

'I'm interested in the one they call Harvey's Folly.'

They chuckled in unison.

'That's nobbut a ruin, it were never finished, I can never understand why they just didn't take it down.'

'It's in a very beautiful spot, if it was finished it could be worthwhile.'

For several seconds they stared at him speechless then the youngest man said, 'Do ye mean you'd like to live in it?'

'Shall we just say I'm very interested. How can I get hold of the man who owns the land and started to build it?'

'That be young Cornelius,' Joe said. ''E never wanted to be a sheep farmer, did well i' cotton 'e did but where 'e is now I don't know.'

'But he must have members of his family living around here.'

'Well the old folk are long gone and the younger folk scattered throughout the Dales. There be 'Enry. 'E's the eldest, lives with 'is wife at Crag End Farm at the top o' the fell.'

'You think he might know where his brother is living?'

''E moight though they've never bin close, that's because Cornelius went away when 'e were a lad and never came back except to visit.'

'I'll call to see them in the morning. Now can I buy you all another drink?'

They accepted the drink and he bade them goodnight. After he had gone they sat shaking their heads. Whoever in their right mind would be interested in Harvey's Folly, just an old ruin across the lake, why even Cornelius had abandoned it. In the meantime Julius was informing his wife that they would call to see the Harveys on their way out of the village and Emily fervently hoped that would be the end of the matter.

Chapter Two

The winding muddy road up to Crag End Farm was pitted with holes filled with water and the big car slithered and lurched until Emily felt convinced they would come to a halt miles from anywhere and that only a tractor would get them out.

Silently Julius agreed with her but at last they could see across the fell a stone house surrounded by a stone wall and several sheds. From the lane it looked almost derelict but as they got closer they could see smoke rising from one of the chimneys and a procession of ducks waddling towards the pond.

'Well at least there's somebody living there,' Emily said caustically.

'You stay in the car and keep warm, honey,' he advised her, easing himself out of the driving seat.

There was no knocker on the stout wooden door so he had to hammer on it with his fist and was rewarded several minutes later when he heard footsteps crossing what he thought was a flagged floor. The door opened on squeaky hinges and a large florid-faced woman stood staring at him.

He raised his hat and smiled.

'I'm sorry to bother you, but are you Mrs Harvey?'

'That I am.'

'My name is Julius Van Hopper and I'm an American from Boston. I hope you can help me, I'm wanting to get in touch with Mr Cornelius Harvey and I believe he's your brother-in-law.'

She stared at him stolidly without speaking and his heart sank. He could feel his smile becoming strained as he looked at her expressionless face and he looked round helplessly at his wife's frozen features in the front seat of the car.

He was about to apologise again for troubling her before turning away when she said, 'We 'aven't seen Cornelius since mi father-in-law's funeral, are you a friend of 'is?'

'No, we've never met, but I do want to see him on business.'

'Ah see,' she said. 'Well all we get is a Christmas card but there's probably an address on that. Yer'd best come in out o' the cold.'

He looked at his wife, shrugging his shoulders and Mrs Harvey said, 'Is that yer wife sittin' in the car?'

'Yes.'

'Well she'd best come in too or she'll freeze to death out there. There's a cold wind blowin' across the fells this mornin'.'

He went to the car to open the door hissing, 'She wants us to go into the farm, we shan't be long, Emily.'

'I'm quite all right sitting here.'

'She's invited us in, we don't want to appear unsociable.'

They were agreeably surprised when they entered the living room where a warm fire burned in the stone fireplace and Emily looked appreciatively at thick oak beams on the ceiling and potted geraniums on the deep window ledges. There was a patterned carpet on the flag floor and a deep pile rug in front of the fire as well as several well-cushioned armchairs.

'I'll make ye a cup o' tea,' Mrs Harvey said, and in spite of their protests that she shouldn't bother she went into the kitchen and they could hear the sound of crockery before she reappeared with a tray on which resided the largest fruit cake they had ever seen.

'Now,' Mrs Harvey said, 'if yer'll just 'elp yerselves I'll see if I can find last year's Christmas cards. We allus keeps 'em until the next lot arrive.'

Both the tea and the cake were excellent and they both mellowed in the warm⟨t⟩ and comfort of the room. They could hear her upstairs, opening and closing drawers and then at last they heard her feet descending the stairs and she came back into the room carrying a large Christmas card in her hands. She handed it to him saying, 'They must spend a small fortune on Christmas cards, theirs is allus the biggest we get.'

'It's a very beautiful card,' Julius admitted.

'I 'ardly knows 'em miself. They've 'ardly ever come 'ere and after work finished on the Folly out there they neither of 'em ever came back.'

Julius surveyed the printed address on the card, a place in Cheshire he had never heard of.

'I don't know this place,' he said doubtfully. 'Have you any idea where it is?'

'South o' Manchester mi 'usband sez, though we've neither of us bin there. I'm sure yer'll find it if ye gets to Manchester.'

He thanked her warmly saying, 'We're on our way to London but I'm sure Manchester won't be a great deal out of our way.'

She was eyeing them shrewdly, expecting him to say more but at this stage there was nothing more to say, so they thanked her again for her hospitality and she stood at her front door until they drove out of the farmyard and along the tortuous lane.

'I want to get to London today and at a reasonable hour,' Emily said adamantly.

'It's not much out of our way, love, I'm sure,' Julius answered quickly. 'We will get to London, we can have a meal on the way. This man can only say yes or no to my wanting to buy his land.'

After several enquiries in different locations they were told they need not go through Manchester but could reach the village in Cheshire quite easily. The fact that it was a small rural village meant they did not have to search long for Cornelius Harvey's abode and soon after noon they were knocking on the front door of a large mellow brick house in what Emily thought was a decidedly pretty village. There was a stone church with a spire that seemed to soar ostentatiously over the cluster of houses that made up the village, and an olde worlde inn sporting windowboxes filled with geraniums.

An elderly lady opened the door to them dressed in a tweed skirt and pale blue twin set and they saw immediately that she was wearing gardening gloves and carrying a garden rake.

Julius smiled. 'I can see we're interrupting your gardening,' he said. 'Are you Mrs Harvey?'

'Yes.'

'Is it possible to see your husband, Mr Cornelius Harvey?'

She stared at them curiously before saying, 'My husband is in the greenhouse, does he know you?'

'No, but I have just come down from Cumberland and I'm interested in some land he owns there. If he would just spare me a few minutes I'm sure he would be interested in what I have to say. My name is Julius Van Hopper and this is my wife. We are Americans, from Boston, New England.'

She opened the door wider inviting them in.

'Perhaps you'll wait in here and I'll tell my husband,' she said, showing them into a room at the front of the house, inviting them to sit in front of the fire.

'What a lovely room,' Emily enthused, 'and how nice to see a fire, the days are growing chilly.'

Mrs Harvey smiled. 'Yes indeed, I thought it was quite cold this morning.'

After she had gone Emily said astutely, 'They don't seem short of money, he'll not need to sell you that land to boost his income.'

'I just want him to give me a hearing, he can't refuse to do that.'

Emily looked round at the pictures on the walls and the ornaments tastefully displayed on burr walnut while Julius stood looking through the window, his impatience growing by the minute.

Recognising it his wife said, 'Perhaps he won't see you, after all he doesn't know you.'

Julius didn't answer. All he was aware of was the silence in the house and the sound of birdsong from the garden outside. After what seemed an age they heard the closing of a door from somewhere in the house and the light clatter of a woman's footsteps crossing the hall outside. The door opened and Mrs Harvey said, 'My husband has been working in the greenhouse all morning, he's just cleaning up before he comes in here. Would you like a cup of tea?'

'Well we don't want to be any trouble, Mrs Harvey.'

'It's no trouble at all. I was going to make one anyway for my husband and myself.'

'We'll never get to London today at this rate,' Emily grumbled after she'd left but Julius had cheered up considerably. It would seem Cornelius Harvey had decided to meet him.

Cornelius arrived at the same time as the tea. Julius had always prided himself on being a fair judge of human nature but in those first few moments he was quite unable to assess whether his host would be amenable or not. Cornelius had one of those grave unsmiling faces that refused to let the world know what he was thinking, and he listened to Julius's enthusiasm for the land across the lake and his ambitions for it without disclosing whether he was remotely interested, so much so that Julius's words faltered to a close and his wife said, 'I really don't think Mr Harvey is in the least interested, dear, why don't we just apologise for wasting their time and get off to London?'

Julius looked across at the Harveys ruefully, but Mrs Harvey said with a smile, 'He's always like this, I never know what he's thinking and I've been married to him for more years than I like to think of.'

Hope revived and Julius said, 'As soon as I saw that place across the lake I fell in love with it. I thought it was some old castle but the natives soon put me right.'

'Ay they would,' Cornelius answered. 'I can understand somebody wanting to build a house there, even finish the one I started, but I can't see some hotel going up there.'

'Why ever not?'

'A great monstrosity of a place would destroy the beauty of it, besides there's no road to speak of and the folk who live round there would have none of it.'

'I'm not in the business of building monstrosities, Mr Harvey. My family have been in the hotel business for a great many years, we're well respected and we have hotels in some of the most beautiful places in the world. If I build a place on that site it will be as beautiful as anything you had envisaged and as for the natives having none of it they'd be fools. There would be employment for a great many of them and trade for their shops.'

Cornelius didn't speak and in some desperation Julius said, 'Do you ever visit the place, if only for sentimental reasons?'

'We never visit,' Mrs Harvey said. 'It was my husband's boyhood dream that one day he would build his little place there, the dream never came to anything.'

'But you made a start, why did you abandon it?'

'Our lives changed. Our son was killed in the first world war, our daughter went abroad and she now lives in Australia. Cornelius was never close to the rest of his family so you see there really is nothing for us any more in that part of the world.'

'But there could be. You could stay at the hotel, at my expense anytime you pleased. You could realise your dream through me. Will you at least think about it?'

He extended his card which Cornelius looked at for several minutes before putting it down on the small table near his chair.

'We're flying back to Boston at the beginning of next week but we'll be in London until then. We're staying at the Savoy, you could reach me there or get in touch after I've arrived home. I'm very keen about this, Mr Harvey, my wife would tell you it's been a long time since I was so enthusiastic about anything. I hope when you do get in touch the answer is yes.'

'You haven't told me how much you are willing to pay for the land?'

'We can go into that when I know you'll be willing to part with it. Think what you can do with the money, a world cruise, travel anywhere and everywhere, all the things you ever dreamed of.'

'My wife and I have very adequate means, Mr Van Hopper.'

'I'm sure you have, but only a fool decides he has enough when there's considerably more on offer. I don't think you are a fool, Mr Harvey.'

Mr Harvey merely smiled, and after handshakes all round, Mrs Harvey was seeing her guests to the door.

As they drove away Emily said, 'She's a different sort of woman to the one we met this morning, I'm not surprised they never kept in touch.'

'I've got the strongest feeling that he won't budge,' Julius said feelingly. 'He's one of those unimaginative Englishmen who thinks as it was in the beginning is now and ever shall be. He won't be able to envisage an hotel in that spot and unusual people wandering around the village.'

'What will you do now then?'

'Let him stew for a few weeks, then when we get back to America I'll write to him again, send him a few brochures of our hotels to let him see the sort of places they are. If he doesn't take me up I suppose I'll have to forget it, but what a pity that will be.'

Julius was not to know that back in Cheshire Cornelius was echoing his words.

'I can't see some ritzy hotel going up in the village,' he said dourly. 'He'll turn the place into a circus, there'll be all sorts of citified folk with their big cars running around the place, the villagers will blame me for it.'

'Well that won't be any different, will it?' his wife said grimly. 'They've blamed you for years for Harvey's Folly, besides it's got nothing to do with the villagers. As it is it's a white elephant, you could be making money out of the land.'

'What do we want money for, we've more than enough for our needs.'

'We have for the way we live. We never travel, we don't even spend much time away from Cheshire. We could travel more, see something of the world, visit Australia to see Josie and her family.'

'They haven't shown much enthusiasm for visiting us, Clarissa.'

'I know, but we don't know how they're fixed, do we?'

'He'll probably go back to America and forget all about it, I doubt if we'll hear from him again.'

Clarissa didn't answer but she had her own ideas about Julius Van Hopper. He'd been enthusiastic, he'd seen something in that derelict property and she had the utmost conviction that they would hear from him again.

His letter arrived a month later, filled with encouragement and accompanied by a wad of glossy brochures in worldwide locations.

Her husband's face was uncompromising as he leafed through them and after several minutes she asked impatiently, 'Well, aren't you going to tell me what you think of them?'

'None of them are what I want for my house. They're glossy, fashionable places that are right enough for where they are, but I don't want them here, and the villagers will resent my even thinking about it.'

'Mr Van Hopper said he wouldn't change any of your ideas and I think he meant it. You don't know anything about his line of business, I think you should go into it a little further.'

He didn't reply, but several days later he and his wife decided they would take another look at the ruin across the lake. He walked alone to the edge of the lake and stared morosely across it at the Virginia Creeper-covered ruin, its turrets shining in the late afternoon sunlight. Sitting in their car his wife was well aware of the thoughts passing through his mind. He would not like the idea of an expensive hotel taking its place, and she got out of the car to join him.

Neither of them spoke and it was only when he turned away that she said, 'Cornelius, why don't you let it go? Look at it, it's a crumbling ruin, in a few years' time it could crumble into dust in one of the winter storms and it will stay there like a dead thing and your name will be the butt of every sarcastic tongue in the village.'

He didn't answer her immediately, and she prompted, 'What have you got against Mr Van Hopper's ideas?'

'If he'd wanted it for a nursing home, a school, anything but some posh hotel I'd have been more than willing to listen to him, it's the hotel I'm against.'

'But why? It would put the village on the map, famous people would come here, it could be a joy for so many people, it's doing nothing for anybody as it is.'

He turned away and she followed him. 'We'll drive up and see my brother and his wife then we'll make our way back. Don't say anything to them about the offer we've had.'

In Boston Julius Van Hopper's disbelief grew that he was being kept waiting while a glum unimaginative Englishman made up his mind. Weeks passed and he decided it was time he forgot about his plans for Harvey's Folly. His father had never been enthusiastic.

'When Americans go to England they go to Stratford-upon-Avon, to London and Windsor, they don't go to the Lake District, there are bigger lakes in this country and if they want to look at castles there are real ones to look at, not some crumbling imitation,' the old man said forcefully.

Emily agreed with him, but Julius had seen in that corner of England the same sort of beauty Cornelius had seen. He had realised its potential and when day followed day without a letter from England his disappointment grew. He received Cornelius' letter with stunned surprise rather than elation, and then to his wife's amazement he took the first plane he could get to England.

It had been a year since Julius had first seen Harvey's Folly, but by the end of September the builders moved in and all the area was agog with the news that an American was building a large hotel where it had once stood. There was plenty of condemnation, a great deal of excitement, and when the winter weather held up work for several weeks there were others who said it would never be finished.

Spring came early to the lakeland fells and now instead of a dirt track road on the other side of the lake a smooth macadam drive was being laid edged with conifers, rhododendron and azalea bushes, and on the other side of the lake the villagers congregated to watch progress. The façade was enlarged, entirely in keeping with Cornelius' ideas, and behind the façade the rest of the hotel was being erected.

Julius spent a great deal of time in the village. He stayed at the hotel in the main street and talked to the locals. He assured them it would be a great asset to the village, find employment for many of them, bring trade to the small shops, and his enthusiasm caught on until they too came to believe in it.

Cornelius and Clarissa were on their way to Australia.

In the summer Julius brought his father and his wife over to see what had been accomplished and although they came with bad grace they were quickly converted into the belief that Julius had created a winner.

'What are you going to call the place?' his wife asked curiously.

'Have you any ideas?' he asked, hoping to include her in something connected with the place.

'How about The Lakeside Hotel?'

'There's several with that name in the area near other lakes.'

'I think The Grand will be too smart.'

'I'd thought of that. I wondered about calling it The Lakes.'

Emily was doubtful. 'Don't you think that is a bit pretentious?' she argued.

'Not really. There'll be nothing in this part of England to touch it, nothing outside London, and nothing in London has the atmosphere of the lake and the mountains. By Christmas we'll be in business, honey, we'll advertise the opening and invite famous people.'

'At your expense, I suppose,' she added dourly.

'Well of course, a sprat to catch a mackerel.'

'Famous people want to be in the centre of things, in London where it's all happening.'

'Famous people want to rub shoulders with other famous people. We'll get them here, as well as other people simply looking for a degree of luxury and good service. We'll encourage the nobility, politicians, theatrical folk and you'll see, in no time everybody will be wanting to stay here.'

'Do you really think the villagers will make them welcome?'

Julius chuckled. 'Have you seen the shops in the village, Emily? They're already advertising local gingerbread and fudge, Kendal mint cake and Lakeland slate. I'm turning this little place into a potential gold mine, in fifty years they'll put up a statue to me in the high street.'

'They didn't do it for Cornelius Harvey.'

'Well of course not. His was a folly, mine's a success.'

'I wonder if he'll ever come to see it?' Emily mused.

'I've offered him a holiday free of charge, for him and his wife, his family too if they come over from Australia.'

'Do you think he'll take you up on it?'

'I'm not sure. He's a man who gives nothing away, a typical north country-man like so many of them around here. He got away when he was young, but nothing in his nature really changed.'

'But he said he was never one of them, all the villagers say so.'

'They're all wrong. He didn't want to be a sheep farmer, but he never got away from his roots. Now come along and tell me what you think of my ideas for the reception area.'

Chapter Three

By the end of November the hotel staff had been appointed. From local people were chosen gardeners and stable hands, chamber-maids, cleaners and maintenance workers. An army of Italian waiters arrived on the scene together with pretty receptionists and secretaries, telephonists and Spanish bartenders. There also arrived a Mr Anton de Roche who had been promoted from the large hotel in Paris to be manager of The Lakes.

Anton de Roche had spent his entire adult life in one hotel after another, rising dramatically from pageboy in Milan to Assistant Manager in Paris.

He was handsome, articulate and diplomatic. Julius regarded him as eminently suitable for his new position and although Anton was not entirely sure that he wanted to exchange the sophisticated delights of Paris for the countrified atmosphere of the English Lake District his views changed dramatically when he viewed its beauty from his bedroom window, and the luxury of the new hotel.

It would not be an easy life. He knew well the jealousies and clash of temperaments that existed between people of different nationalities, their anxieties, their passions and their jealousies and he had learned how to cope adequately without making favourites of any one of them. Then there were the foibles of the guests, their idiosyncrasies; stars with larger-than-life personalities, each one of them guarding fiercely their little place in the lime-light. Then there were the political animals, skilled and experienced in the art of political subterfuge and each one of them eager to use it to advance his or her career.

These were only the famous or would-be famous. There were too the ordinary men and women, each and every one of them seeking something, or hiding something. He had seldom come across a completely honest and ordinary individual. Perhaps he had not found one because the other sort were more interesting, but Anton de Roche was not convinced that they existed.

He poured himself a whisky and soda and looked into the mirror. His reflection showed him a tall, slender, immaculately-suited man with smooth silver hair, and tanned unlined face, whimsical, handsome and strangely immobile.

He knew the sort of show Julius Van Hopper would put on for the opening of the hotel at Christmas. It would be filled with celebrities who had not paid a penny for their board and lodging, but they would spend well in the bars and they would talk about it when they left.

The meals would be lavish, with a great deal of waste. The champagne would flow from breakfast to breakfast and there would be fireworks to light up the winter night. After that there would be dancing to an excellent orchestra until the early hours and there would be flowers in the bedrooms and chocolates on every pillow. The staff would be well tipped and would celebrate the festivities most royally on all that the guests could not eat. In the village across the lake Anton had no doubt families would be sitting down to venison and smoked salmon and other luxuries they had never dreamt of.

In the meantime there was work to be done. To familiarise himself with the rooms of the hotel, his staff and the pecking order of the invited guests. Who would occupy the best bedrooms, who would sit at the most prominent tables and who disliked whom so that they would keep a respectful distance at all times.

After Christmas it would all fall into place. The hotel would close in February so that it could be ready and waiting for the first guests just before Easter, and he would be able to journey forth for his annual holiday in the snows of Gstaad and then south to his beloved Italy.

The villagers were agog with talk of the hotel. They had stood and watched it grow from across the lake and now a great many of them were employed there. Girls arrived home with talk of sumptuous bedrooms with satin bedspreads and carpets their feet could sink into and the men talked about stables larger than the houses they lived in and garages large enough to accommodate a family.

There were those who shook their heads in disbelief and some degree of bitterness, but the shops were being painted and decorated, their window displays were announcing homemade Lakeland Ginger Cake and other homely delicacies, and in village kitchens the women were busy making shortbread, fruit loaves and brandy snaps.

Back at the hotel Julius Van Hopper rubbed his hands with glee. This would be no folly, this would be reality.

The villagers collected early at the edge of the lake on Christmas Eve. The frost had turned the trees and lanes into a shimmering fairyland. A thin film of snow sparkled across the grass and the lake was already freezing under a thin film of ice.

Across the lake the hotel was ablaze with light from every window and from one end of the terrace to the other lamps were lit and there were lights glowing from a giant conifer in the centre of a lawn. On the terrace itself there were tables holding drinks and glasses, and the women guests were wrapped in their furs, the men wearing long overcoats over their dinner jackets.

It was a perfect arctic night with a full moon in a dark blue cloudless sky ablaze with stars and gasps of delight exploded on the terrace and across the lake when the first rocket was launched into the sky, to fall in a shower of silver and gold onto the lake.

Most of the guests had seen it all before in some other corner of the world, but to the villagers it was all new and wonderful. Display followed display until the last firework soared into the heavens and then followed the applause and the laughter before the guests drifted into the warmth of the hotel and the villagers wandered back to their homes, their hearts and minds filled with all they had seen and chattering excitedly like schoolchildren.

'I think that's gone very well,' Julius said proudly to Anton, who smiled and agreed with him.

'I suppose everybody's turned up,' he added.

'Except for Gloria Weston and her escort.'

'Oh well she always makes a late entrance, probably around midnight.'

Anton smiled cynically. Gloria Weston attended everything, from the first night of her films to the opening of such an occasion as this one. She would arrive full of apologies that they had been delayed. Some of the guests would fawn over her, others would pointedly ignore her, it would not matter, there was always another function, another film, another escort waiting to offer his arms, and the man who would bring her tonight would disappear without a trace into oblivion.

The villagers huddled together in the warmth of the village inn with most of them discussing the hotel, its occupants and the firework display.

Old Joe maintained that in all his eighty-nine years had had seen nothing quite like it, but added gloomily that he didn't hold with all the foreigners descending on the village.

'You mark my words,' he said glumly, 'in no time at all they'll be parkin' their big motor cars along the 'igh street and there'll be no room for the rest o' us.'

'I've 'eard they're 'avin' a motor launch to bring guests across the lake,' another man said. 'That means they won't be bringin' their cars and there'll be trade for the village shops.'

'What sort o' trade?' another demanded. 'They won't be buyin' food, they'll be well fed at the 'otel, and what sort o' souvenirs are folk like that aimin' to buy?'

'Well we'll just 'ave to wait and see, won't we? Our Ruby's workin' there in the bedrooms and she says the hotel's goin' to close in February while it's made right for the spring.'

'Does that mean she'll be out o' work then?' another woman said.

21

'Not she. She'll be workin' 'arder than ever to make it fit for the new season's guests.'

'I'd like to be a fly on the wall over there,' Joe's son said with a grim smile. 'The booze'll be flowin' and the dancin'll go on til' mornin'.'

As Julius had predicted Gloria Weston arrived a few minutes before midnight accompanied by a man young enough to be her son.

Anton watched her entrance with world-weary eyes while Julius went forward to meet her, arms outstretched, a broad smile on his face while on the faces of some there were smiles of welcome, others turned away with supercilious disdain.

Her escort danced attention but after the first few minutes he was largely ignored and went to stand disconsolately looking out of the window. Surrounded by rich influential men she had no further need of him, and now it was the turn of a great many wives to feel aggrieved at their husbands' fascination with the new-comer.

At fifty-seven years old Gloria Weston was still a beautiful woman even if her beauty was largely the result of expensive visits to the beauty parlour in whatever country she happened to be living in.

Her fourth marriage, to an Austrian Count, was floundering and he was currently enthralled with a teenage model, a fact totally denied by Gloria. Her last film has been something of a disaster and there was nothing new in the pipeline, none of which seemed to be troubling her as she sashayed her way around the room, pausing to embrace and chat, undeterred by those who preferred to ignore her existence.

Julius, his duty done, had retired to his bedroom. Tomorrow he would fly back to Boston and the family celebrations on Boxing Day. A few expensive presents would quickly placate Emily for his absence on Christmas Day.

In the ballroom Gloria was greeting Anton with outstretched arms and kisses on both cheeks.

'Anton de Roche, you old fox,' she greeted him. 'If I'd known you were to take charge here I'd have booked in for much longer. A weekend isn't enough.'

Anton smiled. He was accustomed to larger-than-life figures and their insincerities.

'Darling Anton,' she was saying. 'I'm definitely coming back here now that I know you're here. I'll be glad to come back when the snow has gone, whatever possessed Julius to find something as remote as this?'

'It's also very beautiful, Miss Weston, perhaps if you were to come here in the springtime you would appreciate it more.'

'Oh I intend to, darling. When the azaleas are in flower, I've heard it's quite beautiful then. What sort of excitement are you planning for your guests?'

'Well there's rock climbing, walking, riding, sailing and rest, haven't you heard of rest?'

'Well of course I have but you know me, the world is an exciting place and I thrive on excitement. There are so many things lined up for me I really won't have much time for rest. This surely doesn't compare with Paris.'

'One doesn't compare it with Paris, it is the difference I find so stimulating.'

'Not for me, darling. I love Paris, London and New York in that order. You can have the rest.'

Anton smiled. 'How would you know if you have never discovered the other places?' he asked gently.

'Darling, I don't want to know them. I suppose you think that's awfully bourgeoise, you're always so superior, Anton.'

'I wouldn't presume to tell you what to like or dislike, Miss Weston. When I was a boy I thought England was the only place to be.'

'I thought you were French, Anton.'

'My father was French and he died when I was three years old. My mother was English. Like I said, I thought there was no place under the sun like England and then one morning in school a line in a poem leapt out at me, "What do they know of England who only England know". I've never forgotten it.'

Gloria was bored. 'Oh well, darling, you to your imaginings and I to mine. I'm a creature of Paris, London and New York, nothing you or anybody else can say can alter that.'

He smiled and bowed. 'I would not attempt to change you. I hope you enjoy your stay at The Lakes.'

'Now you're sulking. And there's another thing, whatever prompted Julius to call it The Lakes? It's awfully commonplace.'

'I know, but it was his idea and it is after all his hotel.'

'Why not The Lakeside or something more romantic like Innisfree.'

'I believe there is already a Lakeside Hotel, and we are not in Ireland. I think your escort is searching for you.'

'He's an absolute doll, you know, too young for me of course but at my age one has to be grateful for young men who dote on you. He'll move on, you know, they always do when I've finished with them.'

He watched her sidling round the room this time with her escort holding her hand firmly in his.

There had been so many of them, spoilt larger-than-life personalities strutting their little role upon the world stage and then falling into oblivion, occasionally surfacing to take part in some unwholesome scandal. Gloria Weston would go on for a while, as long as her beauty lasted, as long as there was some besotted man to pay for her luxuries. In the end it was always the same; scandal, tragedy or oblivion.

Across the room he noticed one of his pretty receptionists being stroked by a stout elderly man and the more she recoiled the more amorous he became. Anton walked across the room to ask her to dance and the man said belligerently, 'I'll have you know I'm a guest here, I don't want staff taking over.'

'I think you will find your wife waiting for you on the steps there,' Anton said calmly, aware of the relief on the girl's face.

The man turned and walked unsteadily to where his wife waited for him. Their meeting was hardly agreeable as she stalked up the staircase ahead of him, while Anton and his partner took their place on the dancefloor.

The girl was very young and Anton said gently, 'I take it he was annoying you?'

'Yes, Mr de Roche. I think he was rather drunk but he's been following me about most of the evening.'

'I don't think he will trouble you again, not now that his wife has appeared.'

He wondered idly how long they would stay up. Half of them had already gone to their rooms but there were the others who would stay as long as there was something to eat and drink. He decided he would not be one of them. The entire staff would have to be up at the crack of dawn to see that everything was in order for breakfast, and as if she read his thoughts the girl asked, 'How long will this be going on?'

He shrugged his shoulders. 'There's no need for you to stay on, you'll need to be up early. I should go to bed if I were you.'

'That group over there have asked me to join them but they're all a little merry,' she answered.

He decided that this was the moment to bring the festivities to a close. They were a group of young people, most of them intoxicated, too amorous, too noisy and when he announced that this would be the last waltz they became loud in their protestations.

Anton was polite, explaining quietly that it was now Christmas Day and that the staff and the orchestra were anxious to get some rest before the onslaught of the morning, in the end his decision prevailed and he watched them slipping and sliding round the ballroom as they danced the last dance of the festivity.

Tomorrow would be a day of feasting, food piled upon food, hot roasting chestnuts and warm mince pies, hot toddies and when the more adventurous could go out into the freezing cold if they felt inclined to walk on the fells.

He stood at the window of his bedroom staring out into the night. A flurry of snow was falling, dry fine snow that fell lightly on the branches of the trees and lay like a white shimmering carpet on the ice that had formed across the lake.

From somewhere in the night a fox barked and across the lake apart from the street lamps the village lay in darkness. Inside those cottages children would be sleeping in anticipation of the gifts they would find stacked round their tree in the morning, and later in the day a great many of them would

24

once more wander to the lakeside to gaze towards the hotel, eager not to miss anything that would be taking place there.

It was so quiet he felt he could almost hear the silence. He was not to know that Julius Van Hopper was finding it difficult to sleep. The hotel was quiet now, most of the guests had probably gone to their rooms. Julius got out of bed and wandered over to the window, pulling back the long velvet drapes and staring out across the lake.

He wondered idly if Cornelius Harvey would take up his invitation and visit the hotel in the spring, and if he would approve or disapprove of all he had done. At least it was alive when before it had been a dead thing, all that was left of a boy's dream. It would be lovely in the springtime, crocuses on the lawns, the azaleas blooming and there would be the launch taking the guests across to the village or around the lake.

He was leaving early in the morning and had been fortunate to get a seat on a plane flying out to America from Heathrow in the late evening. Emily and the family would be waiting for him. His father would be anxious to hear about the hotel, and Boston was a lovely city to spend Christmas in.

He wanted to be back in Cumberland if the Harveys decided to come, he wanted to hear what they thought about it and perhaps he could persuade Emily to come with him.

They'd have a grand opening a few weeks before Easter and the entire countryside would be coming to life. There would be visitors to the mountains, visitors who would be interested in the hotel, come for morning coffee and afternoon tea, then go home to tell their friends what a gem they had found. Oh yes, it was all going very well, and it would improve. The Van Hopper hotels never went down, they only ever went up and up.

Chapter Four

The two young assistants stacking books on the library shelves were vastly amused but they were not malicious. They liked their superior officer, the librarian Mary Styles.

'I wonder if he'll come in today?' Jenny, the younger of the two, asked.

'He didn't come in last week,' answered Helen.

'I know. She didn't lock up until well after six, but the books she'd put on one side for him were still here on Monday morning.'

'Perhaps he was away.'

'Could be. He doesn't usually miss, what time is it now?'

'Half five.'

'Oh well if he's coming he should be here any time.'

Mary Styles was working at her desk. She was nice-looking with light brown hair, green eyes and a pleasant smile. In her late thirties she was a spinster living with her ageing mother.

She looked up expectantly when the door opened, but it was an elderly woman who came to the desk to ask if a certain book had been handed in. When Mary shook her head she said petulantly, 'It's overdue, Miss Styles, I thought it was only to be out for a fortnight.'

'I'm sure it will be brought back before the weekend, Mrs Ashby.'

'Those on the desk are all new, aren't they?'

'They have been ordered, Mrs Ashby.'

'I don't fancy paying to order, I don't think it should be allowed.'

Mary smiled. She was accustomed to Mrs Ashby who moaned about practically everything, from the contents of the books to the time it took to acquire them. At that moment the door opened again and a man came in smiling affably. He was tall and slimly built. His dark hair was silver at the temples and he was good-looking, his smile shy but charming.

'Are those for me?' he asked eyeing the books on the desk.

'Yes, I thought you might be in today, they are the ones you ordered.'

Mrs Ashby sniffed and stalked away.

'I'll take a quick look round, I'm sure you're waiting to lock up and I am rather late this afternoon.'

Her two assistants were already putting on their outdoor clothing and Mary said 'You can go if you're ready, girls, I'll see you in the morning.'

They smiled and hurried out into the late afternoon traffic. They were laughing together as they hurried along the pavement, frivolously surmising that Mary would wish to chat to the man, particularly when Mrs Ashby had followed them out of the library.

Mary watched him meandering along the shelves, occasionally stopping to take out a book before putting it back and moving on.

What did she know about him? That he worked as a bank manager at a bank in the High Street, that he ordered books for his mother and went abroad for his summer holidays. He had told her that he had just changed his car and played golf and when he first became a member of the library she had thought the books were probably for his wife until he enlightened her.

He was the type of man she admired. Nicely spoken, good-looking in a quiet English fashion and smart in appearance. He had a nice voice, low, and gently modulated and she told herself every week that she was a fool to look forward to his visits. His name was Gerald Ralston.

It was almost six o'clock and her sister would be fuming if she was late home. Friday was the only afternoon her sister stayed with her mother until she arrived home. Her mother was demanding, Millicent was impatient and whenever she was late there was an atmosphere in the house.

He had made his choice and approached her desk smiling ruefully.

'I am sorry to have been so long, I've found one or two that I might find interesting. It was kind of you to hang on to these for my mother, I did intend to be in for them last Friday but I stayed away until Sunday evening.'

'Were you on holiday?'

'Just a short one. We were golfing in Troon and decided to drive home through the Lake District. We found the most beautiful hotel on the lakeside and made a detour round the lake to take a closer look at it. We were so delighted we decided to stay there until Sunday.'

'How lovely.'

'Yes it was. Do you ever get up to Cumberland?'

'When my father was alive we went often to the Lake District but I haven't been there for some years.'

'Well I should try to visit this place. The hotel is called The Lakes and they have absolutely everything to entertain the guests. The food was marvellous, we shall certainly go there again.'

'You were lucky to get in at such short notice, wasn't the hotel very busy then?'

'Well at the weekend people come and go you know. After a week on the golf course it was a great place to unwind.'

She stamped his books and watched him placing some of them in his briefcase before he smiled and wished her goodnight.

She was late and the traffic would have built up by this time. He never talked about his golfing companions. He referred to them always as 'we', never by name but she had built up an image of where he lived. Some very nice suburban house in a quiet tree-lined road. There would be a conservatory and a large lawned garden with possibly a dog. If he had a wife she would be stylish and pretty, but somehow or other she didn't think there was a wife, the books he ordered were always for his mother.

When she thought about his mother she pictured her as a charming silver-haired intelligent woman involved with some church or other, well supplied with friends with similar pursuits. Women who played bridge and liked to gossip over their coffee cups, women who drove small expensive cars and went off on holiday together, possibly golfers.

She couldn't really say why she had slotted his mother into this category but Mrs Ralston was quite evidently a very independent woman who didn't mind her son going off abroad and on a golfing holiday. The difference in his lifestyle and her own was painfully obvious.

The first thing she noticed when she turned into the drive was that her sister's car had gone and her heart sank. She was twenty minutes later than usual and as she closed the door behind her she was aware of sounds coming from the kitchen. Her mother never went into the kitchen so she hurried there immediately to find Mrs Scotson, their daily help, busy at the stove.

Mrs Scotson turned round and smiled at her astonishment.

'Your sister's 'ad to go early, Miss Styles, some dinner or other she was goin' to with her husband. She's neither use nor an ornament here, once a week she comes and she can't be bothered to wait until you get home.'

Mary was well aware that Mrs Scotson had little time for her sister, and changing the subject seemed the best idea.

'Has my mother been all right?'

'She's right enough. She's always all right when your sister's here, it's when your Millicent's gone, and with you that she's difficult.'

'Did Mother ask you to stay on? I'll settle up with you now, Mrs Scotson.'

'I've peeled potatoes and set the table. I didn't know what you were 'aving, but I defrosted some steak. Hope that's all right.'

'That's lovely, Mrs Scotson, I'll take over from here. I'll just have a word with Mother first.'

'Settle up with me tomorrow, Miss Styles, I'll get off 'ome now, mi husband'll wonder what's become of me.'

As always her mother sat in her large easy chair in front of the fire, staring morosely into it, and not bothering to look up when the door opened. She was a large woman with iron grey hair, wearing a velvet housecoat and red carpet slippers. She suffered from arthritis and other complaints that seemed endless.

'I'm sorry to be so late home, Mother,' Mary said gently. 'The evening traffic was very bad and I was a little late leaving the library. What time did Millicent leave?'

'She left early. She's going to a dinner tonight, something to do with Eric's firm and she had to get her hair done. She does too much. She has that big house to care for and the children when they're home. She has to keep up with Eric's engagements and there seem to be so many of them, I'm surprised she has the time to come to see me every Friday.'

Mary didn't answer. She was accustomed to her mother's sentiments about her sister's lifestyle. They had always been there.

Her father had always been proud of her ambitions to follow in his footsteps in the town's library and she had studied hard for it. Her mother had been more concerned with Millicent's standing with the well-heeled sons of well-off people in the town and her wedding to one of them had been the highlight of the year, and one which had cost her family dear.

That year there had been no holiday for Mary and her parents but, to Mrs Styles, any outlay paid for her younger daughter was money well spent. Millicent kept her entertained with talk of their expensive holidays abroad, her children's ponies and the parties they went to, whereas Mary could only talk about the people that went into her library, most of them uninteresting, and hardly likely to keep her mother amused.

Mary was fond of her sister. Millicent was pretty, lively and humorous, that she was also selfish and self-absorbed Mary was aware of even when her mother was not.

'Has Mrs Scotson gone?' her mother asked.

'She's going soon.'

'She made me a cup of tea, slammed it down on the table there without a word. I started to tell her about the dinner Millicent was going to and why she'd had to leave early but she wasn't interested. She went out of the door and slammed it behind her.'

'Perhaps she's worries of her own on her mind.'

'Not she. She's simply jealous of Millicent's money and popularity.'

While Mary busied herself with the evening meal her thoughts went out to Gerald Ralston. No doubt he had called to see his mother to give her the library books. She would welcome him with a warm smile and perhaps one or two of her friends would be with her to comment what a kind and thoughtful son he had. Then he would go to his own home, but who would be waiting for him there she wondered?

How would he spend his evening? Go to the Golf Club perhaps to drink with his friends, play snooker or bridge, arrange something for the weekend ahead, or alternatively would he spend it at home? Take his dog for a walk, chat to whomever was there. She could picture him sitting in front of the fire under the lamplight with his book resting on his knee, his dog's head leaning against him, and Gerald's eyes would be indulgent as he gently stroked the dog's head. She couldn't think why she had to picture him with a dog, perhaps he didn't like dogs, perhaps instead there was a fat tabby purring on the hearth. There had to be something, his smile was warm, his eyes were kind.

Absent-mindedly she cooked steak and vegetables, and when they were ready she went back to her mother to ask, 'Are you coming into the dining room, Mother or do you want your meal in here?'

'I'm tired of sitting here all afternoon, I'll go into the dining room.' Then followed the lengthy task of assisting her mother to rise, collecting the rugs she surrounded herself with and helping her slow progress from the room, across the hall and into the dining room.

'Are we having steak again?' she complained. 'Didn't we have it on Monday?'

'No, Mother, we had lamb.'

'Are you sure, I thought it was steak.'

'No, Mother, we haven't had steak for two weeks, you said you didn't like the last steak we had.'

'Then why are we having it tonight?'

'Because Mrs Scotson got it out of the freezer and I thought we should use it.'

She watched her mother picking at her food, pushing it around her plate then setting her plate aside, and she asked gently, 'Aren't you hungry, Mother?'

'You know I don't care for steak.'

'Then what else can I get you? There's bacon and egg.'

'I'm not hungry.'

'I'll be shopping on my half day, is there something special you would really like?'

'Nothing tastes of anything. Millicent brought me chocolates and some gingerbreads. We had them with a cup of tea.'

'That was nice.'

Mary looked forward to Tuesday afternoons. It was half day closing at the library and it was her one chance to look at the shops in the town and have her lunch out. She wasn't aware that her assistants called it the highlight of her week. That and the time she had to herself after her mother had retired for the night.

She felt like a free spirit when she closed the library doors behind her on Tuesday promptly at one o'clock. The High Street was busy with shoppers and it was market day in the town's market just off the main street. It was a sunny afternoon even if there was a chill wind blowing so that people were pulling up their coat collars and seemed glad to escape into the warmth of the shops.

Mary was well known in the town and there were smiles and greetings from a great many people. She usually ate lunch in one of the small cafes but today some strange spirit of adventure prompted her to look at the menu outside the George Hotel.

Was it really the sort of place where a woman could lunch alone? Business men lunched there, Rotarians and Masons, was the dining room at the George really the place where women would chat over their teacups? She was about to turn away when two women came through the swing doors and one of them greeted her with a smile, saying, 'I can recommend the chicken, Miss Styles, we've had it and it was very nice.'

She entered the dining room with a sinking heart. It was crowded with men and with only a handful of women obviously lunching with their husbands. The head waiter approached her with a smile.

'If you're wanting a table to yourself, Madam, you may have to wait a little,' he said.

'I don't mind waiting, or I could come back perhaps.'

'If you don't mind sharing,' he suggested.

When she appeared doubtful he did not press her and their eyes scanned the tables hopefully. It was then she saw that a man eating alone at a table near the wall looked up and smiled at her and she recognised Gerald Ralston.

The head waiter saw the smile and said, 'There is a place at Mr Ralston's table, I'm sure he won't mind if you joined him.'

Silently Mary admonished herself. She was thirty-six years old for heaven's sake, hardly a schoolgirl to feel the warm blood colouring her face and have her heart beating so ridiculously.

He had risen from his seat, but she sat down hurriedly saying, 'Please, Mr Ralston, do carry on with your meal, I'm so sorry to intrude.'

'That's all right, you're not intruding. I invariably eat lunch here, I haven't seen you before.'

'No, I normally eat lunch at one of the cafes.'

He smiled. He really did have the nicest smile.

'Was your mother happy with the books I kept for her?' she asked.

'I expect so. She's pretty busy, she doesn't usually comment.'

She ordered her meal and he ordered cheese and biscuits, then while they waited she said, 'I expect your mother was interested in your golfing holiday and the new hotel.'

'Yes of course, she's always interested in my comings and goings.'

'That is nice. My mother is rarely interested in what I do.'

He stared at her. 'I find that very sad, Miss Styles. You told me she was an invalid, does that mean she doesn't get out much?'

'Oh no, hardly at all. She has very bad arthritis.'

It seemed unbelievable that in the next half hour Gerald Ralston was being made aware of how she lived her life. Her sister's selfishness, her mother's intransigence, her dead father and another life when she had been loved and happy.

31

He listened sympathetically, and the waiter came with his bill and Mary was suddenly lost for words, horrified that she had bored him with a life story that was only important to her. She rushed to apologise but he waved his hand saying, 'No, no, it does one good to talk about things. Really I was very interested, we'll talk some more. When will you next be lunching in town?'

'Always on Tuesday, but this is the first time I've lunched here.'

'Perhaps you'll lunch here again though, the food is very good.'

'Perhaps, Mr Ralston.'

'My name is Gerald by the way.' He laughed. 'I expect you already know that, you did fill my library ticket in.'

'Yes. My name is Mary.'

He smiled again and left her. She watched him making his way around the tables towards the door but he did not turn round.

She was determined that when he came into the library on Friday she would be business-like and circumspect. No more treating him like a confidant, no more treating him as a special customer or offering advice on the sort of books his mother might like.

At five o'clock on Friday afternoon Mary was busy in the office and her assistant was delegated to stamping his books. When he had gone Jenny said, 'Mr Ralston's taken his books, miss.'

Not looking up Mary said, 'Thank you, Jenny, you can get off home now, you worked late on Wednesday.'

She did not see the look that passed between Jenny and Helen when they met outside the office door.

Mary felt rather pleased that she had taken herself in hand.

She kept well away from the George Hotel the following Tuesday and elected to eat lunch in a cafe near the market place instead. For several Fridays she managed to avoid being in the library when he called but she was unable to avoid him in the bakery when she called for her bread.

He stood in front of her handing over the money for whatever was in the cake box and she hadn't realised it until it was too late for her to retreat. He smiled and raised his hat.

'Good morning,' he said. 'Have you had lunch?'

And before she realised it she was saying, 'No, not yet.'

He was waiting for her when she left the shop and for the first time she realised that he was shy, uncertain that she would want to speak to him. It was this quick realisation of his shyness that made her feel suddenly strong.

'I'm going to the George, Mi . . . Mary, could I ask you to join me?'

'Well I was going to lunch at the cafe across the road, the George is a little too grand for me.'

'Oh surely not. It's full of business men and women like yourself, like both of us.'

He was pleading with her, his eyes anxious, and she found herself responding against all her deeper instincts.

She was determined that she would not talk about her life, her mother or
her sister, but she had reckoned without the sympathy in his voice, the kindness in his eyes.

'What do you do for your holidays?' he was asking her.

'Holidays! I spend them in the garden, shopping, I can't go away, Mother
can't walk very far and I couldn't leave her.'

'Wouldn't your sister take her for a couple of weeks?'

'It would be very difficult, she does have her husband and children to think
about.'

'Aren't the children fond of their grandmother?'

'I'm sure they are. They're away at university except for holidays, and then
of course they all go away together. They have a cottage in Cornwall so
Millicent and the children stay there all August and Eric goes down at the
weekends. My mother couldn't stand the journey, she'd be lost there for a
month.'

'Do they ever invite her?'

'Well no. It's difficult, Millicent has three other people to please, I suppose
it's better that I look after Mother, that way there's only me to think about.'

'Doesn't it strike you that it's very unfair?'

'Perhaps.'

'You could put your mother in a nursing home for two weeks, they look
after their old people very well.'

'Mother would never go.'

'Why don't you talk to your doctor, I'm sure he could persuade her.'

'Gerald, you don't know my mother. Would you put your mother in a home
for a fortnight?'

He stared at her in startled surprise. 'Well the circumstances are rather
different.'

'I know. Your mother's probably very independent, very capable and very
healthy. It does make a difference you know.'

'Yes I'm sure it does.'

'When is it your next holiday?'

'Oh there'll be a golfing holiday somewhere, possibly Ireland or Portugal, I
do enjoy those and we'll certainly take another break at The Lakes in
Cumberland.'

Who did he mean when he said 'we'? She longed to ask him. Some woman
who could play golf, some woman he'd known for years because surely if she
had been his wife he would have said so?

'I never seem to see you in the library these days,' he was saying. 'You're
always in the office when I pick up my books on Friday afternoon.'

'Well there's been a lot going on recently. Jenny looks after you very well.'

'Yes of course. Perhaps we could lunch together another day.'

'Thank you, that would be nice, but I must be allowed to pay for myself.'

'There's really no need.'

'But I insist.'

'Very well then. Shall we say next Tuesday at one-fifteen?'

She had never meant it to happen, but week after week she looked forward to meeting him every Tuesday in the George. Their meetings put a spring in her step and a song in her heart and during those weeks when he was away on holiday she longed for his return.

He talked about where he had been. The scenery, the journey, the people in some foreign land like Spain, Portugal and Italy, and he talked about The Lakes. 'You really should go there, Mary,' he enthused. 'Surely your sister would have your mother for a few days, Easter perhaps. When we were there last we met several well-known politicians and there were actresses and film stars staying there, it's a whole new world.'

'It sounds wonderful, but out of the question.'

'Is that why you've never married, Mary?'

She was startled by his question, it was too personal, too searching. 'I've never thought about it.'

'But you're a very attractive woman, there must have been somebody.'

Her face was reflective. Years ago there had been men, boys at the tennis club and those she met at university and later at her job, but after her father died her mother had taken over and the boys had disappeared. They had all been so long ago and now they were unimportant.

He was watching her from across the table, his eyes demanding an answer and all she could do was shake her head and say there was nobody, never had been anybody important, and once more she longed to ask, 'How about you, who is important to you?' If she did he would think she was interested, and there was no point in being interested. Her future was entirely predictable.

When she got back to the library the next morning she went at once to look at the glossy magazine that advertised the most prestigious hotels in the country, and on the first page she found The Lakes.

It looked so beautiful on the banks of the lake, a sort of castle with terraces and turrets, ablaze with Virginia creeper. It advertised golf and horse riding, tennis courts and squash courts, fell walking and rock climbing, there was a ballroom and card rooms and everything to tempt the rich and famous.

A few days Gerald had said, Easter perhaps, and why not? Surely Millicent couldn't refuse to have her mother for just three or four days. She was after all Millicent's mother too. If she didn't ask her she'd never know.

Chapter Five

All thoughts of asking Millicent to have her mother for a few days were swept away when her sister announced that they would be spending Christmas in Florida.

Christmas time was the only time they were invited to Millicent's house and they sat down to eat as a family. This was blamed on the fact that her mother was hardly mobile and hated the taxi ride and refused to be driven in Mary's small car. There was some truth in it. She was invariably ready for the journey at breakfast time and sat fully clothed and clutching her handbag waiting for the taxi to arrive three hours later.

The journey was to the other side of the town and the new estate of large ostentatious houses her sister and her husband had elected to live in. They were all different yet strangely similar with summer houses, large expanses of lawns and garages for two cars. On Sunday morning the children cluttered the roads with their horses and ponies and most of them had huge dogs that Mary's mother found intimidating.

The men were doing well in business, their women were pillars of local charities. They had coffee mornings and bridge parties, most of them had three cars and they all spent their holidays in exotic places.

Mary didn't in the least envy her sister, she was pleased Millicent was happy and well placed, just wished she wouldn't talk about it quite so much, or if she couldn't resist talking about it, at least be prepared to share her good fortune with her mother.

She had only raised the matter on one occasion and never again. Her mother had not agreed with her, indeed she had said, 'I don't want to go abroad with them, I don't want to spend time in their house with them even though it is beautiful. I have you to look after me and I'm happier here with familiar things.'

Gerald Ralston had gone away for Christmas, Madeira, and she had asked rather diffidently, 'Doesn't your mother mind your not being home at Christmas?'

He had appeared momentarily disconcerted by her question, then had said with a smile, 'Oh Mother is well taken care of, she never interferes with anything I do.'

She wished he would talk about his family. If he had brothers and sisters, if his mother had brothers and sisters, if his mother was well, if he had ever been married, but he was beginning to know quite a lot about her when she knew relatively nothing about him.

He was away for two weeks. He had said it would be beautiful in Madeira, the weather would be warm and sunny and there would be a lot of entertainment in a very beautiful hotel. Yes he would be able to play a little golf, and a great thing would be made of Christmas on the island.

For two weeks she ate in one of the cafes she had been neglecting of late, and several people asked where she had been, they had missed her.

She put up a small Christmas tree in the hall and bought a set of lights to adorn it, and on Christmas morning she gave her mother a warm cardigan and a pair of bedroom slippers while she got the usual present from her mother, a pound note to buy what she wanted.

Her mother had no conception of current prices. She never went to the shops and the pound note had stayed the same since Mary left university. Her mother would have been horrified if she had known how much her cardigan had cost.

Some peevish sense of malice kept Mary away from the George Hotel until near the end of January, and on Friday evening she was invariably busy in the office when Gerald came in for his books.

That her assistants eyed her curiously was not lost on her, and she knew that they speculated as to why she suddenly elected to leave Mr Ralston to them.

It was a desolate grey day when she met him walking along the High Street. She was on her way to the cafe across the road, he was on the way to the George, and she couldn't avoid him.

He smiled and held out his hand to wish her a Happy New Year, saying in the next breath, 'Gracious, it's almost the end of January and this is the first time I've seen you since I got back from Madeira. Are you on your way to lunch?'

'No. I've been lunching with a friend at the cafe across the square.'

'Have you fallen out with the George?'

'Well no, it's just that it got so busy over the holidays and I have this friend . . .'

'And you met your friend today?'

'Well yes.'

He smiled and raised his hat. 'I'll say goodbye then, perhaps I'll see you at the George again one of these days.'

She crossed the road, angry with herself. What stupidity had prompted her to lie about the friend in the cafe. There was no friend, only a group of acquaintances and how could she ever go back to the George after this. On Friday afternoon she was back at her desk as usual when he came in for his books and she had to admit that he seemed pleased to see her.

'When is your next holiday?' she asked him as she stamped his library books.

'Well I'm thinking about The Lakes for Easter. You would love it.'

'With your golfing friends?'

'I expect so. My mother enjoyed the last books, she's looking forward to these.'

He smiled and left rather hurriedly, bumping into a lady at the door and they both smiled and apologised.

Dolly Lampeter was a gregarious woman who normally came into the library in the morning, she was a friend of Mary's sister and invariably lunched at the George when shopping in the town, which thankfully wasn't usually on a Tuesday. Mary was quite unprepared for her first words however.

'That's the nice man I've seen you lunching with, Mary. Doesn't he work at the bank on the High Street?'

'Yes. This book is a little overdue, Dolly, I'll have to charge you for it.'

'That's all right, dear. What does he do at the bank?'

'I believe he's the manager.'

'He lives over at Cambourne, doesn't he?'

'I'm really not sure, I only know he lives out of town.'

'You don't know where he lives, Mary, and you appeared to be finding plenty to chat about the last time I saw you lunching together. No need to be cagey with me, darling, I shan't say a word to anybody.'

'There's really no need to be cagey, Dolly. I really don't know Mr Ralston very well. He comes in here for his books and I sat at his table because it was the only seat available.'

'Several times, dear?'

'Yes, several times.'

Her tone was short, but undeterred Dolly prattled on. 'I saw him one afternoon at the garden centre over at Oxbey, he was buying some shrubs and he had a woman in the car. She didn't get out so I couldn't tell if she was young or old. I suppose he's married?'

'I really don't know. We don't talk about personal things.'

'He's rather attractive. It would be nice for you to meet a nice single man with a good job. Millicent has so much going for her and you're stuck with your mother all the time. They had a wonderful time in Florida.'

'Yes, she came to show us her holiday snaps, it looked very beautiful.'

'Did she bring you something nice from Florida?'

'Yes of course, she always brings us lovely presents.'

'How nice.'

It had been a lie. Millicent bought functional presents. A bottle of brandy for her mother, a pure silk scarf for herself, and always with the words, 'I never know what to get you. All the things in the shops were for hot climates and you two would never get to wear them. I know Mother likes her brandy and you'll wear this scarf, Mary, it was very expensive.'

That Dolly Lampeter would tell Millicent about Gerald she felt sure. Dolly wouldn't be able to keep it to herself. She and Millicent were friends, they were also rivals. If Millicent had a new car Dolly had one soon after. They supported the same charities and attended the same functions. If one of them went on an exotic holiday the other had to exceed it the year after.

Having said that, Dolly was warm-hearted with her friends and seldom malicious. She disapproved of Millicent's cavalier treatment of her only sister and was not slow to say so; now Mary hoped fervently she would treat her luncheons with Gerald with some restraint, and as if she read her thoughts Dolly said, 'Don't worry, Mary, your meetings with Mr Ralston are safe with me.'

Inevitably she went back to the George and Tuesday lunch in his company. They talked about his holidays, his golf and his desire to return to The Lakes, and invariably he tried to persuade her to spend some time there.

'You should visit it one day and take your mother,' he said coaxingly. 'I'm sure the library are generous with their holidays, some time when the hotel is quiet perhaps.'

Mary explained that getting her mother out of the house at all was like launching a battleship, and Gerald said, 'Then you really should think of finding a very nice nursing home where you could leave her for a few days. My mother has a friend who constantly spends time in a very nice place and looks forward to going there.'

'I really think my mother would make every excuse under the sun not to go there,' she said steadily.

'Then it really isn't very fair to you, Mary.'

'Perhaps your mother likes travelling and spending expensive holidays,' she said, and was rewarded by seeing his brief smile, then glancing at her watch she said hurriedly, 'I really must go, I haven't finished my shopping.' She smiled and he rose to his feet as she left the table.

For days Mary thought about little else.

The idea tantalised her. Suppose Millicent said she would have her mother, suppose she agreed to go into a nursing home, what would his reaction be? Would he invite her to spend a few days in his company, or would he merely be pleased for her? It never entered Mary's head that she should visit The Lakes at any time other than Easter when Gerald would be there.

It was a dream, nothing more. Whatever plans she made were merely speculation, nothing would come of them. She was foolish to go on meeting him for lunch, chatting at the library when every meeting troubled her foolish heart and made her see that she had fallen in love with him.

Nothing could ever come of it. Her mother had arthritis and a heart murmur, but she was not likely to die of either of them and the weight of the years was overwhelming. Even in the unlikely event that Gerald fell in love with her he couldn't be expected to care for her mother, he had a mother of his own, even when she was an independent and well woman.

The more she thought about it the more wonderful the idea became. Three or four days, that was all she was asking for. To absorb the peaceful beauty of the Lake District and the luxury of the hotel, to be in Gerald's company and discover the things they had in common. To walk the fells with him and sail the lakes, to turn those four days into a lifetime.

She knew it was a dream but she began to shop for clothes more fashionably expensive than any she had ever worn. A new pure camel coat and shoes with higher heels. Cashmere sweaters and tailored skirts, which she hung in her wardrobe as soon as she got home and took out again every day simply to look at.

It was one Friday evening when Millicent came into the kitchen carrying a tray containing their afternoon tea crockery. Mary had just arrived home and had barely had time to take off her outdoor clothing.

Putting the tray on the kitchen table Millicent said, 'She didn't like the scones, she said they weren't homemade.'

'No. I didn't have time to make any this week. Mrs Scotson wasn't in last week, she has influenza.'

'I thought they were all right, but you know what she's like.'

'Will you be here next Friday?'

'I'm not sure. Eric has to go to Gloucester on business, I might just go with him, we like the hotel there.'

'Will you be away at Easter?'

'Easter! It's weeks away, why do you ask?'

'I just wondered?'

'Well, we've nothing planned, it's a bit too close to our holiday in Austria, isn't Easter early this year?'

'I'm not sure.'

'No, I don't suppose we shall be away at Easter.'

'If I decide to go away would you be prepared to look after Mother?'

There, she'd said it, and Millicent's expression was comical to say the least. She was staring at Mary open-mouthed, her eyes wide with shocked surprise, then gathering her scattered wits, she snapped, 'Where on earth are you going? You never go away.'

'I know. It's years since I had a holiday, years since I left Mother, now I really do think that life is passing me by. I should have a holiday, I work hard, I need the change.'

'Mother hates our house, she hates the stairs and we couldn't come here, the kids will be home from university and who knows who they might bring with them.'

'I thought that might be your answer.'

'Where are you going, who are you going with? You've never been interested in getting away before.'

'I know.'

'Have you mentioned it to Mother?'

'No.'

'You've only Mother to think about, I have Eric and the children, and it is their holiday, Mary.'

'They're hardly children, Millicent.'

'No, but you know what I mean. They like to lounge around listening to music, music that Mother can't stand, there would be an atmosphere and then Eric would start.'

Mary didn't answer. Instead she went into the pantry and started looking on the shelves. She had known what Millicent's excuses would be but she couldn't help feeling deep resentment in her heart. It was the first time she had ever asked her sister to care for her mother in all the years of her marriage, it was the first time she had ever looked at a man and wished she knew him better.

All she was asking was four days, and at the end of them they would probably both know that there was no future for either of them.

Millicent was standing idly looking through the window when she returned to the living room. She seemed ill at ease, well aware that she was in the wrong and not quite knowing how she could put things right between them.

Picking up her handbag and gloves she said hurriedly, 'We'll talk about it again, Mary, in the meantime I'll speak to Eric. I have to go, I have a meeting tonight that I can't get out of.'

Her thoughts were in a turmoil as she drove across the town to her home. She knew very well that several of her friends thought she was very lucky to have a sister always on attendance on her mother when she did so little. Indeed Dolly Lampeter who was always outspoken had said as much.

'What will you do if your sister wants to get married?' she'd said quite recently, and Millicent had laughed in reply, saying, 'Good heavens, Mary won't get married, she never goes anywhere to meet men.'

'She meets men at the library,' Dolly had said.

'Well of course, but what sort of men?'

'You'd be surprised.'

Had Dolly known something she hadn't? Dolly'd be at the meeting. Millicent decided to bring Mary into their conversation.

* * *

The opportunity came over coffee later in the evening when Dolly asked, 'Any holidays planned for the Spring?'

'Well no. Every year we talk about winter sports but we've never actually done anything about it. Have you?'

'I'm a sun worshipper myself. I don't really like going away for Easter, it's always too cold for me.'

'I'm not sure what will be happening at Easter, Mary is talking about a few days' holiday at Easter, we have to think about Mother.'

'Does that mean that you'll be having her?'

'Oh, there's nothing definite. She might have second thoughts.'

'I think Mary's looking very happy these days. She's had her hair styled at Jeanette's and she was wearing a quite lovely and expensive skirt last week in the library.'

'I hadn't noticed any change in her hairstyle.'

'You probably never look at her, you're so accustomed to seeing her as she's always been. If you ask me Mary is emerging from her too long hibernation, I rather think we should watch this space.'

'What do you mean by that?'

'Nothing concrete, darling, you know me, always the optimist.'

Her conversation with Dolly troubled her all the way home. Eric sat slumped in front of the television, a whisky and soda on the table beside his chair, favouring her with a brief smile.

She went into the kitchen to make a pot of tea, knowing that he would have little conversation until the football match he was watching was over. That was something else. Her mother wouldn't watch football, she'd talk all the way through it, he would be furious and would probably insist on watching the set in the bedroom for the rest of her stay.

She heard the sound switched off half an hour later and Eric came into the kitchen carrying his empty glass to find his wife sitting at the kitchen table staring into space, a worried frown on her face.

'Something wrong?' he enquired.

She looked up. 'If you can call being asked to have Mother for Easter wrong, then yes, there is something.'

'Us, to have your mother?'

'That's right. Mary would like to take a few days' holiday.'

'When did this arise? She's never wanted to go away, she's always seemed perfectly happy pottering around the garden and shopping in the town.'

'I know.'

'Is she going on her own?'

'I don't know. I said we'd think about it.'

'There's nothing to think about, Milly. The kids will be here and probably some of their friends. Your mother hates the stairs and the entire household would be disrupted.'

'I know. Unfortunately Mary's never asked us before and people talk.'

'How do you mean people talk?'

'Well, Dolly Lampeter for one. She's come out with one or two snide remarks about us being lucky having Mary, that we've never been asked to do our share.'

'It's got nothing to do with Dolly Lampeter. Besides we're a family, Mary's nothing else to do.'

She looked at him doubtfully. 'Maybe she's found something, Eric, something or someone.'

'Ridiculous. She's pushing forty and she's never been remotely interested in a man to my knowledge. Why now for heaven's sake?'

'It does happen.'

'But not to women like Mary with her feet on the ground, a good job and a pension at the end of it.'

'What do I say if she brings it up again?'

'Tell her I'm going away on business and you're all coming with me. Tell her her mother would hate it. In fact if you tell the old girl she'll put the kybosh on it immediately.'

Millicent's face brightened. Of course, that would be the answer. Her mother would never agree to stay with them for four days, it took a lot of persuasion to get her over for Christmas. If Mary mentioned it again she'd suggest they consult their mother.

Millicent didn't waste any time in consulting her mother. Although Friday was her normal visiting day she made it her business to call round on Wednesday morning when Mrs Scotson was busy mopping the vestibule.

Mrs Scotson stared at her in surprise and Millicent said sweetly, 'Are you better, Mrs Scotson, Mary said you'd not been well?'

'Ye' don't usually visit on Wednesday,' was all Mrs Scotson said.

'No. I'm taking some things to the church for their jumble sale. Mother asked if we had anything and I had to pass the door.'

'Well, yer mother's in the living room complaining about the weather, not that she's likely to be going out in it.'

The fact that her mother was unlikely to be in a good humour added to Millicent's expectations.

She listened for a time while her mother discussed the rain, and Mrs Scotson's unsympathetic attitude, and then she said, 'We don't usually see you on Wednesday love.'

'No. I'm taking some things to the church. You know, you asked me to find something.'

'I don't remember. Make us a cup of tea, Millicent and we can have a chat.'

They had been chatting for several minutes when Millicent asked innocently, 'Will you enjoy coming to us for Easter, Mother?'

Her mother stared at her in wide-eyed astonishment which told Millicent that she had got in before Mary had had a chance to discuss it.

'On Good Friday do you mean, just for the day?'

'Oh dear, perhaps I shouldn't have said anything.'

'What do you mean, what's all this about?'

'Hasn't Mary mentioned it?'

'No she hasn't. Why are we coming to you, we never have before?'

'It's only that she thinks she would like to spend a few days away, only four at the most, but she feels she needs a holiday.'

'When did she say that? She's never told me, if she thinks she's palming me off on you she's mistaken. You know I don't like your stairs and besides where is she going and who is she going with?'

'I know very little about it, Mother. I'm sure she intends to mention it.'

'Mention it! Well, of course she needs to mention it. I'm not a parcel she can hand round to please herself.'

Her mother's face was flushed crimson with annoyance, and feeling she'd said enough for the moment Millicent said, 'Mother, I don't want you to worry about it, I'm sure it will all be sorted out quite amicably. I wish I'd never mentioned it.'

'Well of course you had to mention it. It's Mary who is being devious. It shouldn't have been left for you to tell me.'

'Well I must go now, darling, the vicar and his helpers will be setting their stalls out. I'll be in next Friday as usual.'

She couldn't get out of the house quick enough. She could hear Mrs Scotson clattering about in the kitchen and she escaped down the drive before she had a chance to encounter her.

All they could do was wait.

Mrs Scotson found her employer in a furious temper when she called in to ask what she would like for lunch. Then began a tirade on Mary's treachery, her younger daughter's dilemma and her own feelings on the subject. Mrs Scotson listened without divulging her own satisfaction that at last the worm was turning. Mary needed a holiday, she needed time away from her mother, and it was about time that Millicent was being asked to do something useful for her mother at last.

Instead of leaving at five o'clock she decided to wait until Mary got home so that she could warn her about what lay in store.

Mary faced her mother across the dinner table, listening in silence until her mother had exhausted her anger before saying steadily, 'Mother, I couldn't tell you until I made sure you would be looked after. I'm still not sure.'

'But where are you going? Who are you going with?'

'I thought it would be nice to spend a few days in the Lake District, at a very nice hotel I've heard about. I intended to go on my own, after all it isn't a long journey and I'm only talking about a few days at Easter.'

'And what about me? I don't want to go to any hotel in the Lake District.'

'No, Mother, I didn't think you would, that is why I mentioned it to Millicent.'

'You should have mentioned it to me. I don't want to go to them, I don't like their house, it's too big and I don't like their stairs. Besides the children will be home, and I don't always see eye to eye with Eric. He won't want me there.'

Silently Mary agreed with her, but something totally alien to her normal demeanour made her suddenly firm.

'Mother, can you remember when I had a holiday? Not since Father died, and I really do work very hard. Surely you must see that I am entitled to take a few days' holiday without having to explain why I want it or why I asked Millicent to have you. She is your daughter too.'

'She's also got a husband and family. You have no responsibilities.'

'I have you, Mother. Millicent has a good life. She goes everywhere and does everything, if you compare her life to mine I really think you will see that I have very little in my life.'

'You have a good job. I thought you were happy at that library.'

'I am, Mother. I have two girl assistants who go abroad for their holidays, they have a load of boyfriends and loving families. They talk about them, I have absolutely nothing I can talk to them about. They are probably extremely sorry for me.'

'They have no need to be sorry for you. You're probably better educated, more intelligent and you have more respect for the elderly.'

As soon as the meal was over her mother went to bed, disapproval in every line of her limping figure.

Chapter Six

Friday night at the Oxbey Golf Club was Mens' Night. They started to arrive about eight o'clock and stood around the bar swapping stories of their prowess on the links, playing snooker and sometimes bridge. They invariably left well after midnight in happy groups, well pleased with the evening.

Gerald Ralston always arrived just before eight o'clock and he had his favourite place at the bar a little away from the rest of them. They exchanged greetings with him and invariably invited him to join them but always received the same reply, that he would not be staying late so didn't feel he should get into a big school.

He left at quarter to ten, answering their good-natured farewells with his usual bland smile. Most of them didn't comment, but there was always the odd one or two who thought there was more to his departure than met the eye.

'Where do you think he goes at this time?' Tom Barber asked curiously.

'And who is he going to meet?' said John Stedman. 'Do you suppose there's some woman he meets every Friday?'

'I've seen him lunching in the George once or twice on Tuesday. I don't sit near them and I don't think he's seen me,' said Alec Vernon who was a bank manager at the other bank on the High Street.

'You said them,' John persisted.

'Well he does eat lunch with a woman, there's probably nothing in it.'

'What's she like?'

'Nice-looking, refined. She's no dolly.'

'Good luck to him then,' another said. They liked him. He was never controversial. If he made a date to play golf he was always on time, played a decent game without being spectacular and if he didn't join their Friday night school he was always ready to contribute to any event or charity that was on the carpet.

None of them knew very much about him except that he lived in a very nice area of the small town, that he kept his garden immaculate, drove a nice car and had a good job.

He invariably declined to go with them on golfing holidays although they knew for a fact he spent a good many of them playing golf at country clubs. They speculated on his companions but Gerald never enlightened them.

They had other things to talk about besides Gerald Ralston.

Gerald felt sure that they discussed him, mainly because they knew so little about him, and as he drove his car in the direction of his home he permitted himself a wry smile. On the other side of the town he drove down a narrow country lane to a low stone cottage at the end of it.

Lights shone in the downstairs room at the right of the door and as he knocked at the door he could dimly hear the sound of the television. An elderly man shuffled to the door, opening it cautiously, then seeing Gerald opening it wider with a smile.

'We're just listening to the news, Gerald, we've had our cocoa.'

Gerald followed him into the living room where two women were sitting on a sofa pulled up before the fire. On the table in front of them stood three cups and saucers and a plate with three or four biscuits on it. The women looked up with a smile and the man said, 'Would you like a cup of cocoa, Gerald?'

'No, thank you, I'll have a drink when I get home, I expect you're anxious to lock up and go to bed.'

'Ay, well it's late. Shall we be seein' you next Friday, Doris?'

'Yes, about seven-thirty. I'll bring biscuits or cake so don't trouble to get anything,' Doris Ralston, Gerald's mother answered.

She kissed them both briefly then Gerald helped her on with her coat and escorted her out to the car.

'Did you have a nice evening, Gerald?' she asked him.

'Yes thank you, Mother.'

'They're so good to have me every Friday, I really don't know what I'd do without them.'

Gerald didn't answer, but there was exasperation in the swift glance he favoured her with.

The drive to their home took about five minutes and he let her into the house before he went to put the car in the garage. When he entered the living room she had stoked up the fire but even so the room felt chilly.

'I don't like to leave much coal on the fire,' his mother said. 'I know it feels cold but I wouldn't have a moment's peace if I thought a cinder might roll onto the carpet to set the house on fire.'

'We really should get a gas fire, Mother, it would be less trouble all round. You grumble when the coal is bad, you know you do.'

'Yes I do, but I'm afraid of gas, one hears such terrible things, look at those flats in the paper the other day, all of them destroyed and they said it was a gas leak.'

It did no good to argue.

46

'Would you like a cup of tea or coffee?' he asked her.

'No, they both stop me sleeping. What happened at the club tonight?'

'Nothing you'd be interested in, Mother, we just stand around and chat.'

'We could all do that at the Emersons.'

'I know, but they're your friends, Mother. It worries me that you keep them up late, I always have the feeling that they're glad when I pick you up.'

'They both understand how I feel about being left here on my own, and they're glad for you to go to the club.'

'Mother, I've spent an awful lot of money having good locks put on the doors. We have a good neighbour next-door and I'm sure you'd be perfectly safe on your own for a couple of hours.'

'I don't want to talk about it, Gerald, you know how I feel. I think I'll go to bed now. If it's nice tomorrow, Gerald, perhaps we could drive out somewhere.'

'Yes, Mother, I'm sure we could.'

'Are those my library books? It's really very nice of that young lady to keep them for me. I couldn't hunt on the shelves for them and you really don't know what I like.'

He watched while she picked up the three books, staring at the jackets, reading the brief synopses on the back, then choosing one of them she said, 'I'll take this one to bed, it's the thinnest. I don't like reading the heavier ones in bed.'

She kissed his cheek and left him. For several minutes he heard her checking that the front door was locked, checking that lights were out in the other rooms then after a few minutes the closing of her bedroom door.

He poured himself a whisky and soda and settled down in front of the television but he was not watching it. He was wishing he didn't feel this pressing urge to live a lie.

He had a nice home, a nice car and a good job. Something a lot of men would be grateful for, but somehow or other over the years he'd played it wrong.

His parents hadn't been rich. His father had worked as a clerk in the transport offices, his mother had scrimped and saved to make a good home for them and provide him with the best education they could afford, and he had repaid them by studying hard and rising in his chosen profession.

They had been very loving and doting parents and in the early days he'd had a good circle of men friends and there had been one or two girls he'd liked, one particularly that he'd wanted to marry.

When he went away to work in a bank at the coast however she'd met somebody else and when he came home to see his parents she was engaged. He got over her, there'd be somebody else, then he came back to Shropshire and a manager's job at the bank in the next town.

He had looked around the tiny terraced house his parents were living in and decided that they deserved something better. The houses on Rosedale Hill were just being built and on the following weekend the three of them drove round the area and selected the one they wanted. At that time it never entered his head that the day they moved into the new detached house was the day that sealed his fate.

His father had died of a massive heart attack three years later and he could not ask his mother to live alone. He had reached the age of forty and firmly believed he would remain a bachelor. He told himself that he was set in his ways, enjoyed being a single man, and his mother kept his house immaculate with the help of two daily women, she blossomed, joined the Bridge Club and ruled his life.

He had not reckoned on meeting Mary Styles. She was nice-looking and invariably charming, helping him with his books, giving advice when it was asked for but always business-like. He couldn't even think how he had allowed their friendship to grow, now he thought about her relentlessly.

She had been so honest about her family and her life and he had been palpably dishonest about his own. He felt that he knew Mary's mother, domineering, selfish, demanding, and the one sister who did little for them. His sympathy was genuine, he truly believed she should assert herself more, but how had he the nerve to lecture her when he was unable to adopt the same principles.

She asked few questions about his life and yet he knew she was interested and probably longed to ask more. Quite deliberately he had changed his mother's personality so that Mary would not feel sorry for him, and one day, perhaps sooner than later, she would have to know the truth.

To his colleagues at the bank he was simply the manager and they knew little about his personal life. To his acquaintances at the golf club who mainly lived in the same area he was an enigma, largely because he didn't join in their weekends at various golf clubs, or at their house parties. He knew only a few of their wives and when he left early on Friday evenings they could only speculate on where he was going. In the end he doubted if they were interested.

He had told Mary that he was going on holiday in the spring, golf and a few days at the hotel in the Lake District, and then in the summer perhaps to Portugal or Madeira. Why had he encouraged her to put her mother in a home, why was he advising her to do all the things he would never do?

He was playing a game, deluding himself as well as Mary, and it made him feel good, the free and easy man with a good home life, an independent mother who made no demands on him, and with no obstacles to prevent their friendship developing.

Mary was a nice person, she deserved better than this.

Perhaps it was time he cooled those Tuesday luncheon appointments. What would be her reaction if he hinted of a wife, a woman friend he was romantically interested in? He knew she had grown fond of him, and now either way he would hurt her. He would have to sit and watch the shocked disappointment on her face, and the ending of what they had.

He determined he wouldn't mention her mother again. He would accept that there was nothing she could do to change her life, let her see that it was none of his business.

Mary on the other hand resolved that she would keep her conversation with her sister a secret. If by some miracle she was able to spend Easter at The Lakes she would surprise him, and she hoped fervently that it would be a pleasant surprise.

How would he look when she met him in the hotel garden or in one of the public rooms? Would his eyes light up with pleasure or would he recoil in some sort of shock, and what would he say to his friends? She refused to believe that there would be anybody else.

Nothing more was said about her proposed holiday. Her mother refused to think that she had been serious, and Millicent was wary, Mrs Scotson scathing.

'I'd offer to come and look after your mother miself,' she asserted angrily, 'but it is Easter and mi 'usband'll be at home and wantin' to go off somewhere.'

'I wouldn't dream of asking you, Mrs Scotson, of course you must be with your husband.'

'And what about you, ye haven't changed your mind, I hope?'

'I haven't given it much thought. I don't think it will be possible for me to go.'

'Well ye should. There's that nice residential home at the corner of Rayne Avenue. It looks beautiful and I know one woman who didn't want to go there and now she doesn't want to come out. Your mother'd be with women of 'er own age, she'd 'ave company all the time, and I'm sure ye can afford it.'

'Money isn't the problem, Mrs Scotson, my mother is.'

'That sister of yours'll be 'ere talking about their 'olidays and you 'aven't 'ad a 'oliday as long as I've known ye.'

'Well we'll have to see how things turn out.'

'I know 'ow they'll turn out if she 'as anything to do with it.'

It was Gerald showing her pictures of The Lakes that pressurised her. The lake and peaks covered with snow, gardens edging the lake and azalea and rhododendron bushes making a riot of colour lining the paths.

Four days, to be pampered in luxury and aspects of beauty wherever she turned. Four days to be with Gerald and get to know him away from the George hotel and the other diners who smiled and looked upon them as a couple.

She wrote to the hotel to ask for brochures and when they came she pored over them in the evenings when her mother had retired for the night, and on the day her sister visited she left them conspicuously on display on the kitchen table.

She knew as soon as she entered the house that there was trouble, particularly when Mrs Scotson met her in the hall hissing, 'Yer sister went off in a temper slammin' the door behind her. I saw her lookin' at them papers on the kitchen table then I 'eard 'er and yer mother talking afore she went off.'

'Is that you, Mary?' her mother called out from the living room.

Giving Mrs Scotson a resigned smile, she decided to go in to see her mother before she took off her outdoor clothing.

Her mother's face was flushed, her eyes accusing as she said, 'What are those papers our Millicent's been looking at, I thought you'd forgotten about it?'

'I wrote off to the hotel and asked them for brochures. It's a beautiful place, Mother, did you look at them?'

'No I did not. It's impossible and you know it.'

'No, Mother, I don't know it. Like I said before, all I'm asking is four days. Would you like to come with me?'

'Indeed I wouldn't. My days for taking holidays are over, I can't get about and I'd need a whole lot of new clothes for a place like that. I'm not spending money on such things at my age.'

'Then there are two alternatives, Mother. You can go to spend a few days with Millicent and her family or you could have a few days at a very nice residential home.'

Her mother's expression was once again comical with surprise. 'Residential home, me!'

'Why not, Mother? I would find you a lovely one where you would be well looked after, where the food is good and where you'd have plenty of company. I know several people who go into them for short stays so that their children can have holidays.'

'How? How do you know about them?'

'Well I chat to people in the library. There is a very nice one at the corner of Rayne Avenue.'

'That was old Doctor Clarson's house, it was sacrilege to turn it into an old people's home.'

'It would have been worse if they'd left it standing idle for much longer. They'd been trying for years to sell it, most people don't want large houses these days, they need too much looking after.'

'Well I don't hold with it, and I certainly don't want to go there. If you decide to go away I shall stay here and Mrs Scotson can come in and look after me.'

'It's Easter, Mother, Mrs Scotson will want to be with her husband.'

50

'Then I shall stay here on my own.'

'I'm afraid I shall speak to Doctor Elton who will no doubt insist that you go into a home if Millicent won't have you.'

She was not surprised to find Eric's car outside the house when she arrived home from work the following day. It was apparently going to be a family meeting.

They sat in the living room with Mary on one side of the fireplace and her mother, Millicent and Eric ranged across from her. It had evidently been designed that way, making her feel she was on trial for her life.

'Now then,' Eric said reasonably, 'what's this about a holiday, Mary? Why now when all these years you've never really been interested?'

'I've explained to Mother and Millicent that I would like to spend a few days away at Easter, that I've never been interested before doesn't mean that I haven't thought about it. That I did nothing was incredibly foolish of me.'

'Well, we shall be away at Easter, the kids want to go to Spain for the holiday.'

'Millicent didn't mention it, so apparently it is something that has been arranged since I talked about my holiday.'

'Well yes. The kids are at university so we don't get to chat over things at the house, most of it's done by correspondence.'

'In that case, Eric, I suppose Mother will have to go into a residential home, it will only be for five days at the most.'

'I told you the other evening that I wouldn't go,' Mrs Styles said belligerently.

'Then I'll ask Doctor Elton if he can get somebody to live in for the time I'm away.'

Three pairs of eyes stared at her in amazement and then Millicent said, 'You really do intend to go then?'

'Yes, I really do.'

'That hotel in the Lake District is very expensive,' Eric said dourly. 'A smaller hotel would suit you better.'

'You think I'll be out of my depth at The Lakes?'

'Probably. It'll be filled with people who dress for dinner and when did you ever buy clothes for an occasion?'

'Well, I have to admit it was a long time ago, I shall have to look around for something.'

'And what a waste of money that will be,' her mother said bitterly.

'Are you staying for a meal?' Mary asked. 'You're very welcome.'

'No, we'd best be getting off,' Eric replied. 'I have a meeting at the club this evening and the traffic will have built up.'

For the rest of the evening Mary was treated to her mother's long silences until she decided to go to bed just after nine o'clock.

When she had gone Mary looked again at the hotel brochures, at the list of attractions including the ballroom and her heart sank. Had she really been sensible in thinking about Easter at The Lakes? They wouldn't be her sort of people, and she needed to buy at least two decent gowns for the evening, gowns that would probably be pushed at the back of the wardrobe when she got home, and remain there for the rest of her life.

She thought about Gerald. She had asked questions about The Lakes without disclosing that she might go there. He had been enthusiastic about the place, the scenery, the food, the entertainment and the variety.

'You should try it one day,' he had said with his grave sweet smile and then had changed the subject because he felt sorry for her, because he thought she never would.

There was nothing of interest on the television and she could hear the rain beating against the window and the dismal sound of the wind. It rained in the Lake District and the wind blew savagely across the fells and the mountains, but in the hotel there would be music and laughter, conversation between people enjoying themselves. If she made the effort now, perhaps her family would begin to understand that she might do it again.

She took a notepad and an envelope out of the drawer in the writing bureau and sat down to compose a letter. They were probably booked up, if they wrote to say so that would be an end to her problems.

She read the letter through and sealed it in the envelope then she folded the brochure and went to put it away. For another long moment she stood looking down at it, then with an impatient shrug of her shoulders she went to the telephone and dialled the number of the hotel.

A woman's voice answered her and in the background she could hear music and conversation. She asked if she could make a reservation, and after a few minutes the voice said, 'Thank you, Miss Styles, you will be arriving on the Thursday before Good Friday in time for lunch and leaving on the following Tuesday, one single room. Will you please confirm?'

It was done. She tore up the letter she had written and wrote out another in confirmation of her booking. For better or worse she would be a guest at The Lakes hotel for Easter, whether it would be a joy or a disaster was in the lap of the gods.

Chapter Seven

Coping with the heavy build-up of traffic in the few days prior to Easter meant that Stuart Mansell was saved the trouble of thinking too deeply about his secretary's curt goodbye as he had left his office at Westminster to drive north to his constituency.

The Easter recess hadn't come soon enough. There would be those in his constituency who were scathing at his lack of attendance there in recent months, some of them thought London was a few miles down south and there were others who blamed him for the fact that the government was slipping badly in the polls.

He'd call a few meetings in his surgery and persuade his wife to spend a few days in the country, the weather forecast wasn't bad, The Lakes might not be a bad idea.

Reluctantly he thought about Alison Gray. She'd been his secretary for fourteen years and they'd been lovers for almost all of that time. He'd been newly married when he first became a member of parliament for the north country town he had been brought up in. His father had been a solicitor, well known in the town, and his mother had been a leading light in the local Inner Wheel. He'd received his early education in the town, and after leaving university he too had gone into law, but politics had always been his dream.

His wife Sybil had been largely content to remain in the north, particularly after the children were born and he had tried to get back there whenever possible. He had been very lonely in those early years and Alison had been there and readily available. She was pretty and intelligent, she understood his work and his ambitions, but recently it somehow wasn't enough for her. She sulked when he went north, she sulked when his wife came to stay in London so that they could attend functions together, and she no longer asked questions about those times he travelled north, not even when he explained that he needed to see his constituents. Today had been a good example.

She'd been busy at her desk, hardly bothering to glance up at him when he went to collect the things he needed to take to his constituency. He'd looked at her anxiously from time to time but her face was frozen with resentment. He'd been afraid to ask what she was doing with herself over Easter, afraid of her caustic wit and the accusation he read in her eyes.

He knew now that nothing he did was enough for Alison. His marriage, his children, his standing in the community no longer counted, instead Alison only saw the long years of being there when he wanted her and the necessity for her to become invisible at those other times.

It was all building up to something, he knew. Whether she was walking out of his life or demanding recognition. Either way it wouldn't be easy.

His career would be on the line, his wife of many years and their children. And what would those north country people with their respectable attitudes to life think about an M.P. who could forsake his wife and family for a woman they had never heard of? If the newspapers got hold of it there would be mayhem. He thought about the people he would be meeting during the recess.

People who had voted for him, a local boy with a respectable family behind him. And Sybil, his wife, the daughter of a local builder who poured money into the town's coffers and employed a great many of the town's populace.

He thought back across the years to his early days in Westminster. Flushed with the success of his campaign, he had been arrogant, Alison had been another conquest and never in a million years had he thought that one day he would have to think about making a choice.

He wasn't the only one of course, affairs were usually light-hearted, seldom serious. Nobody bothered as long as they could be hidden under the carpet, but only let an M.P. fall out of line and the Prime Minister would come down on him like a ton of bricks and bang would go any prospect of promotion. That wasn't the end of it, however, after it came to light his marriage was at stake.

He was fond of Alison, she'd always been supportive, a nice girl, a great colleague, but he'd never been frightened before. Perhaps it was time he talked to Sybil about her, explain that he'd been lonely in London without her, tell her that it was a recent thing, not something that had been going on for years.

She'd be furious, she'd probably threaten him, but in the end she would be the good loyal wife he'd always relied on. For all their sakes she'd be true to him, and if Alison was going to be difficult his wife would stand like a bulwark behind him.

His thoughts moved on to the idea of spending a few days at The Lakes. They'd been there for a long weekend soon after it opened and they'd been very impressed. He'd pamper her in luxury, buy her some nice present in the expensive shops in the hotel and he'd grovel, if grovelling was necessary.

It was late afternoon when he drove into the driveway of the large stone house he had acquired on the outskirts of the town. There were lights in the hall and the rooms on either side of it, and he was surprised to see Sybil's car waiting outside the front door. He surmised that she probably had some meeting she needed to attend but the kids would no doubt be in.

Parking his car on the drive he took only his briefcase, leaving his suitcase in the boot. He was closing the front door when his daughter greeted him from the door of the drawing room saying, 'Hi, Dad,' before turning to go into the room.

He followed her and saw that she was stretched out on the rug in front of the fire, not even bothering to look up, and slightly exasperated he said, 'When did you get home from university?'

'Yesterday, Mother met me at the station.'

'And is Jeremy home?'

'Today. I thought it was Jeremy coming when you came in.'

'Look at me when I'm talking to you, Lesley, it's months since we've seen each other, one would think we'd met yesterday from your attitude.'

She stared at him in surprise. He was an indulgent parent, hardly ever raising his voice to them, and he was already regretting it from the hurt little girl look on her face.

'Sorry, Daddy, you're in a bad mood.'

'I'm not in a bad mood, but I've had a long drive and it would be nice to receive a little welcome at the end of it. Is your mother going out?'

'I thought she'd telephoned you in London to tell you.'

'Tell me, tell me what?'

'Grandfather's had an accident, she's got to go there.'

'What sort of an accident?'

'They're up at the cottage in the Dales, he's fallen and broken his leg. Granny doesn't drive so she says they can't cope, Mother'll be away all over Easter.'

'What about me, what about us?'

'I'm going walking with a crowd from the tennis club, somewhere in Scotland and Jeremy's going with the Wrights to Cyprus. Didn't Mother tell you?'

'If she rang me this morning I'd probably already left. Where is your mother?'

'Probably packing. She had a luncheon date earlier on, she hasn't been in long.'

He turned back into the hall and at that moment his wife came running down the stairs dressed in her outdoor garments and carrying a small valise.

'Hello, darling,' she greeted him, kissing his cheek gently. 'Has Lesley told you what has happened?'

'She's told me your father's broken his leg.'

'Isn't it awful? They only went up there two days ago and he had to go out in the garden in the pouring rain. The path was slippery and he fell. His leg's broken in two places, they've set it but he's got to stay put in hospital for a while and Mother's on her own.'

'How long are you expecting to be away?'

'Darling, I don't know. Mother doesn't drive and we'll have to visit him in hospital. You haven't arranged anything for Easter, I hope?'

'I thought we'd have a few days in The Lakes.'

'Quite impossible now, darling, you could come up to the cottage though.'

'Well, I don't know. I shall have a few surgeries here and there'll be meetings. I've got a lot of work on here, the house will be quiet, I might just get on with it in some degree of peace.'

'I hope you're not too disappointed, Stuart, it can't be helped. We'll talk about holidays later, somewhere really nice where we haven't been before. Daddy'll be very contrite about me having to leave you, but thank heavens the children have arranged to be away. You can cope, I know, I'm sure you'll be eating out anyway.'

'Lesley said you telephoned me earlier in London.'

'That's right. I gave a message to Alison, didn't she tell you?'

'No. I only saw her for a few minutes.'

'Even so. I thought she was the secretary to end secretaries.'

'It's always pretty hectic before the recess, she'll be ringing me, I think.'

'Why should she? It's too late now anyway.'

'I'll offer a suitable chastisement.'

'The fridge is stocked with food and there are plenty of eggs and fresh milk, you'll be fine, darling.'

He took her suitcase and went with her to her car. It had started to rain and pulling a dour face Sybil said, 'Oh dear, the rain's coming down and I do hate that journey across the Pennines. I'll telephone you when I arrive, I'll be able to give you the latest news on Daddy.'

Damn Daddy, Stuart thought belligerently. Daddy had put a kybosh on the entire holiday. He'd be here on his own, working, talking to people he didn't want to talk to, listening to their woes and their dire thoughts on the government he represented, and he'd promise them the earth to get rid of them.

Lesley came running out of the house and Sybil embraced her swiftly.

'Have a lovely time in Scotland, darling, and try not to be too adventurous. Tell Jeremy I'm sorry to have missed him, and tell him to enjoy his holiday. Your father will see that you both have sufficient money before you leave.'

They stood in the thin drizzle of rain while she drove out onto the road, then after a brief wave of her hand she was away.

Lesley ran back to the house and Stuart followed. He felt abandoned. His wife had gone away and tomorrow the children would have gone too. Surely this was why he'd needed Alison, the loneliness, the vulnerability.

Lesley was in the kitchen making coffee and looking up with a bright smile she said, 'Mother's left something in the oven for you, Dad, steak pie I think, we had it for lunch.'

'How much money are you going to need?' he asked her.

'The others are taking twenty pounds each. We're staying in hostels and they don't cost much.'

'Twenty pounds won't be nearly enough.'

'Mother paid for my train tickets and we've paid half towards the hostels. It's only spending money, Dad.'

'Well I'll give you forty. I don't want you roughing it all the time and one never knows what other incidents might crop up!'

She grinned at him. 'Mother said you'd fuss about the money. Honestly, Dad, there's really no need to give me more, but if you feel you must.'

'I do.'

'Grandfather's paid for Jeremy's trip.'

'That was nice of him.'

'I suppose so. What will you do all on your own here?'

'I shall have plenty to do, surgeries, meetings, it's not going to be much of a holiday.'

It was almost midnight when Sybil telephoned to say she had arrived.

Her voice was contrite. 'Mother's coping very well, a neighbour took her to see Dad in hospital this afternoon and he's bearing up. They say he could be home in a few days but of course his leg is in plaster and he'll be on crutches. But I can't abandon them, darling.'

'No, of course not.'

'I've been thinking, Stuart. Why don't you find a friend and play some golf, either at the club or get away for a few days?'

'Away!'

'Well yes. You won't have a surgery over Easter, three or four days at some country club is just what you need to get the pace of Westminster out of your system.'

'I don't know . . .'

'Well, the way things are I don't think I'll be home for several weeks. Father says he'll stay here until his leg heals, he seems quite taken with the way they've handled him at the hospital and he won't be able to drive for some time.'

'I'll think about it, Sybil.'

'You do that and let me know what you decide. Has Lesley asked you for the twenty pounds?'

'I'm giving her forty.'

She laughed. 'I felt sure you would. You spoil her.'

'You'll ring and let me know what is happening?'

'Well of course, darling, and do think about what I've said, a few days

57

playing golf would be the very thing for you. And, darling, I am sorry not to be there, there won't be a day when I'm not thinking of you.'

'And I you, darling. Goodnight.'

And that is what they would do, think about each other, in the meantime he poured himself a whisky and soda, sat in front of the television to watch the news and thought about Alison.

What would she be doing at this moment, and was she still angry?

Alison was seething.

She looked around her tiny flat with some degree of disenchantment. Shaking the rain from her raincoat, her shopping waiting to be unloaded, the petals of the spring flowers dropping onto the table top, and from the windowpane the steady pattering of rain.

Over the years she had come to dread holidays because that was the time Stuart returned to the bosom of his family and she was left alone to spend it in any way she pleased.

His wife had telephoned in the morning to say she had to go away but quite deliberately she had kept the news from him. It gave her some perverted sense of satisfaction to think he would be arriving home to an empty house, or at least, a house without the presence of his wife.

She was thirty-eight years old and a spinster. When they'd first met she was twenty-five and in a junior position at Westminster and from the moment she laid eyes on him she had fancied him. He was tall and slender, extremely good-looking, clever and evidently going places. When he wanted her she was always there and to count up the number of times she'd seen his wife would only take the fingers of one hand.

He'd never put it into words but she'd always believed that when the children were off their hands he'd leave his wife and come to her, of late however she'd refused to believe it.

He was nowhere near as attentive, he never spoke of the future, if she did he cut her short and rapidly changed the subject, at thirty-eight years of age she realised she'd wasted most of her best years on a dream that was unlikely to reach fruition and it was something she had to think about.

She put away her shopping, cramming tins into the kitchen cupboard, stacking the refrigerator and the acrimony increased. Why should he be allowed to get away with it? Didn't she have some rights, shouldn't those years count for something?

She was dreading the few days ahead. Most of her friends were married or in some sort of stable relationship. She had one or two girl friends who were more interested in their careers than men friends but they were a rarity and in retrospect she didn't want to be like them because they were the type of women men didn't admire.

She knew that her married friends regarded her association with Stuart as a disaster waiting to erupt, the others thought she was a fool to allow him to dictate her life, but for him she could have done more, moved on into a better position, earned more money.

She resented her bitterness. She couldn't exactly remember when she had started to feel this way. At first there had merely been disappointment that she remained his mistress when she wanted to be his wife, but more and more now she was coming to feel anger and a desire to hurt him, to seek vengeance.

She supposed she must start to make a meal but she wasn't really hungry, so instead she made a cup of coffee and raided the biscuit tin. People were remarking that she'd lost weight, that she was worrying about something, and she'd taken to eating a snack lunch in her office rather than joining the others in their lunch hour.

Bitterness had the power to make her feel ill, she'd seen it in other women involved in similar relationships to her own. She'd thought it couldn't happen to her, she was too sane, too intelligent, but intelligence had nothing to do with it, her life was a mess and she'd only herself to blame.

A sharp knock on her door brought her out of her reverie and when she opened the door she found her nextdoor neighbour standing there, her arms filled with flowers.

Tracie Sutcliffe was young, pretty and obviously happy. She smiled as Alison opened the door wider to invite her in.

'I heard you come in,' she said, 'I do hope you don't mind, Alison, but I'm off to Cornwall tomorrow morning and I was wondering if you'd look after these for me.'

Alison took the flowers saying, 'They're beautiful, was it your birthday?'

'No, just a year since Alan and I met. It seems such a shame to leave them in an empty flat to die.'

'How long are you away for?'

'Well, until after Easter. I'm going to stay with the family, Alan's coming for Easter.'

'They might not live until you get home.'

'Oh that doesn't matter. You'll have the pleasure of them and I somehow didn't think you'd be away.'

'I've just made coffee, would you like some?' Alison asked.

'I'd love some, Alison, but Alan's waiting for me in the hall. We're going to a show.'

'How lovely.'

'I'll put the flowers on this coffee table, they cheer the room up a bit, don't they?'

Tracie hovered within the door, wanting to say more, wanting to leave, but indecisive, as though Alison's mood and the cool atmosphere of the room troubled her. She did not know Alison well although they had been neighbours for eighteen months. She had seen her bringing a man to the flat and seen them leaving together, but at those times all they had exchanged were the briefest of greetings.

'There,' Alison said brightly. 'The flowers are lovely, I only bought a small bunch and in any case I was loaded up with shopping.'

Tracie smiled. 'Will you be home for Easter?'

'I'm not sure, possibly.'

Tracie's eyes strayed to where a huge gaily coloured parcel lay propped up on the settee, and with a bright smile she said, 'Well at least you've got an early Easter present. That looks interesting.'

Alison smiled.

When there seemed nothing else to say Tracie turned away and after a brief farewell she ran lightly down the stairs. Alison heard them laughing in the hallway before the closing of the front door.

She stood looking down at the flowers, early tulips and daffodils and she saw that Tracie had left the card with them. Idly she picked it up to read the inscription, 'To my darling Tracie, with all my love, Alan.'

Stuart sent her flowers for her birthday and when he'd been home for several days. Usually roses, but he never wrote, With all my love, always it was the same, 'To Alison, with love from Stuart'. Stuart's love was divided, between his wife and children, his mistress and himself.

She sat on the settee staring into space, wishing she was in a better mood, wishing she could be philosophical, she'd been able to be at one time, now all she could be was angry.

She picked up the lavishly decorated parcel which an expensive shop had had wrapped and delivered. On it was a label, 'Not to be opened until Easter'. Easter when she would be alone, Easter when she'd be counting the days for the recess to be over and for Stuart to be back in London.

She leapt to her feet suddenly, after throwing the parcel across the room where it lay dejectedly on the carpet.

60

Chapter Eight

The afternoon surgery was over, the people were leaving. They'd been the usual hotchpotch of moaners. Dissatisfaction with education, their pensions, housing, crime. A good many of them had told him bluntly that they hadn't voted for him, neither were they likely to, and he had answered them with a charming smile, assuring them that it was his duty to represent them all whether they voted for him or not.

He did his best in the face of prejudice, bloody-mindedness and often sheer hostility, and of course there were the compensations of being with his own kind, people who bolstered up his courage and his pride. To these people he was all things to all men.

After the first afternoon he had returned home well pleased with himself and then the rot had set in. The house was empty.

He had forgotten to set the central heating and it felt cold, facing him was the prospect of cooking a meal, there'd been no time for a decent lunch, and it had to be something quick like bacon and eggs.

As he set about laying the kitchen table he could hear the telephone ringing in the hall and he went quickly to answer it.

Sybil's voice hailed him from the other end. 'I was hoping you'd be in, darling, we're just back from the hospital. How did the surgery go?'

'Oh the usual.'

'Nothing really interesting?'

'Old Mr Berbridge was there as usual complaining about his pension, his neighbours and the state of the pavements.'

She laughed. 'Well at least you can always rely on having one constituent in attendance.'

'One I could do without. I never satisfy him.'

'Well of course not, darling. He wouldn't be happy if you did.'

'How is your father?'

'Much better. He's hobbling about the ward on his crutches and hoping to come home next week.'

'Well that's good. Why don't you bring them both home, wouldn't he get just as much care here as over there?'

'I've suggested it. Mother says she doesn't think he'd be happy on the journey and she likes it here. I don't think either of them will budge.'

'Have you told them that I am home?'

'Well yes of course I have. They think you could come here for Easter.'

'Well of course I can't, the cottage is too small for the four of us, and your father and I always argue. That wouldn't do him any good.'

'Stuart, I do hope that you'll get away to play some golf, you'll only sulk if you stay at home and I'll feel guilty.'

'Well, you must admit, Sybil, you're putting your parents before me as usual.'

'No, Stuart, it's not as usual, usually I put you first. I didn't make Daddy break his leg, I didn't build this wretched cottage and I didn't agree to stay here without telling them it was unfair to you. My hands are tied.'

There was a long silence and then he capitulated. 'All right, darling, I'm sorry. I hope to see you soon.'

'Did the children get off all right?'

'Yes, I saw Jeremy for all of five minutes, long enough to give him some money. I took Lesley and her pals to the station.'

'That was nice of you, darling. I'll be in touch, but do let me know what you decide to do about Easter?'

He returned to a kitchen filled with smoke. He had forgotten to turn the jet down and he was no longer interested in bacon and egg.

In the living room he switched on the television and settled down in front of the gas fire which had now come to life. There was a pile of glossy magazines on the long table in front of him and idly he picked one or two of them up and started to leaf through the pages.

You couldn't open a magazine these days without finding a page devoted to the expensive joys of staying at The Lakes. The photograph of the hotel looked idyllic. Cool Pennine stone and red Virginia creeper, long sweeping lawns and blooming azalea bushes, the peaceful lake and the joys of sailing, he and Sybil would have loved it there, now thanks to her parents' stupidity he was here and she was there and there was nothing either of them could do about it.

He thought about Alison. She'd be in London in that poky flat seething with annoyance. In actual fact the flat was not all that poky, he supposed and she had good taste in furniture and he'd been generous. He should telephone her, but perhaps it was better not to. He didn't want to listen to her anger, he didn't want it putting into words. He'd wait a day or two, ring her before Easter perhaps.

Alison put the remainder of Tracie's flowers in the waste disposal unit and washed the vase ready to give back to her when she returned from Cornwall.

Flowers were a waste of time with central heating and Tracie'd probably had them a few days before handing them over.

The room looked strangely empty without them, she'd get some more before Easter, the barrows were piled high with spring flowers at this time.

It was Saturday morning, the week before Easter and her mind was busy with all the things she could find to do in London. She should make an effort, go to the pictures, walk in the parks, anything except stay in the flat thinking about Stuart, building up the resentment.

The telephone was ringing in the living room and she hesitated about answering it. Let him think she was out, let him think there was somebody else, but then it might not even be Stuart, she had to answer it.

Her heart lifted at the sound of his voice, when even at the same time she felt like slamming down the receiver.

'I wasn't sure I'd find you in, darling, it's such a lovely day. I've been thinking of you a lot, how are you?'

'I'm all right.'

'It's been pretty hectic here, surgeries two or three times and evening meetings, they've been well attended too, that's a good sign surely.'

She didn't answer, and hurriedly he said, 'Have you opened your present?'

'No, I've been following instructions that it hadn't to be opened until Easter.'

'Did I really say that?'

'Either you or the shop.'

'Well, please don't obey it. Open the parcel and enjoy it. What are you doing for Easter?'

'You know what I'm doing for Easter. I'm here at home waiting for the day when I start work again.'

'I have a better solution.'

'What is that?'

'Why don't we spend it together?'

She sank down weakly on the nearest chair and the silence seemed interminable to the man waiting at the other end of the line, presently she heard his voice saying, 'Alison, where are you? Answer me.'

'Does this mean that your wife is still away?'

'Yes, I know I've got the devil of a nerve to be asking you but I've missed you so much, Alison, I can think of nothing I'd rather do than spend Easter with you, we have a lot to talk over.'

'We never talk, Stuart.'

'I know, there never seems to be the time, but I promise you we will. You are free for Easter, I suppose?'

'I just said so.'

'Have you heard of The Lakes up in Cumberland? It's expensive, beautiful and romantic.'

'Everything in fact to tempt you and me?'

'I think so, darling.'

'Well, I'm not sure, it's something I have to think about.'

'Surely not. In any case we'd be lucky to get reservations if we leave it too late.'

'I still have to think about it, Stuart.'

'How long do I have to wait?'

'I'll think about it over the weekend, after all it has come as a bit of a surprise, something I wasn't expecting.'

'I know. I'll telephone you tomorrow evening, I can't leave it any longer to make a booking.'

'As what?'

'I beg your pardon?'

'As what, Stuart, am I going? Your secretary or something else?'

'I'll telephone you tomorrow evening and hope you're in a happier frame of mind. Goodbye, darling.'

Oh but he was maddening. Of course she wanted to go, there was nothing in her entire life she wanted more, but just for once couldn't she have said no, bring him to earth, make him realise she had a life of her own.

She picked up the parcel from the settee and started to pull off the wrapping paper. She stared at the huge pink Easter bunny with its long floppy ears and the box of expensive continental chocolates that had fallen onto the settee.

She sat down with the bunny on her knee, her tears falling onto its soft pristine fur, hugging it against her yearningly but it was a poor substitute for Stuart. She'd been hating the lovely spring day because she was alone and would have been happier in the rain, now there was the prospect of spending Easter with him and she knew that his reasons for inviting her were purely selfish. The self-centredness of a spoilt child whose family had deserted him and he had to have something and somebody.

Stuart himself couldn't believe that he'd actually asked Alison to spend Easter with him. He'd done it in a fit of pique because he was lonely.

Tomorrow was Palm Sunday. He'd go to church with the local dignitaries in the Mayoral procession, at one with the town's most prominent citizens, and the congregation of the Parish Church would largely consist of those who had voted for him.

A good few of them had made tentative enquiries as to how he expected to spend Easter when they knew his wife was away. He had simply said he might play some golf somewhere, and already he was regretting his telephone call to Alison.

They'd spent long country weekends in the South where they'd been pretty sure nobody would recognise him, but he'd mentioned The Lakes and he began to think about the well-heeled members of his constituency who might conceivably have thoughts on The Lakes too.

He'd chat to them, make a few enquiries, accept their dinner invitations, that way he'd soon know where they intended to spend the Easter weekend, and if he discovered they were heading towards The Lakes he and Alison could go somewhere else.

Sybil wasn't being fair. Her father was back at the cottage even if he was on crutches, and they had a good neighbour who would have seen them all right for the weekend. After Easter he'd be returning to London and she could have returned to the Dales.

He had sensed Alison's frustration and to be fair she had every right to be angry, at the same time she'd always known there could be nothing more to their relationship. He'd been a married man and a father when they met, he'd never lied to her and if she hadn't liked the set-up she'd had every opportunity to end it. He shied away from the fact that that wasn't strictly true, there had been those times when he'd hinted that one day things might be different.

He didn't think for a single moment that she wouldn't come.

There was a buffet lunch laid on for the Mayoral party in the Mayor's parlour after the church service and they were all doing justice to the excellent lunch the Town Hall had laid on.

From his vantage point near the door where he was engaged in conversation with the vicar Stuart eyed the guests. Which one of them might be likely to be spending Easter weekend at The Lakes? He decided if anybody it would be Lionel Clarke, the local solicitor. He had a thriving business in the town, his wife was a very rich woman and they ran a very expensive car. His opportunity came when he saw Lionel returning to the buffet for second helpings, and excusing himself from the vicar decided to join him.

'Nice buffet,' he commented as they stood together.

'Yes, always is.'

'Nice service too, the vicar didn't go on too long.'

'No. Here over Easter, are you?'

'I'm not sure. Thought I might get away for a few days to play some golf.'

'Not a bad idea if the weather prospects are good. Sybil not coming home for Easter?'

'Actually no. The old man isn't too good.'

'Oh, I'm sorry to hear that. Hard luck on you though.'

'Yes. We were hoping to spend a few days at The Lakes in Cumberland, but I'm afraid his accident has put the kybosh on that. Do you know the place?'

'Yes. We were there for Christmas, the entire family, the kids as well as the in-laws. It cost a bomb.'

'So you're not thinking of spending Easter there?'

'Absolutely not. If it had just been me and Jill I wouldn't have minded but

I can't afford it for all the family. One has to draw one's horns in somewhere and we're having a new garage.'

'I see.'

With a smile Lionel moved away and Stuart continued to survey the room over his glass of wine. The women had formed groups of their own while the men dallied with business acquaintances or golfing friends. His eyes fell on the short prosperous figure of Councillor Daniel Hanley.

Hanley was a likely contender for The Lakes. A rich self-made man who had recently been elevated to the Council and who gave ungrudgingly to the town's coffers. He had made his money in haulage and a great many other pursuits. If anybody could afford the hotel it was Hanley.

Stuart was well aware that he had a very recent supporter in Councillor Hanley. When Hanley was working his way up he'd voted for the opposition, once arrived he changed his allegiance to the Conservative Party, and Stuart always had the feeling when they spoke together that he was weighing him up. Hanley was no fool, he would have to tread carefully.

He sauntered round the room, stopping occasionally to chat to this group and the next then catching Hanley's eyes had stopped to say, 'Nice lunch,' as he had to Lionel.

Hanley nodded. 'Oh ay, the Town Hall can do us proud on these occasions.'

'Business booming, Councillor?'

'Can't grumble.'

'Away for Easter, are you?'

'I've left it to the missus. How about you?'

'I'm not sure, I'm afraid, Sybil's away with her parents, the old man isn't too good after his accident.'

'Get away, he'll live to be a thousand, he just wants pampering.'

Stuart warmed to him.

'Well you know what it's like, all the family spoil him.'

'So what are you doing for Easter?'

'I'm not sure. We were hoping to go up to The Lakes in Cumberland for a few days, now I'm afraid it won't be possible. Know the place at all?'

'One or two long weekends. Nice place, expensive, but it's not for us at Easter.'

'You prefer somewhere warmer?'

'My eldest son's getting married on Thursday and then the rest of us are off to Malaga.'

'Is your son marrying a local girl?'

'John Broadhurst's lass. It'll be a big do, thank God I'm not having to pay for it.'

Councillor Hanley's face was dour and Stuart's eyes followed his gaze across the room to where John Broadhurst and his wife were the centre of a crowd of the town's richest citizens. John Broadhurst was the son of a moneyed family, his wife the daughter of another, they were old money, old gentry.

Geraldine Broadhurst was a tireless worker for local charities, a pillar of respectability within the parish church and something of a snob. They were both members of the golf club, rode with the local hunt and Geraldine was a great socialite. Her bridge parties were famous as were her coffee mornings and idly Stuart speculated as to what she thought of her one daughter marrying the Hanley boy.

The Hanleys were newly rich, money made in trade, and it showed. He tried to recollect if he had ever met Hanley's boy or the girl but he met so many people as he went his rounds, and the young were not overly interested in politics anyway.

'I suppose the town will be coming to a standstill on Thursday,' he said with a smile.

'Well the wedding's in the morning and Broadhurst is having the reception at his place, if you're likely to be around I'm sure they'll want to invite you. I just hope we can get away early, we're off to Spain in the evening.'

'I doubt if I'll be here on Thursday, I'm hoping to go off for a few days to play golf.'

'Oh well, don't be surprised if they invite you. Most of the town will be there.'

Mention of the wedding came later from Geraldine.

'Will you be joining us on Thursday, Stuart? Sybil said if you were available you would accept our invitation.'

'I didn't know anything about it. You know she isn't at home?'

'Yes of course, but you'll be here won't you?'

'I don't think so. I'm thinking of going away on Thursday.'

'Well the wedding's at eleven and the reception at our place, plenty of time to go away later. Where are you thinking of going anyway?'

'I thought perhaps The Lakes in Cumberland.'

'Really. John and I thought of it, but then this wedding surfaced and we didn't give it another thought. I expect we'll get there later in the year.'

'I was hoping Sybil and I could go, but she's not likely to get away from Yorkshire.'

'And will you go alone?'

'That doesn't trouble me. I go to quite a lot of places alone, one meets people.'

'Well of course, but I've been telling Sybil for years that she's really very lucky that you don't mind being in London when she's up here. I suppose it's all part and parcel of the job.'

He smiled and moved away. In a little while he'd be able to make an excuse to leave. Some of them were already drifting away and the buffet had served his purpose. None of them would be likely to be at The Lakes, he'd sussed out the ones who could afford the place and none of the others were in the running.

As he left the room he smiled across to where Geraldine was chatting to a group of her women friends and she called out, 'Try to come, Stuart, we'll be very disappointed if you don't.'

It was the empty house that made him decide to telephone Alison on Sunday evening. He did it with some trepidation but was reassured when her voice seemed more friendly than of late.

'I'll be tied up most of the morning,' he lied, 'that's why I'm ringing you tonight. I hope you have some good news for me, darling.'

'When are you thinking of going?'

'I thought Thursday afternoon or evening, that will give you time to get the train and I'll meet it in Kendal.'

'You don't want me to meet you at the hotel?'

'Well no, it's off the beaten track and I felt sure you wouldn't want to drive all the way on your own. It will be Easter and the traffic could be heavy.'

Her voice became warmer, lifting his spirits.

'How long are we intending to stay?'

'I thought until Tuesday morning, Wednesday at the latest. I have a meeting here on the Friday and then I'll be thinking of returning to London at the weekend.'

'What about your wife?'

'Sybil's still in Yorkshire. She's encouraging me to get away.'

'But not with me, Stuart?'

'No, obviously not. Darling, we have to talk about us. Why don't I meet you in Kendal around three o'clock?'

He'd promised her they would talk, but how many times had he made that promise? The empty house depressed him, at the same time he felt he was at the top of a slippery slope descending into chaos.

He would go to the Broadhursts' wedding, it would take his mind off things. He'd enjoy a good lunch, listen to all the boring speeches and present the happy couple with a decent cheque before driving off to meet Alison.

Chapter Nine

Geraldine Broadhurst stood in the centre of a group of women consulting her diary. In a crowd Geraldine always stood out as the most elegant, the cool unruffled look of neutral colours and uncluttered good taste.

She was an attractive woman in her early forties. Her figure was as slender and graceful as it had been in her youth and there was not a shred of grey in her dark hair. Her face was always exquisitely made up and the townswomen speculated how much it cost to keep her in such a pristine condition. They would have been surprised to learn that it cost very little. Geraldine was both artistic and resourceful, she knew how to make the best of herself.

'I really don't have any time this week for bridge or golf,' she informed her companions. 'With the wedding next Thursday there really is too much to do. I'll be happy to get back to normal afterwards.'

They all understood, and across the room she caught her husband's eye sending the intimation that it was time they were leaving.

'Will Stuart Mansell be there and is Sybil coming back?' a friend asked.

'I invited him but he may be away. I'll telephone him later to see if he's decided one way or another.'

They waved their farewells and she hurried across the room to join her husband. On the way Councillor Hanley said jovially, 'Well it won't be long now before we're related. Everything going to plan?'

'Oh yes, I think so. Isn't Mrs Hanley with you?'

'No. She's got a bit of a cold. She wants to be fit for the wedding so she decided to stay indoors this morning.'

'Do tell her I hope she'll soon be better.'

John was waiting impatiently near the door. He didn't like the Hanleys any more than she did and as she hurried to meet him she was well aware of the speculation they were leaving behind them. The wedding of her daughter Debbie and Tod Hanley would be the talk of the town for some time to come. Most of the town had been stunned when their engagement had been announced.

Debbie was their only child. She was beautiful, clever and spoilt. They'd sent her to the best girls' school they could find, a school where she'd mixed with royal and aristocratic girls freely and from where she'd acquired excellent examination results that could have sent her to university.

Instead she'd decided she wanted to find a job. She didn't want to go to university, she wasn't career-minded.

She'd faced her parents over the breakfast table, her pretty face mutinous as she listened to her father encouraging her on the paths open to women that had never been possible before.

'But I don't want a degree,' she'd insisted. 'I don't want to study for years and then move into some boring job I don't really want.'

'Then perhaps you'll tell us what exactly you do want?' he said acidly.

'I want a job now and I want to have a little fun. The girls at the tennis club have jobs, they work in offices and do other jobs and in the evening they have time for parties and dances. They go away for long weekends and they always seem to be doing something.'

'You would enjoy university,' her father cajoled. 'You'd meet girls there, and boys of similar background.'

'That's what it's all about isn't it, background?'

'Don't be silly, Debbie. Eventually, you'd be better paid than any of the girls you meet at the tennis club, you'd have a career for life, not some temporary job until you decide to get married. It's cost your mother and me a great deal of money to send you to that school, we wanted to do the best for you.'

'I could do any of the jobs my friends have, I'm going to shop around.'

So shop around she did and in the summer after leaving school she went to work in the office of the town's largest engineering works, a very prosperous firm since Daniel Hanley was elevated to the board room.

On the outskirts of the town the firm owned several acres of land which they had turned into a cricket field, several tennis courts and a very opulent pavilion where dances were held on a regular basis in the winter months. It was at one of these dances that Debbie Broadhurst met Tod Hanley.

Tod was good-looking, tall and broad-shouldered, a keen rugger player and mad on football. He was usually the life and soul of the Saturday hops and most of the girls had a crush on him. When he singled Debbie out for attention she became the envy of the rest of them.

They went everywhere together and were thought of as a pair. Debbie's parents were horrified, Tod's parents displeased.

'What do you want a girl like that for?' his father admonished him. 'She's a spoilt little minx without a brain in her head. You'd do well to look around for a decent girl who'll make you a good wife, all that girl's good for is spending money and dressing to kill.'

'She's a nice girl, I'm not interested in anybody else,' Tod had said.

'Well I'll tell you for nothing that the Broadhursts won't want you for a son-in-law. They're a couple of snobs, they've never had to work for their money like I have and they look down on the likes of us, they think we're common, and I think they're old hat, the world's moved on since the likes of John Broadhurst meant anything.'

'You're jealous,' his son had stormed. 'You're jealous because they are somebody, they're cultured and you're not.'

'I could probably buy and sell them out though, think about that.'

'There's more to life than money.'

'Oh you think so do you, well I'd advise you to think again. It's money that's educated you, that buys your cars and runs them, it's money that's helping you to entertain that young woman.'

'I do happen to be working at the factory.'

'But it's me who's subsidising you. What you earn won't keep that girl in the manner to which she's been accustomed, and her father will know it. Have you met them?'

'Once or twice.'

'And did they make you welcome?'

'Of course.'

Debbie was suffering similar strictures from both her parents.

'We didn't educate you to be serious about the first boy you've met. Tod Hanley is not the man for you, he's vain and insufferably boorish. He's a lot like his father and we don't want it to go any further.'

'You don't know him. He's nice, all the girls like him, he's the most popular boy at the club.'

'And the club is made up of boys like him. It does not have our approval, Debbie.'

But the friendship went on and blossomed. The close confines of her expensive school had not equipped Debbie to see the shallowness of her times with Tod. His obsession with sport and the endless times she sat shivering on the edge of some field watching him sprawled in the mud.

The dances at the club showed off his prowess as a hard drinker who could hold his liquor. His friends encouraged him, and she stood with the rest of them in total admiration.

When she chastised him he sulked, but there were the other times when his open good humour charmed her and her parents despaired.

They gave dinner parties where she met other young men, the sons of friends, quietly spoken young men who were studying for a career in medicine, politics, all sorts of pursuits Tod had never heard of. He felt himself superior, he was working, he had a job in his father's firm, he was earning money, not sitting on the sidelines waiting for some unheard-of Utopia.

The other men let him talk. They didn't dislike him, they thought him vaguely immature and wondered what on earth Debbie Broadhurst saw in him. One or two of them invited her out, to tea dances, to May balls and point to point races but Tod was around with his handsome rugged face jeering at them, flattering her, sure of himself.

At the beginning of August Tod went off with three golfing friends to Portugal and the rest of his family went to Malaga, Debbie sulked.

Her parents placated her with a new sports car and a horse, neither was enough to bring the smiles back to her face and when her parents set off for a week's holiday at The Lakes in Cumberland she refused to go with them. Halfway through the week she arrived, bored from being on her own and they duly extended their holiday when she decided she loved the place and found a boy to drive with, dance with and pay her attention.

Her parents were delighted. He was charming, an only son with prospects and working for his stock-broker father. Two days before they were due to go home Tod arrived, demanding and wheedling, the holiday was over.

On the morning of Debbie's nineteenth birthday she came down to breakfast wearing an engagement ring which she proudly showed to her parents and received a taste of their righteous anger.

Tod had not asked her father's permission to the engagement, she was too young, he was unsuitable to be their son-in-law but the outcome was that Debbie said they would either elope to get married or she would leave home to move in with Tod's parents. She would not have been so confident if she could have heard the comments being expressed at the Hanleys' establishment.

Debbie was a spoilt brat. She would not make him a good wife, she'd know how to spend his money and probably end up like her mother, a fashion plate and total snob.

Nothing the older generation said made the slightest difference. Tod and Debbie were two young people who knew everything, wanted everything and wanted it now. The two families were aware that if they didn't accept the situation they lost their children.

The wedding was fixed for Easter and the invitations were sent out. Both families were well aware that people talked. There were two camps, each of the opinion that the engagement was a disaster.

It seemed all the town turned out for the wedding. Those who had not been invited lined the church path and scrambled over the tombstones in the churchyard, but the array of guests was considerable.

Mrs Hanley regarded the guests on the other side of the aisle and hoped her own attire was suitable. It had cost more money than she'd ever spent on an outfit in her life and she wasn't too sure that she'd spent wisely. She was a large woman and she thought something darker might have been more appropriate. As it was she'd chosen a jade-green heavy georgette dress and jacket and an extremely large black hat adorned with jade flowers.

When Geraldine Broadhurst arrived wearing uncluttered beige her heart sank. Her son turned round and grinned at her, and she thought how wonderful he looked in his morning dress. Debbie was a lucky girl to have got Tod, there wasn't a man in the church with his good looks or popularity.

Geraldine turned to smile graciously at the Hanleys across the aisle. She considered Mrs Hanley to be a little overdressed, but Tod looked well enough. She had to admit he was good-looking and had a fine physique.

Councillor Hanley stared straight ahead, he was thinking how much the wedding had cost the Broadhursts, it seemed they'd invited everybody who thought they were somebody, even the Member of Parliament was present.

The organ struck up the bridal march and the vicar was leading his choir along the aisle. From behind there were already gasps of admiration at the sight of John Broadhurst proudly escorting his daughter, a vision of beauty in white Honiton lace, followed by four bridesmaids in pale blue lace and a pageboy in white satin. The small boy looked self-conscious, the girls self-assured, and Debbie looked up with a smile as Tod stepped out to meet her.

The photographs were taken on the lawn outside the Broadhursts' house and the guests were relieved to be indoors drinking their first sherry, and out of the keen wind that blew across the lawn.

The Hanleys and the Broadhursts stood with the happy couple to receive their guests. Everything had gone without a hitch, and as they followed their guests through the hall and into the dining room Daniel Hanley had to admit that the Broadhursts had style. The table was sparkling with cut glass and silver, and along each length great bowls of red roses had been placed.

'This'll have set you back a bit,' Councillor Hanley remarked to his host.

'Yes well, she's our only daughter, one has to make it an event.'

'If we can contribute in any way, you only have to ask.'

'Thank you, but that will not be necessary.'

'I see our M.P. is here without his wife.'

'Yes, she's away with her parents. I think he has to leave early.'

'Joining her, is he?'

'I'm not sure, either that or he's off to play some golf.'

The guests were scanning the place names on the tables and Councillor Hanley made his way to the top table where he was sitting next to Geraldine. The bride and bridegroom were applauded to their seats at the table and everybody seemed to relax.

Stuart sitting at his place near the top table found he was in a position to watch the rest of the room. Catching Geraldine's eye he smiled and she whispered, 'I hope the speeches don't go on too long, you'll be wanting to get away pretty soon?'

'Well I do have to go back to the house to change out of these things.'

He knew them all and he thought that largely they liked him. He was that breed of politician capable of being all things to all men, he could converse at the highest level with men with money and high standing and he could come down to earth just as easily with those others who called a spade a shovel.

73

Geraldine was thinking she had little to say to Tod sitting next to her.

He didn't seem to have very much to say to Debbie either and she found herself worrying. She'd been aware of it for some days now, Debbie's sulks, their voices raised in argument until somebody went into the room they were occupying, then the arguments ceased.

She'd asked Debbie if anything was wrong but her daughter'd smiled brightly saying, 'It's nothing, Mummy, we just can't agree about something at the moment, Tod'll come round.'

'Does he have to, darling, can't *you* come round?'

'Not this time, Mummy, this is something that matters to me, this time Tod has to be the one to agree.'

She hadn't mentioned it again, Debbie was being very charming to her new mother-in-law and her gaze moved benignly over the heads of her guests.

Everything had gone well, the meal was superb, the champagne flowed, the best man's speech was witty and fulsome in his praise of the bridesmaids and now it was Mr Broadhurst's turn to talk about his daughter, her sweetness, their love for her, their joy at her happiness, and beside him Geraldine felt a certain numbness that it wasn't quite true.

Stuart made his excuses to leave, but most of them looked as if they were intending to stay for some time. He'd said his farewells to his hosts and his favourite people, wishing he could stay until the bride and groom departed for their honeymoon but saying that reluctantly he had to leave.

His last question had been to the happy couple as to where they intended to spend their honeymoon.

Debbie had merely giggled girlishly, saying it was a secret, not even the parents knew, Tod had stood with his arm round her waist, his expression non-committal.

At last he was driving north on his way to meet Alison's train at Kendal and the sun was shining. The lakes would look beautiful on such a day, white clouds scudding across a blue sky above the mountain tops, The lakes would be alive with pleasure craft and the streets of the villages teeming with fell walkers. Easter could be enchanting in Cumbria, and there was nowhere on earth more enchanting than The Lakes. He'd thought it worth every penny during his last visit, he'd give Alison a few days she'd never forget.

He'd told her they had to talk about themselves, but she'd probably forgotten. They would fill their days so that there was no time for talking and very soon now he'd be heading back to London and nothing would have changed.

He had time to drink a cup of tea in the railway cafe and then he spent some time at the magazine stall. He didn't meet a single soul that he knew and as he waited for the passengers to alight from the train he looked impatiently along its length until he saw Alison stepping down onto the platform.

As always she looked wonderful. She was as attractive now as she had been the first time he had seen her. Long dark blonde hair reaching her shoulders where it curved up deliciously at the ends. She was tall and slender, elegantly dressed as always in a long camel coat, a pure silk jade green scarf knotted casually round her shoulders.

People looked at Alison, she had an air about her that men found irresistible and women envied. When she saw him she raised her hand to wave and she smiled. With an answering smile he went forward to meet her, taking the suitcase she carried and putting his hand under her elbow to guide her through the crowd.

'What was the journey like?' he asked. 'The train looked a bit crowded.'

'Yes it was. People going away for Easter.'

'You'll love The Lakes, Alison.'

'When were you there?'

'Oh it's some time ago, soon after it opened actually. I always wanted to go back there.'

'This won't be like the last time, Stuart.'

'What do you mean, darling?'

'The last time you were with Sybil, this time you'll be with me.'

His complacency shattered a little. 'Actually, darling, there were a few of us, I simply liked the hotel, the company wasn't all that brilliant.'

She smiled. She'd put him on the defensive, and it wouldn't be the only time during the weekend ahead. He'd said they had to talk and talk they most certainly would. The days of being available were over, this time something concrete had to come out of their relationship.

Chapter Ten

The long black car was forced to ease its way along the busy high street of the lakeland village which gave local people plenty of time to see its driver. They stared after it as it wound its way along the street before it started to climb the hill towards the stately pile of Alveston Hall. The lord of the manor had come home

Andrew Alveston sat for a long time in his car after he had brought it to rest before the imposing doors staring up at the stone façade of the house with its tall mullioned windows and graceful chimneys. He might have left it yesterday. The gardens were immaculate, it was as though Alveston was set in a time warp as unchanging as the fells surrounding it and for the first time in years memories were crowding in upon him.

Ten years was a long time to have stayed away from the home he loved and the scenery of his boyhood. The decision to come home had not been an easy one and now he was reluctant to walk through that heavy oak door and into a past burdened with tragedy.

There was no need. He could turn the car round and go back the way he had come, but while he hesitated the door was opened and his butler came running down the stairs, his face warm with smiles, his hands outstretched in greeting.

Andrew opened the car door, and Grant called out, 'I saw the car coming up to the house, sir, somehow or other I felt sure it was you. Welcome home, sir.'

The two men shook hands and Grant said, 'I'll get somebody to help with your luggage, sir, I'll take some of it.'

Other servants had appeared on the doorstep, men and women, all wearing broad smiles of welcome and Andrew went forward confidently, none of his staff must know that he was desperately afraid.

They behaved as though he'd only been out of the house for a morning's drive. The doors of the drawing room were flung open and one of the servants was putting a match to the logs piled in the large stone fireplace.

'The rooms are cold at this time of the year,' Grant was saying. 'The fire is waiting to be lit.'

It seemed that nothing in that graceful room had changed. Later he would face his ghosts, but in the meantime Grant was asking if he wanted breakfast.

'No thank you, Grant, I had something on the road.'

'Coffee, sir?'

'Yes, coffee would be very nice. Has the staff changed much?'

'Hardly at all, sir. One of the gamekeepers left and two of the housemaids, that's all.'

'Why did they leave?'

'The girls left to get married and they moved away. The gamekeeper left to buy a shop in the village, quite a nice little earner with the hotel.'

'Hotel?'

'Yes, sir, The Lakes. On the site of Harvey's Folly just across the lake.'

'I don't much like the sound of that, Grant.'

'Oh you will, sir. It's very expensive and nothing was spared to make it appear very beautiful from this side of the lake. A new road on the other side of the lake has been made and the guests are very circumspect. There is no rowdiness, sir.'

'I'll take a look at it. Does it bring trade into the area?'

'Well, yes it does, sir. The shops are busier and the inn. I'm sure they'd make you very welcome, sir, if you decide to visit.'

'I'll think about it.'

'Will you be occupying the same bedroom, sir?'

'I think not, Grant. I'll have the room I had as a boy overlooking the fells.'

'I understand, sir.'

After Grant had left him he went to stand at the window. The view was beautiful, the lake and the far mountains, the formal gardens and the drive lined with azalea bushes. Soon now they would be coming into flower edging the drive with blossoms in every shade from orange to deep tragic crimson.

In all the years of his self-imposed exile he had thought about the beauties of this place and longed to come home, and yet he had been a coward, afraid to face the past, afraid of the memories it evoked.

In every room of the house memories would crowd in, memories of growing up, schooldays and holidays, friendships he had laid aside and Olivia. Olivia would be everywhere and his mind went back to those early days when he had loved her, refused to see the emptiness behind the exquisite beauty of her face. Olivia, his beautiful child bride and all the pain that came after.

Always when his mind went back to his years with Olivia he shut the memories out, but now that he was back in his home he had to face them, only by facing them honestly could he start to live again. He had a duty to this old house and the legacy his forebears had left for him, as well as to the people who relied on him for their livelihood.

He looked at the photographs standing on the grand piano. Nothing had been changed, it was almost as though he had left the house yesterday for they were photographs of his parents, himself as a laughing schoolboy, a much loved child, and then his heart quickened as he looked at another photograph of himself standing with a group of men and women, all of them in evening dress and he had his arm around a girl who was looking up at him with smiling affection. He'd thought he was in love with Stella Brampton, on that night they had just announced their engagement and it had been a night of rejoicing. His parents and hers had been delighted, his future stretched before him clear and uncluttered with disappointments.

The wedding was arranged to take place in the early spring and Stella had chosen her bridesmaids, two small nieces, the daughters of her brother William, and two grown-up ones, one an old school-friend, the other her cousin who was coming from Singapore where her father was a British diplomat.

In those weeks leading up to the day of the wedding he and Stella hardly seemed to have time to talk. Their wedding was the talk of the village and already the vicar was arranging rehearsals. They were only waiting for the missing bridesmaid to arrive.

He remembered that morning when he looked across the room at Olivia arriving with Stella for the rehearsal. Love at first sight had always seemed a ridiculous thing to him, fairytale stuff, but on that morning when he looked at Olivia nothing else had mattered, would ever matter. She was beautiful, but it wasn't that, it was something else, some strange compulsion that made him feel that he'd known her for a thousand years, that he'd been waiting all his life for her to come into it.

In the days that followed he'd been miserable, a man neither his parents nor his fiance knew, and yet what came after had been inevitable. His engagement to Stella was over. The scandal of it swept through the village and far beyond and the following spring he had married Olivia, quietly, in the presence of his parents and hers, and later that year Stella had married Jonathon Clarke, the man he had chosen to be his best man at his wedding to Stella.

Almost immediately Stella and Jonathan went to live in Kenya. That same year Andrew's father had died from a massive heart attack and his mother went to live with her sister in Cheltenham. He was the master of Alveston and he settled back down to a life of country pursuits, with a vast estate to run and he had believed Olivia would be as dedicated as himself.

Olivia had hated every moment of it. She was an only child of parents who travelled the world and she'd been spoiled. Olivia liked expensive hotels and foreign glamour, expensive shops and lengthy cruises, and most of the time she was bored.

More than anything Olivia wanted love. That he should love her endlessly and to the exclusion of anything else. Her insecurity demanded constant expression of it, and if he failed there followed the tantrums and tears that he became increasingly unable to cope with.

She made scenes whenever he entertained guests and spoke to other women, even when they were old friends and the wives of his friends. She would not have Stella in the house whenever they came to England on leave and when their Christmas cards arrived she immediately tore them up and threw them in the fire.

She fell out with his friends one after the other and the staff too felt insecure. She made favourites and then discarded them, Andrew felt increasingly that he was living with a volcano waiting to erupt.

He was patient with her because he loved her, but even love can only stand so much and Olivia realised it before Andrew that there was no love, she had killed it.

Now life with Olivia became impossible. She took lovers, neither was she particular where she found them. He never knew the men she entertained when he was away, but at home there were the men who worked on the estate, members of the staff who were afraid to antagonise her, and others who succumbed and then were dismissed. Andrew was loyal, his servants were loyal, but they all knew that eventually the happenings that went on at the hall would be common knowledge in the village.

Olivia demanded a ball on New Year's Eve and Andrew invited old friends who he hoped would come to show him that he was still one of them, that memories of the past were dear, and Olivia invited a raggle-taggle of people he had never met and they did not mix well with those he had invited.

He had never seen her looking more beautiful, at the same time she drank too much, laughed too loudly and flirted outrageously. In the early hours of the morning he missed her. By this time many of the guests were leaving and he searched the house frantically so that she could join him in bidding them goodnight. It was mid-morning on New Year's Day when they retrieved Olivia's body from the lake.

Andrew believed that memories of that morning would be with him for the rest of his days. The house and the grounds were crawling with police. He was questioned along with any guests remaining at the house as well as the servants. They demanded the names of all those present at the ball but he was unable to give them the names of a great many of Olivia's guests and the stolid long-suffering silences from the police officers asking the questions both angered him and distressed him.

The results of the post mortem disclosed that Olivia had been strangled before her body had been thrown into the lake, and then the questions became worse, more personal, at times accusing. It was one of the game-keepers who came forward willingly to say that he had seen her ladyship in the park that night in the company of a man he did not know and they appeared to be quarrelling.

The police hinted that he had come forward to protect his employer or one of the people known to him, but after long diligent hours spent trying to trace her activities in London they arrested some man Andrew had never heard of, but whom he remembered had been a guest on the evening of the ball.

Some of Olivia's jewellery was discovered in his possession and then followed the long months of waiting for the trial, the uncertainties and the pity of those he knew and of the village overlooked by his ancestral home.

For whole days the newspapers thrived on the scandal and then something else took its place and people started to forget. Andrew was unable to forget. All he could think of was that he had to get away, neither was he concerned if he ever came back, and for years he travelled the globe, and when he grew tired of a place he simply moved on. He did not go to Kenya. He could not bear to look into Stella's wise sad eyes and remember what he had done to her. He had loved her, she was to have been his wife, and there were many who said fate had paid him back for the unhappiness he had caused her and in his heart he knew it was true.

After a discreet knock on the door Grant came in to inform him that a fire had been lit in his bedroom and his suitcases had been unpacked.

'Will you want to eat dinner in the dining room, sir, or in the smaller room your father preferred?' he asked gently.

'In the smaller room, Grant, and nothing too elaborate, I'm not very hungry.'

'Very well, sir.'

'I don't want any fuss, Grant, I don't want the servants to think they have to dance attention on me all the time. What do you do in your spare time, Grant?'

'Well I like to walk on the fells, and I do a little sailing in a friend's boat, and a little fishing.'

'And what were you intending to do this evening?'

'I play chess with the vicar, sir, but if I telephone him to tell him it isn't convenient he will understand.'

'Under no circumstances must you telephone him. I'm not a child, Grant, I don't need constant attention. What do the other servants do?'

'Well some of the girls go down to the village hall, one of the hops they have, Wednesdays and Saturdays I think, sir. Very popular they are with the younger people, and the inn is a good meeting place.'

'I'm sure it is. Well whatever they do with their time I wish them to continue doing it. If the time ever comes when we get back to entertaining visitors I'm sure they won't let me down.'

'Indeed not, sir.'

'I'll eat at seven-thirty tonight, Grant, that won't inconvenience you?'

'Not at all, sir.'

He was glad the servants were going out. He wanted to look round the house without anybody watching. He wanted to relive the past, face his ghosts.

On his return to the kitchen Grant shook his head sagely in response to the housekeeper's keen questioning stare.

'He doesn't want anything to change. We can continue to do whatever we've been doing in his absence.'

'Is he likely to stay, Grant, or do you think he'll be off on his travels again?'

'I don't know, the next few days will tell.'

'You'd have thought ten years would have got her and the past out of his system. It was all a terrible mistake, time to pull himself together and look forward instead of backwards.'

'I agree, Mrs Stokes. We shouldn't judge, we only know the half of it.'

'He should have married Miss Brampton, she was beautiful, just as beautiful as her cousin, and a far better person. I wonder if he ever thinks of her?'

'I'm sure he does.'

Grant moved away into the pantry, he too was thinking of Stella Brampton. It had been twelve months ago when he walked through the park and saw a woman strolling idly along the margin of the lake. He had stared at her curiously. People looked through the gates, they did not come through them to stroll in the grounds, and there was something about the woman that seemed vaguely familiar.

He crossed the grass towards her and was only a few feet away when she turned and stared into his face. Before he could speak she favoured him with a strangely sad half-smile, then she turned away and walked quickly in the direction of the gates. He had recognised her immediately, Stella Brampton was as beautiful as he remembered her.

He knew that he would not tell Sir Andrew of her visit, such incidents were best forgotten by the likes of him.

Andrew ate his solitary meal and after Grant had cleared away he went into the drawing room and sat for a while watching the television. Grant came in to tell him he was going into the village and after wishing him goodnight closed the door softly behind him. Andrew listened to his footsteps crossing the hall and the closing of the heavy front door. The time had come to face his past.

From somewhere outside the house he could hear laughter and the sound of women's voices, probably the women servants going off to their village dance, but even so he paused at the door until he felt assured the house was his to explore without interruption.

Only a few lights had been left on in the hall and he climbed the shallow staircase gingerly, afraid to look at the portrait at the head of the first flight of stairs. He need not have worried. Instead of Olivia's portrait somebody had had the good sense to put his mother's portrait there, serenely beautiful, a gentle beauty that had seemed so right on the wall of Alveston.

He was remembering how beautiful Olivia had looked on that last fateful evening, and how strange. In the light from the chandeliers her face had been a delicately-tinted golden mask. Blue, blue eyes, almost too blue to believe. The small straight nose in the perfect oval of her face. The black hair, dark and tumbled, a bird's wing of it curling down her cheek and along her white throat.

There had always been a faint Oriental cast to Olivia's face. The artist who had painted her portrait had gone a little overboard with her mouth as he had with her eyes. It was ripe red, crushed-strawberry red, the lips soft and full and moist. He could remember her long lithe body, the high rounded breasts, the gown that had moulded it like a second skin until it fell away in deep folds around her feet.

Surrounding her on that last evening had been an aura of excitement, a strange devilry as she danced and flirted with her guests, and he had been aware of their embarrassment as they stood in silent groups watching her performance.

He'd been distant with her, annoyed with the way she was behaving and she had accused him of being boring and without imagination. Those were the last words she said to him before she waltzed off with somebody else.

Now in this silent house she was everywhere. He could hear her laughter, her quick light footsteps in the hall and the sound of her shrill harsh voice raised in temper, accusing and bitter.

In the bedroom he had occupied as a boy his suitcases had been unpacked and his clothes put away. A fire burned in the grate but even so the room looked as spartan as he remembered it.

A boy's room. Cupboards filled with tennis racquets and other things dear to a boy's heart, and on the walls long photographs of school pupils in several different years. He had no difficulty in finding himself in their midst, a laughing cheerful young boy in striped blazer and later at university the same boy grown tall and confident.

There was nothing in this room to remind him of Olivia. The boy in these pictures had looked forward to the future with confidence and assured promise. He loved his home and his parents, he had good friends and life had seemed something to look forward to with joy. When Stella came into it he had believed his life would be complete, and then with Olivia everything had changed.

He looked round the master bedroom and felt nothing. He was unable to remember the good times, unable to see her beauty without remembering the despair but somehow it all seemed to have happened to another person, a being outside himself. In this room he could believe that Olivia was truly dead.

He returned to the warmth of the drawing room and poured himself a whisky and soda. On his way here he had truly believed he would not be able to settle down, now he realised that he was tired of running away. It was time to re-enter the world of the living.

He knew that in the village there would be speculation on how long he would remain at Alveston. He meant to show them that the past was truly dead, there had to be a future.

He picked up a country magazine from the table near his chair, leafing through the pages idly until he came to several pages dedicated to The Lakes and he stared with interest at the photographs of what he had always known to be Harvey's Folly. In the coming days he would acquaint himself with what went on there, even though he was unsure if he approved of the place.

Sleep did not come easily on that cool April night and he lay staring up at the ceiling where the branches of the trees made a pattern. The night was very still. Occasionally he recognised the lonely hooting of an owl and the barking of foxes, and at one point he heard laughter, probably from the servants returning home from their dance.

Across the lake there would be revelry in the hotel ballroom, soft music accompanying conversation and he frowned a little. He could not conceive that a fashionable hotel had been built on the site of one of his favourite places. The villagers had laughed at Harvey's Folly but he had always had some sympathy for Cornelius Harvey who had loved the spot so much he had badgered Andrew's father to sell him the land. Andrew had never been able to understand why his father had agreed to it, but the castle had come to nothing and now some other person had seen its potential as a site for some hotel.

In the next few days he would let the village know he had come home, visit his tenants, seek out his friends, even take a look at the hotel across the lake. His return would be a nine days' wonder, then something or somebody would come to take his place.

Chapter Eleven

The sun shone out of a clear blue sky the next morning when Andrew walked to the stables. He was unsure what he would find. He had given no instructions about the care of the horses but he felt sure his land agent would have seen to things. If nothing had changed at the house why should anything have changed on the estate?

A groom came forward to meet him as he crossed the yard and he recognised him immediately. Old Henry Forshaw had been with his family since he left school and he was still here, smiling a welcome, his weather-beaten face wreathed in smiles.

'I'm glad to see ye 'ome, sir,' he said.

'Glad to be home, Forshaw. Dare I hope that there's a horse suitable for me to ride? It's been a long time.'

'That it 'as, sir, but there's old Major there, in need of exercise and it's almost as though he's been expecting ye.'

Andrew's face lit up as he looked across the yard to where the old horse stood with his head over the gate looking out across the yard. Was it recognition he saw in his calm brown eyes, or expectancy that he might be taken out for a canter? Gently he caressed the horse's soft muzzle and ran his hand along the long satiny neck, and Forshaw smiled, 'I reckon 'e knows ye, sir, they 'ave their memories, I'm sure,' and as if to prove his point there came an excited barking from across the yard and a black labrador came running for his life, leaping up at Andrew excitedly.

A lump came into Andrew's throat when he remembered he'd gone off without a second's thought. He'd thought of nothing but his own pain, nothing about the people and creatures who had loved him, obsessed with his own anguish and bitterness.

'You've looked after them well, Forshaw,' he said at last, and Forshaw smiled.

'That I 'ave, sir. I knew you'd come back one day, I knew you'd come 'ome. Shall I saddle up the 'orse, sir?'

'Yes please, Forshaw. I'll take a ride over the fells.'

'They'll be glad to see ye in the village, sir, nothin much 'as changed unless it's the hotel. The village'll be crawlin' wi' strangers at Easter when they come to stay at the hotel.'

'You don't sound very happy with the idea, Forshaw.'

'Oh they don't bother us, sir. Mostly they're very nice ladies and gentlemen, some of 'em foreign and they do bring trade into the village, but I used to like the old ruin of 'arvey's Folly. It 'ad a sort of enchanted look about it.'

Andrew smiled. 'You have the soul of a poet, Forshaw. That's what I always thought: as though one day the place would come to life as a fairytale palace, not as some modern hotel.'

'Oh well, the gentleman that bought it 'as done 'is best with it. It's a beautiful sight fro' this side o' the lake, nobody could dispute that.'

'I'm very surprised Harvey consented to sell him the land, even if he didn't want it himself. Grant didn't tell me who bought it.'

'An American gentleman, sir. One or two of 'em in the village 'ave met him. He's stayed at the village inn and the landlord says he's generous and very friendly. Most likely 'e'll be over for Easter, I 'ave 'eard that Cornelius 'Arvey and his missus are likely to be visitin'.'

'I wonder what he'll think of it?'

'I wonder. Well now, sir, 'ere's the horse all ready and waitin' for ye. Enjoy your ride, sir.'

'Thanks, Forshaw, I will.'

It was good to feel the cool lakeland breeze on his face as he cantered across the fell, good to step across the ancient stone bridge which crossed the rippling stream and gaze out to where the mountain peaks rose dramatically across the lake and he found he could still recognise them, Scafell Pike and Skiddaw, Great Gable and Pillar. Snow still lingered on the peaks and the sunlight fell in shafts of gold on the dark crags and forests of evergreens.

Nowhere in his years of travelling had he come across anything more beautiful than the sight before his tear-dimmed eyes.

Anger and pain had sent him running away, now he was regretting the years he had wasted when he could have been here where he belonged, with people he knew instead of strangers and as his eyes swept across the fells he caught sight of homesteads he had known and he was remembering Christmas Days of the past when he had driven with his father to distribute gifts of wine and Christmas cheer to his tenants. Always they had received them into the warmth of the kitchen where bright log fires burned in the hearth and he had been plied with hot mince pies and huge portions of Christmas cake.

Those people who had known him as a boy would have been reluctant to recognise the man he had become, the man who had abandoned the woman he was expecting to marry, to marry instead a woman none of them had known and who had never wanted to know them.

These honest country people had never expected to hear of the events they had been subjected to on that New Year's morning. Tragedies of that sort did not happen in peaceful lakeland villages to people they had looked up to and respected for centuries.

Would they be able to greet him normally without thinking about the past and about Olivia?

He could see her now riding through the village on her black horse, her head held high, looking neither to right nor left, her profile etched against the sunlight, her black hair restrained under her riding hat, her beauty alien and distant.

Those local people had known that their lord's wife had little or no time for them. From the first days of her coming she had made it clear and in their turn they paid her no homage, they regarded her as an upstart and the backlash of their hatred had passed over him. Now he could only hope that they would forget those few months and remember him as a boy, as a young man who had been happy in their midst, before he had taken leave of his senses and closed his eyes to reality.

He turned his horse and galloped down the hillside towards the lane, perhaps tomorrow he would walk down into the village.

He was aware of the embarrassment he had created as he stood at the bar in the village inn. He had recognised a great many of the people sitting round the room and standing at the bar and in answer to his smiled greeting they had answered him respectfully, while averting their eyes. It was left to the village's oldest inhabitant Joe Grimshaw who had come into the bar accompanied by his son and an old lurcher dog.

'It's nice to see you looking so well, Grimshaw,' Andrew said affably, and the old man rewarded him with a self-satisfied smile.

'And it's nice to see ye back 'ere, sir, after all these years. 'Ope this time yer've come to stay.'

'Well for some time at least.'

'Nay, lad, yer can't run away forever. This is where ye were born, this is where yer belong.'

'You're probably right.'

'And what does yer lordship think o' the changes around 'ere? Now we've got a posh 'otel right where 'Arvey's Folly used to stand. I've often asked miself what yer father'd 'ave thought about it, and you too if ever ye came back 'ome?'

Andrew laughed. 'I'm not very sure I agree with it, Joe, but I haven't seen it yet. What do you think about it?'

'Well at first I didn't 'old with it, now I'm used to it. It's brought trade into the village, put us on the map and found work for a great many of us.'

'So I believe.'

Joe chuckled. 'If it wasn't for the 'otel yer'd think we had nothin' to talk about. Mi two great-grandchildren are employed there, they keep us entertained with the comin's and goin's.'

'I'm sure they do. How are they employed?'

'Mary's a chambermaid and Dolly's workin' in the kitchens.'

'Waiting on tables?'

'Bless ye, no, sir. They 'as Italian waiters and cooks too, and one or two Spaniards to boot. I've told mi great-grand-daughters that I don't want 'em bringin' any o' that lot 'ome. Allus flirtin' wi' the village girls they are and the girls are encouragin' 'em.'

Andrew smiled. He could well understand the advent of handsome Italians and Spaniards into the lives of properly brought up village girls some of whom had never set foot outside the area.

Now that Joe had broken the ice, others joined the conversation and mellowed considerably when he ordered drinks all round. They had never really known much about him since he left university. They had known him as a child, riding round the estate with his father, but his adult life had been alien to them. His sudden marriage to a woman none of them had known and the scandal that followed, then the years of absence and the aftermath of tragedy.

Olivia had never been one of them. She had detested country pursuits and the sort of things his mother had enjoyed. Her involvement with the villagers had been a chore, never a pleasure, and she had been unpopular. He found himself remembering her funeral.

The churchyard had been crowded. Newspapermen had jostled each other around the gravestones and the villagers had looked on with stone-like faces, angry that scandal had brought such notoriety to their village, unsympathetic at the demise of a woman they had neither liked nor respected, and angry with him that he had seen fit to marry her.

As he left to go out into the night Joe's last words were, 'Let the memories die, sir, yer'll soon pick up the pieces. I'm right glad to see yer back.'

It had not been as bad as he had thought it would be. They would go back to their homes and relate the events of the evening to their wives and families. Given time his life would fall into place.

His thoughts strayed to the Easter weekend ahead. He had never really liked Easter. It was usually cold and windy and a strange melancholy had always seemed to pervade the house and village with Good Friday's religious services commemorating the ancient tragedy.

Several mornings later his butler placed the morning post beside his breakfast plate and in answer to Andrew's smiling, 'Good morning, Grant,' said, 'It is a good morning, sir, I think we are in for a nice Easter.'

Andrew leafed through his post and after staring at one particular envelope embossed with gold lettering and a crest said, 'Well, what have we here?'

He passed the envelope's contents to his butler with a wry smile. 'News travels fast in these parts, Grant, what do you make of that?'

Grant stared down at the embossed invitation and Andrew said, 'My return has evidently reached the proprietor of The Lakes since he's seen fit to invite me to dinner on Easter Saturday, now I must think of an excuse not to attend.'

'But why should you, sir, unless you have something else planned for the evening?'

'It's hardly my scene, Grant.'

Grant handed the invitation back without comment, and as he moved away Andrew said doubtfully, 'You think it would be churlish to decline the invitation?'

'I think you would be agreeably surprised if you decided to accept, sir. There is nothing at the hotel which could cause you to wish you hadn't gone there.'

'Have you been there?'

'On one evening, sir. I was invited by the vicar to celebrate his silver wedding. Everything was first class, there was absolutely nothing one could feel dissatisfaction with.'

'I can't think why they've invited me.'

'A nice gesture I think, sir, to welcome you home.'

Andrew smiled. 'I can see that you think I should go, Grant, that it would be discourteous of me to decline.'

'I think it would be a very pleasant way of spending Easter Saturday evening, sir, unless you had something else in mind.'

'I haven't, Grant. I'll think about it.'

Later that morning Andrew rode his horse through the village and made his way to the lake. Those he had met on the way afforded him smiles of greeting and quaint country salutes and he was aware of a feeling of wellbeing, strangely absent in recent years.

He halted his horse where the banks rose gently above the lake and from where he could see the new jetty and a discreet car park partly hidden by shrubs. He might at first have thought that nothing had changed until his eyes became accustomed to the fact that there were people strolling in the gardens across the lake and that others were sitting on the long terrace outside the hotel.

The Virginia creeper still twined lovingly against the façade and the entire building seemed to blend with the distant hills and the forest of evergreens.

He was remembering his father's display of antagonism, angry at his own stupidity in allowing Cornelius Harvey to purchase the land, and then his reluctant admission that the man had not abused the privilege. His father had approved of Harvey's concept of how he wanted his house to be. Harvey's dream had come to nothing, but from his vantage point across the lake Andrew could find nothing incongruous in what it had become.

He supposed it would do no harm to accept the invitation, after all what else would he be doing?

He informed his butler of his decision to accept over dinner that evening and Grant decided not to inform him that the hotel would be blessed by the visit of a film actress and the horde of photographers that would be waiting for her arrival. By Easter Saturday the lady would be settled in and hopefully the horde would have taken their pictures and left the area.

He reckoned without the villagers' avid interest in the lady and the fact that those employed by the hotel had already informed their families of her arrival, and if royalty had been visiting they couldn't have been more enthusiastic.

There were mixed feelings in the kitchen at Alveston Hall as the house-keeper shook her head doubtfully about her employer's invitation to eat dinner at the hotel.

'There's that actress woman coming, he'll not take kindly to be associating with the likes of her,' Mrs Stokes said dolefully.

'I doubt if he will be expected to spend time with the lady,' Grant said firmly. 'She will no doubt have her own coterie around her, people who admire her, people who want to be seen with her.'

Mrs Stokes sniffed derisively. 'Four husbands she's had and the Lord knows how many men living with her. Do you think she's attractive?'

'I confess the lady has some earthy attraction, Mrs Stokes, but I doubt if the master will be taken in by it.'

'I should think not indeed. The woman's brash, it would be nice if he could meet some nice lady like Miss Brampton, he can't spend the rest of his life alone.'

Grant decided it was time for him to retire gracefully. He had his own thoughts about Stella Brampton. She'd been a visitor in the area, he'd seen her himself and he doubted if she'd been staying with the people she'd known in the area. She'd seen fit to walk in the grounds, thereby evoking old memories, with a bit of luck she could be visiting The Lakes over Easter, then he remembered that Stella Brampton was a married lady and his hopes sank.

Andrew replied to the proprietor of The Lakes accepting the invitation to dinner on Easter Saturday but he had little enthusiasm for the event. His mind went back to other hotels he had visited over the years, hotels that were expensive and where a great many people went to be seen and to display their wealth and fame. People he liked preferred smaller hotels in out-of-the-way places and now here was this one on his own doorstep and he doubted if it would be any different from others he had despised.

As Easter drew nearer he began to have regrets about accepting the invita-tion. His friends were amused by it, and Daphne Carmel was quick to say, 'Why don't we all go to lend support, poor Andrew will be quite out of his depth with that film actress and the crowds she gathers around herself.'

They were all in agreement that the least they could do was give him some support, but when Daphne's husband rang the hotel to book a table he was politely informed that the dining room was completely booked up for the evening, indeed for all the Easter weekend.

They plied him with invitations, saying he would be bored with the evening at The Lakes, encouraging him to cancel it, but some strange stubbornness made him decline. After all what was one night, and he had no legitimate excuse for staying away.

When Grant heard the guests encouraging him to get out of it he hoped silently that the master would ignore them. None of them had a part to play beyond friendship in Andrew's future. They were all couples and the women who were single had not attracted Andrew in the past and were hardly likely to do so now.

Mrs Stokes had an altogether different opinion.

'They're quite right,' she asserted. 'That actress woman will make a play for him as soon as she hears of his title, hasn't she already had her name linked with one peer of the realm?'

'Don't you credit him with more sense?' Grant said calmly.

'I don't credit men with much sense at all when a woman of that sort sets her cap at them.'

Grant smiled. Mrs Stokes had set ideas about men in general. She had married briefly in her youth, a man she thought little about and who had conveniently died at the age of thirty-six. Since then her opinion of the opposite sex had been noticeably unsavoury.

In the village itself Andrew noticed that the shops had a festive air, their windows decked out with Easter eggs and Easter bunnies. Window boxes filled with Spring bulbs bloomed wherever he looked and moored at the jetty he caught his first sight of an elegant steamship, 'The Lady of the Lake'.

When he remarked upon it to his butler Grant merely said, 'She's a beautiful little vessel, sir, she must have cost a small fortune.'

'Nothing but the best, eh, Grant?'

'Exactly, sir.'

As he rode across the fells on the week before Easter he became more and more aware of the hustle and bustle in the village itself. The buzz of more traffic: from his place high up on the fell he could see the steady arrival of it along the road on the other side of the lake.

It was evident many of the guests would be leaving their cars on the village side of the lake and sailing across to the hotel on the steamer waiting for them, but he had already decided that he would take the long way round when Easter Saturday came around.

When he called at the inn that evening the landlord was quick to tell him that Cornelius Harvey had arrived that very afternoon in a car driven by his wife, and he had been seen later driving up to his brother's farm where they were obviously visiting.

'Will this be the first time he's visited the hotel?' Andrew asked curiously.

'I do hear so, sir. 'E probably didn't 'old with it, and now 'e's come to see what a mess they've made of it.'

'It looks very well, I doubt if he'll be disappointed.'

'Well no, sir. It's well patronised, and the people come back again and again. Old Joe saw him walkin' across the fell with 'is brother, lookin' very well 'e says, 'ardly changed at all.'

'The Harveys were an extensive family I seem to remember.'

'That they were, sir. It were Cornelius who was the odd one out. I didn't live 'ere in them days but I've heard the villagers talkin'. 'Ave ye bin up to the hotel yet, sir?'

'No, I'm afraid not. That is a treat in store, I think.'

'Well yes, sir. I keep tellin' the missus we should take a look at it but we're kept pretty busy 'ere. We might just do it though, one weekend when we've closed the doors.'

'Yes, why don't you? Goodnight, Jarvis.'

It was dusk as he walked along the village street to where he had tethered his horse and a crowd of children were standing near it, offering the horse titbits of chocolate and sweets. They ran off as he approached but he raised his hand and waved in their direction.

The long evening stretched ahead of him and there was a strange emptiness about it. He would read or watch television. He would delay going to bed because it seemed such a waste, at the same time he had come to resent the sound of laughter from the grounds outside as the girls came home from their dance.

It seemed to Andrew that everybody in the world had more to do with their lives than himself. He had thought running away was the answer, new sights, new pursuits, new people, but in the end he had realised there was no place to go except home, no way to forget except by reconciliation with familiar things that had meant something before Olivia.

The house no longer reminded him of her. Her sojourn at Alveston had been fleeting and she had never belonged, yet at the same time there were moments when he felt her teasing presence close to him, when he was afraid to look around in case she stood behind him and he could look into the dangerous madness of her eyes.

He tried to remember those other days when she had seemed sweet and normal, days when her beauty had enchanted him, obliterating other memories that shocked and tormented him, so that in the end he could only remember the bad days, the days when her tears and tantrums had sent him reeling from her in abysmal despair.

He became impatient with himself. He put on an air of normality he did not feel, for Grant's benefit and the benefit of all those people who had felt sorry for him. He was remembering that after the tragedy the entire village had hidden under a cloud, when friends and villagers alike could hardly believe that something so terrible had happened to a family they had respected.

Now the village had returned to normal and this was how he remembered it from his early years. It had taken considerably longer for him, but he was recovering. Life had to go on, and he had to prove to himself and everybody else that he had what it took to put the past behind him.

Chapter Twelve

Stuart and Alison were enjoying the drive. The countryside was welcoming with daffodils along the hedgerows and as yet it was a little early for the build-up of Easter traffic. Stuart was glad he'd had the good sense to leave the wedding festivities in good time.

'How was the surgery?' she asked him.

That was the nicest thing about Alison, she was genuinely interested in his work. She had a brain, unlike some of the dolly birds that attracted some of his colleagues, and Stuart was convinced a good many of them envied his association with his secretary.

'Well, you know,' he answered her, 'the usual moans about pensions and education. Most of them have an axe to grind and it is difficult trying to be all things to all men.'

'I'm sure you manage it very well, Stuart.'

He looked at her quickly but her face was expressionless.

'Well, it is difficult, darling. Some of them are well off, others are on the bread-line. One thing they all agree about is that they don't want the new trunk road that will cut through part of the constituency.'

'It's nice that they agree about something.'

'Yes, of course. I was at a wedding earlier today, quite a select affair, even if I'm not very sure that they're entirely suitable for each other.'

'Why is that?'

'Well the girl's father is old money, upper-crust family background and the groom's father is a self-made man. Rich now, but from an obscure family background. He's made his money in haulage and the building trade whereas the girl's family had it handed down to them. I hope it works out.'

'Didn't your wife want to attend the wedding?'

'I don't really know. She's tied up with her parents, she didn't seem particularly put out at missing it.'

'Didn't they want to know why you were leaving early?'

'There was too much going on. I said I'd probably go somewhere to play some golf.'

'I've heard about The Lakes, isn't it supposed to be very stylish?'

'Well, yes. I'm sure you'll enjoy it.'

'I've brought cocktail dresses and one or two evening dresses in case they're needed. Are there likely to be people here that you know?'

'Maybe. We can spend some time in the morning doing a little work if you like.'

'So that having your secretary with you will not seem too unusual?'

They were embarking on slippery ground and it was the last thing he wanted.

'Alison, you do know that an M.P. has work to do during his vacation, his work never stops, but there will still be ample time for us to enjoy ourselves.'

They were booked into separate rooms, not even on the same floor. It had never been any obstacle before, and in public their association would be entirely business-like. The other guests probably wouldn't be interested, and there was more media interest in London, they were hardly likely to be milling around some village in the Lake District.

He brought the car to a halt in the car park across the lake and Alison gazed across to where the hotel looked particularly beautiful in the late afternoon sunlight. The sky was already tinged with hints of rose as the sun was sinking to rest, and the towers and turrets of the hotel were tinged with pink which vied strikingly with the dark green conifers that formed its backdrop.

'We can park here and sail across the lake or we can drive round and park at the back,' Stuart said. 'I see that the launch is there at its moorings.'

The launch looked particularly inviting and the captain and crew were already stationed on the jetty in anticipation of people arriving early.

'Do you suppose they're waiting for us?' Alison asked.

'For anybody who wants to take the steamer, I should think.'

That was the moment when a small mini-bus arrived in the car park and out jumped several newspaper men, and almost immediately they were followed by a white Rolls Royce which they rushed to surround.

'Damn, damn, damn,' Stuart said testily. 'Who the hell is this? It's the last thing we want at a place like this.'

Alison looked up at his face, dark with anger, his expression one of vindictive fury.

Her own resentment was of a different sort. Nothing had changed. She was still the other woman, the mistress to be kept apart and no amount of talking would ever change it. Stuart had no intention of informing his wife about her, his fury at this new development said as much.

A woman was easing herself out of the rear seat of the Rolls, and they recognised her immediately. Not a day passed without Gloria Weston's photograph occupying the front page of some newspaper or magazine, even when she was no longer young and seldom featured these days in either stage, film or television.

Now the media were more concerned with her penchant for younger men, her lifestyle, her money, and Alison had to admit she was still an attractive woman, from across the car park at any rate.

Gloria was wearing a dark mink coat over a beige dress and her hair blowing in the breeze was dark blonde and luxuriant. She was smiling, well pleased with the attention she was receiving, and happy to pose for the photographers. A young man had left the car and was standing uncertainly at the door but at a sign from Gloria he went to stand with her and she was encouraging him to smile.

She moved towards the launch followed by the journalists and Stuart said hastily, 'Come on, we're not sailing in that thing with them, we'll drive along the far shore and reach the hotel that way.'

Perversely Alison said, 'I thought it would be rather nice to sail there, terribly romantic, don't you think?'

Stuart merely scowled and returned to his car.

'You know who she is, I suppose,' he said.

When she didn't answer he said, 'I can't think why everybody is still remotely interested in that woman. She hasn't made a decent film in years and that last silly television programme she made was a disaster. How old do you suppose she is?'

'I'm not sure, but she can still apparently pull in the crowds.'

'I hope she's not hugging the limelight all through the weekend.'

'She could conceivably take the limelight off you, Stuart, you'd like that I'm sure.'

He scowled. 'I don't merit the limelight. I'm a hard-working M.P., she's past her sell-by date.'

Gloria was well-pleased by her reception. The villagers had flocked to the banks of the lake to jostle together while they watched her boarding the launch. She smiled and waved to them, and already on the other side of the lake guests strolling in the grounds and sitting in the lounges were staring at the small steamer coming to rest at the jetty.

Mrs Cornelius Harvey sat in the window enjoying her afternoon tea and as others flocked to the window she rose from her seat to join them.

'Who is she?' she asked another woman standing beside her.

'Gloria Weston, the film actress,' she was told.

Of course she'd seen her picture a good many times in the papers but she couldn't ever remember seeing her in a film. Obviously, there was that television programme, but Cornelius wouldn't watch it so she'd missed a great many episodes. She returned to her afternoon tea. She didn't know where Cornelius had got to. He was probably wandering about outside, familiarising himself with the gardens and he had that face on him so that she wasn't sure if he approved. She would give him time to make up his mind before she asked him, they had only arrived the evening before so it was early days.

Clarissa thought it was beautiful. Their bedroom overlooked the lake and it was beautifully furnished and carpeted. The bathroom was everything a bathroom should be and there was soap and shampoo provided as well as exquisite towels and a basket of fruit in the bedroom.

Mr Van Hopper had greeted them charmingly, given them a table in the restaurant where they could see everything, and the food has been wonderful.

Cornelius said the hotel wouldn't compare with others they'd stayed in in Sydney and Kuala Lumpur when they went to see their daughter, but it was better, and every bit as grand as the Mandarin in Hong Kong.

Of course Cornelius wouldn't agree. He still thought of this corner as his, if the Queen had elected to build a house here he wouldn't have accepted that it was better than his dream.

Gloria Weston by this time had swept into the reception area and Anton de Roche was greeting her, bowing professionally over her outstretched hand.

'Anton darling,' she exclaimed. 'You're still the handsomest man I know. I was wondering if you'd still be here.'

Anton smiled, before eyeing the young man standing behind her.

'This is James,' Gloria said. 'I told him he couldn't possibly think of spending Easter all alone in London, I do hope you've given him the nicest possible room.'

'I think he'll be well suited, madam.'

'Is the hotel full?'

'As always.'

'And looking absolutely beautiful. Have we anybody famous staying here?'

'Most of our famous guests come here hoping to be left alone,' Anton said with a smile. 'They are anxious to get a little peace and remain anonymous.'

'But not me, darling,' Gloria said. 'I love the limelight, where would I be without it?'

'Where indeed?'

'So, there is nobody of note?'

'Not that I am aware of.'

By this time other guests were arriving in the reception area and Anton said, 'Perhaps your companion would like to register, Miss Weston. If you need anything you only have to ask.'

His eyes swept over the group of people standing uncertainly near the door. He recognised Stuart Mansell immediately but not his companion. Mr Mansell had stayed at The Lakes with his wife soon after the hotel had opened so he knew this young lady was someone else. They were staying in separate rooms which didn't mean a thing but he felt sure Mr Mansell would enlighten any interested party and the enlightenment would be entirely circumspect.

He went forward to greet his guests. Two elderly people who seemed a little overawed, Mr Mansell and his companion, and a lady who stood looking round her uncertainly, a lady who smiled at him charmingly and a little unsure.

Minutes later Mary Styles looked around her bedroom with evident pleasure. From the rose velvet curtains to the deep-piled carpet on the floor it was charming. Her view from the window overlooked the forest of evergreens and the distant mountains. She had not asked for a lake view because they had been rather more expensive and she was already having qualms about the money she was spending on only a few days.

Mr Mansell had helped her with her luggage at the car park and she had recognised him from photographs she had seen in the daily paper. He had been delightful, his companion had been equally so and her introduction to the hotel couldn't have been more cordial.

The manager had suggested that she should go down for afternoon tea which was already being served so she removed her coat, refreshed her make-up and left her luggage to be unpacked later. Most of the tables were already occupied but an elderly lady sitting alone at a table in the window smiled at her graciously and Mary asked if she might join her.

'Please do,' Clarissa said. 'I'm expecting my husband but there is plenty of room. I can't think where he's got to.'

Mary looked around the room quickly. There was no sign of Gerald but she hadn't been sure when he was arriving, probably in the morning of Good Friday. The lady was smiling across the table.

'Is this your first visit?' she asked her.

'Yes. It's a beautiful place, isn't it?'

'Yes it is. Have you just arrived?'

'Yes. I came this afternoon thinking the roads would be less crowded than in the morning.'

'So did we. I believe the hotel is fully booked, more people will be arriving tomorrow morning.'

At that moment an elderly gentleman joined them and the lady looked up with a smile saying, 'I've been wondering if you'd join me for tea. I'll ask for some more hot water. This is my husband, Cornelius Harvey,' she explained. 'My name is Clarissa.'

Mary held out her hand. 'I am Mary Styles.'

'Are you here alone?' Clarissa asked.

'Yes. I think perhaps a friend will be arriving tomorrow.'

'Well, what do you think of the place, Cornelius?'

'It's all right, I suppose.'

When Mary looked at him in some surprise Clarissa laughed.

'He's not sure about the hotel because he was brought up here and he once contemplated building a house on this plot of land. Nothing came of it and he resents the fact that somebody else built on it.'

'Not at all,' Cornelius said, 'I merely resent the fact that it's this place.'

'Oh surely not, Mr Harvey,' Mary said. 'The hotel is very beautiful, there is nothing to take exception to.'

'Nothing you or I could take exception to,' Clarissa said with a smile. 'But my husband would object to everything and everyone with a stake in this place.'

'I'm sure you will like being here,' Mary said gently. 'By the time you leave you will see how beautiful it is.'

Cornelius helped himself to scones and butter, favoured her with a brief smile but remained silent.

Mary looked around her. The sound of conversation and the tinkling of crockery, music played softly in the background, gentle lighting from lamps placed on small exquisite tables, and outside through the windows the mist beginning to lie low across the water.

There were largely family groups enjoying afternoon tea and couples chatting to other couples and she felt singularly alone. Clarissa Harvey was being kind, endeavouring to include her in conversation and her husband by this time was mellowing as his wife gently teased him out of his rather foolish objections to the hotel.

As soon as tea was over she made an excuse to leave them and Mrs Harvey said, 'Do join us this evening if you are on your own.'

She spent the next half hour moving from one room to another, lost in admiration at the artistry that had gone into the furnishing and embellishment of the hotel. Everything was in perfect taste. The colours, the flowers, the ambiance and as she returned to the foyer she saw the lady who had arrived with the Member of Parliament standing rather forlornly looking up the long curving staircase as if she was waiting for someone.

Mary smiled at her and Alison smiled back.

'Have you been taking a look around?' she asked.

'Yes. I'd heard it was beautiful, but I hadn't quite expected this. Is it your first visit?'

'Yes.'

'I've been hearing about it from a friend who is arriving later, he was very enthusiastic, now I know exactly why.'

'Have they given you a good view?'

'I'm at the side overlooking the fells and the mountains. I get a corner view of the lake. I should think every view from any window is wonderful.'

'Yes. I'm overlooking the lake on the second floor.'

'That must be very nice.'

They exchanged smiles again and Mary started to ascend the stairs. The girl had said *I* have a view of the lake so obviously she was not his wife. Mary wasn't unduly curious, she had too much on her mind.

Suppose Gerald arrived with a group of men and felt embarrassed by her presence? She should have told him she intended to spend Easter at The Lakes and left it to him either to stay away or arrive as planned, now the situation could be difficult.

On the ground floor Alison was seething with impatience. Stuart had gone to his room in something of a temper without telling her the number and without asking her hers. She would have liked afternoon tea but was reluctant to enter the room where it was being served in case he was looking for her and she had no intention of asking for his room number at the reception desk.

Obviously the newpaper men had upset him, even when, as yet, the only person they were interested in was the actress. When she'd said as much to Stuart all he'd said was, 'If they get a sniff of scandal they'll be on to it like a pack of hounds.'

'Are you suggesting we leave then?' she'd asked him.

'I'm suggesting we don't give them anything to write about.'

Nothing had changed. Suppose the newspaper men hadn't been there, how would they have talked? He'd have fobbed her off yet again with talk of the future that they only had to wait for, play it by ear, now was not the time but it would come as surely as Christmas.

She'd listened to it over and over again, accepted it and gone on loving him. The only chance she had of ever becoming more than a mistress to him was if Sybil Mansell found another man, or found out about her husband's infidelity and threw him out. If the scandal came to light and it became a political problem then Alison had no doubt Sybil would stand by him. They would present a united front to the electorate and probably all would be glossed over as a temporary fall from grace but never a catastrophe.

Anton de Roche made it a rule never to forget the name of any of the guests and approaching Alison with a charming smile said, 'Are you looking for the tea lounge, Miss Gray?'

'I was wondering if Mr Mansell had come down.'

'I haven't seen him. Why not go in there and I'll tell him where to find you.'

'Thank you, I will.'

His eyes followed her across the room, a tall elegant woman, and something in him felt strangely saddened.

He'd seen so much of it over the years. Girls in love with men who used them to bolster up their pride and too besotted to realise it. Silly young girls with ageing Casanovas, mostly with too much money. Young men escorting and flattering women whose youth had left them years before, but left them with enough money to buy sex and attention.

It was girls like Alison Gray he felt most sorry for. Girls who were in love, sacrificing their youth and ambition for some hoped-for dream that in the end would crash around their ears.

The men who had professed to love them invariably went back to their wives, wives who forgave their indiscretions because at the bottom of it was money, and the girls disillusioned and miserable were mostly blamed. The woman tempted me and I fell, must be the oldest excuse in the world, Anton reflected, and a small cynical smile came to disturb the urbanity of his features.

Stuart Mansell stepped out of the lift gazing rapidly round the foyer, he had expected her to be here waiting for him as always, and the fact that she was not afforded Anton a brief feeling of pleasure.

Stuart frowned at the sound of laughter coming from the lounge where Gloria sat in one corner with her young escort surrounded by people who found her amusing. His eyes swept over the room and Anton approached him with a smile. 'If you are looking for Miss Gray, Mr Mansell, she has gone into the tea lounge.'

Stuart nodded. 'How long is Miss Weston intending to stay here?' he asked.

Anton shrugged his shoulders. 'We never know. She usually books in for several days but rarely stays the entire length. She will probably only stay over the weekend.'

'And we shall be plagued with that retinue of newspaper men, I suppose.'

'They do not appear to be bothering any of the other guests.'

Stuart frowned. 'They will when they've exhausted everything she can do for them.'

'That should not worry anyone with nothing to hide,' Anton said calmly, and when Stuart looked at him sharply he was met with a bland smile.

Alison sat at a table near the window and as Stuart took his place beside her she said, 'I've ordered tea, I wasn't sure if you'd be here.'

'I'm not looking forward to hearing that woman's voice over our tea,' he snapped. 'Does she ever let up?'

'Some of them seem to be amused by her.'

'Well I'm not.'

For several minutes there was silence, and as she poured the tea he stole a glance at her face. It was wearing the expression he had come to dread, and gathering his wits he said, 'I'm sorry to be in such a dire mood, darling, but I wanted this weekend to be special. I didn't bank on somebody like that being here and the place crawling with newspaper men.'

'And they're causing you more annoyance than Gloria Weston,' Alison said. 'You're afraid they'll get around to us.'

'Well I don't want things to get out this way. Surely you can understand that.'

'I understand everything very well, Stuart.'

Chapter Thirteen

The wedding guests were standing around in groups waiting for the bride and groom to appear so that they could be sent off on their honeymoon with their good wishes.

The bride's mother was distinctly unhappy. She had sat through the wedding breakfast sitting next to the bridegroom and he had barely addressed a word to her, neither had he spoken to his new wife but had sat with a little boy's sulky look on his face and Geraldine was aware of Debbie's set expression and the fact that she had ignored him.

Something was wrong. Tod's father too was aware of it. He wasn't unduly surprised. His new daughter-in-law was accustomed to getting her own way, she'd been well and truly spoilt and while his wife was dewy-eyed about the proceedings he was considerably less so.

He looked across the room at Geraldine's strained expression, but she was looking at her husband engaged in conservation with Josie Martindale, and he had heard rumours about their involvement.

Upstairs in her bedroom Debbie was being assisted into her going-away outfit by her bridesmaids who were drooling ecstatically over the pale green dress and jacket lavishly adorned with pale cream mink.

The bridesmaids were not aware that anything was amiss. They had enjoyed their day, been flattered by a number of young men who were expecting to see more of them, and now they were anxious to join the rest of the wedding guests downstairs.

The young pageboy had eaten too much and was curled up asleep under one of the tables while his mother searched frantically for him, and there was a hearty cheer as Debbie and her new husband arrived in their midst.

'Have you enough money?' Tod's father asked, pulling his son to one side.

'Yes thanks, Dad, everything's paid for.'

'Aren't you going to tell us where you're going?'

'It's a secret. Debbie wants it that way.'

'Well you know your mother and me are off to Spain later today, we'll be away for two weeks. How long will you be away?'

'I'm not sure. Debbie made all the arrangements and her father has paid for it.'

'Have you had any say in it at all?'

'Not much. I wanted to go to Spain.'

His father didn't comment. To the Broadhursts Spain would be considered bourgeois. Not quite their scene.

Meanwhile Debbie's mother was asking anxiously, 'Is something wrong, darling? Tod was very quiet over lunch.'

'Nothing's wrong, Mummy, he'll see for himself how wonderful it is when we get there.'

'You mean he doesn't want to go to this place you're going to, didn't you discuss it?'

'Well, of course. He wanted to go to Spain and I didn't. He's been to Spain once this year already and his mind doesn't stretch much beyond it. He'll be all right when he sees how beautiful everything is.'

'But where, darling?'

'It's a secret, Mummy, even Tod doesn't know. I wanted to surprise him.'

At that moment her father joined her asking, 'Are you all right for money, love?'

'Yes thank you, Daddy, you've been very generous.'

Geraldine favoured him with a caustic smile.

'Josie Martindale looks positively frightful in that red colour, fancy choosing red for an Easter wedding, and with her colouring,' she said.

Her husband looked across the room at the offending outfit and remained silent. The red dress and large red hat certainly stood out amongst the other attire, but Josie was able to carry it off, she had great style.

The guests were milling round Debbie's new sports car. They had elected to travel in that instead of Tod's large lumbering car that ate petrol.

Tod was driving however, and as he sat behind the wheel for the first time that afternoon he was smiling.

John Broadhurst was wishing the day was over. He had indigestion and the guests were still milling around and showing no inclination to leave. All he wanted was to go upstairs and get out of his morning suit and into something more comfortable, and whenever he looked at his wife she looked away quickly, smiling brightly at whomever she was talking to and ignoring his evident signals of distress.

Josie sidled up to him, a smile on her attractive face, her eyes under the wide red brim of her hat smiling at him provocatively.

'It's been a fabulous day, John,' she enthused. 'Debbie looked absolutely beautiful, you must be very proud of her.'

He smiled.

'Where are they off to?'

'We don't know, she wouldn't tell us.'

'How wonderfully romantic.

'I see Stuart Mansell left directly after lunch. Is he joining Sybil, do you know?'

'I understand he was golfing for a few days.'

'I wonder who with.'

There was a half smile on her face and John reflected that if anybody knew who Stuart Mansell was golfing with it would be Josie. Her husband was twice her age, singularly unperceptive where his wife's comings and goings were concerned, and Josie had an eye for the men.

She had a lively sense of humour and few women friends. She had a sharp tongue, often malicious, but she was good company, the sort of company most of the men enjoyed.

His wife joined them, and after eyeing Josie over said, 'I like the dress, Josie, red suits you.'

'I fell in love with it. It was frightfully expensive, I daren't tell Clive how much I paid for it. I wasn't sure about red for a wedding though.'

'I think it looks very well.'

The two women smiled at each other. Geraldine had lied and Josie was well aware of it.

'How long are our guests staying?' John asked plaintively. 'It's getting late and there's a lot of clearing up to do. Can't we give them a nudge?'

'Hardly, darling. The caterers will do the clearing up, I'm just glad to see them enjoying themselves.'

'I want to get out of this monkey suit and into a sweater for the rest of the evening. I have terrible indigestion.'

'You ate too much and probably drank too much. Where are your tablets?'

'Upstairs in the bathroom.'

Josie laughed. 'I think Clive and I will set an example and leave,' she said. 'If one or two of us drift off the rest of them will get the message. Thank you for a lovely day.'

They watched her walking across the room, occasionally pausing to speak to one or another of the guests, then collecting her husband. The Martindales disappeared into the dusk.

'I don't know why you don't like Josie,' John complained, 'she's always agreeable company.'

'Too agreeable,' his wife said caustically.

'There was no need to mention the dress, particularly as you didn't much like it.'

'I was being polite.'

'You were being two-faced, Geraldine, and what do you mean about Debbie and Tod falling out? I thought they looked perfectly happy when they drove off.'

'He'd had time to recover. I didn't imagine it, John, they'd had words.'

'Well whatever it was let's hope they patched it up.'

Tod felt more relaxed than he'd felt all day. He liked the feel of Debbie's new car and it couldn't half move. Debbie was looking particularly enchanting and wherever they were going at least Debbie was happy.

He spared a thought for his parents getting ready to fly out to Malaga and for a moment the frown returned. He hadn't a clue where Debbie was taking him to, but they hadn't required passports so it was evidently somewhere in England or Scotland. Scotland at Easter would be vile with those long dreary lochs and mists, besides it would be freezing, and they'd passed the roads heading towards Wales some while back. They were driving north so where on earth was there?

Deciding to overcome his early churlishness, he said, 'Everybody seemed to be enjoying themselves today, Debbie.'

'Except you, darling,' she replied.

'Well, wouldn't you have been cross if I'd done it on you? There they were all of them asking where we were going and I couldn't tell them.'

'Of course not, honeymoons are only important to the people concerned, they shouldn't have asked you.'

'Well I'm the bridegroom, I had a right to know.'

'I wanted to surprise you.'

'It's Easter, Debbie. If we'd gone to Spain the weather would have been lovely. You could have sat in the sun and swum in the sea.'

'We can do that some other time. Where we are going is the most romantic place I've ever been to.'

'In England!'

Debbie smiled.

'It'll be dark when we get there wherever it is,' Tod complained, 'and too late to get an impression.'

'There's tomorrow and all the other tomorrows,' Debbie replied confidently.

She stole a look at his face, young, good-looking, confident and for the first time she began to have qualms. Suppose he didn't like it, suppose he went about with a sulky face. She'd seen him in such a mood when everything was not going to his liking. She'd wanted a honeymoon she would remember for the rest of her life, Tod could change all that so that she would remember it for the disaster it was.

'I'd like you to tell me where we're going,' he said petulantly. 'I feel I'm driving blind. We're headig for Kendal so I suppose we're going to Scotland.'

She didn't answer, and in some exasperation he snapped, 'I don't like this, Debbie. It's almost dark, I don't want to be arriving in some Scottish town in the dead of night.'

'We're not going to a Scottish town,' she said softly.

For several minutes there was silence, then he said, 'Don't tell me we're spending our honeymoon in the Lake District. I can think of nothing worse, cold and damp, probably rain and nothing to do but walk.'

'Why don't you just wait until we get there.'

The rest of the journey was taken in silence and Debbie's heart sank. Light rain was falling on the windscreen and a thin eerie mist swirled along the road ahead.

Debbie was beginning to have misgivings. Perhaps they should have gone to a warmer climate at this time of the year and come to the Lake District in the summer. Then they could have left the car and sailed across the lake in the new launch, Tod would have liked that, as it was they would have to drive along the narrow drive at the other side of the lake and he would not be able to see how enchanting the hotel looked from the east bank.

The silence was heavy with resentment. 'You'll have to tell me where we're supposed to be going,' he said, 'this is new to me.'

They were approaching the village now. There were lights from farmhouses on the fells and from some large building set well back from the road showing lights from one or two windows. 'Is that where we're going?' he asked as they reached the lodge house and large wrought iron gates. 'It doesn't look very prepossessing.'

'That is Alveston Hall, I doubt if the lord of the manor will be expecting us.'

Her tone was brittle, in tune with the resentment he was arousing in her.

The village shops were closed but lights streamed out into the gloom from the village inn halfway along the high street and Tod slowed the car down.

'Is the car park at the back?' he asked.

'This isn't where we're staying.'

'You mean we're driving on into the fog?'

'It isn't a fog, Tod, it's only a light mist. We haven't far to go.'

By the time they reached the lake however the mist was considerably thicker and only a faint glow shone across the water from the hotel.

'Where now?' Tod asked.

'Drive on, I'll tell you when to take a left turn.'

She could have wept. It was never going to be like this. She had thought he would look across the lake and gasp with delight at the scene before them, instead there was this murky darkness and increasing rain. Tod cursed under his breath as a sheep wandered aimlessly across the road and he had to brake hard to avoid it, after that he relapsed once more into sulky silence until she told him to turn left at the junction ahead.

There were passing places along the drive but they met no-one and eventually the road widened and they were driving into a car park shadowed with great trees and through the gloom above them could clearly be seen the hotel and the lights shining eerily into the night.

He stared at her in stony silence, then after a long uneasy moment he said, 'Have we arrived?'

'Yes. We walk up the path there through the trees, there will be somebody to help with the luggage.'

'You'll probably need an umbrella. My new suit and yours are going to be ruined.'

The foyer was largely deserted since people were in their rooms changing for dinner and Anton came forward to greet them.

'The honeymooners,' he deduced correctly, giving instructions to a porter to go down to their car for their luggage after handing him the car keys, and taking in at once the young man's petulance and the girl's uncertainty. A good judge of character, Anton summed the couple up immediately. The young man was brash, good-looking, unaccustomed to the surroundings he found himself in, yet well supplied with money. The girl was different, it was obviously not destined to be a union made in heaven.

'If you want anything in your room before dinner,' he said genially, 'you only have to ring. We have given you the bridal suite on the first floor with a beautiful view of the lake, and dinner starts at eight o'clock. Most of the guests are already changing for dinner, that is why the place looks oddly deserted.'

Debbie smiled. 'I'm sure we're going to love it.'

Tod said nothing at all.

Minutes after, they stood in the middle of the bridal suite staring around them and even Tod showed an element of dismay.

A pale oyster carpet covered the floor and there were oyster pink velvet drapes at the large windows and glass chandeliers hanging from the ornate ceiling. Debbie wandered round enchanted while Tod took an apple out of a large basket of fruit and proceeded to bite into it. Then he flung open the large doors and stepped out onto the balcony.

Mist swirled across the lake and Tod said dourly, 'It looks like a scene out of Dracula.'

Standing beside him Debbie said, 'It's dark, Tod, it will look altogether different in the morning. Did you remember to pack your dinner jacket?'

'Yes. It's archaic. We stayed at the best hotel in Marbella and didn't need a dinner jacket.'

Debbie was unpacking, taking dresses out of her travelling case and flinging them across the bed while he gazed on in sulky silence.

There was a discreet tap on the door and Tod went to open it. A smiling waiter stood there holding a tray on which reposed a bottle of champagne and two wine glasses.

'With the compliments of The Lakes,' he said, and Tod, looking rather bemused, placed the tray on the table beside the vase of orchids.

106

'I don't suppose you got champagne at the hotel in Marbella,' Debbie said sharply.

'We wouldn't have thanked them for it, we all preferred beer in the bar.'

Debbie faced him squarely while he poured out the champagne. 'We're here for a week, Tod, I hope we're not going to quarrel all the time. You're not giving it a chance.'

'I should have been consulted.'

'I know. I'm sorry about that, I just thought you'd be as thrilled with the place as I was, it was meant to be a wonderful surprise, now I can see that it isn't.'

She took the glass and raised it. 'Here's to you, darling, happy wedding day.'

He stared at her solemnly. She really was very pretty and he had surely pulled off the catch of the season. He'd left a few broken hearts behind him when Debbie entered his life, he'd make the best of the honeymoon, in the summer they'd go to Spain.

They were the last to enter the dining room and they made a handsome couple, Debbie in her new dark blue evening dress and Tod in his immaculate dinner jacket. People smiled as they walked to their table, surmising correctly that they were newly married, and across the room a young man sitting with a group of people smiled and Debbie smiled back and gave a little wave.

'Who is he?' Tod hissed.

'His name is Peter Cavendish, he's a stockbroker. I met him in the summer when I was here with my parents.'

'Did you go out with him?'

'We went sailing once or twice, and I danced with him in the evenings. He's nice, I'll introduce you later on.'

'I've never asked you to hobnob with any of my old girlfriends.'

'Darling, he wasn't a boyfriend, just somebody I met on holiday. There was nothing going on.'

'I'll take your word for it.'

It wasn't Tod's scene. Expensively dressed women and men in dinner jackets or white tuxedos that proclaimed they'd holidayed in warmer climates or cruised. Most of the guests were older than himself and the ones that weren't he regarded as toffee-nosed. Tod was accustomed to being the ringleader, he certainly wouldn't be in this crowd.

'I think I'll give Mother a ring later on,' Debbie said softly. 'I think they ought to know where we are.'

Tod didn't answer. Debbie's old man was paying for everything, he supposed he had a right to know where his money was going.

He looked round the room with interest, meeting the shocked gaze of a man sitting with his back to the wall in the company of a young woman and

Tod whistled under his breath, 'Gosh, it's our M.P. Don't look now, Debbie, he's sittng over there with his back to the wall.'

'He left the reception early,' Debbie said. 'He probably told Mother he was coming here.'

'He's with a woman, but it's not his wife.'

'Don't stare at them, Tod. It's probably perfectly innocent.'

'Not it. She's a lot younger than him, and they know each other very well.'

'How do you know?'

'Well they seemed to have a lot to say to each other before he spotted us.'

'Somebody you know?' Alison asked softly.

'Only the couple who were married earlier today,' Stuart answered tersely.

She felt a sudden urge to laugh. Nothing was going right for Stuart, first Gloria Weston and now the happy couple. It would be very interesting to see how he was going to extricate himself from this one.

The girl had turned round to smile, and Alison met her smile with one equally as bright, while Stuart merely nodded his head curtly.

He'd be lucky to get through the weekend with his reputation intact, and she didn't care in the slightest.

Chapter Fourteen

It was two o'clock in the morning and Geraldine Broadhurst was in the kitchen making herself a cup of tea. Her daughter's telephone call had unsettled her and she hadn't been able to sleep.

That they were at The Lakes in Cumberland had amazed her. She knew at once that it wasn't Tod's scene and she was surprised that Debbie had even thought it might be.

Debbie's voice had been bright and confident. They were going into the ballroom to dance and they'd had champagne in their bedroom, of all things, the Bridal Suite equipped with flowers and fruit.

'What does Tod think about it?' Geraldine had asked.

'He's very impressed, Mummy.'

'Are you sure?'

'Well of course, and guess what, Mummy, Mr Mansell our M.P. is here.'

'Really. Did Sybil join him after all?'

'He's with a girl, older than me but younger than Mrs Mansell.'

'Has he seen you?'

'Well yes, at dinner.'

'I wonder who she is, try to find out, darling. I must say he's a dark horse.'

'She looks very nice, they're probably just friends, or they've only just met.'

'Yes, well. Enjoy yourselves, darling and give our love to Tod. I hope the weather improves, it started to rain here soon after you left.'

'It was drizzling and the mist came down. I expect tomorrow it will all have gone. Give Daddy my love.'

'He's asleep in his chair, shall I wake him?'

'No, of course not. I'll see you both at the end of the holiday.'

Her husband had been dismissive of Stuart Mansell's companion.

'I don't want you saying anything,' he'd said sharply. 'There's probably nothing in it, she might be the wife of one of his golfing friends, or somebody he's just met. He has to eat with somebody.'

'Not at The Lakes, people on their own usually dine on their own.'

'Well, it's not coming from us.'

'Sybil Mansell is a friend of mine, if he's playing around she has a right to know, particularly as she's looking after her old parents.'

'Suppose you say something and he's not playing around, a right fool you're going to look. He'll demand an apology.'

'And I'll be glad to give it.'

'No, Geraldine, I won't have it. He's too much to lose, he wouldn't dare put his career on the line.'

'Other men more important than Stuart Mansell have done it.'

'And if he's any sense he'll have learned from their mistakes.'

'Gloria Weston's at The Lakes, the evening paper was full of it.'

'It's a pity they can't find something more important to write about.'

'Well if they find some M.P. misbehaving they'll latch on to it, news of his ladyfriend needn't come from me.'

'Did Debbie say if Tod was enjoying it?'

'Apparently so, although I hardly think it's his scene.'

'No, I wouldn't have thought so. Perhaps he's beginning to mature.'

What was it then that was preventing her going to sleep? She'd even taken one of her insomnia tablets and it hadn't worked.

She was remembering the atmosphere between her daughter and her new husband at the reception, and she was thinking about Stuart and his lady friend. A few days' golfing indeed, and he'd been so suave about it. Looking a little bit lost without his wife, charming Geraldine with his smile, and leaving the reception with a certain regret that he didn't really know what he was going to do with himself.

If he was playing around she hoped it would get into the papers, Sybil thought he was perfect, and she'd been too trusting by half.

She was not to know that Tod's father was having similar thoughts as the plane they were flying in was winging its way across France to Spain.

He didn't like flying, he was of the opinion that if God had meant people to fly he would have given them wings, and the flight had been bumpy. They still had their seat belts fastened.

His wife had drunk two brandies and was gently snoring in the seat beside him. He reckoned he knew his son very well. Wherever they'd gone to Tod hadn't been looking forward to it, largely because he didn't know their destination; Tod loved the Med, and Spain in particular.

He'd married the wrong girl. He'd played around for years with Bill Brewster's daughter and she'd have been far more suitable as a wife. True she didn't have Debbie's background or her beauty. She was however a nice jolly girl with a sense of humour and they'd been at parties at the Brewsters' when Janet had done the cooking. He doubted if Debbie could boil an egg.

Bill Brewster and his wife had been very cool at the reception, and he'd heard from another source that Janet had taken Tod's marriage very badly.

You just couldn't tell young people anything, they knew it all. That wedding must have set the Broadhursts back thousands, nothing had been spared, but none of it had erased the scowl from Tod's face or the impatience from his wife's. He wondered where they were. Evidently somewhere within driving distance and when they left England the heavens had opened. It was foggy and pouring down.

At The Lakes Tod and Debbie were joined by a group of younger people who were intent on dancing the night away. Whereas Tod felt he should remind her that they were on their honeymoon and there was something better to do than dance. They eventually made their exit amid good-natured laughter and several risque innuendos and for the first time that day Tod was happy. This after all was what he was good at, or so innumerable young women had told him.

Alison had left Stuart in conversation with two men at the bar. He brought her drink over and excused himself on the grounds that they were discussing something rather important and he'd join her in a few minutes. That had been almost an hour ago, he hadn't even noticed her leaving the bar.

He knew the number of her room. She knew exactly what he would do. He would go to his room, see that the bed looked as if it had been slept in, then when he thought the corridors were quiet he'd climb the stairs to her room. He wouldn't trust the lift, there might be others using it, and if he met people on the stairs he would smile disarmingly and hope they wouldn't know his room number.

Outside her window the view looked distinctly eerie. Mist still swirled across the lake and the lights from the village street could not be seen. She could just distinguish the white launch at its moorings below the gardens and there were no sounds from the other rooms because they had been expertly sound-proofed.

She could almost believe that she was in some strangely different world instead of a large hotel that was pulsing with music and conversation. She spared a thought for the young honeymooners wrapped in each other's arms, and for the only two ladies who had dined alone. At first she had thought they were sisters, they resembled each other, but when they occupied separate tables she knew she had been wrong.

She looked at the clock on the table besides the bed. It was one o'clock on Good Friday morning, something entirely perverse made her go to the door to lock it. Let him go back, she didn't want him to make love to her tonight, if she wasn't more important than his drinking acquaintances he needn't bother. She was fast asleep when half an hour later Stuart turned the knob on her door and stood there astonished to find it locked.

111

He tapped on the door. She had locked it by mistake, surely she hadn't meant to lock it, but from inside the room there was no sound. He waited several minutes, then after looking along the corridor nervously he beat a hasty retreat to the stairs.

The weekend was a disaster as far as Stuart was concerned, with the presence of the media and the honeymooners. Alison was in a mood and he had promised her more than he could offer.

He had no means of knowing how Sybil would jump if his affair with Alison came to light, and there was his career. Westminster was his life, and he'd tried to be a good and useful Member, what else did he know? Besides there were the children to consider.

He had to end his affair with Alison Gray, but it wouldn't be easy, to see her every day and know that his feelings for her were still strong. She was a good secretary, she kept the wheels of his political life running smoothly and he didn't want to lose her, maybe that was the answer though, there would be a queue of men waiting for Alison but would she go lightly or would she make him suffer before she left?

He thought about her sleeping like a baby with her bedroom door locked when for him sleep was impossible.

Tomorrow he'd make it his business to speak to the honeymooners, explain to them that his work had to go on even during Easter and he'd invited his secretary along so that they could accomplish the backload. They'd believe him, after all they were little more than children.

Meanwhile in the Bridal Suite only the bride lay awake while Tod slept the sleep of the well content.

She had known he would be a competent lover, she'd heard it often enough from his friends and the girls he had dallied with. The girls had been envious when she captured him, his friends assuring her that he was a prize to be treasured.

So, why wasn't she sleeping in his arms like a contented cat instead of being burdened by the nagging feeling that there had to be more. She thought about their union clinically. Tod had been competent, experienced, but where was the tenderness? She eased herself out of the bed and went to stand at the window. Dawn was creeping across the lake bringing to life a flock of wildfowl streaming across the water, and through the early mist the distant view of the mountains.

Tod had made love to her like he'd made love to many others, selfishly, easily forgotten until the next time, and she'd expected so much more.

She'd felt sorry for Janet Brewster who had been his girl before she had come onto the scene. She had known Janet was unhappy, she'd felt sorry for her, but Janet must have been content with the little Tod gave her. Debbie felt anything but content.

Her mind went back to the wedding ceremony and the reception afterwards. The girls who were envious, Tod's sulky little boy face and she found herself remembering his words to his father when he'd asked if Tod had enough money. 'Oh sure, Dad, there's plenty of kelp where I'm going.'

The wedding had been a great extravagance, there was a new detached house waiting for their return and the honeymoon had been paid for, Tod had every reason to feel cocksure.

Further along the corridor on the first floor another guest lay sleepless.

Mary Styles was thinking about her mother in the residential home she had taken her to in the morning. She would be hating it. It hadn't mattered that her room was charming and that there was a small balcony overlooking the rose garden. The Matron had received her kindly, asking what she would like for lunch, assuring her that she was welcome and would have a delightful Easter weekend.

Her mother had sat with a frozen face, hardly bothering to turn her head when she left the room.

'It is a beautiful place, Mother,' Mary had tried to reassure her. Mrs Styles had merely said, 'It's well enough, you go and enjoy yourself, don't think about me put in here like an unwanted parcel.'

'It isn't like that, Mother. You wouldn't come with me. You couldn't go to Millicent's and I really do feel I need this holiday.'

'I know I've been a burden to you, the sooner I die the better for all of you.'

'That's nonsense, Mother.'

'I've felt sorry for other women whose children put them in homes rather than look after them, I thought it would never happen to me, my children would never be like that, now I know how wrong I was.'

'You're only here for a few days, Mother.'

'So you say, but you'll be wanting to go off again when you've had a taste of it. I'll be in and out of here until I'm dizzy.'

'I can't talk to you when you're in this mood, Mother. Millicent said they'd call in to see you before they go away, and you'll make friends here. I'll call for you on Wednesday morning.'

'When are you coming back?'

'Tuesday afternoon. I might get held up on on the road and it could be too late to call for you. I'll be here after breakfast on Wednesday.'

'And then you'll be leaving me again to go back to work.'

'On Thursday, Mother, the holiday will be over.'

She'd thought about her mother on the journey and the days leading up to Easter when her sister and her husband had stayed aloof yet privately condemning, and her mother had been difficult.

She'd lunched with Gerald the day before he'd left for Scotland and he'd said, 'What will you be doing at Easter, Mary?'

'I'm not sure.'

What a stupid thing to say. Why hadn't she had the courage to say she was putting her mother in a home so that she could spend the weekend at The Lakes? Why had she been so afraid of his reaction, either delight or dismay?

She couldn't have been wrong about him. He did like her, he sought her company more and more, and yet there was something intangible that prevented him asking for more. He never invited her out at the weekends and she put it down to the fact that he believed she needed to be with her mother.

What would his friends think? Would they be allowed to spend some time together and would they tease him unmercifully? Two people, no longer in their first youth, meeting in this most romantic place, unexpectedly! Would they believe it?

She was one of the first to arrive in the breakfast room. She had dressed carefully in her new tweed skirt and twin set and as she passed the only other guest dining alone she knew she had chosen wisely. She had noticed the other lady on the evening before, a woman of about her own age, expensively but beautifully dressed, a pretty woman with dark blonde hair framing a cool patrician face.

They had exchanged smiles, and this morning a pleasant greeting. She was near enough to see the rings on the other woman's fingers, one of them a wedding ring, the other a large solitaire.

She wondered idly if she was a widow, but then Stuart Mansell was entering the room, taking his place at the table near the wall and staring moodily at the newspaper in his hands. There was no sign of his companion of the evening before and Mary was never one to look for scandal. She assumed correctly that they occupied separate rooms.

When Alison arrived at the breakfast table forty minutes later she smiled brightly and for a brief moment he lifted his head up from his newspaper and mumbled a terse good morning.

A person more worldly than Mary Styles might have been intrigued, Mary thought they were merely acquainted. The newspaper man dining with his colleague thought otherwise.

'I think we might have something there,' he murmured with a sly smile.

'They arrived yesterday,' the photographer replied. 'Isn't he Mansell the M.P.?'

'Yes, but who is she?'

'You mean she's not his wife?'

'Definitely not. I've seen Mrs Mansell and I'd know her again.'

'Have we exhausted Gloria Weston then?'

'A few more pictures perhaps. She's not giving us much material, she's not with anybody of note, she'll have to do better at the usual functions she attends, Ascot for instance.'

Debbie and Tod arrived together and the young man sitting with his parents several tables away greeted her with a warm smile.

114

'Doesn't he have a girlfriend, is that why he's here with his folks?' Tod demanded.

'I should think he has several. He's very nice and he has a good job.'

'What sort of a car does he run?'

'I think he had a sports car the last time I met him.'

'Of course, he would have.'

'You're being very childish, Tod, you don't even know him.'

'I know his sort. All money and nothing else. What are we doing today, what does anybody do around here?'

'There's a notice board in the reception area advertising all sorts of things to do, sailing, fishing, walking, climbing. There's a swimming pool in the hotel and there's horse-riding if you feel up to it.'

'Horse-riding has never been my forte.'

'The entire district is beautiful, we could drive somewhere, take a look at some of the other lakes.'

'We haven't exactly looked at this one yet.'

'Well, that is what we could do this morning. We can sail or we can walk, I'll leave it to you.'

The sulky little boy look was back on his face and her exasperation increased, not just with Tod but with herself. She was remembering all the warnings she had received from her parents, warnings she had chosen to ignore and now she was facing the truth of them.

He looked through the window mournfully. 'Have you thought that we could have cruised to the Caribbean for what we're paying for this?'

'For what my father's paying, do you mean?'

'All right, for what your father's paying.'

'And you're not giving it a chance, Tod. You would rather be in Spain, you've made that very clear, and when we do go there I promise I won't go on and on about it like you're doing about this place.'

'My parents will come back as brown as berries, we'll be lucky to escape pneumonia.'

His eyes surveyed the room mournfully until they fell on Stuart Mansell and his companion.

'They're not having much to say to each other,' he said with a cynical smile on his face.

'Don't let him see we're even interested,' Debbie cautioned him, 'after all we don't know who she is.'

'The Mansells think they're everybody, living in that big house, lording it at every event in the town and telling us all how to behave and conduct ourselves.'

'I'm sure he's never said a wrong word to you.'

'Your father thinks he's perfect, everybody fawns round him whenever he takes the trouble to visit. It's time people woke up to the fact that he's no different to anybody else.'

115

Debbie was wishing that she hadn't told her mother that Stuart Mansell was here. Her mother was a friend of his wife's, but surely she wouldn't say anything to her about the woman he was with. Mrs Mansell was very nice, she did a lot of good in the town and it would be dreadful to make her unhappy over something that was perfectly innocent.

'I'll go and take a look at those notices in the reception,' Tod said.

They could have looked at them together but Debbie watched him go without saying anything. If they looked at them together Tod would decide, anyway, and that she could finish her second cup of coffee without having to look at his sulky face was preferable.

Mr Mansell and his companion were very quiet, Tod was right. The girl was pretty in her casual clothes. She seemed totally unconcerned with his pre-occupation with the morning paper, and his sulky expression reminded her of Tod's. Perhaps one day she too would be able to treat his moodiness with the same kind of indifference.

Alison was well aware of the interest bestowed upon them by the two journalists, contributing she felt sure to Stuart's annoyance.

'I'm going out for a stroll,' he suddenly informed her. 'I feel like a breath of fresh air. I'll see you later.'

Two pairs of eyes watched him leave the room, then they were turned on the girl left sitting alone. Alison allowed her eyes to meet theirs with bland indifference, amused when they were the first to look away.

She knew in her heart that the affair was over and half of her felt bitterness at the way it was ending. The other half felt a sense of sudden power that she could make him pay and suffer for those wasted years.

Chapter Fifteen

The breakfast room was almost empty and Tod had not returned. Debbie was angry and people were looking at her, smiling politely when they passed her table. What could he be doing?

In some exasperation she picked up her handbag and left the room. She expected to find Tod at the reception desk but there was no sign of him, instead she found him outside on the terrace chatting animatedly to three other young men dressed in climbing gear. When he saw her he made hurried excuses to his companions and ran quickly up the steps towards her.

'I'm sorry, Debbie, we got talking, did you get tired of waiting?'

He was smiling down at her, putting his arm round her waist and walking her into the hotel. She had seen him like this before, usually when he was going off somewhere with his friends and he expected her to be accommodating.

'Well,' she demanded, 'did you look at the brochures?'

'Yes, and then I got talking to those chaps. They're set on climbing Helvellyn and they wanted to know if I'd done any climbing. You must admit it's a perfect day for it, no mist, clear views everywhere.'

'What did you tell them?'

'Well I told them the truth, that I'd climbed in Germany and was almost at the top of the Matterhorn when the weather beat us. I told them we were having another go next year.'

She was not prepared to make it easy for him.

'They were so full of themselves, Debbie, I couldn't let them get away with it.'

'So, what is this leading up to?'

'They said they could lend me the gear if I'd go with them. You didn't tell me where we were heading for, Debbie, or I could have brought my own stuff.'

'I suppose that means you'll be away all day, Tod.'

'I also told them you were a great sport and that you wouldn't mind.'

His handsome cajoling young face was appealing. He wanted to climb Helvellyn regardless of the fact that it was the first day of their honeymoon and incredibly she didn't mind. At that moment it was preferable to spending a day when he would sulk that she'd made objections, that there was nothing for them to do and she suffered his sudden enthusiastic hug. The relief in his expression spoke volumes.

'I'll show them what climbing is all about,' he said with a warm smile. 'You'll see, darling, tonight we'll all be able to celebrate.'

She was staring across the gardens to where several people had gathered on the jetty and Tod said quickly, 'Why not go down to the boat, love? You love sailing and it looks as if several other people have the same idea.'

'Perhaps I will,' she replied, smiling up at the young man who had joined them to urge Tod to hurry, they were ready to leave.

She waited while they piled into a Land Rover and watched as they drove out of the car park, then she made her way to the jetty below.

She was joined on the steps by Alison who smiled at her affably.

'Going down to the boat?' she asked.

'Yes, but I don't know where it's going.'

'Across to the village for those who want to go there and then around the lake, I believe. I think some of the passengers are wanting to go to church as it's Good Friday.'

'Yes, of course.'

They walked on in silence and Alison reflected that men were the very devil. She had watched Tod driving off with his new acquaintances and here was this pretty girl left to amuse herself, as she was being told to do. She'd seen Stuart strolling through the grounds, walking as if his life depended on it with a set expression on his face and she'd seen the two newspaper men sitting on the terrace watching him.

They were boarding the boat and Mary accepted the seat next to the other lady who smiled at her in the friendliest way.

'It is a lovely morning,' Mary said, 'I was hoping it would be.'

'Yes indeed. This is how one should see the Lake District, so often it is covered in mist.'

'Have you been here before?'

'Yes twice. It really is a beautiful hotel. The first time I came out of curiosity, the second because I'd enjoyed it so much.'

'I suppose you will keep on coming back?'

'I'm not sure. Do you know the area well?'

'No, hardly at all. I came with my parents to Windermere when I was a child, but this is the first time I've been back.'

'I've spent a lot of my life in Cumberland but I live a great distance from here now.'

'Really, where is that?'

'My home is in Kenya, I shall be going back there tomorrow.'

'Are you travelling alone?'

'Yes. I simply want to look around the village once more, relive old memories if you like.'

'Of course. Would you mind very much if I came with you?'

'No, I should like that.'

Mary had been troubled all morning. She did not want Gerald to find her in the hotel rooms or even in the gardens as if she had been waiting for him. She wanted to meet him by accident so that she could tell him she had been exploring with a companion, that way he would know that she was not relying on him for companionship, her independence would be protected.

Her companion introduced herself as Stella Clarke and she was a good guide around the village and the paths that edged the lake. They wandered up to the old stone church that dominated the village and the murmur of prayer came to them across the churchyard gay with daffodils. From the top of the High Street they looked up at the imposing pile of Alveston Hall and Mary said, 'I noticed that building when I drove along the road there, it's a beautiful place. Do you know anything about it?'

'Alveston Hall. It is the home of the Alveston family, I'm not sure if any of the family are in residence. Lord Alveston has been travelling abroad for a great many years.'

'You know him?'

The other woman's smile was sad and reflective, before she answered simply, 'I did know him once, some years ago. People lose touch.'

Mary decided to ask no questions, she felt they would not be welcomed by her companion and they turned to retrace their steps to the village.

'There is a small shop in the village that sells home-made gingerbread and mint cake,' Stella said. 'I promised to take some back with me, they send it all over the world so they will be able to wrap it for me.'

'I'll take some home for Mother, she loves gingerbread,' Mary said.

The shop was doing a good trade and eventually the queue dispersed, Mary waited for Stella to place her order and she looked round the shop with interest at decorated boxes and shelves filled with home-made sweets and chocolates. It was then she noticed the well-dressed portly man standing near one of the shelves, who appeared to be watching her companion with some degree of interest. When Stella turned however Mary stepped forward to ask for her gingerbread and it was only when she turned to leave the shop that she found Stella in conversation with the man.

He was saying, 'I wasn't really sure it was you, Mrs Clarke, I thought I saw you in the village a year ago but I wasn't sure.'

'I did come here for a few days then.'

'Did you know that the master had come home?'

'No. How is he?'

'He seems very well. He's eating dinner at the hotel tomorrow evening, he'll be delighted to see you.'

'I'm afraid I shall have left the hotel by then.'

'I am sorry. Why not visit the hall this afternoon, that's if you have the time, Mrs Clarke.'

'I doubt that, Grant. Do please give him my best wishes.'

'When I tell him you are in the area I'm sure the master will want to see you. Could I ask him to come down to the hotel?'

'I'd rather you didn't, Grant, I'm sure you can understand why?'

He nodded sadly. 'Are you travelling alone, Mrs Clarke?'

'I'm afraid so. My husband has M.S. and is unable to travel. He will be waiting for all my news when I get home.'

'I am sorry. He was a very nice gentleman.'

They smiled and shook hands but Stella seemed entirely preoccupied as they made their way to the jetty.

Mary had sensed another tragedy behind the polite exchange of greetings between her new friend and the man, something unspoken, some memories of sadness that a meeting between his employer and Stella would rekindle and which Stella for one was not ready for.

Alison and Debbie had climbed the lower slopes of the fells and sat on a stone wall watching the display of boats sailing across the lake. Debbie didn't quite know what to make of this lovely sophisticated woman who was staying at the hotel with the man she only knew as her Member of Parliament, and Alison was well aware of her embarrassment.

Lightly she asked, 'I suppose you'll know Mr Mansell quite well?'

'My parents know him better than me. He was at our wedding.'

'Yes, he told me. Mrs Mansell is staying with her parents, I believe.'

'Yes.'

'I'm his secretary at Westminster.'

'I see.'

'I've been his secretary for a good few years, we work well together. I've met his wife on a few occasions, she doesn't spend much time in London.'

'No, she doesn't. She's very nice, she does a lot for the church and other things around home.'

'In other words she's a pillar of society.'

Debbie didn't answer. Behind the other girl's words she sensed real and deep resentment. She would prefer to be wandering around on her own but without hurting the girl's feelings she couldn't suggest it. It was left to Alison to say, 'They're coming out of the church now, I think I might go along there and look inside. Do you want to come with me?'

'Well, if you don't mind, I'd really rather wait up here until the boat comes in, then I might just take a trip round the lake.'

'Right then. You're very wise, the lake is beautiful. See you later.'

Alison understood Debbie's wish to be on her own since she too had been doubting the advisability of their being together. They were both hurting, both feeling badly done by. She wasn't really interested in looking inside the church, she'd simply thought it was a good idea to move on.

There were people waiting on the jetty for the boat and, making up her mind quickly, Debbie hurried along the path towards the jetty. She smiled at the two ladies she'd seen on the boat earlier that morning and was about to speak to them when a voice said, 'Hello, Debbie, on your own this morning?' and she turned to see Peter Cavendish smiling down at her.

'Yes, Tod's climbing Helvellyn.'

'I take it he's the boy you're engaged to?'

'Was. He's now my husband.'

'Really, I'm sorry, when was this?'

'Yesterday.'

She was aware of his perplexity and astonishment that a young man so recently married could leave his new wife to climb a mountain and she felt strangely angry at it.

'I really didn't mind, Peter. Tod is always energetic, he has to be doing something and it's my fault that we're here.'

Peter Cavendish was well aware of the sudden hostility in Debbie's eyes and decided to change the subject. She was not to know that he was feeling strangely unbalanced by the news of her marriage. He had liked her rather too well during those few days they had been together in the summer. He had known she was engaged to be married but last night when he had seen her in the hotel restaurant he had felt envious of Tod's good fortune in being with her. The chap was an insensitive bounder to go off climbing and leave this gorgeous girl to find her own amusement.

'How do you intend to spend your day?' he asked her evenly.

'I thought I might sail round the lake.'

'Well we're heading back to the hotel right now, the boat has already done its morning cruise. I believe there will be another after lunch.'

'Then I might do that.'

'It's a beautiful lake, one only really realises just how beautiful from the water.'

That was the moment Peter decided he would take another cruise in the afternoon.

Mary and Stella walked up from the jetty and Mary stole a quick glance at the cars parked below in the car park. She could not find Gerald's among them so he had evidently not yet arrived.

'I think I'll go to my room and start packing,' Stella said. 'Thank you so much for your company, perhaps we'll meet over lunch.'

'Yes of course, that will be nice.'

Mary had sensed her remoteness on the voyage back. Before meeting the man in the shop she had been ready to talk about the area and what Mary should see, afterwards she had been thoughtful, her mind engaged on other things connected with the past. Mary was intrigued. That she knew the lord of the manor was evident, and the man she had spoken to had expressed his disappointment that she was leaving so soon. Somewhere along the way Mary sensed a mystery.

As she took a seat on the glass-fronted terrace she was able to look down on the car park and the garden where Stuart Mansell was in conversation with two men.

The conversation was light-hearted.

'Is this your first visit to The Lakes, Mr Mansell?' one of them was asking.

'No, I've been here several times.'

'A very peaceful and tranquil change from the hectic trauma of Westminster.'

'It should be, actually this is a working break.'

'Really.'

'Really. Just because I'm no longer at the House doesn't mean that work has stopped. My secretary is up to her eyes in it, the poor girl is hardly thinking of this as a holiday.'

'Your secretary, sir?'

'Yes, Miss Gray.'

'I thought the young lady went off in the boat, sir.'

'She did. It's Good Friday, the poor girl has to have some time to herself.'

'Doesn't Mrs Mansell care for the Lake District then?'

'My wife was here with me last year, this year unfortunately she's looking after her sick father. It's given me the opportunity to do some much-needed research.'

'How long do you intend to stay here, Mr Mansell?'

'Simply for the Easter break. I rather think you've asked enough questions for one morning and I doubt if my activities would interest your readers. I lead a very busy but dull life.'

With a brief nod he moved away followed by two cynical pairs of eyes.

Where was Alison? She'd not returned on the boat and that meant she'd not be back for lunch. The holiday had been a mistake, she was playing up and there were these two news hounds. They'd evidently exhausted Gloria Weston, but where was the woman, she'd hardly escaped out of her room for more than half an hour. She'd had her meals served there and that little weaselly man she was with hardly merited a line.

Stella Clarke sat on her bed surrounded by the clothes out of her wardrobe but she was not thinking about packing her suitcase. She was thinking about Andrew.

His butler would return to the hall and would in all probability tell his master that he had met her in the village. She didn't want to see Andrew. A long time ago he had hurt her terribly, married her unstable cousin and as a consequence suffered an awful tragedy.

She had been happy with Jonathon, dear solid Jonathon who had never possessed the charm and dash of Andrew, but who had loved her steadily and unwaveringly even when he knew Andrew still possessed her heart.

Time had worked its magic. She had put Andrew firmly in the past where he belonged and she had come to appreciate Jonathon's calm healing worth. That he had developed M.S. was a terrible blow to them both, but he had accepted it without bitterness, allowing her to travel where she wished, and she could remember his voice saying gently, 'This is my life, darling, you still have yours, and I want you to live it as fully as possible. I know you're coming back to me, and I shall be here waiting for you.'

No memory of the past was going to trouble her on that journey back. She thought nostalgically of that long white house with the scents and sounds of Africa surrounding it, and Jonathon waiting for her in his favourite chair on the balcony, his face alive with joy when she embraced him.

Whatever had prompted her to come back here? She had told herself over and over that nothing of the past remained so why this need to torture herself now with memories that were too painful. Olivia had never been right for Andrew, that beautiful spoilt mercurial girl with her beauty and her needs.

Although she had been in Kenya when his marriage tumbled around his ears friends had been quick to write and tell her what was happening to him. He had hurt her sorely but she had never wanted him to suffer as Olivia was making him suffer.

She made her decision quickly. She would have lunch and then settle her bill. She would order a taxi to take her into Kendal and the train that would take her to London, by this time tomorrow she would be on her way to Nairobi.

It did not take her long to pack, she would ask them to send a boy up for her case while she ate lunch and then she would leave immediately afterwards. If Grant told Andrew that he had seen her she felt sure he would come to the hotel and she couldn't face him. The past was over and done with, there was no point in resurrecting any part of it.

Mary was surprised to find her new friend already wearing her travelling clothes and seeing her surprise, Stella said quickly, 'I've decided to travel immediately after lunch, I'd much rather travel in the daylight.'

'Are you driving into London?'

'No. I've been using taxis, I've asked the hotel to order one here to take me into Kendal.'

'I would have driven you there if you'd asked me.'

'I couldn't possibly ask you to do that. This is your holiday, I'm sure you don't want to spend it driving me about.'

'I really wouldn't have minded.'

'That really is very kind of you, but I thought the taxi was a good idea. I should eat a good lunch, it may be quite late when I get another meal.'

Mary was wise enough not to ask questions. Her companion quite evidently wanted to leave and leave quickly.

She looked round the dining room. Mr Mansell the M.P. was eating alone and there was no sign of the two journalists. The young girl was also dining alone although the young man she had been with on the boat had smiled down at her as he passed her table and had glanced at her several times from where he was sitting with two other people.

Most of the tables were full and she had met only a handful of the guests but she was wondering about the stories she could fill her library shelves with concerning her fellow guests.

There was the elderly man sitting with the pretty girl who was quite evidently not his daughter.

A second old man had a servant who followed him everywhere to place rugs around his knees. Then even as her eyes roved around the room there was a sudden commotion round the door and Gloria Weston appeared standing on the threshold, surveying the room with a practised eye.

She was wearing skin-tight white ski-pants and a white sweater, embroidered in beads which Mary thought more appropriate for evening than luncheon. She was alone, disdaining the table the head waiter ushered her towards so that those nearby could hear her say, 'No, no, not that one. I prefer to sit near the wall where I can see what's going on.'

As she passed Stuart Mansell's table she gave him a bright smile to which he responded with a curt nod, and Stuart thought angrily, where had she been that morning when the newspapermen had interrogated him?

Stella gathered her handbag, saying, 'I'm leaving now, Mary, do enjoy the rest of your holiday.'

'Thank you, I hope you have a good journey home.'

Gloria scanned the menu. She was angry. Her companion was sulking and had refused to go down for lunch, preferring to lie on his bed with a bottle of whisky, and she was fed up with his tears and tantrums. She'd have done better to come to The Lakes alone. She stole a quick glance at the man on the next table, morose and good-looking, and alone.

Chapter Sixteen

Driving down from Scotland, Gerald Ralston was in a reflective mood. Taking his mother with him to a country club where groups of men played serious golf, couples enjoyed their golf and the evenings' entertainment and where there was laughter and camaraderie around the bars in the evening hadn't really been for either of them.

This holiday had been her concession. In the summer he would take her abroad on the sort of holiday she enjoyed. They would hire a car and take long drives into the countryside, but this holiday had been for him, and they had booked two single rooms, complete with television and where they had both retired after dinner in the evenings.

His daytime companions didn't know how he spent his evenings. They regarded the presence of his mother with something like curiosity and they asked no questions.

On those mornings and afternoons when he had not played golf they had toured the countryside, and now they were on their way to the Lake District and his mother was wearing a self-satisfied smile. The next few days would be more to her liking.

'Do you think there'll be some entertainment at The Lakes?' his mother asked.

'I expect so but I'm not really sure. There will be dancing of course and bridge for those who want it. I'm sure something will be laid on.'

'Well neither of us are interested in dancing. I shall play some bridge of course. I wish you were interested, Gerald, it's so social.'

He thought about Mary Styles. She would be shopping in the town, caring for her mother, taking short country drives, and she would perhaps think about the marvellous time he would be having at The Lakes.

'I suppose we ought to call somewhere for lunch,' his mother was saying.

'I thought we'd press on, Mother, we ate a good breakfast and we can order something when we arrive.'

'Just as you like, Gerald.'

He felt sorry for Mary because her life echoed his own. It was years since he had looked at a woman with rather more than interest because he believed it was useless to do so. Even now he told himself that their friendship was born out of some sort of pity, nothing more.

Their friendship would have to end of course, there was no future in it for either of them, and yet he knew that when next he lunched at the George or went into the library his eyes would search for her, his day become brighter because for those few moments they had been together.

'Are we driving up to the hotel?' his mother asked.

'Well yes. I'm not sure if the boat will be there to take us across and there's the luggage to see to.'

'I should leave your golf clubs in the car, you'll not be playing here, I hope.'

'No, Mother.'

'Some of the shops are open, wouldn't you think they'd be closed on Good Friday.'

'I suppose they have to make hay while the sun shines.'

'Even so, Good Friday should be observed.'

The village street was busy with fell walkers and people enjoying the afternoon sunshine. Village shops were doing a lively trade and all along the straggling High Street stone urns were gay with daffodils. Gerald's heart lifted. He loved the atmosphere of The Lakes, its refined good taste, the warm softly lit lounges where people sat around chatting and exchanging anecdotes, where silent-footed waiters attended smilingly to their wants.

'I hope they've given us nice rooms,' his mother was saying. 'I don't particularly want a lake view, I think the rooms overlooking the mountains are nice.'

Personally Gerald preferred the lake views.

'I'll change with you, Mother, if I've got the mountain view and you're looking out onto the lake.'

'There are a lot of people here, the car park is nearly full.'

'There's plenty of room, Mother, and some of the guests will be out.'

In the lounge overlooking the car park and the gardens, Mary was sitting with Cornelius and Clarissa Harvey. They had been entertained to drinks by the owner of the hotel who seemed highly gratified that Mr and Mrs Harvey were enjoying themselves.

Mary had never met an American before but he had been humorous and pleasant, enquiring if she was enjoying herself and expressing the hope that she would return.

Her eyes were scanning the car park watching the cars coming and going, and halfway through the afternoon she could feel the hot blood colouring her face at the arrival of Gerald's car moving slowly along the line of cars until it found a place to drive into.

She watched him leaving the car, walking round to the boot from which he took out several pieces of luggage, then she watched him walking to the passenger's door and holding it open.

Her eyes opened wide at the sight of a woman easing herself out of the seat, a slender quietly dressed woman but from this distance she was unable to assess her age.

Her heart was fluttering wildly. This was something she had not expected, for never once during the time she had known him had he mentioned a female companion.

She watched them climbing up the path towards the gardens and then a man went forward to take their luggage and they followed him into the hotel.

She wanted to go into the foyer but common sense kept her back. She was here because she had wanted to be here, not because he had encouraged her, and why should it matter that he was not alone?

Mrs Harvey was looking at her curiously. 'Are you all right, dear, you look a little flushed?'

'Yes thank you, Mrs Harvey.'

Mrs Harvey had followed her gaze, seen the man and woman leaving the car and she had the feeling that Mary knew them and something about their presence had disconcerted her.

She would never know how she managed to remain in her seat and make normal conversation and it was Mrs Harvey suddenly hunting in her handbag saying, 'I haven't got my spectacles, I must have left them in the dining room. Will you get them for me, Cornelius?' that brought her to her feet.

'I'll get them for you, Mrs Harvey, I know where you were sitting.'

'Would you, dear, I am sorry to trouble you.'

'It's no trouble, Mrs Harvey. I'll get them now.'

Mrs Harvey watched her go. How quickly Mary had said she would go for the spectacles which were actually residing in her handbag. She had sensed Mary's preoccupation. Mary's thoughts had been with that young man and his companion and she had merely supplied an excuse for her to go into the foyer.

Mary hurried through the room and arrived in the foyer in time to see Gerald leaving the reception desk while his companion waited near the lift. For the first time she realised that she was not young: a small slender woman, smartly dressed, neat rather than fashionable. As Mary moved towards the restaurant her eyes met Gerald's and surprised in them disconcerted astonishment.

She smiled and went forward to speak to him, while he stood looking at her suddenly tongue-tied.

'Hello, Gerald, have you just arrived?' she asked.

'Why, yes. How long have you been here, Mary?'

'I came yesterday, I'm here until Tuesday.'

'What about your mother?'

127

'I did what you suggested. She's gone into a very nice residential home for a few days. Did you enjoy your holiday in Scotland?'

'Yes, it was very nice.'

His eyes slid nervously towards the woman staring at them from the wall, and in some confusion he said, 'I'd like to get rid of the luggage, perhaps we'll meet at dinner, Mary.'

She smiled, allowing her eyes to stare across at the woman he was with, and Gerald said quickly, 'My mother is waiting for me, we have to sort our rooms out.'

She smiled, suddenly light-hearted. He was with his mother, so it was all right.

For a few seconds he watched her walking towards the restaurant. She looked very nice in her beautifully cut skirt and pale pink twin set and as he reached his mother's side, she hissed quietly, 'Who was that woman you were talking to?'

'She's your librarian, Mother. Her name is Miss Styles, she chooses those books you're so fond of. You'll be able to thank her for them now.'

'I surely don't need to thank her for doing her job. Is that all you know about her, that she works in the library?'

'I see her shopping in the town, I've had lunch with her once or twice in the George.'

'I thought you lunched with men.'

'Well the tables were full so the waiter showed her to mine.'

'What do you know about her?'

'She's unmarried and lives with her mother.'

'Is her mother here with her?'

'I only spoke with her for a few minutes, Mother, I don't know who she is with.'

They both had rooms at the side of the hotel overlooking the gardens and the fells, and after inspecting the bathroom, the bed linen and the curtains Mrs Ralston decided the room was adequate.

'I shall have a rest before we go down for afternoon tea,' she said. 'They'll be dressing for dinner.'

'I suppose so, Mother. There's no need to make a fuss.'

'I've brought the clothes I took to Madeira, if they were good enough for Reids in Madeira they're good enough for The Lakes.'

'I'll see you later then, Mother.'

'What are you doing now?'

'Unpacking. I'll see you later.'

He unpacked quickly, putting his shirts away tidily, hanging his clothes and assortment of ties in the long wardrobe. The afternoon was his to do as he liked but the rest of the weekend would be dominated by his mother.

He felt sure that Mary had come to the hotel on his recommendation and he was beginning to feel like a rat in a trap. He should have been honest with her from the outset instead of pretending all was well with his life.

He looked for her in the lounge but the day was fine and sunny and there was only an elderly gentleman sleeping in a quiet corner and two elderly ladies playing some sort of card game. He next went to the conservatory where he saw Mary sitting with an older couple. The other woman was doing most of the talking but Mary appeared to be enjoying the conversation, occasionally laughing aloud, and then their eyes met.

He smiled, and after a few moments Mary made an excuse to leave her companions to join him.

'I was so surprised to see you here I didn't get a chance to say very much in the foyer,' he said. 'When did you make up your mind to come?'

'You made it sound very inviting, I've been thinking about it for some time. Mother was the stumbling block.'

'And what have you done with your mother? I know you said a residential home but how did you manage it?'

'With great difficulty. Her doctor helped convince her that it was an extremely good home and I needed a holiday.'

'Good for you.'

'Are you waiting for your mother to join you?'

'No, she's resting. We don't live in each other's pockets.'

'No, so you told me. It's a lovely afternoon, would you like to walk in the gardens?'

'Yes, that would be nice.'

'You enjoyed your holiday in Scotland?'

'Very much. I enjoyed the golf and the comradeship in the bars.'

'Does your mother play golf?'

'No, but she always finds women friends to chat to.'

He was still lying to her, it was a compulsion he couldn't escape from but there was no other way.

'It must be very nice to have a mother like yours,' Mary said thoughtfully. 'Always to know that whatever you do she'll understand and support you.'

He nodded. 'Yes it is.'

'I'm tempted to ask why you've never married, your mother sounds like a person who would have made an ideal mother-in-law.'

'Perhaps I'm a very selfish animal, Mary. I live a very rich full life and I wish every person could be the same. We go on hoping that nothing will change, at least I do.'

With every word it seemed to Mary that her hopes were crashing around her ears. She had secretly believed that she was living in a dream world but having her dreams shattered so suddenly by a cruel complacency was like the twisting of a knife in her too vulnerable heart.

'It must be nice to feel like that,' she said, her voice little more than a

129

whisper, and relentlessly he said, 'Well yes it is. Now that you've made the break, Mary, don't lose it, take other holidays, travel abroad, you have a good job, there's no need for you to stand on the sidelines waiting for something to happen.'

She turned to stare at him, and some remnant of pride came to her assistance. 'Is that what you think I've been doing, Gerald?'

'You've missed an awful lot, Mary.'

'I wish I could say I too lived a rich full life but you know it wouldn't be true. I hope it doesn't change for you, Gerald, with arrogance like yours I would be afraid of tempting providence.'

He stared at her, surprised by her vehemence, but before he could say another word she said, 'I must get back to Mrs Harvey, they've been very nice to me since I came and I'm afraid I left them in rather a hurry.'

Her smile was tremulous, but her shoulders were straight and square as he watched her hurrying back along the path towards the hotel.

She did not go back to Mrs Harvey, instead she went up to her bedroom where she dissolved into tears. She'd been a fool to read more into their weekly meetings than they meant. She was simply a woman he liked to chat to, an agreeable companion, not someone who was likely to disturb the rich full life he was so fond of.

Snatching her coat from the wardrobe she went out of the room and out of the hotel. People were waiting at the jetty for the boat and she joined them without really knowing where she was going. She went to stand alone at the ship's rail and when the boat reached the jetty for the village she joined the few people leaving her.

Blindly she walked quickly along the crowded street and up the winding road leading onto the fell. She was seeing nothing of the golden sunlight on the sweeping fell, nothing of the primroses shyly peeping out from the hedgerows or the purple cloud resting on the summit of Blencathra until suddenly the screeching of tyres brought her out of her reverie and a car that had come suddenly round the bend had mounted the banking to avoid knocking her over.

She stared at it in dumbfounded surprise and the driver easing himself out of the front seat. He stood looking down at his car in some dismay then turned his angry attention on her.

'Do you usually walk in the centre of the road when you can see the bend in it?' he demanded. Then in a quieter voice, 'Stella, is that you?'

She looked at him in silent surprise, then he said, 'I'm sorry, I thought you were someone else. Are you all right?'

'Yes. I'm so sorry. It was my fault. Is your car damaged?'

'A bent wing, that's all.' He was about to return to his car when she suddenly burst into tears and in some consternation he said, 'You're frightened. Here, get into the car, tell me where you want to go.'

He had walked towards her to take her arm, and the sobs continued making her feel ashamed. 'No really,' she managed to say, 'I'll be quite all right to go back on my own. Please see to your car.'

'The car isn't a problem. Tell me where you want to go.'

'I'm staying at the hotel. I can go back there on my own, I'm perfectly all right.'

He had backed the car out onto the road and she stared at the damaged wing uncertainly.

'Please let me pay for the repair to your car,' she said.

'Get in the car, the incident has obviously unnerved you, what you want is a stiff drink or a sweet cup of tea.'

His voice was commanding and by this time he was holding the car door open for her and his expression brooked no more arguments.

She had expected him to drive down to the village street but instead he was driving upwards towards the fell and very soon they were driving through tall iron gates and along the long drive leading to Alveston Hall.

He was standing with the car door open waiting for her to get out, and this time he smiled.

'Come into the house,' he commanded, 'I'll order some tea and you shall tell me what you were thinking about down there on the road.'

Grant came forward with a smile to receive them, a smile that faltered when he viewed Andrew's companion.

'We'd like some tea, Grant, and whatever else you can rustle up, the lady's had a fright and she's a bit shaken up.'

He ushered her into a large beautiful room that overlooked the gardens at the side of the house and an oblique view of the lake. She looked around her with surprised delight, 'But this is so beautiful,' she said. 'I thought it was a lovely house when I drove up here.'

'Perhaps we should introduce ourselves,' Andrew said looking down at her. 'I am Andrew Alveston and this is my home. Now tell me who you are.'

'My name is Mary Styles. I'm staying at The Lakes until Tuesday. I live in Carling, a small town in the West Midlands.'

He nodded, without saying whether he knew Carling or not, and Mary said shyly, 'You thought I was somebody else down there on the road?'

'Yes. A woman I used to know and who is staying at the hotel.'

'You called me Stella.'

'Yes, that was her name.'

'I think I may have met her. I had breakfast this morning with a lady called Stella and we went into the village together. A woman at the hotel asked me if we were sisters, we had the same colouring and the same height.'

'Yes, you are very like the Stella I remember.'

'She left the hotel after lunch to return to Kenya. She told me her husband was an invalid.'

131

'Poor chap. I remember him too, he was a friend of mine many years ago.'

She looked into his eyes, grey eyes under dark hair threaded with silver, at a cool remote face, tanned and handsome. She judged him to be in his mid forties, and in turn he was looking at a pretty face surrounded by light brown hair, unremarkable except for a straight gaze from unusual green eyes and a mouth with gentle curves.

The interruption came with Grant pushing in a tea trolley laden with a silver tea service and trays of sandwiches and scones. Grant poured out the tea, placing cups and saucers on small walnut tables and inviting them to help themselves from the trolley.

Mary thanked him with a smile, and he left them chatting amicably.

Back in the kitchen the housekeeper was ready with her questions.

'But who is she, Grant, you say she's very like Miss Stella?'

'She is. They were together in the village. She could be some relative but I don't think so. The master said he'd almost run her down in his car.'

'Well he drives too fast, I've always said so. It's all right in the grounds but those country lanes are treacherous. Are they getting on do you think?'

'She seems a very nice lady, Mrs Stokes, an acquaintance nothing more.'

'Oh well, it has to begin somewhere.'

Women were all the same, thought Grant, too romantically minded, always looking for intrigue when there wasn't any.

'Would you like to look around the house?' Andrew asked her.

'Oh yes, I'd love to.'

They walked together up the wide curving staircase and stood looking at the portrait of his mother.

'She's a very beautiful woman,' Mary said softly.

'Yes. She is still a beautiful woman.'

'She doesn't live here?'

'No. She doesn't even visit me very often these days. She has many happy memories of this house, but unfortunately a great many sad ones.'

'Oh, I'm sorry.'

He showed her the long picture gallery and the library, the dining room which he said he seldom used, and the ballroom.

'It must be lovely to attend a ball in this beautiful house,' Mary said.

'Yes, I remember a great many of them with pleasure.' He did not tell her of the one evening that had cost him years of loneliness and haunting sadness.

'Are you enjoying your stay at The Lakes?' he asked her as they walked to his car.

'Very much, it really is quite beautiful. You haven't been there?'

'No. When I came back here I was amazed to find that a hotel had been built on that site, I'm agreeably surprised that it has style.'

'Oh yes, you should really see it for yourself.'

'I've been invited to eat dinner there tomorrow evening.'

He didn't elaborate on the invitation or that he expected he might see her there. They mostly drove in silence and Mary was surprised to find the village street quiet and that dusk was descending on the fells.

He drove her to the back of the hotel and she thanked him for his kindness saying, 'I hadn't realised it was so late, I'm sorry to have been such a nuisance.'

He smiled, got back into his car and drove away.

Chapter Seventeen

Debbie and Peter stepped onto the gangway when the boat docked below the hotel. They had enjoyed each other's company and a delightful afternoon cruising the lake and wandering about the streets of Keswick where the boat had docked for an hour.

The Lakeland town had been busy with holiday-makers and they had wandered along the narrow streets lined with shop windows filled with paintings of the district, exquisite watercolours and oils, some painted by local artists.

There was one of the hotel with its backdrop of mountains, showing the red Virginia creeper lovingly covering its walls and looking more like a medieval castle than a modern hotel.

'I'll probably buy that one before we go back,' Debbie said confidently.

'They have a rather larger one in the hotel lounge, haven't you seen it? Peter said.

'No, but this size will suit me better.'

As they boarded the boat to take them back to the hotel Debbie reflected with some dismay that she had hardly spared Tod a thought all afternoon. But she saw that the Range Rover was parked in the car park and she looked at her watch with some surprise to see that it was after six o'clock and the sun was already setting.

'I'd no idea it was so late,' she said. 'Tod and his friends are back, he'll be wondering where I am.'

'He surely won't have expected you waiting for him all day in the hotel,' Peter said reasonably.

'I left the key at the desk so he'll have been able to pick it up.'

She seemed a little troubled and Peter said, 'He'll probably be waiting for you in the bar or one of the lounges. I'd take a look in there before you go upstairs.'

They could hear laughter as they walked towards the bar and for a few moments they stood together in the doorway looking across to where a group of young people were sitting together. Tod was not amongst them and they were about to turn away when one of the young men said, 'It really was hilarious, we told him we'd never climbed before, we just thought we'd let him show off.'

'And did he?' a girl asked.

'Well of course. He led the expedition and we did as we were told. We didn't inform him we'd climbed the Materhorn and most of the other Swiss peaks, I'll tell him before we leave.'

Everybody laughed and Debbie turned away, her face flaming. As she looked up at Peter helplessly he knew she was close to tears and he said sympathetically, 'Don't mind them, Debbie, I know them very well, it will have amused them to string Tod along.'

She smiled tremulously. 'I must go, Peter, he's probably in the bedroom.'

She turned away and almost ran towards the lifts.

Peter knew all the people sitting in the bar. They were acquaintances not friends, but he knew how they spent their holidays, climbing on the continent, the father of one of them had a yacht in the Med and they were busy with sailing regattas and racing stables. They had jobs in the city and too much money. Tod would be a child in their hands and as he walked to the bar one of them called to him, 'Join us, Peter.'

'No thanks. It's almost time to change for dinner.'

They were always the last to enter the dining room, making a laughing entrance so that people looked up indulgently, they were young people having a good time, filling their days with pleasures denied to older and staider guests.

Peter sipped his Martini and one of the boys called out to him, 'We've climbed Helvellyn today, Peter, ever done it yourself?'

'Yes, but not for some time.'

'Scafell Pike tomorrow if the weather holds out.'

Peter merely smiled. He could imagine Tod in their company, a small town boy with new money. No doubt the centre of attraction in his home town but with this street-wise crowd strangely out of his depth. Tod would have no idea that they were laughing at him, amused at his pomposity, but Debbie knew.

Debbie stood in the bedroom uncertainly. She could hear Tod singing in the shower, evidently well pleased with the way his day had gone.

She opened the wardrobe and took out the dress she proposed to wear that evening and hunted in the drawer for the appropriate underwear. She heard Tod moving about in the bathroom and then he was smiling at her from the doorway saying, 'Ah, you're back, I promised we'd meet up with them in the bar later, if that's all right with you, darling?' he added the last bit as an afterthought.

'Don't you want to dance?' she asked him.

'Dancing ancient and modern. No thanks, we'll have more fun in the bar. Aren't you going to ask if we managed to climb Helvellyn?'

'I heard that you had, they were discussing it in the bar.'

'You'll never believe it, Debbie. They had all the right gear but they'd never climbed anything higher than Downey's Hill before. I showed them how it was done and they were quite content to let me lead the expedition.'

'Did they tell you they hadn't climbed before?'

'It was evident.'

She had the utmost urge to tell him not to be such a fool, that they'd been toying with him, laughing at his bragging but she remained silent. After a few minutes she said lightly, 'I think I'll take a bath now, Tod, and change.'

He didn't answer, he was searching in the wardrobe and not once had he asked her how she had spent her day, indeed it was much later when they were on their way downstairs that he said, 'What did you do today?'

'Sailed round the lake and took a look at Keswick.'

He took it for granted that she had been alone and Debbie reflected that his conceit was so immense it would never enter his head that she could possibly have spent her day with another man. With this in mind her anger grew.

'We're among the first,' Tod commented. 'I expect my friends are still in the bar, perhaps we should have gone there first.'

'This is our honeymoon, Tod, surely we don't need to spend it with them.'

'I'm only suggesting a drink in the bar, Debbie, why are you so against them?'

'I'm not.'

'We've had a smashing day, they've asked me to join them again tomorrow but of course I told them I'd have to mention it to you first.'

She stared at him in disbelief, and he rushed to say, 'You owe it to me, Debbie. You hauled me up here without even telling me where we were heading, and I do think the holiday should be a two-way affair, some of it for me, some of it for you.'

'So you want to go with them tomorrow, where?'

'They want to climb Scafell Pike. Heaven help them, it's more dangerous than Helvellyn, I'm up to it, I'm not sure about them.'

'And if I said I didn't want you to go you'd sulk all day and make my life a misery.'

'No, but I would think you were being very unfair.'

'Then of course you must go, Tod, if you don't Scafell will never be the same again.'

'There's no call to be sarcastic.'

'I'm rather more than sarcastic, I'm furious, and I don't want any dinner.'

True to her words she gathered her handbag and marched out of the dining room. At that moment she felt that she hated him, his selfishness, his egotism, then humour came to her rescue and she had to agree with him that she hadn't consulted him about the holiday.

136

As she marched through the hall Anton de Roche summed up the situation accurately.

Anton de Roche was a student of human nature, in his profession he had to be. His staff believed he knew accurately the foibles, likes and dislikes of every guest at the hotel and every employee. He also knew their eccentricities and exactly what was going on.

As he watched Debbie marching through the foyer, her head held high, bright spots of colour on her cheeks, he thought cynically that they were a couple too young to be married, too unsuitable and he could have wagered a bet that the marriage would not last. He would give it a few months and they would both be complimenting themselves that they were well out of it.

He turned his attention to the young woman walking through the swing doors.

Stuart Mansell had informed him that he was here with his secretary since he needed her assistance on some quite important piece of legislation he was working on. Anton believed him, even when he was quite sure the two were lovers. The girl was beautiful and she had great style. Anton thought that like Debbie Hanley she was wasting the best years of her life.

Stuart Mansell had a good and loyal wife who would undoubtedly stand by him through thick and thin, he was not the man to jeopardise his career for this girl, even when he was very fond of her.

Where had she been all day? She had not been in for lunch and Mansell had lunched alone with a dour look on his face. Now she was standing at the desk to collect her key and he smiled at her asking if she had enjoyed her day.

'Yes thank you, Mr de Roche. There was a coach going to Ullswater so I took a ride on it. We were late getting back but fortunately I met some other guests in the village who gave me a lift back.'

'There is plenty of time before dinner, I don't think Mr Mansell is down yet.'

'Even a secretary gets a holiday on Good Friday, Mr de Roche.'

He smiled.

'Well of course. Do you enjoy being a secretary to a Member of Parliament, a quite prestigious Member of Parliament?'

'It has its moments, I've worked for Mr Mansell for a great many years. I wonder sometimes where it is leading and if I should look around for something else.'

Whether it was the job or the affair that was leading nowhere he could only hazard a guess, but her expression was pensive and at that moment a girl came to the desk to hand in her key. She smiled at them and Mr de Roche said, 'This is Miss Harknell, Miss Grey, soon to be leaving us, I'm sorry to say. You're off home now, Cathy?'

'Yes. I've left everything in order and I'll be back in a week's time.'

He smiled. 'Enjoy yourself,' he said.

137

Alison asked curiously, 'What does she do here?'

'She is my secretary, and does secretarial work for any of our guests who might need it. I recruited her from another hotel because I knew she would be an asset to us here. She is leaving in July to get married.'

'I see.'

'To one of our guests she met here, an American. She is going to live in Boston.'

'I should think her job here would be very interesting, lots of variety.'

'Exactly. A job that might suit you, I think.'

'Do you really think so?'

'Well of course. Meeting people, a great deal of variety, a beautiful environment. The situation becomes vacant at the end of June, would you be prepared to think about it?'

'I might.'

'Think about it before you leave, I shall very soon be looking around for a replacement for Miss Harknell.'

She smiled. 'I'm leaving in two days' time, but I will think about it.'

She had changed quickly for dinner and was about to leave her room when there was a discreet tap on her door and on going to open it she found Stuart standing there, looking somewhat uncomfortable.

She held the door open wider and he walked into the room.

'When did you get back?' he asked her.

'About half an hour ago.'

'Where did you go to?'

'I took a coach to Ullswater.'

'We could have gone there tomorrow.'

'But not if the two journalists are around, Stuart. As your secretary we don't have that sort of relationship.'

'You're very sarcastic, Alison.'

'I know. I can't help it.'

'Are we ready to go down for dinner?'

'Of course.'

They left the room and walked down the staircase in silence. To Anton standing in the hall they presented a singularly distant couple. Something had to break soon, he couldn't expect to hold out forever.

Tod Hanley passed their table on his way out with a curt nod and Alison surmised correctly that something had gone wrong between him and his wife. There was no sign of Debbie in the restaurant.

The two newspaper men were sitting in their usual place just within the room and the room was filling with several newcomers.

Gloria Weston swept past their table followed by a small slender man who paused to pick up Alison's napkin with a toothy smile and the scent of his after-shave lingered long after he had joined his companion.

Standing on the threshold of the restaurant Mary Styles surveyed the room for a glimpse of Gerald and his mother, and with the hope that they were nowhere near her.

She found them at last, sitting near the wall on the other side of the room and gratefully she went forward to her table. While her meal was served she debated how she would spend the evening ahead.

She got her first real view of Mrs Ralston, a small woman with immaculately coiffeured silver hair and wearing a dark blue dress and several rows of pearls. They seemed to have little to say to each other and some of her anger towards Gerald evaporated.

She had been open with him, talking about her mother as it was and she felt a strange sort of pity that he had been unable to be as honest with her. Pride had been at the bottom of it, he had not been able to put into words the fact that his mother ruled his life, that beyond her there was nothing.

She wondered what they were doing for the rest of the evening. There was dancing in the ballroom for the younger end. In the music room there was entertainment from a pianist and a local singer of some repute, and there was bridge and snooker. She didn't know if Gerald played bridge but he had told her that his mother played.

She couldn't avoid meeting them in the hall where they were looking at the noticeboard outside the music room and Gerald turned just as she reached them.

She smiled, inclining her head in their direction, and Gerald stepped forward to say, 'Mary, I'd like you to meet my mother. This is the lady who chooses your library books, Mother.'

Mrs Ralston gave her a cool smile. 'Oh yes, Gerald told me you were staying here. Are you alone, Miss Styles?'

'Yes.'

'How brave of you to come on holiday alone.'

'I hope I am choosing the right books for you, Mrs Ralston.'

'Well yes, some of them I like better than others. Nobody can please everybody I'm sure.'

'Are you going to the concert?'

'Well we were just thinking about it. I would really like to play bridge but Gerald doesn't play very often. Do you play, Miss Styles?'

'I'm afraid not.'

'Oh you should, it's a very social game.'

'I believe so.'

'Well, Gerald dear, I suggest we go along to the bridge room, you can watch the play for a while and then if you get bored you can always play snooker, he plays at the golf club, you know,' she added with a little smile.

At that moment Mary spotted Mr and Mrs Harvey and smiling across the room at them she said hurriedly, 'I can see two friends over there, if you'll excuse me.'

'We're going to listen to the music, dear, join us if you've nothing else you'd rather be doing,' Mrs Harvey greeted her.

'I'd love to join you, Mrs Harvey.'

'Well we're not energetic enough for dancing and neither of us play card games. I wonder if that young man's wife isn't well, we saw her leaving the dining room and she looked a bit upset.'

Mary turned to see Tod strolling into the bar and Mrs Harvey said, 'He doesn't seem too concerned, perhaps I was imagining it.'

Tod's friends of the afternoon greeted him with smiles, making room for him to pull up a chair.

'Well, are you coming with us to climb Scafell?' he was asked.

'I'd like to. Debbie's playing up a bit so I'll have to placate her before I can make any promises.'

'Oh, you'll manage her all right, we've got our womenfolk tamed.' The laughter was general, and Tod said shortly, 'She's gone upstairs, I'll have a drink with you then I'll see what it's all about.'

Several drinks later Tod decided to see if Debbie intended to join them. One look at her face told him she had been crying, but she was sitting in front of the dressing table mirror trying to repair the ravages the tears had wrought.

She didn't look round when he entered the room and he went to stand behind her looking at her face through the mirror.

'I don't want us to quarrel, Debbie,' he began. 'You don't want me to leave you to go climbing, and I didn't want to be here. Can't we compromise?'

'How do we compromise, Tod? I don't want to spend all evening with your climbing friends, you dislike ballroom dancing and you'd hate the musical entertainment. You're right, we should be in Spain where you would be loving every minute and I wouldn't know the difference.'

'I thought you liked Spain?'

'I put up with it because you liked it and because I was in love with you.'

'Well I'm in love with you and I'm putting up with the Lake District.'

'No you're not, Tod, you're doing your own thing, and you have time for me when it's over.'

'Oh well if you're going to adopt that attitude we might as well not bother going down again.'

'You go down and make your arrangements about tomorrow, I shall go to bed.'

He stared at her doubtfully before he reached out and brought her into his embrace. Tod thought his kisses would make everything all right, obliterate the hurts and when she pulled sharply away from him he only held her closer, whispering endearments against her ear.

'I'll be back in a jiffy, darling, and we'll both go to bed. They're leaving on Easter Monday and we'll have the entire week to do whatever you want to do, just let me have tomorrow, darling, I've half promised and they're relying on me.'

He left her with a bright encouraging smile and he would return to make love to her. That would be her reward for Scafell, and in that moment she knew that all through their married life Tod would think it was enough and the resentment grew and festered as she lay in bed waiting for his return.

In the music room Mary sat with the Harveys listening to a young man playing the piano, haunting beautiful music exquisitely played and later the young soprano who was making a name for herself in Grand Opera.

Mrs Harvey conveyed the information that the hotel had paid an extortionate fee to enable the guests to hear them.

Gerald appeared in the music room halfway through the performance, taking his seat at the back. He had left his mother at one of the bridge tables where she had managed to make up a four, and he knew that for the next few hours at least he would not have to dance attention.

If things had been normal he could have spent this time with Mary, but it was better like this, he could stop pretending.

His mother would be gratified that one of her opponents at the bridge table was a Member of Parliament, she would dine out on it for months, he was not to know that sitting in front of him Alison was reflecting that this was a weekend she could have done without.

Tomorrow they would have to talk, she was ready to go home.

Chapter Eighteen

Most of the hotel guests slept well that cool April night. They had dined well and enjoyed the evening's entertainment, and now only a handful of them lingered in the bars or sat chatting in the lounges. The rest of them had long since sought the comfort of their bedrooms.

Only a few of them stared sleepless into the darkness.

Alison had wished Stuart a cool goodnight in the foyer and he had watched her striding resolutely up the staircase, disdaining the crowded lifts.

This was not at all the sort of weekend he had planned. He understood her anger and realised the time had come to make up his mind either one way or another. For years he had been promising her that one day it would be different, when the children were grown up and able to face things, when he was strong enough to face Sybil with the news that he had fallen in love with somebody else. He knew now that he would never be strong enough.

Sybil was his wife and he loved her, even when he was no longer in love with her. He owed her everything. Her father was a prominent person in the borough he represented, it was thanks to her family that he had been elected, if he was to leave her they would replace him at the earliest opportunity.

If he didn't have Westminster what would he replace it with? He was a political animal. He was a solicitor by profession but he no longer had a practice and he would have great difficulty in getting back into it. When the chips were down he had to think about himself and his family.

Alison would be all right. She was a good secretary, it might be a good idea if she was to move on, and he had no doubt there were a great many other men who would be only too willing to have her work for them. The worst part of it all was how to tell her.

Meanwhile Alison was pacing her bedroom rehearsing what she would say to him. She was the one who had to tell him that it was over, that their affair had run its course, but what could she put in its place?

Did she want to stay at Westminster where she would see him every day, hear about him, still loving him in such a way that she would be willing to drift back to him on his terms?

Gerald had sat listening to his mother going on and on about the charming Mr Mansell she had played bridge with. 'Such a nice man, Gerald, and so interesting. I asked him if his wife minded him playing bridge while she listened to the concert, but he said she wasn't his wife, she was his secretary and they were on a working weekend.'

Gerald merely thought Easter was an odd time to be with his secretary, working weekend or not, but he didn't put it into words.

He had seen Mary in the music room sitting with the elderly couple she seemed to be spending time with. She had looked particularly elegant in a dark blue evening gown. In contrast to the larger-than-life actress, Mary looked a lady, the sort of woman he admired.

At first his mother had been disposed to ask questions about Mary. How often did he see her? Why wasn't she married? Who did she live with? But on each occasion he had said he didn't know, in the sort of voice that seemed totally disinterested and now she had stopped asking questions. She was feeling reassured.

It had always been like this whenever there had been some woman he had chatted to, even at the country clubs he had taken her to, and when the woman had in all probability been married to one of his golfing opponents.

His father had been a quiet sort of man who lived for his garden and his work. His mother had always had her own way and because his father had spoilt her he had made her into a tyrant. She always thought she was right and his father had gone along with it. He had never known what a legacy of bitterness he was building up for his son.

Gerald had come to think that he would never get married, was too old and set in his ways to contemplate it, and then Mary had come along.

Mary would never forgive him for his arrogance, that his rich full life was enough. He had made her feel important to him, and in those few fleeting moments he had crashed her world around her ears.

He had enthused about the hotel, to such an extent that she had been brave enough to insist that her mother should go into a home so that she could spend time with him, and this was how he had repaid her.

For the first time in days Mary was not thinking of Gerald, she was thinking of the strangeness of her day.

She was reliving the moments she had spent being escorted around Alveston Hall by the man who owned it. He had been courteous, charming, a little puzzled by the distress he had found her in, but asking no questions. It was something Mary could tell her mother when she was in a mood to listen to it. The gracious rooms, the tasteful furnishings, the exquisite valuable pictures and ornaments. It would find them something to discuss, because more and more these days there seemed so little to talk about.

She was picturing the face of Gerald's mother, weighing up her appearance putting a mental price tag on the gown she was wearing. How Mrs Ralston would have enjoyed being a guest in Lord Alveston's home, but she would never know Mrs Ralston well enough to tell her about it.

They would all go home after the holiday and Gerald would come in the library every Friday to pick up his mother's books, they would exchange pleasantries but there would be no more intimate Tuesday lunches at the George Hotel, no more advice from Gerald to live her own life, no more enthusiasm for The Lakes, not now that she had seen it for herself.

In the room along the corridor Alison lay in bed with a book open in front of her. She was not reading, instead she was thinking how she was going to bear the weeks and months ahead. Everybody would know that the affair was over, and she would have to make up her mind if she could go on working for him or seek other employment.

Her thoughts turned idly to Anton de Roche's suggestion that she might be interested in a post at the hotel. She had not given it any serious thoughts, now she began to wonder what it would be like.

She thought about Anton de Roche. She could picture him in lace ruffles or in a suit of armour, his keen aristocratic face slightly satanic under his sculptured hair, always urbane, invariably charming. What sort of man would he be to work for?

In a place such as this she would meet other men, men with good positions, men with money, men with potential.

She laid her book aside, her last thoughts before she put out the light were that in the morning she would make some enquiries about what she might expect from a job at The Lakes.

It was almost dawn and Debbie stood at the window staring out into the morning. She opened the long glass door and stepped out onto the balcony, only to retreat back into the room when a gust of wind brought the rain splashing down onto her nightgown.

The lake lay in front of her grey and glassy and a dark mist covered the mountain tops. On such a morning surely they would not attempt to climb Scafell Pike, but if they did not Tod would complain about the weather, that there was nothing to do only read the newspapers, and she found herself hoping that the mist would lift and that sunlight would illuminate the mountain tops.

It was Easter Saturday. The fells and the villages would be busy with visitors, she could take the hotel steamer and go to Keswick to pick up her picture, she could browse around the village shops looking at articles made from Lakeland slate, or visit the woollen centres to look at hand-knitted sweaters and hand-woven tweeds. It would have been nice if they could have gone there together, and her thoughts strayed to Peter and how he intended to spend his day.

In her exclusive suite on the first floor, Gloria Weston helped herself to another gin and tonic. She was bored and slightly drunk.

The holiday had not gone according to plan. She had arrived to be feted by those who admired her and she had been surrounded by photographers, all that was to the good, but it had been a façade she had been unable to build on. She was old hat, too old, people had moved on and the parts were not coming in any more. She was too old for main roles and unwilling to see herself in second place. Somewhere along the line she had to come to terms with the fact that one couldn't go on living with past glories forever, something else had to replace them.

The journalists were still around, but these days they were more interested in that M.P. and his companion. They chatted to de Roche in the hope that he might pass on some gossip but they were barking up the wrong tree. Anton de Roche was incorruptible, they would learn nothing from that source.

Her thoughts turned to Jamie Broughton no doubt fast asleep and steeped in alcohol.

Jamie had been a mistake. It wasn't as though there was anything between them, he was more interested in boys than women, and he had ceased to amuse her. He was costing her money, she was paying for his booze, his hotel bill and his shoddy flat. That would have to stop as soon as they left the hotel. No doubt, there would be more tears and tantrums but Jamie Broughton was unimportant, he'd get over it. She had to find somebody better than Jamie but she had to put her own house in order first.

Perhaps she should accept that minor part in the new television soap. She could build on it, be nice to the producer, show all of them that Gloria Weston was still a power to be reckoned with.

She went to the mirror and ran her fingers along her throat, tracing the lines under her eyes and across her forehead. Make-up would obliterate them, and she still had a figure that could show clothes off to their best advantage. Whatever people said about her, give her the right clothes, the right jewels and sable, no little glamour puss could hold a candle to her.

She topped up her drink and went to sit in her chair staring out through the window. Rain splattered the glass and she shivered delicately. The scenery was depressing her, mountains and lakes were hardly the sort of scenery to make her feel confident, she'd feel better when she returned to London.

She could do something with that part, Mother of the Bride, and the bride was beautiful, an up-and-coming young actress making a name for herself. Still she was known, her public would expect something from her, she wouldn't be content to turn the role into something obscure, she'd make suggestions, appear at her most beautiful.

If she came to The Lakes next year she'd be back on the map again. Everybody else would be here to see her.

Over the breakfast tables guests were shaking their heads lamenting that the sunshine of the last two days was missing, and instead Easter Saturday had started with torrential rain and mist.

Tod's face was morose and Debbie said, 'I suppose this means climbing Scafell is off?'

'Not necessarily. We'll see what the morning brings, the mist could lift, rain isn't a deterrent.'

'You mean you'll actually consider climbing if it is still raining?'

'We'll see. What else is there to do?'

She had to admit that there was nothing to do that would please Tod.

Peter passed their table with a polite greeting, and Tod muttered, 'I wonder what he does to pass the time?'

'Oh, I rather think he manages very well, he knows the district.'

'Bully for him.'

'He comes here several times during the year.'

'Doesn't his mind stretch to anything else?'

'I'm sure it does, he likes the district and he's enough money to go elsewhere if he wants to.'

Tod scowled making Debbie well pleased with her remarks.

They read the morning papers and drank coffee, and by mid-morning the rain eased off and a thin watery sun peeped out from darkly leaden clouds. Tod's spirits lifted and when one of his climbing companions passed their table he said brightly, 'Looks as if we'll be climbing after all.'

'Rather, if the mist stays away we'll be off in about half an hour.'

'Right, I'll meet you on the terrace.'

'The mist will probably come down again,' Debbie said. 'It looks far from promising.'

'Then we'll come back,' Tod said.

'Where are you starting from?'

'We're driving over to Westdale, that's the best starting place. Tonight we'll be celebrating, champagne with dinner.'

She stood in the gardens to watch them drive out of the car park. It had started to rain, thin driving rain that hung like mist across the lake and she turned and walked back into the hotel. If this weather continued surely they would not attempt to climb Scafell and her thoughts were confirmed by Mr de Roche saying, 'I hardly think they will do any climbing today, Mrs Hanley, it is going to be one of those unpredictable days the Lake District is famous for.'

She smiled. The day may be unpredictable but Tod was not. If he wanted to climb Scafell it would take a little more than mist to prevent him. He played golf in a thunderstorm and swore there had been no rain on the golf course, he made the weather to suit himself.

As she walked towards the stairs she met Mr Mansell who smiled at her saying, 'We're in for a wet spell, I think, Debbie, what will you be doing with yourself?'

'Tod has gone climbing, Mr Mansell, I was hoping to go into the village.'

He smiled. 'It's hardly climbing weather. Are you enjoying your stay here?'

'Yes thank you.'

He merely smiled and moved away.

As Debbie walked up the stairs she resolved to inform Tod during the evening that Mr Mansell was with his secretary, that might put an end to the snide remarks he had been making.

Stuart hung about the foyer until Alison emerged from the lift and he went forward to meet her.

She always looked so right in everything she wore. This morning she wore a businesslike suit and cream silk blouse. Her dark blonde hair was tied back from her face and as always she was exquisitely made up. He was aware that he still desired her. He had meant this weekend to be one when he made love to her every moment they were alone together. He meant to reassure her again and again that he loved her and that one day things would be different, but nothing had worked out as he planned.

Now there had to be a reckoning, his reassurances would fall on stony ground. There was a cool determined look on her face and as they walked together into the restaurant he wondered when it would come to a head. Would it be when they were sitting over a meal or would she demand to see him privately? He hoped it would be the latter so that perhaps once more he could persuade her to wait.

Across the room he could see the two journalists eating breakfast and their sudden interest when Gloria Weston swept into the room with the man she had elected to bring with her. They too were distant, eyeing each other warily like two adult cats and Stuart reflected grimly that perhaps that association was also on its way out.

They ordered breakfast and sat for a few moments in silence, it was Alison who finally said, 'We haven't talked, have we, Stuart? In fact we haven't done anything except sit together like two polite strangers?'

'It wasn't meant to be like this, Alison.'

'I know. It was meant to be a weekend like all the others that have gone before. The time for talking is over, isn't it?

He stared at her mournfully without speaking.

'Stuart, you are never going to leave your wife and your children. You would like us to go on indefinitely as we are but I can't agree to it, it's already gone on too long.'

'You know I love you, Alison.'

'It isn't the sort of love I want, Stuart, it's entirely on your terms. You're a family man, I'm simply the other woman in your life and I derive nothing from it except uncertainty, doubt and resentment. I'm leaving you, Stuart.'

'Leaving me! How are you leaving me?'

'I'll not leave you in the lurch, I'll work out my notice until you've found a replacement for me, then I shall move on. Our lovelife and our business life are over.'

'Where will you work, are you going to work for Denison?'

'You wouldn't like that would you, Stuart? You know he's been sniffing around for years.'

'I can't stand the chap.'

She grinned at him. 'I can't stand him either so I'm not going to work for Denison. I'm getting out of Westminster, I've had enough of politics to last me a lifetime, besides if I stayed there I'd see you every day and I have to get you out of my system. It won't happen overnight.'

'So you haven't fallen out of love with me, Alison?'

'I never said I had, but I will, and hopefully sooner rather than later.'

'But what will you do?'

'I'm not sure. You'll know when I finally leave Westminster for good.'

They finished their breakfast in uneasy silence. Stuart had no appetite and he watched with some dismay as she nonchalantly buttered her toast as if the ending of their affair meant little.

He held her chair as she rose from the table and they walked side by side out of the room. She favoured the journalists with a swift smile and in the foyer Stuart said, 'Are you wishing to leave today or do you want to stay on until Monday?'

'I think I'd like to stay, Stuart, but I'll quite understand it if you want to get away.'

He was hesitant, a frown on his good-looking face and staring up at him she was miserably aware that she still loved him.

'You haven't got your car, Alison, I drove you here from the station.'

'You needn't worry about that, Stuart, I can get a taxi into Kendal and get the train from there. I'm never helpless, you should know that.'

He stood besides her with an indecisive frown on his face and Alison prompted, 'Why not go home, Stuart, you could telephone your wife, perhaps by this time she'll be ready to come home.'

He thought about Sybil and the empty house. He'd be alone and miserable, thinking about Alison and the end of their long affair, and he'd be resentful about Sybil's absence. Suddenly he made up his mind.

'I'll stay here as we planned it, Alison, I'm not leaving you here alone.'

'Thank you, Stuart. What will you do today?'

'What do you want to do?'

'Don't bother about me, I have plans.'

He stared dejectedly through the long windows that looked across the expanse of lake saying, 'God, what a miserable day, it's not even fit for a drive out somewhere.'

'I'll see you for lunch then?' she said with a little smile.

'I suppose so.'

He watched her walking away from him across the foyer, going to speak to a man behind the desk, and he turned away so suddenly he collided with a woman standing behind him.

Apologising profusely he saw that it was his bridge companion of the evening before, who greeted him warmly, saying to the man standing beside her, 'Gerald dear, this is Mr Mansell the gentleman I played bridge with last evening. This is my son, Mr Mansell.'

The two men shook hands and Mrs Ralson said, 'What an awful day, we were hoping to go off on the boat but I hardly think it's a good day for it.'

'No indeed. There'll be no good views across the lake today but the village shops will be busy.'

'Yes of course but there's nothing we need to buy.'

'Oh well, enjoy your day anyway,' Stuart said with a smile and turned away.

'I told you he was nice,' Mrs Ralston said. 'I expect he's a very good M.P.'

Gerald was not listening. He was looking across the room to where Mary was standing at the desk selecting postcards. After choosing some she was looking down at them pensively and following his gaze his mother said sharply, 'I want some cards to send to some of the bridge ladies, Gerald, I'll get them later.'

'The weekend will be over if you don't get them quickly,' he said.

'Oh well I'll get them now. Keep two places in the lounge for us, dear.'

She joined Mary at the counter and Mary smiled down at her, wishing her good morning.

'Not a very good one,' Mrs Ralston said. 'We were hoping to go on the lake but I believe it's still raining. When are you leaving for home, Miss Styles?'

'On Tuesday morning.'

'Are you travelling by car?'

'Yes.'

'How strange that we should meet you here, Gerald didn't know you were coming?'

'No, he didn't.'

Mary smiled at her and turned away. The woman was so transparent. That Gerald should know the comings and goings of any woman would be unacceptable, was this really his rich full life?

Chapter Nineteen

Debbie sat in the lounge staring morosely through the window when Peter joined her late in the afternoon. The rain was coming down now in a steady downpour and it was impossible to see the opposite bank of the lake.

'Penny for them,' he said with a smile.

She turned to look at him. 'I was wondering when they were coming back,' she said softly. 'Surely they can't be up a mountain in weather like this.'

'They're probably sitting in the Wastdale Hotel hoping it will clear. It's a meeting place for climbers and fell walkers, they'll have a lot to talk about.'

'Have you climbed Scafell Pike, Peter?'

'One summer when I came with some chaps from the university, it's a formidable peak. Has Tod ever climbed it?'

'No.'

'Oh well, I wouldn't worry too much, they're probably on their way back.'

But she did worry. Tod was courageous, he was also foolhardy. He'd be the one to spur them on even if he was less experienced, he didn't know that, and they'd be egging him on and laughing at him. At that moment she was furious with them all.

The boat had taken people across to the village in spite of the rain and now they were walking back through the gardens huddled under umbrellas and looking thoroughly dejected. Most of the guests had decided to stay indoors. In the hotel there was conversation and laughter, afternoon tea and music.

Stuart Mansell sat in a corner of the lounge with his face buried in a newspaper, there was no sign of his secretary. That nice Miss Styles was having afternoon tea with the elderly couple and the owner and his wife and they appeared to be enjoying themselves by the sound of their laughter.

Mrs Ralston and her son sat at another table near the window, he staring morosely through the glass, his mother doing needlepoint.

Peter ordered afternoon tea for himself and Debbie.

Alison had made an appointment to see Anton de Roche in the late afternoon and now sat opposite him in his opulent office on the ground floor.

She felt inordinately nervous, which was something new to her, and he was aware of her nervousness as he talked pleasantries in an effort to put her at her ease.

At last she asked, 'Did you really mean it when you thought I might be suitable for work here, Mr de Roche?'

'Yes, of course I meant it. As soon as you stepped into the hotel I found myself wishing that I could find somebody like you. You are the sort of young lady who would be an acquisition here.'

'And I would be working for you?'

'You would be my secretary but there are a team of you. You could be asked to do secretarial work for one of our guests, would that be a problem?'

'Of course not. My duties have been many and varied at Westminster.'

'And is Mr Mansell willing to let you go, have you broached the matter to him?'

'Yes, this morning.'

'He has offered no objections?'

'It is my life, Mr de Roche.'

For several minutes she sat silent, then looking him straight in the eyes she said, 'Mr Mansell and I were rather more than friends, it was not entirely a business relationship, we have been lovers for many years. The affair is going nowhere. There have been times when I thought things might be different but not anymore. Stuart is married with a family. His wife's family have some standing in his constituency, he needs them far more than he needs me. Getting a new secretary will pose no problem, getting a new lifestyle is something very different.'

'I understand.'

'I have told him I will stay until I can safely hand over my duties to somebody else. You did say you would not be needing a new secretary until the summer?'

'June would be ideal so that you could spend a little time with Cathy before she leaves in July.'

'You call her Cathy?'

'Yes. Would you prefer it if I referred to you as Miss Grey?'

'No, I would like you to call me Alison, it might help me to feel more at home here.'

'Then that is it, Alison. You are coming to work for us here in June and I am sure you will be very happy here. We run a contented ship, the owner of the hotel makes sure of that, and I am not an ogre. I think you will find me easy to work for as long as you do your job.'

They smiled at each other, and rising from her chair she held out her hand which he clasped firmly in his, then he ushered her out of the door.

She could hardly believe that she had come to the hotel to spend a loving

few days with Stuart and had ended up with a whole new life. She would tell
him over dinner, he would have difficulty in believing that she had replaced
him in every way so soon.

Andrew stood at the window looking out into the wet misery of the late afternoon. He was wishing with all his heart that he had not accepted the invitation to dine at The Lakes. The journey would be a miserable one, he would
not know a soul and he would have preferred to spend the evening sitting in
front of the fire.

He wondered idly if his visitor of the previous afternoon would be in evidence, probably she had made friends and would not be dining alone.

Several visitors had come and gone during the day. First the local vicar
with an urgent invitation to morning service on Easter Sunday, then a party of
three friends who had heard that he had come home and had been anxious to
see him. They had come with news of old friends, old pursuits and pressing
engagements to dine with them, hunt with them, weekend with them.

He was picking up the pieces much to his staff's gratification, they were
not to know that he could still hurt, still grieve over past miseries.

He wondered what particular anxiety had troubled his guest of the previous
afternoon so that she had walked blindly into the path of his car. It wasn't
only the very young who agonised over love, it could well be that Mary
Styles was suffering from some disappointment in that direction.

She had reminded him of Stella. She had the same straight gaze and
uncluttered style. The same light brown hair with auburn lights in it, the same
tall slender figure. No wonder Grant's eyes had lit up when he held the car
door open for her.

Grant thought it strange that Stella should want to come back to the lakeland fells, but she had been raised here, there were other memories for her
than the ones they had shared.

She had gone back to an invalid husband and Andrew reflected sadly on
the strong virile young man he remembered and whom Stella had eventually
fallen in love with.

How strange were the twists and turns in life, the joys and sorrows, the
people who came and went across the years. He was reconciled to spending
his future alone, he had made one terrible mistake there had to be no more.

At the hotel people were thinking about going upstairs to change for dinner
but still Debbie sat on in the lounge staring in the dusk.

Peter was reluctant to leave her.

'Try not to worry, Debbie, I'm sure they're already on their way back,'
said gently, and although she smiled her eyes were dark with anxiety.

'I'll go upstairs to change presently,' she said. 'I'll hang on here a little
longer, I'll see you later.'

He left her, and meeting Anton de Roche in the doorway he shook his head and Anton said, 'I think I should telephone the Wastdale Hotel in case they have news of the climbers. If they're still in the vicinity perhaps I can reassure Mrs Hanley.'

The news he received was far from reassuring. The climbers had gone off to climb the peak as planned and they had not returned. The weather at Wastdale was very bad, thick mist and driving rain, and they were already being searched for.

Common sense told him not to worry Debbie with the news until something more concrete came to light.

She looked round the lounge to find it deserted apart from one old man asleep in his favourite chair. She had to find something to do, even if it was only bathing and changing for the evening. They were all saying how much they were looking forward to the ball planned for the evening, indeed anything to shut out the remembered misery of the day, and it was after all Easter Saturday.

Tod would be full of apologies, he would blame the weather, his companions, anything except his own stupidity.

Mrs Ralston was complaining about the ball.

'Not everyone cares for dancing,' she said stiffly. 'There are elderly people staying here, surely some of them would prefer to play bridge.'

'I'm sure you'll find someone, Mother,' Gerald reasoned.

'What will you do?'

'I haven't decided. Watch the dancing perhaps. See if anybody would like a game of snooker.'

'Does that Miss Styles dance?'

'I haven't any idea, Mother.'

'Well I wouldn't be too anxious to ask her to dance, being your librarian she might read more into it than you intend.'

'Really, Mother. What has being our librarian anything to do with it? She's a very nice woman I see around the town and in the library, she won't be expecting me to ask her to dance.'

His mother looked at him sharply. It wasn't often Gerald answered her so heatedly, and seeing her look Gerald said quickly, 'I'll look in on the dancing, Mother, but you know it's not exactly my scene. I'm sure you'll manage your game of bridge.'

When did he ever dance these days? He never went to the dances at the golf club and when they went on holidays it never occurred to him to go into the ballrooms, either in the hotels they stayed in or on cruise ships.

Some feeling of perverse humour made Alison select her most glamorous evening gown, the one Stuart liked above all others. A jade green confection in heavy silk which vied deliciously with her blonde hair and eyes the same colour as the gown.

She would make him see what he would be missing in the months ahead, she would give him something to remember her by.

He was waiting for her in the foyer when she went down to dinner, his eyes strangely brooding as he looked down at her.

'It's a little too early to go into dinner,' he said. 'Shall we go to the bar?'

She nodded. 'A quiet corner please, Stuart, there's something I want to tell you.'

'You select the corner then, I'll get the drinks,' he said giving her an anxious look.

There were few people in the bar as it was early, and as she waited for him to bring the drinks to the table she caught sight of Debbie Hanley walking slowly towards the stairs. Leaving her bag on the seat she hurried out of the bar to speak to her.

'Haven't they come back yet, Debbie?' she asked.

Debbie shook her head. She looked grey with worry.

'Oh I'm sure they'll be all right, they'll be sheltering somewhere.'

Debbie nodded. 'I expect so,' then with another bleak smile she went towards the lifts.

Alison returned to the table where Stuart was setting out the drinks and seeing her concern he said, 'I suppose they're not back yet. Hanley's an arrogant young fool, far too sure of himself and a bit of a show-off.'

'Surely they won't have climbed the peak.'

'I wouldn't put it past them.'

'Poor girl, she's terribly upset. He shouldn't be climbing at all on their honeymoon.'

'No. Now what do you want to tell me?'

'I've got another job.'

He stared at her with the utmost astonishment. 'A job! Where?'

'Here. Working for Mr de Roche and anybody else in the hotel who wants secretarial work.'

'I never heard anything more insane. What about your flat? What about Westminster? They can't possibly match your salary here.'

'You don't know that, Stuart. I can sell my flat, and I can either live in here for the time being or get somewhere locally.'

'Haven't you gone into your salary?'

'No, I didn't even think about it, I simply wanted to get away from London and from you.'

He winced. 'Don't you think you'd better see about your salary before you do anything else?'

'Mr de Roche knows the sort of job I've held down and the sort of salary I've been getting. London is expensive, there'll not be the same expense here,

154

after all what is there to spend money on? I'll have my car and I've enough clothes to sink a ship.'

'When did all this arise?'

'Accidentally. I met his secretary who is leaving in June to get married, he happened to mention that her job would be coming up and I was interested. I shall enjoy being here, I shall enjoy the peace and I shall meet people.'

'Men, you mean?'

'Obviously, and women too. My object in coming here is not to meet men. At the moment I feel I've had a surfeit of men.'

'Does that mean that you will stay with me until June?'

'With the exception of the holidays you owe me.'

'Alison, it will be a disaster. You love London, burying yourself in the country will not be the answer, you'll come to hate every minute of it.'

'You *hope* I'll hate every minute of it. We'll see. It could be my salvation, yours too. My staying in London and working for somebody else at Westminster would be a disaster, you'd be there breathing over my shoulder, we'd make the effort to leave each other alone and we'd fail. I can't face months and years of hanging on hoping for better things, Stuart, it has to end and this is the best way to end it.'

He looked down at her beautiful determined face and he knew she meant it. Their affair had run its course, it was time to move on.

Anybody seeing them together sipping their drinks in companionable silence could be excused from thinking that they were simply two people who knew each other very well and were content in each other's company. From the ballroom came the first sounds of the orchestra and Stuart said glumly, 'Do you want to go in there?'

'Yes of course. Why can't we go out in a blaze of glory? Dance the night away and enjoy ourselves.'

'Are you ready to go into dinner then?'

'Why not.'

The two newspaper men watched them enter the restaurant with speculation. They were two people who had given nothing away in the few days they had been together, now for the first time since they arrived they seemed like a pair. So thought Gloria Weston, as she watched them take their place at their table.

She had thought it might be an idea to cultivate Stuart Mansell during the course of the evening, but now she wasn't so sure. The girl he was with meant something to him, forcing them apart might prove too difficult.

She was alone, her companion of the last few days had been told to stay where he was, that she didn't need him and he was sulking. As far as Gloria was concerned the weekend had done nothing to add to her reputation and the sooner things got back to normal the better it would be. She looked around the room with interest, followed by dejection.

The gown Mary Styles was wearing had been a great extravagance. It was elegant and she looked well in it. Gerald's eyes followed her slender figure as she walked towards her table. The dress was heavy sage green georgette and the colour suited her soft brown hair. Gerald thought it looked gentle and ladylike and his mother remarked caustically, 'I wouldn't have thought her position at the library could afford such a dress.'

'She's the head librarian, Mother, she has a very responsible job.'

'But this hotel, and that gown, Gerald. She's hardly in the same league as that M.P.'s wife.'

'That is not his wife, Mother, that is his secretary.'

His mother looked at him in shocked surprise. 'Who told you that? Of course she's his wife.'

She was looking at him indignantly but at that moment the head waiter was ushering a tall distinguished man between the tables to his seat against the wall and as he reached Mary's table she looked up and the man paused with a slight bow and words were exchanged.

'Who do you suppose that is?' his mother asked. 'They seem to know each other.'

'I have no idea, Mother.'

Mary felt confused by the encounter. Andrew had greeted her charmingly, his smile warm, before he went on to his table.

After she had eaten she would go into the lounge, perhaps Mr and Mrs Harvey would be there, but most of the guests would make their way to the ballroom. Tonight was the highlight of the Easter weekend and most of the guests were attired for it.

In the meantime Gerald was speculating on who the man might be who obviously had met Mary before and to his chagrin his mother was saying to their waiter, 'Who is the gentleman who has just come in? I seem to know him from somewhere.'

'That is Lord Alveston, Madam, from Alveston Hall.'

Of course Mary didn't know him, he had simply greeted her out of courtesy and his mother was saying, 'I don't suppose he's interested in the dancing, I wonder if this is the first time he's been here?'

Gloria Weston was trying to remember all she had ever heard of Andrew Alveston. She had been a young starlet when she was introduced to Olivia, Lady Alveston at a cocktail party in London. Her Ladyship had been elegant and beautiful, treating Gloria to a long cool look out of speculative eyes. In those days Gloria had been beneath her notice, simply a young actress hobnobbing with the famous in her desire to rise to the top.

There had been a scandal, that much she remembered. The papers had been full of it. Her ladyship's body being retrieved from the lake in the grounds of Alveston, her husband had been a suspect, and then another man had been accused of it and hanged.

Now here he was alone on Easter Saturday and her spirits revived.

Stuart Mansell too was regarding his lordship with some degree of satisfaction. Here at any rate was somebody else those damned journalists could get their teeth into.

Mary finished her meal but saw that Mr and Mrs Harvey were only just sitting down with the owner of the hotel and his wife. Her spirits fell. She did not want to intrude, they had been more than kind, but she did not want to sit in the ballroom like the proverbial wallflower.

She dawdled over her coffee. Gerald and his mother were still eating, no doubt Mrs Ralston would retire to the bridge tables but if they went into the ballroom would Gerald ask her to dance? She couldn't imagine that he would, after all, what would they talk about?'

Making up her mind suddenly she pushed her coffee cup aside and rose from the table. As she passed the Harveys' table, Mrs Harvey said, 'How nice you look, Mary, shall we see you in the ballroom?'

'I'm not sure, Mrs Harvey, perhaps.'

She smiled and passed on.

In the foyer she could see young Mrs Hanley in earnest conversation with Mr de Roche. They both seemed upset and in the next moment he was showing Mrs Hanley into his office behind the desk. She remembered that Mr Hanley had gone off climbing and she hoped nothing was wrong. It had hardly been a day for climbing mountains.

She was standing looking up idly at the noticeboard when a voice beside her said, 'Are you looking forward to the rest of the evening, Miss Styles?'

She looked up into Andrew's dark eyes smiling down at her and she blushed nervously.

'I was wondering what to do with myself,' she said softly.

'I thought the hotel laid on entertainment for all its guests,' he said.

'Well, I'm not a bridge player and I don't have a dancing partner so the choices are rather limited.'

'Then I suggest we go into the bar and join each other in a drink. I'm a little out of practice with my dancing but perhaps you'll put up with me.'

'Thank you, Lord Alveston, you are very kind.'

'My name is Andrew, and yours is Mary, I think?'

She smiled, and together they walked into the bar.

Chapter Twenty

Anton de Roche placed a glass of sherry on the small table beside Debbie's chair and went to sit behind his desk. She was pale and tearful, and unfortunately he had no good news for her.

Anton had telephoned the Wastdale Hotel only to be informed that the climbers had gone home early except for four young men who were attempting to climb Scafell Pike, that had been before lunch, the weather had been bad and the mist had come down. Other climbers had tried to dissuade them but one young man had been particularly insistent, none of them had returned to the hotel and men who knew the mountain were helping to search for them. When they had any more news they would telephone.

'You shouldn't be alone here waiting for news,' he said anxiously. 'Would you like me to telephone your parents?'

'But they'll have such a long drive,' Debbie persisted.

'Even so, I think they would like to be informed.'

'Tod's parents are in Spain.'

'Well they are probably perfectly safe and sheltering somewhere, but I do think your parents should be here. I have their telephone number, they have been guests here several times.'

She did not attempt to argue with him, and after a few minutes she heard him talking to one of her parents. He called her to the telephone and she was listening to her father's voice asking anxiously, 'What's wrong, Debbie?'

She explained quickly, and immediately her father said, 'We'll drive up there, Debbie, it's a foul night but we'll be up there in an hour or so. Try not to worry, I expect by the time we get there Tod will have arrived back.'

'You are very welcome to remain in here, Mrs Hanley,' Anton said. 'I expect it is preferable to having people commiserating with you when in all probability nothing dreadful has happened.'

'Thank you, Mr de Roche.'

'As soon as I have any news I'll come in to tell you. Hopefully your husband will be the one to come in to tell you.'

Outside in the foyer all was normality. There was music and laughter, the gathering together of a crowd of people intent on enjoying the evening ahead and Anton circulated among the guests urbane and smiling.

He saw that in a corner of the bar Lord Alveston and Miss Styles were deep in conversation and that Mr Mansell and Miss Grey were walking into the ballroom, it would appear that for this evening at least they would be together.

Gloria was leaving the bar with a sullen look on her face. What could that quite uninteresting woman have in common with Andrew Alveston? They appeared to be finding plenty to talk about and he had merely favoured her with a quiet smile. She did not think he even knew who she was.

Anton read the signs well. She was a star, perhaps a fading one, but not in her opinion, and she was alone. A few years ago, perhaps months ago she would have been feted, the other guests would have flocked to be seen with her, dance with her, but her star had waned, they were no longer interested.

'I hope you're going to ask me to dance, Anton, there's nobody else I want to dance with,' she said sulkily.

'Perhaps later, Miss Weston, I'm not free at the moment.'

'Oh well, if I'm still around whenever you're free perhaps we'll dance.'

She would no doubt find somebody and he wondered idly what the man she had brought with her was doing. His staff had already informed him of the empty whisky bottles they retrieved from his bedroom, his decrepit appearance and the disarray in his room.

He felt a sudden rush of compassion for Gloria Weston. She was probably older than Mary Styles but Mary would accept the years gracefully, retain her poise and her humour while Gloria had fought against them and would continue to do so. He wondered idly where Andrew Alveston had met Miss Styles but he was pleased that they were obviously enjoying each other's company, the owner had cautioned him to look after his lordship and see to it that he was enjoying himself.

'At least the traffic's light,' Geraldine commented as they drove northward through driving rain and heavy cloud.

'Anybody with any sense wouldn't be out on such a night,' her husband replied tersely.

She had thrown a few things hurriedly into a suitcase while John was seeing to the car. His thoughts on the journey were angry.

'What sort of a young fool is he to go climbing on his honeymoon?' he snapped.

'I told you there were problems but you didn't listen,' Geraldine said. 'Anyway when did Tod ever please anybody but himself? I suppose we should let his parents know.'

'I hope there'll be no need for that, he'll probably be back by the time we get there and I'll be giving him a piece of my mind.'

'I wouldn't do that if I were you, we don't want to make things worse.'

'They couldn't be worse. It's not my idea of a pleasant Easter Saturday driving to the Lake District in this weather. I'll tell you another thing, they've called out the Mountain Rescue Team and they'll not be thinking too highly of Tod and his pals at the moment.'

'Will they know where to look for them?'

'They'll know Scafell Pike, but it won't be easy to find anything in driving rain and the mountains covered with mist.'

'Don't go on, John, Debbie will be upset enough as it is.'

John remained silent. The driving rain and slippery road needed all his attention. Now and again oncoming headlights shimmered through the windscreen sending up spray so that the windscreen wipers could barely cope.

The powerful car ate up the miles but the narrow mountain roads were hazardous as they neared their destination and in sudden pools of rainwater the car swerved frighteningly. Through the mist and across the lake they could vaguely see the lights of the hotel and John muttered, 'We don't want to miss the turn off, keep a look out for the signpost.'

In silence they drove along the margin of the lake until suddenly Geraldine said, 'Now, to your left, this is the road.'

The scene that met them when they entered the hotel was one of festivity. Men and women in evening dress stood in groups and from the ballroom floated the sound of an orchestra.

People stared curiously at two people arriving late on Easter Saturday dripping with rain, but immediately Anton was there to take them into his office. There should be no unusual disturbance to trouble the guests or their enjoyment.

Debbie rushed into her mother's arms and, over her head, Anton shook his head sadly, 'There has been no news, I'm afraid, of course the weather will hamper whatever the Rescue Team is doing. We shall simply have to wait. I've arranged for a room to be prepared for you, Mr Broadhurst, perhaps you would like a meal? It can be served in here.'

'I'm not hungry, how about you, Geraldine?' her husband asked.

'No. A cup of tea would be nice, the journey was very unpleasant.'

'I'll arrange for it. I'm sure you want to talk and I have to get back to the guests. Please ring for anything you want.'

As soon as he had closed the door, Geraldine asked, 'Whatever possessed him to go climbing in this weather, and on your honeymoon too?'

'He got friendly with some other men and they encouraged him.'

'I don't suppose he needed much encouragement, he was always a show-off.'

'Not now, Mummy, please,' Debbie pleaded.

She was saved from further recriminations by the arrival of a maid with the tea, and to change the subject her father said heartily, 'What did Tod think of the hotel?'

'Not very much. He would have preferred to go to Spain.'

'I wish you'd told us where you intended to spend your honeymoon, Debbie, I would have told you it wasn't Tod's scene. What have you done with yourselves since you arrived?'

'I went on the boat yesterday and took a look around Keswick.'

'Did Tod go with you?'

'No. He climbed Helvellyn with the same group. I met up with Peter and we strolled around Keswick together.'

'That nice boy you met earlier when you were with us?' her mother demanded.

'Yes. Mummy, don't look like that. Peter's nice and very kind, we just happened to be on the boat together and we knew each other.'

'And I suppose you told Tod where you'd been and with whom.'

'Yes of course.'

'And he didn't mind?'

'What was there to mind about?'

By this time Debbie was thinking it hadn't been a very good idea to send for her parents, but after giving his wife a warning look her father said, 'But you have enjoyed most of it, love?'

'Oh yes, it's been great.'

'Is Stuart Mansell still here?' her mother demanded. 'I had a telephone call from Sybil, she's hoping to come home after Easter. She said she'd been speaking to Stuart on the telephone but she seemed a bit vague about his whereabouts.'

'He's on a working holiday, Mummy, she's awfully nice.'

'Who's nice?'

'Alison, his secretary. They don't spend much time together, I've been into the village with her, but they're probably working most of the time.'

Geraldine's eyes met her husband's over Debbie's head and he shook his head to tell her to say nothing more. Whatever the Mansells were up to was not their business, and he didn't want his wife involved.

'I'm not sure we brought the right sort of clothes for this place,' Geraldine said. 'Everybody's in evening dress and all I've packed is a silk afternoon dress and a couple of skirts and twin sets.'

'We're not here to socialise,' John said testily. 'We're here to look after Debbie, and when the people out there know why we're here they'll not be expecting you to be a fashion plate.'

At that moment the telephone rang shrilly and they all looked at each other in startled dismay.

The door opened and Anton came in, going immediately to answer the telephone. They sat with their eyes glued on him, listening to his voice answering briefly, saying at last, 'I see, so there's nothing more to be done tonight. You'll start again at daybreak and keep me informed. Thank you.'

'You heard?' he asked quietly.

'Why have they called it off, does that mean the men have to spend the night on the mountain in this weather?' John demanded.

'I'm afraid so. The mountains are dangerous, those men who are out looking for them should not be asked to put their own lives at risk, they've already been searching several hours. The mist is down, but you can rest assured the search will start again at daybreak.'

'How about the men Tod was with?' John asked. 'Don't they have womenfolk with them?'

'There were girls with them yesterday evening in the bar but they are not staying here, they were merely girls they knew, perhaps they're staying in another hotel, I don't know, only that they are not here.'

'So they came here as a climbing party?' John persisted.

'They've stayed in the hotel several times to go climbing, they were experienced, at least one of them was.'

Deep anger surged in Debbie's breast. These were the men who had urged Tod to go with them, laughed at his bumptiousness, egged him on, now they were all out there in the cold misty night and other braver men were risking their lives to find them.

'Your room is ready now if you'd like to go up there to unpack,' Anton was saying. 'I've asked Doctor Latimer to come in to see you, Debbie, he's suggested a sleeping draught to help you to sleep. There's nothing you can do, nothing anybody can do until the morning.'

In the luxury of the bridal suite Debbie looked around her with pain-filled eyes. Tod's pyjamas lay folded on the bed, in the bathroom were the toiletries he had used that morning, in the wardrobe were his clothes and the golf clubs he had insisted on bringing.

It would have been the same if he'd met golfers instead of climbers. He'd have challenged them to a game, proving to himself and to them that he was the best, but at least the golf course would have been a safer place than the treacherous Scafell Pike.

She tried to remember what she knew of it. The deep dark Wastwater lake and the rugged screes. The highest mountains in England surrounding it, Pillar and Great Gable, Scafell and the Pike. She remembered seeing that lake in all its gloomy grandeur, it had looked haunted, even when she was seeing it on a day bright with sunlight and white tossing clouds. She could imagine it on a night like this when misty shadows turned into wraiths that floated mysteriously across the lake's surface.

Cumberland's lakes were beautiful, dotted with lush islands where peaceful Lakeland cattle waded in the shallows and where graceful trees dripped their branches into the placid waters. Wastwater was different, grander, more primeval, a lake of brooding sadness, and with her thoughts sad and strangely bitter Debbie fell into a dreamless sleep.

It was the maid serving her with breakfast that roused her, and then suddenly all the trauma of the day before was back with her and she asked sharply, 'What time is it?'

'Nine-thirty, Mrs Hanley, Mr de Roche said we were not to disturb you.'

'But I should have been disturbed, are my parents awake?'

'Yes, madam, they're downstairs with Mr de Roche. Please have your breakfast first.'

The girl gave her a swift sympathetic smile before leaving the room.

Debbie poured tea and rushed into the bathroom. While she was eating a slice of toast she hurried into slacks and a sweater, then snatching up her handbag she hurriedly left the room. As she passed Stuart Mansell's room he was locking the door and he looked up at her with a sad smile, 'How are you, Debbie? There's no news yet I'm afraid.'

'Have you seen my parents, Mr Mansell?'

'Yes, I saw your father earlier on when we were looking at newspapers.'

'Did he tell you there was no news?'

'Yes. You'll find them in the lounge.'

He walked with her to the lift, then said hurriedly, 'I've forgotten something, Debbie, I have to go back. Please go on ahead.'

It had not been his intention to go downstairs, he had promised Alison he would change then go back for her. He had spent the night in Alison's room and the last few days might never have happened. He had made love to her with all the old ardour she remembered and she had responded as if there had been no sulky quarrels, no angry resentment, and yet he knew in his heart it was her way of saying farewell, the end of the road, after this weekend they would be nothing more to each other than working colleagues, and his heart was filled with a painful regret.

She opened her door and went naturally into his arms.

'Alison,' he murmured against her hair, 'it needn't be like this, not when we care too much, not when there's no need to end it.'

Quietly she pushed him away.

'Last night was wonderful, Stuart, tonight can be wonderful, tomorrow we're going home. You are not having the best of both worlds and I am not spending the rest of my life wondering where you are, if you'll call, when I'm going to see you outside office hours. It's over.'

'I can't fight you on this, Alison, it isn't possible.'

'No, it isn't. When I saw you speaking to those two people last night from your constituency I knew I was doing the right thing, you were so anxious to make it plain to them that we had been working very hard over the weekend, that I was your secretary of a great many years, and you were quick to call me

163

Miss Grey. I'm not sure the woman believed you, I should work on her at your earliest opportunity. She's a friend of your wife's, I believe.'

All the time he had been making love to her he had been telling himself that it needn't end. They still had a few months when they would meet every day, he would make her see that they couldn't split up, they still meant too much to each other, but he was afraid of the determination in her eyes, the assurance that she could live without him.

'How do you want to spend the day?' he asked her. 'It's still misty out there and the sky's decidedly grey.'

'You mean you don't want to avoid the newspaper men today?' she asked with a small smile.

'With a bit of luck they'll have something else to think about today with men lost on Scafell.'

'You really are an insensitive bastard, Stuart. One of those boys is in your constituency, you went to their wedding, for heaven's sake, and all you can think about now is your own skin.'

'Well, of course I'm concerned about the boy. I'll have a much better chance of showing my concern without them breathing down my neck. I'll talk to the Broadhursts and then we'll see what the weather's like.'

She followed him out of the door and turned to lock it. Stuart wouldn't change. Why hadn't she seen it before she fell in love with him?

As they walked down the staircase Stuart said, 'Come with me and I'll introduce you to the Broadhursts.'

'So that they can be told I'm your poor secretary who's been inveigled into spending a working weekend, no thanks.'

When Stuart walked through to the lounge Alison went to the desk to pick up a newspaper. She smiled at Mary Styles and noticed that she was wearing a camel coat and seemed ready to brave the elements.

'Are you going across the lake?' she asked.

'I have a friend picking me up, we're driving to Ambleside, I do hope the mist lifts.'

'The nice man you were dancing with last evening?' Alison asked.

Mary smiled.

Gerald came to the desk accompanied by his mother to pick up their newspapers. He favoured Mary with a bleak smile but his mother was rather more affable. She literally beamed. 'Did you enjoy the dancing last evening with Lord Alveston, Miss Styles? You were the envy of every lady in the ballroom, except you of course,' she gushed to Alison.

Mary and Alison merely smiled, but unabashed, Mrs Ralston went on, 'I wonder what sort of a day we're going to have, have you been out, Miss Styles?'

'No, not yet.'

'But you're going to venture out, I'm sure.'

'Yes. We're driving to Ambleside.'

Mrs Ralston arched her eyebrows and besides her Gerald cringed. This was his mother at her worst, enquiring, too friendly, embarrassing him as she had so many times in the past.

At that moment Stuart joined them and Mrs Ralston said with a smile, 'We're just talking about the ball, Mr Mansell, I saw that you and this young lady here were enjoying yourselves.'

'That's what it was all about, wasn't it, and now we'll see what the weather is going to do to us.'

Taking Alison's arm he moved away and with a brief smile Mary followed to join Andrew who was coming through the door.

'I think you're probably right about Mr Mansell, if she'd been his wife he'd have corrected me,' Mrs Ralston said.

'How do you want to spend the morning, Mother?'

'I suppose we could drive off somewhere, Ambleside perhaps.'

'We'll take a look at the newspapers, by that time the day may have improved. We'll go into the lounge.'

People sat around in groups. Conversation was hushed, and there was an atmosphere of waiting for something to happen. Mrs Hanley sat with her parents and those sitting near to them kept their eyes averted, afraid to intrude upon a misery that was too apparent in the pale, tear-streaked face of the girl.

Alison watched Stuart's air of compassion with grim amusement. This was what he did best. These were his constituents and he was here to give them moral support and comfort. They would remember all this when the next election came along.

If she was being unfair to him he deserved it, but she had to admit that she had once fallen heavily for that charming compassion that she no longer believed in.

Chapter Twenty-One

On the banks of Grasmere Mary and Andrew sat in the hotel window looking out at the view. During the morning the mist had lifted and a pale watery sun shone through, tinting the gentle beauty of the lake with pale gold and Mary felt she must pinch herself to confirm that it was real.

What was she, a small town librarian doing, in the company of a peer of the realm? They were comfortable together, they made each other laugh, they talked about a great many things and never once had she felt inferior or subservient.

He had asked her about her life and with her usual honesty she had told him about her mother. That she had had to be positive about taking this holiday and he had said quietly, 'But there have to be others, Mary, you can't swear your life away at your age to a lifetime of caring for your mother with nothing else.'

'I tell myself that, I should have asserted myself years ago.'

'What made this time so different?'

'I met somebody, I was honest with him, apparently he was not so honest with me.'

'And are you still smarting from that?'

She had had to consider. At last she realised that she was not, Andrew had given her back her pride, her self-esteem. At the same time their friendship was going nowhere. She would go back to her library and her shopping in the small town on Market days. She would go back to caring for her mother, storing up all the interesting bits of her daily life that she thought might interest her mother, the occasional arguments with her brother-in-law and Millicent's extravagances that amused her.

What did she know about Andrew? He was reticent about himself and yet she sensed in him a sadness, a history of remembered pain. He talked about his house, his land, the horses he loved and his life as a boy growing up in the area, but then she was aware that a line had been drawn between boyhood and manhood. Something had happened in Andrew's life that had been

166

painful and she asked herself if it could have been Stella? Had Stella rejected him in favour of the man she had married and who was now an invalid?

He was aware of her eyes, honest and questioning, and yet although she had told him about herself he was unable to talk about the past. When this weekend was over Mary would go back to her own life, they would probably never meet again.

He felt a strange sort of irritation with the man who had been dishonest with her, what sort of a man was he?

There was something very decent and wholesome about her, something Stella had had, and she was not to know that she brought back to him all the heartache and anger he had caused Stella.

'Did you say you were leaving on Tuesday morning?' he asked.

'Yes. I want to get unpacked, do a little shopping and then pick Mother up.'

'She'll be anxious to see you?'

She smiled.

'Tomorrow if you like we could drive over to Ullswater, the lake is very beautiful, that is if you would like to of course.'

'Yes, that would be lovely.'

'We'll get on our way then, we'll drive around Windermere and get back to the hotel before dusk. Perhaps you will have dinner with me this evening?'

'Yes thank you, I'd like that.'

She liked him, she was happy in his company, and yet as she sat besides him in the car she felt again that elusive barrier and she puzzled as to what it could be. Some other woman he loved, some tragedy from his past, or that strangely English barrier born of class. She stole a look at his face, remote, handsome, and he turned his head and smiled at her, at that moment the barrier disappeared.

He left her at the hotel doorway and immediately she entered the hotel she sensed that something was wrong. There was an air of sadness reflected in the faces of those standing in groups in the foyer. Their voices were subdued, there was no laughter.

The lounge doors were closed and as she stood there perplexed Anton de Roche came to speak to her.

'The lounge is closed for the moment, Miss Styles,' he said softly. 'Tea is being served in the billiard room and the library.'

'Is something wrong, Mr de Roche?'

'I'm afraid so. They have recovered the body of Mr Hanley from the mountain this morning, and another climber is in hospital suffering from multiple injuries. Mrs Hanley is in the lounge with her parents and the police, Mr Mansell is also with them.'

Mary stared at him in horror. 'Oh that poor young girl, she has only been married a few days,' she cried.

'I know, it is a tragedy. They should never have attempted to climb in such weather, it was stupid and it happens all too often.'

'Will Mrs Hanley be allowed to go home?'

'She is going to the hospital with her father to identify the body, then there will have to be an inquest and all the usual formalities. In the meantime I think she will wish to go home.'

'How about the boy's parents?'

'They are in Spain but they have been contacted and I'm sure will soon be on their way home.'

He smiled and moved away.

She did not want tea. She would go up to her room and change but the evening ahead would be tinged with sadness for the young girl whose marriage had been all too brief and ended with tragedy.

As she waited at the lift she was joined by Alison Grey. The girl looked preoccupied but when Mary spoke to her about Tod's death she said quietly, 'Yes, it's terrible, I'm glad her parents are here.'

'It seems incongruous that the holiday period will go on as if things are normal but I've already sensed an air of depression in everybody.'

'Yes, the activities will be very subdued, I'm sure. Are you dining in the hotel this evening?'

'No, I've been invited to dine out, and you?'

'I'm not sure. Mr Mansell is with the Hanleys, he is their M.P. so obviously he wants to help all he can.'

'Yes of course.'

Alison had not been long in her room when there was a tap on the door and Stuart entered.

'I hope you won't mind, Alison, but I shall be dining with the Broadhursts this evening, dinner will be served to us in some small room somewhere. They're absolutely shattered by all this, there was nothing else I could do.'

'I'm sure they'll be glad of your company, Stuart.'

'Yes well, one has to do one's bit at a time like this. I'll see you later this evening.'

He made as if to take her in his arms, but she turned away to pick up a jacket from off the bed and he stared after her doubtfully when she went to put it away in the wardrobe.

For a few moments he hesitated near the door, then with a brief smile he left.

Alison sat on the edge of her bed. She'd been involved with politics long enough to understand that as far as Stuart was concerned this was business. His sympathy for Debbie Hanley was real enough, but coupled with it was his ambition. He had to be seen doing the right thing, some gesture, some act of kindness, anything that his constituents would remember when the time came for voting.

She was cynical and bitter and she was ashamed of her feelings. She couldn't help it, playing second fiddle to everything else in Stuart Mansell's life had been a bitter pill to swallow and her resentment had built up over the years. She had gone into it with her eyes wide open, ignoring the warnings from her mother so that they had hardly seen each other for years, now she knew that every word her mother had uttered was true.

She thought about Mary Styles. Tonight she would be dining out with her lord but would there be anything else? She doubted if Mary would make the same mistakes she had made, Mary was a wiser woman, she would know that nothing lasting would come out of her friendship with his lordship.

She met Mary in the foyer where she was waiting for Andrew to arrive and she thought how nice she looked. Elegant in beige, her camel coat thrown loosely over her shoulders.

So too thought Gerald Ralston, waiting for his mother near the dining room door. He thought about the times they had lunched together, a discreetly dressed business woman carrying her shopping basket, soft brown hair hidden under a soft felt hat, her smile warm and welcoming and here she was going confidently forward to meet her escort for the evening.

Of course it wouldn't last. Perhaps in the weeks and months to come he'd run into her on the street, the library on Friday afternoon, perhaps recover something of their old friendship. Of course it would be on a different footing. Mary would know the truth about his life, but surely friendship was not impossible.

'Here you are, Gerald,' his mother said as she joined him. 'Are you ready to go into dinner? I see that Miss Styles is dining out this evening.'

'Really? I hadn't noticed.'

'I do really think she's blossomed out during the last day or so. I wonder where the girl and her parents will be dining, surely not in the room with the rest of the guests?'

He was accustomed to the way his mother's mind switched from one subject to another, and as they passed into the dining room she smiled at Alison Gray. At their table she said, 'She appears to be dining alone, Mr Mansell will probably be with his constituents, I was told he was their M.P.'

His mother had a genius for finding things out about people. Normally her prattle passed over his head but somehow tonight he felt irritated by her. Her bright bird-like eyes scanned the tables in the room and he felt sure she knew something about the people sitting at every one of them.

There was only one day left and he wanted to go home. The weekend had not been a good idea, and yet there had been so many weekends in his life exactly like it. This was different because Mary had been here, and heaven help him, he'd been the one to put the idea into her head.

Although a small group of musicians played in the ballroom very few people were taking advantage of it. Instead they sat around in groups in the lounge, or retired to the library to read magazines and other reading matter.

At Alveston Hall Andrew was entertaining Mary to dinner. They ate in the small dining room waited on by soft-footed servants and a benign butler. The meal was beautifully cooked and exquisitely served and Mary wondered what it must be like for Andrew to spend his life surrounded by luxury and waited on every day by such devoted staff. Why then should there be times when she discovered a hint of sadness in his smile and a puzzling reticence when they talked?

He was happiest talking about his travels abroad and Mary who had never really been anywhere listened to him entranced.

At the end she asked a question which she wished immediately she had never asked.

'Why did you stay away from here for so long?'

For too long there was a waiting silence and looking into his eyes she was aware of an uncomfortable reluctance to speak, and hurriedly she said, 'I'm sorry, I shouldn't have asked, please tell me more about your travels.'

She watched his hand twirling his wine glass and she knew his thoughts were miles away, unconnected with her and with his travels, concerned only with a remembered pain.

She felt uncomfortable. She had intruded into something he wanted to remain private and as she reached out for her wine glass her embarrassment caused her to knock the glass over. She jumped to her feet, apologising profusely for her clumsiness and Andrew said sharply, 'Don't worry, Mary, really there's no need. Here, I'll get you another glass.'

He was aware of her pink embarrassed face, and he said gently, 'When we've finished dinner there is something I want to show you. I discovered it in one of the attics a few days ago.'

They drank their coffee in the drawing room and she listened to the charm of his voice talking of everyday things in an endeavour to restore the peace they had enjoyed earlier. After enquiring if she would like more coffee and hearing her decline he said, 'Then perhaps you'll come with me and I'll show you the secret of Alveston House.'

Curious, Mary walked with him up the wide curving staircase to a door at the end of a long corridor when he produced a key and unlocked the door. They were in another long passage with a staircase at the end of it, and Andrew switched on a series of lights as they walked along its length.

Her heart was beating quickly. She had the strangest feeling that she was about to discover things that had been shut away for reasons of sadness and betrayal, things that had brought the anguish into his eyes and the remoteness into his voice.

At the end of the corridor he led the way up the narrow curving stairs to a door at the top which he opened with another key and they were in a lofty narrow room holding bric-a-brac: gilt tables and chairs, pictures leaning against the walls, rolls of old carpeting and rugs, and at the other end another door.

The room behind it was empty except for a large picture leaning against the wall and Andrew switched on the light so that she could look at it.

She was looking at the portrait of a woman, young, very beautiful, with black hair and eyes like pieces of chipped jade. She could not tell if the woman was English, because her face had a strange oriental cast, but the gown she wore was beautiful, swathing her tall slender figure in folds of gleaming silk.

He was staring down at her curiously and when she looked up Mary felt suddenly tongue-tied. What did he want her to say?

Faced with his silence at last she blurted out, 'She's very beautiful, Andrew, who is she?'

'Olivia, Lady Alveston. My wife.'

'Your wife!'

'Yes.'

'Where is she, doesn't she live here?'

'She's dead, Mary.'

'Dead! Oh I'm so sorry, how long has she been dead?'

'Many years. She died on New Year's Eve and the next morning her body was retrieved from the lake. She had been strangled.'

Mary stared at him in shocked surprise, and putting his hand underneath her elbow he escorted her out of the room, switching out the light and locking the door behind him.

Without another word they made their way back to the drawing room where he poured out a whisky for himself after asking her what she would prefer.

'Nothing, thank you,' she answered.

'I'm so terribly sorry,' she said again, 'No wonder you went away for so long, it must have been awful coming back.'

'Yes, perhaps that was the worst of it. I wasn't sure it would work out.'

'Are you still in love with her?'

His eyes were strange as they looked into hers, then giving a harsh laugh he said, 'Love! When I went away I hated her, perhaps I still do, Olivia was a harlot, a witch. That I ever laid eyes on her was a disaster.'

'But you married her?'

'Yes. She was Stella's cousin and we only met just before my wedding day to Stella. You can guess the rest.'

'But the pain has to go, Andrew, you can't let it destroy the rest of your life,' she said, even though all the time she felt her words were trite and meaningless.

He smiled gently.

'You told me you'd never done anything, Mary, never really lived, and yet there's been no torment in your life, no great tragedy to make you a different sort of person. That is what tragedy does to you, Mary. Once I was a contented happy sort of man expecting life to continue in its calm, even vein, and when it didn't I felt that the entire world had conspired to let me down. Perhaps in the end, Mary, you can take comfort from your nice steady life.'

'Perhaps, I never thought about it, I just accepted it.'

'Then for the rest of the evening we'll forget about Olivia, I'm always glad to forget about her, relegate her to the past where she belongs, it's only now and again when my old devils haunt me and I get the impression that they'll go on haunting me as long as I live.'

'Only if you let them,' she said softly. 'Did you say we were driving over to Ullswater tomorrow?'

For a long moment he stared at her, then he laughed, and pulling her to her feet he put his arms around her and whispered, 'Dear sane normal Mary, I've been very happy with you these last few days.'

He held her close against him so that she could feel the beating of his heart. He did not attempt to kiss her and when he released her he did it gently, holding on to her hand and smiling down into her eyes. It was a moment she felt she would remember all her life.

Back at the hotel Stuart found Alison sitting in the lounge leafing idly through a magazine and he went to sit beside her.

'We're off to the hospital now, Alison, I've decided to accompany John Broadhurst and his daughter, it's the least I can do.'

She nodded, and he said somewhat anxiously, 'They're returning home tomorrow and I think I should go too. I'm sorry, Alison, it's something none of us expected.'

'When will you leave?'

'Early. Immediately after breakfast. I'll leave you some money for a taxi into Kendal to catch your train. I'm so sorry about this, but you'll have no problem I'm sure.'

'Of course not.'

'I'll come up to see you as soon as I get back.'

She didn't answer and she watched his tall figure striding through the lounge.

Debbie waited with her father in the car. Her face was expressionless, she couldn't feel anything, not even the knowledge that her brief marriage was over and at nineteen she was a widow with her young husband dead and waiting to be identified in some hospital she'd never heard of.

Stuart Mansell joined them and they were driving off into the darkness.

172

There was no conversation on that journey. Stuart Mansell drove and John Broadhurst held his daughter's limp hand in his own. His thoughts kept going back to the pomp of their wedding, she had looked so sensationally beautiful that morning and so many people had surrounded them all intent on enjoying the day.

Tod's parents were on their way home, tomorrow would be the awful task of meeting them, he was glad Mansell had agreed to go home with them.

In the hospital they were taken to the mortuary and Debbie looked down at the still white form of her husband. She could hardly believe that this was Tod with every expression eliminated from his face. All the brash humour, the firm smiling mouth and laughing eyes.

John looked at his daughter anxiously. There were no tears, she stood like a statue looking down at the boy she had adored. She was too young, too young to face the immediate future and he looked too young to be dead.

In a short while they were driving back to the hotel in silence. In the foyer Stuart wished them goodnight after agreeing to meet them for breakfast, then he made his way to Alison's bedroom. He tried the door but it was locked. He went quickly downstairs and took a brief look in the lounges, the ballroom where a few couples danced, and in the library, then he went back to her room and knocked again. He could see the light under the door.

Alison sat in a chair in the window staring back at the locked door. She heard his voice whispering plaintively, 'Alison, please open the door, we have to talk.'

Carefully she stubbed out her cigarette in the ashtray and took off her negligee, then she climbed into bed and turned off the light. They had done all the talking they needed to do. It was over.

From underneath the door Stuart saw the light go out and after a few minutes of waiting hopefully he turned away.

In the Broadhursts' bedroom Geraldine sat in bed reading her magazine. She looked at her husband expectantly as he turned to lock the door.

'Is Debbie all right?' she asked.

'Yes, she's still in shock. Nothing registered.'

'Not even when she saw Tod?'

'Not even then.'

'I suppose we'll have to meet the Hanleys tomorrow?'

'Yes, the sooner the better. There's nothing else to be done, there'll have to be an inquest and a funeral, then hopefully she'll pick up the pieces and get on with the rest of her life.'

'I hope so. I hope to God she's not pregnant, that would surely be the living end.'

He stared at her. Trust Geraldine to think of something worse that could happen. Tod had always been irresponsible, he hoped getting his wife pregnant hadn't been one of his scatter-brained ideas.

'Mansell's coming back with us in the morning,' he said. 'It's jolly decent of him, I think.'

'What about the girl?'

'What girl?'

'His so-called secretary.'

'For heaven's sake, Geraldine, she is his secretary, and don't you go stirring it with Sybil. The man's been a tower of strength, we should be grateful.'

'I am grateful, I just don't think it's fair on Sybil if she's some girl he's having an affair with.'

'I can't think he's seen much of her these last twenty-four hours, he's been dancing attention on us.'

'We vote for him, don't we?'

'We do, and how cynical you've become. Forget the girl, remember your gratitude. He's coming back with us and if Sybil comes home she'll find him there waiting for her.'

'And he'll soon be off to London and *she'll* be waiting for him there.'

He looked at his wife with the utmost exasperation.

'I've told you to forget it, Geraldine, we've other things to worry about than Stuart Mansell's love life, real or imaginary.'

She looked at him in pitying silence. Men were so obtuse about things they didn't want to think about.

Chapter Twenty-Two

Alison was handed an envelope at the reception desk the following morning and she immediately recognised Stuart's handwriting on the front of it. She decided to read it over breakfast but gathered that he had already left the hotel with the Broadhursts.

The letter informed her that he had tried to see her the evening before but found that she had retired early. That part of the letter held a vague reproach that she found amusing. He was leaving very early with the Broadhursts and enclosed twenty pounds which would pay for her taxi into Lancaster to catch her train for London, and he had settled the hotel bill. He looked forward to seeing her in Westminster after Easter and apologised again for leaving her to make her own way to the station.

The letter was terse, and yet it held a vague feeling of regret. If Stuart had found her door open the evening before she knew what would have happened, they would have ended the day in each other's arms for the usual night of shared passion. There had been so many of them, and in all honesty she had enjoyed the ecstacy even when it had often been followed by feelings of resentment.

It was Easter Monday, what would she do with her day?

On her way out of the restaurant she passed Mary Styles coming in and they paused to chat.

'Has Mr Mansell left?' Mary enquired.

'Yes, very early this morning.'

'What are you going to do with yourself?'

'Take a cruise around the lake perhaps, I think it's going to be a lovely day.'

'Yes. How sad that the bad weather brought such tragedy. Are you leaving tomorrow?'

'Yes. I shall have to ask them to get a taxi for me at the Reception, my train goes from Kendal.'

'Well I'm driving to the West Midlands, I can give you a lift into Kendal.'

'Oh yes, that would be lovely. I don't know what the taxi situation is here, I'd much rather travel with you if you're sure I'm not being a nuisance.'

'Not at all. I shall be leaving immediately after breakfast if that's all right with you.'

'Yes it is. I'll see you at breakfast tomorrow.'

Mary was looking forward to driving to Ullswater with Andrew. After his revelations of the evening before she felt more comfortable with him, it was as though he'd become more human, a person who had suffered, a person who was reaching out for companionship and understanding.

After today they would both return to their familiar lives, far removed from one another, two people who had met by a strange sort of accident and enjoyed however briefly a few days of joy. Tomorrow would be her mother, Mrs Scotson's views on the world in general and her sister's probings about her holiday. Then there would be the library with its quiet routine and her two assistants with their stories of boyfriends and the problems that came with them.

On Friday afternoons there would be Gerald but the pattern of their friendship would have changed irrevocably, they could never go back to the old camaraderie, his rich full life had proved to be a farce, but the hurt that had prompted him to tell her about it had not gone away.

Some normality had returned to the life of the hotel. People had not forgotten the tragedy of the last twenty-four hours, but they had not known Tod, it was something that had happened to somebody else, regrettable but life had to go on.

It was a procession of three cars that drove into the driveway of John Broadhurst's home later that morning. John and Stuart were driving their own cars. Geraldine was driving her daughter in Debbie's car.

Wearily they got out of their cars and Geraldine called out, 'Are you coming in for coffee, Stuart? The entire town will be aware of things now, the papers will be full of it.'

Throughout the journey Debbie had sat beside her mother staring straight ahead through the windscreen, but Geraldine suspected she was oblivious to everything. They had not exchanged a single word.

Stuart followed them into the house uneasily, and when Geraldine again suggested coffee he said quickly, 'If you don't mind, Geraldine, I'll get off home. I'll telephone Sybil, she'll probably have seen the papers and might have decided to come home today. If she does we'll call round this evening, and I'll have to call on the Hanleys.'

'Oh gracious yes. They'll be home now. What a homecoming for them.'

'I'll telephone them,' John said quickly. 'We'll have to go round there or invite them here.'

'I don't want them to see Debbie like this,' her mother said sharply. 'She's like a Zombie, no tears, simply nothing.'

'She's in shock, anybody can see that.'

'Well there'll be plenty of tears from Mrs Hanley, Tod was the light of her life, nothing will ever be the same again for her.'

It was true. Debbie was young and the young healed, to Tod's mother the premature death of her son would be a disaster that would never go away.

Stuart was glad to leave. The town was dead as he drove through the empty streets with all the shops closed for the holidays to his home at the opposite side of the town. Tod's parents lived within walking distance of his home and he was not looking forward to meeting them. Daniel Hanley's large Volvo stood outside the front entrance and he parked his car behind it. For several moments he stood hesitantly on the doorstep before ringing the bell, and almost immediately he was aware of footsteps behind the closed door and when it swung open he stared into the sombre eyes of Daniel Hanley.

He stared at Stuart in surprise before inviting him in, and Stuart was quick to say, 'I was staying at The Lakes when it happened, I came back this morning with the Broadhursts.'

Daniel nodded curtly. 'Good of you, Mansell. How's the girl taking it?'

'I don't think everything has fully registered yet.'

'I suppose there'll have to be an inquest and all the other formalities before we can have the funeral. The Missus is taking it very hard, she's in bed, taken some sleeping pills. We've been travelling most of the night.'

'You managed to get a plane back without too much trouble?'

'Yes that was no problem, the problem was that the plane was delayed with engine trouble and was late taking off.'

'I'm sorry, there's usually trouble when you least want it.'

'Are the Broadhursts expecting us to go over? If they are I'll probably go alone.'

'Perhaps that would be best.'

'I suppose it's too early to offer you a drink, but there's coffee.'

'No thank you. I'd better get off home, my wife should be coming back today.'

He was glad to get away. He was glad he had not had to face Mrs Hanley, poor woman, she would find difficulty in coping with the next few days and the days that came later would never be the same. She had been so proud of Tod, his popularity, the bold handsome boy who had filled her days with his good humour, his enthusiasm for life. Tod and his father had both borne her along with them even when she had never really been like either of them.

Clara Hanley had always been a shy, self-effacing woman who had never quite got used to the fact that her husband had made money, money that had launched them into small town society in which her son had been a shining light.

Debbie would recover, but Debbie was angry. Grief was making her angry. She was angry with Tod, that she had loved him, married him and that he was

177

dead. There had been no need for him to die, no need for him to climb that stupid mountain.

She didn't want to be a widow at nineteen. She wanted to go to dances and parties, not stand out like some freak in her widow's weeds when all around her other girls were enjoying their youth and vitality. Tod had done this to her, Tod had ruined her life.

Stuart picked up several days' mail from behind the front door and the hall looked depressing. A weeping fig tree was living up to its reputation and a vase of wilting flowers stood on the hall table. The daily woman had evidently not been near the house for several days and it felt cold. Surely the woman had not turned off the central heating, the beginning of April was hardly midsummer.

He took his suitcase up to the bedroom and started to unpack. The entire house had an unlived-in air, and before attempting to unpack the suitcase he put a call through to Sybil's parents and was rewarded by hearing his father-in-law's voice.

'This is Stuart,' he said tersely. 'Are you feeling better?'

'Yes, I'm getting around more, Sybil left after breakfast she'll be arriving shortly. Terrible news about young Tod Hanley.'

'Yes, terrible.'

'Give them our condolences, I expect you'll be going round there.'

'Yes, probably this evening.'

'That's good then. It will do them good to see that you care.'

'When are you likely to be coming back?'

'Oh there's no hurry. When you've gone back to London Sybil said she'd come up here again.'

'I see. If Sybil's on her way back I'd better light some fires, the house feels very cold.'

'Have you been away then?'

'For a few days. I'll be in touch again, goodbye.'

After he'd unpacked he set about lighting a fire in the lounge and the dining room, then he looked in the larder to see if there was anything suitable for a light meal. He found eggs and cheese and decided to make an omelette.

He needed to do some thinking.

Sybil would want to know where he'd spent most of Easter and he had to tell her the truth, if he didn't the Broadhursts would.

John Broadhurst could be relied upon to be discreet, but Geraldine was a different matter. In the role of Sybil's friend she would warn her about Alison and what she didn't know she was capable of inventing. He had seen her eyes filled with speculation as they had eyed Alison up and down, and when he had said that she was his secretary at Westminster her eyes had hardly echoed the smile on her lips.

He had to get to Sybil before they did and as he ate his solitary meal his mind was busy with possible explanations.

He had only just cleared the table and washed the crockery when he heard the sound of a car on the drive and then Sybil's key in the lock.

He went out into the hall to meet her, and immediately she burst into tears.

'Poor Debbie Broadhurst and Geraldine,' she sobbed, 'I couldn't believe it when I read the news in the paper. Have you spoken to them?'

It was the best opening he could have hoped for.

'Fortunately I was on the spot when it happened. I travelled home with them.'

She stared at him. 'What do you mean, on the spot?'

'I was at The Lakes. As soon as the boy was missing they sent for John and Geraldine and I was there to give whatever comfort I could. Of course everything was terrible. It was night when they arrived and the search for the climbers had to be called off until the next morning. They were found then, one climber badly injured, Tod was dead.'

'And Debbie?'

'Absolutely shocked. The poor kid's only been married a few days, and a widow at nineteen. I called on the Hanleys this morning, they were flown back from Spain. Mrs Hanley's in a terrible way.'

'Of course. She idolised Tod. What were you doing in the Lake District, Stuart?'

'Well I told you I'd probably go away for a few days to play some golf but something else cropped up. I got a phone call from Alison Grey, she's leaving me, taking another job in the summer. I drove up there to try to talk her out of it. Alison's a damned good secretary, she's worked for me a very long time, I couldn't imagine what she was thinking about.'

'But why The Lakes, what has that got to do with it?'

'The job's at The Lakes, working for de Roche. She obviously sees some sort of glamour in it and she's fed up with politics. I couldn't budge her.'

'Did she leave with you?'

'No. I left her up there. The job comes up in the summer so it does give me a little time to get a replacement.'

'Oh well, you won't have any trouble I'm sure. Isn't there a typing pool you can get a replacement from?'

'There is, but good secretaries are hard to find, particularly one like Alison. She's worked very well for me, plenty of other chaps have envied me, however if that's what she wants there's nothing I can do about it.'

'Well of course not. She obviously doesn't know when she's well off. I really do think we should go round to the Broadhursts, Stuart, what do you think?'

'I agree. I told them we'd be round this evening.'

'And the Hanleys?'

'If you like. Perhaps not tonight though since Mrs Hanley is unwell, I hardly think the poor woman will be ready for visitors.'

'No, perhaps not.'

'Have you had anything to eat, Sybil? I rustled up an omelette.'

'Mother insisted that I ate a good breakfast before I left, I'll eat something later on, I expect all the restaurants are booked up for Easter Monday. Was The Lakes very busy?'

'There was plenty going on. The weather was mixed so I didn't play any golf and the ballroom was hardly my scene without you.'

'Was there anybody interesting staying there?'

'That film star Gloria Weston with an army of photographers around her.'

'Who was she with?'

'Some weaselly little chap who seldom came into the restaurant and looked half-plastered most of the time. She's not the glamour girl she used to be and she's not pulling in the crowds.'

'Anybody else of note?'

'Oh yes. Lord Alveston is back in the area. He came into dinner on Easter Saturday and he came into the foyer several times to pick up a woman friend. One would have thought he'd had enough of women to last him a lifetime.'

'Well yes. There was all that scandal surrounding his wife. Who was he with at The Lakes?'

'I thought she was on her own but apparently not. A rather nice reserved sort of woman. Obviously a lady.'

'Oh well, perhaps he's found somebody else. Alveston Hall is very beautiful, it's nice to think he's come back to it. Nothing else to tell me?'

'No. The American owners were around. I'm not sure Alison's going to enjoy working for de Roche, he's one of those charming remote sort of chaps, one never knows what he's thinking.'

'Well she's evidently thought it over!'

He nodded.

Now let Geraldine do her worst. He'd told Sybil a half-truth but it was enough to allow her to put Geraldine in her place if she decided to malign him.

He wondered what Alison was doing on her own. She'd surely exhausted the village and the trip around the lake. It was his guess that she'd go to bed early and leave immediately after breakfast. In a short time they'd both be back at Westminster, he had a few months to convince her to stay where she was well off.

It was late afternoon when the Broadhursts telephoned to invite them over for dinner. Stuart suspected it was because they needed to be with somebody rather than a sudden urge to hold a dinner party.

Indeed, as was to be expected, dinner was a dismal charade. John and Stuart made desultory conversation, Geraldine's eyes constantly strayed

180

towards her daughter sitting like a stone statue while occasionally Sybil dabbed at her eyes.

The subject of the inquest and the funeral to come was ignored and soon after ten o'clock they made a move to leave, it was then that Geraldine said, 'Wasn't it fortunate that Stuart should have been staying at The Lakes, he was a tower of strength.'

'Yes indeed,' Sybil said. 'He's been telling me his secretary is going to work at The Lakes, for Anton de Roche, some time in the summer.'

'Really?'

'Yes. He's a bit put out about it, she's been with him for many years. He was hoping to dissuade her but apparently her mind's made up.'

'Quite a change from Westminster, Stuart, whatever has possessed her to go in for something so different?'

'Well we all like a change. Now I'll have to look for a replacement.'

He looked Geraldine straight in the eye and smiled.

After they had left Debbie went immediately to her room and John said to his wife, 'He well and truly spiked your guns, old girl.'

'I wonder how much truth there is in it?'

'Quite a lot I should think. If he's told Sybil his secretary is leaving him, how is he going to tell her she's staying on? No I rather think he's being entirely truthful even when there is possibly a great deal more behind it.'

'I still maintain he's been cheating on Sybil.'

'And I believe we should stay out of it. We've enough on our plate to worry about, the next few days are going to be horrendous. Poor Clara Hanley, she's the one who needs our sympathy.'

'And how about Debbie, she's the young widow?'

'I know, but Debbie will pick up the pieces, and sooner perhaps than we think, it's the boy's mother who will find it hard to live with.'

Mary Styles was finishing packing her suitcase. From below, the sound of music floated up from the hotel's ballroom and she went for a few moments to stand at her window. Lights flooded out into the gardens and from across the lake lights in the village gleamed fitfully in the darkness.

Some of the Easter guests had already left, most of the others would be leaving in the morning. Next weekend there would be a new crowd, perhaps a quieter crowd enjoying the amenities of The Lakes out of season.

She had settled her bill and all that remained now was to eat breakfast and drive home. Her last day with Andrew Alveston had been a joy. She had loved Ullswater's three reaches and the daffodils that bloomed thickly on every bank. There would never be a time when she could read Wordsworth's poem without thinking of one of the happiest days of her life.

She had stood with him in the hotel foyer and he had held her hand, gently, smiling down at her, and then the Harveys had joined them, wishing her a pleasant journey home, that they would hope to see her again in the future, and somehow the moment had been lost. After that Andrew had bowed over her hand, and after echoing their sentiments had left her to go to his car.

It was over, consigned to history, a memory she would relive many times, but only a memory. Tomorrow would be reality and her mother.

A few doors along the corridor Alison Gray snapped the lid of her suitcase shut and started to brush her hair. She had had a long conversation with Anton de Roche when she had assured him she would not change her mind about the position he offered, and yet she couldn't help comparing him with Stuart. What sort of a boss would he be? He was urbane, charming, somehow remote, and yet his grey eyes had smiled down at her with friendly ease.

He was attractive, impersonal and she knew nothing about him as a person. She had learned her lesson, there would be no more intimacy between her and the man she worked for, whether Anton de Roche was married or not, it was a vow she meant to keep.

It was raining when they left the hotel soon after breakfast, a soft gentle rain that lay on the wind and echoed the dismal thoughts in their hearts.

At the station in Kendal Alison thanked Mary warmly for the lift. There were thirty minutes before her train was due and she said she would buy newspapers and perhaps have a coffee, then Mary got back in her car and after waving to the girl standing on the pavement drove out of the station yard.

It was early afternoon when she drove along the high street and the pavements were crowded with shoppers after the Easter break. She drove along the low hill towards her home relieved to find the front door open which told her Mrs Scotson was already indoors.

As she left her car Mrs Scotson came out to help her with her luggage.

''Ave ye enjoyed yourself?' the good woman asked.

'Yes, thank you, Mrs Scotson, I've had a lovely time.'

'Yer sister's back, she 'phoned but I told her ye 'adn't got in.'

'I'll get unpacked, Mrs Scotson and put everything away then we'll have lunch, I promised Mother I'd pick her up in the early afternoon.'

''Ay well, no doubt she's waitin' for you very impatiently.'

Mary smiled before she took her luggage upstairs.

Mrs Scotson stared after her with narrowed eyes. There was something different about her, and it wasn't just the fashionable camel coat and the unusual high heels on her brown shoes. She smiled grimly to herself, the next few months would be interesting, she had the feeling that things were about to change, perhaps not immediately, but give it a few months or so. One taste of freedom wouldn't be enough for Miss Mary Styles.

Chapter Twenty-Three

Alison arrived at her flat at the same time as a man bearing a huge bouquet of pale pink roses. She took them from him and stared down at the card attached to them, Welcome Home, Alison, Stuart.

Of course he'd had to send them from a florist in his home town, his constituency, and as always discretion was the word.

She opened the door with her latch key and as she turned to go inside a voice hailed her from the door across the passage and she turned to see Tracie in the doorway to her flat.

'Are you just arriving home?' she asked.

'Yes, you too?'

'Well about half an hour ago. The flat looks so unwelcoming, I expect yours will too.'

'Here have these,' she said thrusting the flowers into the other girl's arms. 'They'll brighten up the place.'

'But I can't possibly, they'll brighten up your flat too.'

'They'll depress me. Every time you look at them think how lucky you are to have Alan, at least he's unattached.'

Tracie looked at her doubtfully and Alison urged, 'Go on take them. Alan would have sent you red roses, these had to be pink.'

'But they're beautiful, Alison.'

'I know. It's just me being difficult.'

'Have you had a nice time?'

'Yes. I've landed myself another job starting in the summer, so I'll be putting the flat on the market.'

'Really. Is it your flat then? Gosh I'm sorry, I just thought . . .'

'It is my flat. I bought it with money my father left me, it's not a bad little place, I should be able to sell it.'

'Of course you will, if I hear of anybody I'll let you know.'

'Please do. Enjoy the roses.'

She felt strangely aggravated that Tracie had thought Stuart had bought the flat for her, actually it had been the one thing they had argued about.

Possession of the flat made her too independent. Stuart had suggested he should rent a flat for her in a more fashionable area but she'd resisted, her job and her flat were exclusively her own.

The Easter Bunny he'd sent her grinned at her complacently from the other chair so she picked it up and stuck it unceremoniously behind the settee. It would take more than an Easter Bunny to make her forget the last few days, even when she knew in some ways she was being unreasonable.

There had been a tragedy, that poor young girl's husband was dead and Stuart did have a duty to assist his constituents, particularly when they were friends.

In just over two months' time all this would be behind her, she'd have a new job, a new existence and no foolish act of hers would spoil it.

Mary Styles had given her her telephone number but there seemed no reason to ring her. Mary had spent four happy days with her aristocratic new friend and now it was over, Alison suspected neither of them were in the mood to mull over the events of the Easter weekend.

Mrs Scotson was putting away the crockery and Mary was preparing to go for her mother when the telephone bell shrilled from the hall and Mrs Scotson hurried to answer it.

'It's your sister,' she called upstairs, and as Mary went to take the receiver out of her hand she hissed, 'I thought she'd ring, can't wait to find out how things are.'

'I thought you'd be home,' Millicent said sharply. 'When are you fetching Mother?'

'I'm going for her now.'

'Well I'll be round on Friday morning. I can't come before then, I have things to see to.'

'Very well, I'll tell her.'

'Did you enjoy yourself, what was the weather like?'

'Mixed, but I did enjoy it.'

'Oh well no doubt I'll be hearing all about it on Friday.'

'You'll probably have left by the time I get home, the library stays open longer on Fridays.'

'So it does. Well some other time then.'

Driving the short distance to the residential home where she had left her mother gave her little time to reflect on anything beyond the fact that life was catching up with her, real life, not the unreal ambience of the last few days.

The matron met her in the hall, saying with a bright smile, 'You'll find your mother waiting for you in the lounge at the back, Miss Styles, we've all had a lovely Easter, you'll be hearing all about it.'

Her mother sat facing the door, dressed in her outdoor clothing, her black felt hat pulled firmly down over her hair, clutching her copious black handbag and with her weekend case at the side of her chair.

There were several other people in the room. Two elderly men were playing dominoes and a woman was fast asleep in her chair.

Dutifully she kissed her mother's cheek saying with a bright smile, 'Here I am, Mother, you look very well, I hope you haven't been waiting long.'

'You said early afternoon.'

'It is early afternoon. Is there anybody you want to say goodbye to before we leave?'

'I've seen everybody I want to see.'

'The matron says you've all enjoyed Easter.'

'It was all right, I suppose. Is Milly home?'

'Yes, she's coming in to see you on Friday.'

'Not before?'

'Well Friday's her day but I'm sure she's anxious to see you and hear all your news. Now come along, I've got your suitcase and the car is outside.'

'Is Mrs Scotson at the house?'

'Yes, she'll be there when you get home.'

'That woman who is asleep in her chair only came in yesterday. It's impossible to hold a conversation with her.'

'Perhaps she isn't well.'

'There's a few of them like that. They make you feel ill even when you're not.'

'Well you're going home now. As soon as I've unpacked your case we'll have tea and you can tell me all about the weekend.'

'There's nothing to tell. I suppose Milly wanted to know about yours.'

'There wasn't time, Mother.'

Her mother preferred to sit in the back seat of the car and as they drove out through the gates onto the main road she could see her mother's face in the driving mirror, wearing a familiar scowl, unprepossessing.

'There's no leg room in the back of this car,' she complained.

'It's big enough for me, Mother and you don't particularly like motoring.'

Nothing further was said until they arrived at the house and Mrs Scotson came out to assist Mary to get her mother out of the car. She was taken immediately to her favourite seat in the living room and Mary left Mrs Scotson to arrange her cushions.

She unpacked her mother's case and sorted out the things that needed laundering and put the others away. She felt close to tears. Perhaps it had been a terrible mistake to have gone away, to enter for a brief while into something completely at variance with her normal existence. If she'd never experienced the last few days she wouldn't have known what she was missing, now memories were making her unhappy, unwilling to face what before had been normal.

In the kitchen Mrs Scotson was busy buttering scones and arranging them on a plate.

'She doesn't seem any happier,' she commented. 'She's not saying much about the home.'

Her mother was doing it deliberately. Every time Mary tried to tell her something about her brief holiday she listened half-heartedly and spoke of something else, mostly some trivial episode of life at the home, it was only when Mary spoke of seeing Gloria Weston that a spark of interest showed in her face.

'I didn't like that last thing she was in,' she complained. 'She's always playing a silly woman, is she like that in real life?'

'I didn't speak to her, Mother, she's fashionable but perhaps not quite so glamorous as she appears on television.'

Of Andrew she said not a word, and when she talked about the tragedy of Tod Hanley's death her mother merely said, 'Well it's silly of those men to go climbing mountains, particularly in this climate.'

Her assistants at the library were rather more interested in her holiday, but although she spoke of the hotel, the Lake District and some of her fellow guests she did not speak of her meeting with Andrew.

Promptly at half-past-five on Friday evening Gerald came in for his mother's library books, and she was well aware that from behind her, two inquisitive pairs of eyes watched eagerly for any signs of familiarity.

Gerald's visit was brief. He looked at the titles of the books, said his mother would probably approve, asked if she'd had a good journey home and departed.

The two girls exchanged glances. It was evident that the weekend had brought them no closer, indeed if anything they seemed further apart.

Mary's sister Millicent however was still at the house when she got home and then the questions came thick and fast.

'Well, was it worth putting Mother in a home? Didn't you feel a bit out of things, particularly if there was dancing? Were there any spare men? Is the hotel as luxurious as it's cracked up to be, and how about that climbing tragedy, surely that would have put the damper on things?'

After Mary had finished answering her questions she said airily, 'We might spend a few days there in the summer, just out of interest you know.'

Andrew Alveston's butler placed the morning paper besides his breakfast plate announcing at the same time that the inquest on Tod Hanley had taken place and a verdict of accidental death had been established.

'It happens every year,' he went on. 'Young men killed on some mountain while other men risk their lives to look for them. There ought to be a law against it.'

'I take it you don't approve of men climbing mountains, Grant,' Andrew said with a slight smile.

'Not in bad weather I don't, sir, and not when it puts their lives and the lives of others in danger.'

'You're probably right.'

Andrew was remembering the last time he had seen Debbie Hanley standing with her parents in the foyer of The Lakes, and Mary had said sadly, 'She's such a child to find herself a widow, they've had no time together.'

That was what people had said about himself and Olivia, but they had actually had two years, the longest two years of Andrew's life. Instead of going to the stables that morning he went instead to the attic and he took with him an axe. He knew what he intended to do.

He stared at Olivia's portrait and the portrait stared back at him, it seemed to him that there was a small secretive smile on the red seductive mouth, that the green slanting eyes were daring him to destroy it, and he had thought he had forgotten the anger that brought the axe down on that beautiful smiling face. After the first blow it was easy, nor did he finish until the picture lay in ruins at his feet.

He informed his butler over lunch that he had destroyed the painting and faced with Grant's thoughtful stare he said brusquely, 'Get rid of it, Grant. It should have been got rid of years ago.'

'I know, sir, I didn't think it was my place.'

'I should have got rid of it, Grant, I can't think why I didn't. In all those years I stayed away I never once thought of it.'

The few days he had spent in the company of Mary Styles had been happy ones. He liked her sense of humour and the sheer normalness of her attitude to life, even when he became increasingly aware that her life had been a backwater, a backwater she had accepted with a fortitude most women would have baulked at.

They had said their farewells easily and he had made no promises to see her again. Mary had accepted those few days as being all there would ever be, two people who had been drawn together for a few days and who would each retire into their separate worlds when those few days ended.

He thought about her from time to time. At work in the library, shopping in the small market town where she lived, administering to her mother in a life he knew nothing about.

He was not aware that his brief friendship with Mary was mulled over by his butler and his housekeeper many times over the days that followed the Easter weekend.

'She seemed like a very nice lady,' Mrs Stokes observed as they drank their morning coffee. 'He seemed happier than I've seen him for weeks, now 'e's back to moping about the estate or riding that 'orse of 'is over the fells.'

'Miss Styles has gone home. I don't even know if he has arranged to meet her again,' Grant said firmly, but Mrs Stokes persisted.

'He married that upper crust girl who did him no good whatsoever, I suppose he's lookin' for the same sort.'

'I don't think he's exactly looking for anybody, Mrs Stokes.'

'Well he should be. This place needs a woman's hand. He needs a wife to bring it to life, to entertain his friends and bring a smile back onto his face. Why doesn't his mother talk to him about it?'

'I rather think her ladyship has given it up as a bad job, the master will go his own way. Perhaps there will never be a new mistress for Alveston.'

'He's thrown out Lady Alveston's portrait from the attic, destroyed it with an axe,' he added.

'Well that's a start at any rate,' Mrs Stokes said firmly. 'I never liked the thought of that portrait lying upstairs, it was as if she was still around the house, whenever I went into the attics I had the feeling that she'd come striding out of that far room, fixing me with those green eyes of hers, demanding this, that and the other. Now I can feel she's truly gone.'

Grant didn't answer but he knew the feeling well. Her light amused laughter and the sound of her high heels on the stairs. The expression in her unusual green eyes, half-taunting, half-burdened by some strange amusement only she could be aware of. He had been younger then, and only too aware of the provocation in her red curving lips, and the perfume that lingered whenever she was in the room.

He had witnessed her toying with men, friends who came to the house, workmen on the land and the house servants. Aware always of her beauty and her power, and underneath her chilling devilment. He remembered the night they had found her dead, and he had been unable to feel either sorrow or regret at her passing.

'You're very pensive this morning, Grant,' Mrs Stokes observed. 'You were miles away then.'

'I was thinking of something else.'

'You were thinking about her.'

He got to his feet and stood for a few moments looking down at her. Olivia Alveston had fascinated every man she met, and at the same time she had repelled them. He had been there when Andrew's mother had left the house shortly after Olivia's death, and he had heard her say to her son, 'You must try to forget her, Andrew, she was the most devious being I ever met in my life, one day you will see that for yourself.'

Over her head his eyes had met Andrew's and were surprised to see in them a strange and haunting misery.

Stuart and Alison had seen each other briefly since his return to Westminster after the Easter recess. She was the perfect secretary, seeing that his papers were always at hand when he needed them, dealing with his correspondence, and life went on much as it had done before, except that he no longer came to her flat in the evenings, and their conversation if at all was business-like.

He informed her stiffly that he was returning to his constituency on Friday morning to attend Tod Hanley's funeral the following day, and as an after-thought added, 'I don't suppose you've had any more thoughts about leaving in the summer?'

'Well, of course. My appointment has been confirmed by Mr de Roche, here, you can read it for yourself.'

He took the letter she handed at him and glanced at it briefly before handing it back.

'So, when do you intend to leave?'

'Mid-June, I thought, that will give me time to see to things at this end.'

'How about the flat?'

'I've had an offer for it and I think I'll sell.'

'Suppose you decided to return here?'

'I don't think I will. I'll have burnt my boats, won't I, besides what is there to come back for?'

'I can't think de Roche will be the easiest person to work for.'

'Why do you say that? I thought he was perfectly charming.'

'It's his job to be charming. There's always another side.'

'I've noticed.'

'I'll need to be thinking of a replacement soon.'

'You won't have any trouble, half the secretariat is waiting to work for you, I can get you a shortlist if you like.'

He scowled. 'I'll choose my own shortlist, Alison, if you don't mind.'

She smiled, and with a brief nod he left her, slamming the door behind him.

It hadn't been easy. There were too many memories, too many years, too much left to abandon it lightly, but she'd come this far, there was no turning back.

He'd be at his best at Tod Hanley's funeral, the perfect friend, the kindest, and revelling in the part he had played in the tragedy. His constituents would already have learned how wonderful he'd been in the crisis and he'd probably added a larger contingent of votes, even from the opposition.

She wished ardently she didn't feel this way about him. She still loved him, and he had a great many good points, unfortunately they were so much mixed up by his bad ones she'd never quite known which was which.

London could be a lonely place, these last few months had shown her just how lonely, but what was she walking into? She was a townie. She'd never grown up surrounded by green fields and sloping fells. She was accustomed to city traffic and dark intimate restaurants, crowds of people and noise, but what was left for her in London? She couldn't end things with Stuart and remain in London. They'd drift back together, and the old agonies would begin all over again. Nothing would change.

She looked around her flat. She didn't want her furniture and the new owner had seemed interested in buying it. She'd keep the pictures and some of the china and reading lamps. The flat wasn't home anymore, it was simply a place to lay her head until she said goodbye to London then she looked at Stuart's wretched Easter Bunny with its vain, self-satisfied expression leering at her from a corner of the settee and the tears fell afresh.

Who knew whom she might meet at The Lakes and Stuart had never tired of telling her that she was a beautiful girl, a man's girl, lovely, intelligent, funny too. The sort of girl a man liked to be seen with. That intelligence had not been in evidence when she'd fallen in love with a married man, at least that was something she would never do again.

Driving north Stuart felt irritably angry with life in general. He hated funerals, and this one would be more harrowing than most. He thought Alison was making a disastrous mistake and he'd been away a week, who knows what mischief Geraldine would have been up to in his absence. Geraldine was one of his wife's best friends, how much of Alison's presence at The Lakes could she have divulged to Sybil?

The wretched windscreen wipers were having a hypnotic effect on him so he opened the window but was glad to close it when spots of rain fell on his cheek. This time tomorrow it would be all over. Funerals were bad enough when the deceased was old and weary with life, not somebody like Tod with all the world to live for.

Chapter Twenty-Four

Mrs Ralston was entertaining her two oldest friends to tea and sitting across from them Gerald felt cynically amused to see the blank expression on both their faces. His mother had talked them to death for most of the afternoon.

'Why don't you both make the effort to come with us the next time we go?' she said brightly. 'You would love the hotel, and you'd enjoy being looked after and waited upon. It really isn't much of a change when you take that old cottage on every year in August, cleaning and cooking, you have to do that at home.'

'We love the cottage, Doris, I don't think we'd like hotel life,' Aunt Edith said. He'd called them Aunt Edith and Uncle Maurice ever since he was a child. Aunt Edith had been his mother's schoolfriend and Uncle Maurice had been their nextdoor neighbour. They had remained a contented country-loving couple on Maurice's local government pension and displayed no envy whenever his mother embarked on her display of pretension.

'We met the most interesting people,' she went on. 'A member of parliament made up our bridge four one evening, a most charming man, and quite handsome. He was with a girl, not his wife, his secretary we were told, but of course he was no doubt there on business, I don't think for a moment there was anything going on. We didn't think so, did we, Gerald?'

'I wasn't interested, Mother.'

'Then there was the young lady who saves my library books. A very nice girl, Gerald has had lunch with her, and she's very kind saving my books for me. She spent the entire weekend going about with Lord Alveston so it's my guess she is rather more than a librarian. But then, girls do find jobs these days, don't they, even when they're members of the aristocracy?

'You know her very well, don't you, dear?'

Gerald squirmed. The expression on their visitors' faces became rather more vacant, but his mother went blissfully on.

'I've really been thinking I might meet you in town one day, Gerald, some Friday so that I can go into the library with you to thank her for being so thoughtful.'

'I rarely see her in the library these days, Mother, she's busy in her office. Mostly it's one of the other assistants who sees me.'

'But we'll ask for her, dear. She's been so kind, I think it would be a very nice gesture to invite her to have tea with us one day soon.'

'There's really no need, Mother, when she saves your books for you she's merely doing her job.'

'I know, dear, but I've met her now. I want to show her how grateful I am for this special service, she would appreciate it I feel sure.'

'In that case, Mother, why don't we invite the postman, the girl in the post office and the man who fills the car up?'

His mother stared at him in surprise, and for the first time during the afternoon their visitors shook themselves out of their stupor.

'Really, Gerald, what is the matter with you? All I want to do is extend a little courtesy, it's not like you to be so difficult.'

'I think perhaps we ought to be getting off now,' Maurice said quietly. 'Shall we see you as usual on Friday evening, Doris?'

'Well yes of course. I wish my bridge friends would come one evening but they all seem to have other things planned for the evenings. Of course I'm the only one who is a widow. Gerald will bring me round on his way to the golf club.'

They accompanied the couple to the door and Gerald walked with them to his car. Maurice had never owned a car, never been interested in learning to drive and they sat in the car waving to his mother who stood at her front door to see them off.

As they drove the short distance to their home Gerald asked, 'Are you sure you don't mind Mother coming round every Friday? She's perfectly safe in the house you know, we're well protected with good locks on the doors.'

'We don't mind,' Maurice said.

'It means your leaving the golf club awfully early,' Aunt Edith said. 'We feel badly about that, but neither of us likes to stay up late.'

'I know that, Aunt Edith. It bothers me sometimes.'

'You mustn't worry, Gerald, we like having your mother, she's always full of news about some person or another, and we live a very quiet life.'

They had arrived at their front gate and Gerald left the car to assist Maurice out of the front seat since he suffered from arthritis.

It was Sunday, a soft balmy Sunday at the beginning of May and the links would be busy with golfers. He seldom played on Sunday afternoon because their Sunday visitors needed a lift home, and then his thoughts turned to Mary Styles.

He had spoken the truth when he had said he seldom saw her in the library these days. His books were always waiting for him, chosen as meticulously as ever, but it was one of the junior girls who attended to him, smiling coyly, her eyes snapping brightly and no doubt wondering why her superior officer had handed the duty to her.

Sometimes on Tuesdays he spotted Mary around the shops but she never lunched at the George now, and whenever they did meet on the road she afforded him a serene smile and that was the end of it. He hoped his mother would change her mind about visiting the library with him, and her idea of inviting Mary to tea was preposterous.

Mrs Ralston was not a woman to change her mind. She had been vastly intrigued by Mary's friendship with Lord Alveston, a little chat over the teacups, a little charm and motherly interest would not come amiss, and she might learn a little more.

She would not tell Gerald she intended to go into town on the next Friday afternoon or he would try to put her off, instead she would take the bus and arrive at his office halfway through the afternoon. She would tell him she'd finish her shopping, call for him later so that they could visit the library together, it would not take her long to assess whether Mary was responsive to her friendship, but of course she would be. She was probably attracted to Gerald anyway, most women were, even when he had shown little interest in any of them.

It was almost half-past-five on Friday afternoon and the two library assistants were busy stacking the shelves with returned books and wishing people would make up their minds what exactly they wanted so that they could get off home.

Mary sensed their impatience. They had things to do on Friday evenings, the pictures, some night spot, boyfriends to see, but she busied herself in the small office and left them to see to their customers. She knew that they speculated on why she no longer greeted Gerald when he called, she was therefore very surprised when Helen popped her red head round the door to announce that Mr Ralston and a lady were asking for her.

'A lady?' she asked in some surprise.

'Yes, Miss Styles.'

Two round pairs of eyes watched as she walked to the counter and Mrs Ralston greeted her effusively while Gerald stood awkwardly at her side.

'I've been shopping in the town,' Mrs Ralston said, 'so I thought I'd call in personally to pick up my library books and to thank you once again for looking after me so well.'

'It's no trouble, Mrs Ralston, it's my job,' Mary said evenly.

'That's what Gerald said, but these little kindnesses make our lives so much nicer I think. I would like to thank you, Miss Styles, and I was wondering if you would come to tea one Saturday or Sunday, next weekend perhaps.'

'That's very nice of you, Mrs Ralston but I have an invalid mother who is left alone all week, so you see I do really have to spend time with her at the weekends.'

'Couldn't you bring her along? We would make her very welcome, I'm sure a little change would do her a power of good.'

Mary's eyes met Gerald's over his mother's head and she sensed in them a strange misery. She felt sorry for him. For weeks she had raged against herself and her naivety in thinking that he cared for her, and the high-handed way he had brushed her aside. His life was as empty as her own, but where she had been honest, his pride had not allowed him to be.

His mother was looking at her with a bright smile expecting her to accept her invitation with some display of pleasure but Mary knew she couldn't.

She had answered her with a half truth. Even if things had been different her mother would not have wanted to go, and for the first time she felt some degree of relief in her intransigence.

'My mother suffers from arthritis and she has a bad heart,' she explained gently. 'It really is very difficult for her to get about and for me to manage her.'

'Gerald would pick you up, of course, I am sure between you you could manage your mother very well.'

'But my mother does not like people to see her like that, she feels a nuisance. I am really very sorry, Mrs Ralston, but I simply can't accept your invitation. I do thank you for asking me though.'

'But you managed to leave your mother at Easter, and that was for four days. This would be for one afternoon.'

'My mother went into a residential home at Easter and she was very well looked after. We have a very good daily woman who sees to her when I'm at work, I couldn't ask her to come at the weekends.'

'I am sorry, I was so looking forward to repaying a little of your kindness to me. So every time you want to see that very nice gentleman in the Lake District will mean putting your mother in a home?'

Mary's smile was stiff, her words stilted. 'I must ask you to excuse me, Mrs Ralston, the girls are anxious to get off home and I do have to close the library up. Thank you once again for your invitation, I am sorry I can't accept it.'

There was nothing more to be said, and for the first time Gerald spoke saying, 'Come along, Mother, we're keeping Miss Styles from her work.'

All the way home she went on and on about it.

'Did you see how she clammed up when I mentioned Lord Alveston?' Mrs Ralston said tartly. 'Surely you remember the scandal of Lady Alveston's death, it was in the papers for weeks, that woman knew a lot about it, it's more than likely she was involved and moved down here to get away from it.'

'That's nonsense, Mother. Miss Styles knew nothing about the hotel until I mentioned it casually one day over lunch.'

'I'm not talking about the hotel, Gerald, I'm talking about the scandal concerning Lord Alveston, the hotel came much later, but everybody living in those parts knew about it. She was using her mother as an excuse for not accepting my invitation, she didn't want us to talk about the holiday and who she spent her time with.'

'There was no reason to talk about it, it was none of our business.'

'If it was so unimportant then why did she mind so much?'

'I'm quite sure she didn't mind. She does have an invalid mother who doesn't get out much. I might be a bit later tonight, Mother, there's a meeting at the club, not just the usual social evening.'

'But you don't usually go to the meetings, you're not on the committee.'

'I know. It's about alterations to the club house and the course. You'll be perfectly safe in the house on your own, Mother, I'll lock up well before I leave and I won't be all that late.'

'No. I'll go to your Aunt Edith's as always, just get there as soon as you can.'

They drove the rest of the journey in silence. His mother was preoccupied with her own thoughts and his were full of resentment. He was remembering Mary's annoyance at his mother's insistence, the way she had rebuffed her when Andrew Alveston had been brought into the conversation, she was probably blaming him and hating him for it.

He hoped his mother would now let the matter drop.

Mary watched her two assistants go off chattering as usual, possibly chattering about her since she felt sure they had missed nothing from their hidden place behind the bookshelves.

Her meeting with Gerald and his mother had disconcerted her. She had not understood why Mrs Ralston was being persistent in inviting her to tea, and then suddenly she realised the woman wanted to talk about her friendship with Andrew during the Easter weekend, a subject she would no doubt dine out on with her bridge friends.

She could imagine Mrs Ralston regaling them with stories of an old tragedy, telling them that she had met Lord Alveston, indeed that they were personal friends of a woman he was interested in.

The thought gave her some cynical amusement. She was never likely to see Andrew again, or The Lakes.

As she drove through the evening traffic she thought miserably of the weekend ahead. Her mother had been more morose than ever since she got back, refusing to talk about her time at the residential home, and Millicent was coming to the house more often and filling her mother's head with all sorts of nonsense.

She found Mrs Scotson ready for departure. Her dark felt hat pulled down over her newly permed hair, her shopping basket filled to the brim so that she felt she had to explain. 'Yer sister came round, Miss Styles, so I was able to get out to do a bit o' shopping. She brought some flowers, I 'adn't time to put them in a vase, I thought you'd do it later.'

195

'Yes of course. What time did my sister leave?'

'Around five, she said she wanted to get back afore her husband got 'ome.'

'I'll see what mother would like for her tea.'

'Well, yer sister brought cakes and biscuits. She allus does that these days.'

'Perhaps she doesn't think I'm feeding Mother enough.'

'Who knows what she thinks, and what they talk about,' Mrs Scotson finished darkly.

Her mother was more communicative than she had ever known her. She talked about the home, the entertainment they had had, the days out by coach when they were looked after very well and where there was an excellent assortment of meals.

Mary listened in some amazement, saying at last, 'You never spoke about the home before, Mother, I thought you would enjoy the experience when you got used to it, are you telling me you wouldn't mind going there again?'

'I didn't say that. It was all right that's all.'

Her mother was looking at her with an expression she couldn't read, a strange sly expression and Mary asked, 'Has Millicent said anything about your stay there?'

'Milly! No, why should she?'

'Only that this is the first time you've spoken about it and Mrs Scotson said she'd been visiting this afternoon.'

'I gave Mrs Scotson the afternoon off, told her to be back before Milly left and before you came home. She misses nothing, that woman, and we could talk in peace without any interruptions.'

'I hardly ever seem to see my sister, she visits when I'm at the library and she's always gone when I get home. Has she any news?'

'Only that the children are costing more and more money and they need it for their education.'

'I'm sure they do, but their father has a very good job. They take very expensive holidays.'

'He works for it.'

'Well of course. I'm not complaining, Mother, I'm pleased that they're seeing the world now that they're of an age to enjoy the experience.'

'Milly keeps me entertained, you never have any news.'

'We were invited out to tea this weekend by two people I met in the Lake District. I didn't think you'd want to go.'

'You're right, I don't. Who were they?'

'A Mrs Ralston and her son Gerald. They came into the library to invite us.'

'Why would they do that?'

'Like I said, Mother, I met them at The Lakes. Mr Ralston comes into the library every Friday for his books, today his mother was with him.'

'Is that the man you had lunch with in the town?'

'Why yes. How did you know about that?'

'Milly told me. That Dolly Lampeter told her. I've been waiting for you to tell me yourself.'

'There was no reason why I should. Mr Ralston is simply a member of the library, he's hardly a personal friend. You can tell Millicent I hardly know either of them, in case she's concerned about it, Mother.'

Her reply had been terse and her mother looked at her sharply.

'You've said I hadn't said much about the home, you've said even less about your weekend in the Lake District.'

'I told you the hotel was lovely and I'd enjoyed myself, Mother, there was really nothing else to tell you.'

'All the same, it was funny that you should want to go so badly, and he was there with his mother.'

Her mother was watching her with narrowed eyes but she made herself meet them innocently. With wry amusement she thought that if things had been different and there really had been something for Gerald and herself, how could she ever have realised it, and how could he?

'I'll go and make tea, Mother,' she said gently. 'Is there anything you particularly fancy?'

'Milly brought cakes and biscuits, I'm not hungry, you get something for yourself.'

Milly had never been so considerate before. Now she came several days in the week and always with some delicacy she knew her mother might fancy. Mary thought about the sister she had grown up with, always self-centred, always with one eye on the main chance and never doing anything for anybody unless there was some reward at the end of it. Why was she suddenly being the dutiful daughter?

Gerald consulted his watch surreptitiously. The meeting had gone on longer than he had thought it would and one of the members was now on his feet and well launched into a lengthy discourse on exactly how he thought the golf-course should be changed.

The man sitting next to him sighed.

'We'll not get away before midnight now that Lawson's on his feet,' he said wearily. 'You don't usually stay so late.'

'No. I shall have to leave before the meeting's over, I'm afraid.'

'We're off on holiday in the morning, let's make a discreet exit as soon as he eases up.'

Lawson showed no signs of easing up. He was enjoying himself and Gerald's desperation grew.

He felt annoyance with his mother that she had insisted on going to their friends, and he felt unease that he was keeping them up. His mother would be furious. She would be talking them to death and when she ran out of conversation she would telephone the club. Indeed the interruption came several minutes later when one of the stewards informed him he was wanted on the telephone.

'Do you know what time it is, Gerald?' she accused him. 'They're wanting to go to bed, both of them are half asleep and I've a good mind to call a taxi.'

'You know you won't go into the house on your own, Mother, I told you I would be late.'

'But not this late.'

'I didn't know how long the meeting would last.'

'Well I suggest you get away now. One of the other members will tell you what you've missed.'

There seemed no point in returning to the room where the meeting was still going on so he left the club to go for his car. He was opening the car door when the man who had been sitting next to him passed on his way to his car, saying cheerfully, 'The arguments are going on and on, I managed a quiet exit. Nothing wrong, I hope?'

'No. I was expecting the call.'

'We'll hear all about it in due course, I expect.'

'Well yes, I suppose so. Goodnight.'

Gerald squared his shoulders in anticipation of the meeting to come. It had been one hell of a day.

Chapter Twenty-Five

Stuart Mansell sat at the kitchen table drinking his third cup of coffee while he waited for his wife to make up her mind about the hat she proposed to wear for Tod Hanley's funeral.

He stared at her in some exasperation when she appeared in the doorway to see if he approved.

'For heaven's sake, Sybil, it's a funeral we're going to, not Ascot,' he snapped.

'I want to look right,' she said stolidly. 'How about this one?'

'It looks all right to me.'

'Better than the other one?'

'They both looked all right to me.'

'I'm not sure.'

'Does it really matter? We're going to pay our last respects, we're not his nearest and dearest. You look fine, and it's time we were going.'

'Geraldine is such a one for weighing everybody up and she always looks exactly right.'

'So do you, now come along, Sybil. We don't want to make an entrance by arriving late.'

She was wearing a neat clerical grey suit and white silk blouse. The hat was a light grey straw adorned with a white silk band and it suited her better than the previous black floppy hat adorned with feathers. Before she could change her mind yet again he hustled her through the lobby towards the front door.

She smiled up at him. As always he looked elegant in his dark grey suit and black silk tie. Grey suited his classical features and his dark hair which had turned silver at his temples and which gave him a distinguished severity.

They drove in silence to the Broadhursts' house which was already surrounded by cars.

'You'll have to put it round the back,' Sybil advised, 'we have to leave room for the funeral cars.'

'If you hadn't kept changing your mind about the hat we'd have been able to leave it at the front,' he said testily. 'I suppose we can get into the house at the back.'

'We can walk round to the front, Stuart. That's the way everybody else is entering.'

'Do you want to get out of the car here?'

'No, I'm coming with you. I don't want to stand on the front step waiting for you.'

The conversation was subdued, but these were the wedding guests dressed more sombrely and Geraldine was coming towards them with hands outstretched and tears glistening in her expertly made-up eyes. Wearing deepest mourning, as always she looked elegant from her wide-brimmed black hat to the narrow pointed court shoes on her feet.

'We've hired three large funeral cars,' she said hurriedly. 'Most of them will use their own cars but we'd like you both to travel with us, you've been such good friends. The Hanleys will go in the first one, we'll go in the second and the relatives in the third.'

'And Debbie?'

'She'll go with the Hanleys of course.'

'How is she bearing up?'

'She's still in shock, poor darling. It would do her good to cry but she seems incapable of registering any emotion whatsoever. Mrs Hanley's never stopped crying and look at the Brewster girl over there, she couldn't be more desolate if she'd been in Debbie's shoes.'

The Brewster girl had her arms wrapped round Tod's mother and they were both sobbing uncontrollably to Geraldine's utmost disdain.

John Broadhurst came to shake hands with them.

'I'll be glad when this morning's over,' he said ruefully. 'We can't do anything more. Ah, here's Debbie now.'

Debbie was wearing a black skirt and hat with a white tailored jacket. She looked composed, tearless and very beautiful. For a brief moment her eyes flicked over Mrs Hanley and the sobbing girl in her arms, her expression was faintly contemptuous.

There would be a great many girls in the churchyard, relics of Tod's conquests. Janet Brewster had almost nailed him until Debbie had made her appearance, now she was at his funeral at the invitation of his parents.

Geraldine stood with Sybil Mansell, surveying their guests. As always Josie Martindale stood out from the crowd in expensive and sophisticated black so that Geraldine murmured, 'Really, there was no call for her to wear deepest mourning, it's rather ostentatious, don't you think?'

'It looks new to me,' Sybil whispered.

'Oh I'm sure it is. Somehow or other she's always controversial.'

Josie smiled across the room at them, and Geraldine hissed, 'She gets most of her clothes from Jeanette's in the High Street, keeps them going I shouldn't wonder.'

'What exactly does her husband do? I've never been sure.'

'Dabbles in stocks and shares, John says. Successfully from his wife's extravagances. It looks as though the cortege has arrived, people are moving forward. You'll be with us, won't you, Sybil? John and Stuart are waiting for us near the door.'

There was no sign of Debbie and as they entered the second car they could see that she sat at the back of the first one between Mr and Mrs Hanley.

Geraldine said sharply, 'That Brewster girl has been making quite a show of herself, after all it's been over between her and Tod for ages, she'd do better to keep a low profile.'

Nobody spoke.

Janet Brewster stood amongst the others, red-eyed and tearful, while her parents moved protectively nearer.

'I'll be glad when this day is over and we can get back to normal. I think we should try to get away for a while, take Debbie on a cruise somewhere. I love that place in the Lake District, I only hope when all this is behind us we'll feel able to go back there,' Geraldine murmured.

Mrs Hanley wept unconsolably throughout the service in the parish church and at the graveside looked ready to collapse. It was unbelievable that this was the funeral of her son, the boy who had delighted her with his brash good humour, his prowess in every sport he undertook, his rugged handsome face and figure.

Across the open grave Geraldine bit her lip nervously. Why couldn't Debbie show some emotion? She stood like a marble statue, her face cold and expressionless, clutching her spray of red roses until Geraldine reminded her to throw them onto the coffin.

But Debbie was not a marble statue, inside she was churning with anger. Tod had done this to her, Tod who had wanted to show off in front of men he didn't know and he hadn't cared that he had left her alone, to amuse herself in any way she could. Now she was a widow. There would be no parties because people would think it was unseemly to invite her, no escorts because it was too soon, and it seemed easy to believe that her life too had ended.

People were looking at her in uncomfortable silence, and Janet Brewster was sobbing wildly beside the desolate form of Tod's mother.

She wanted this day to be over, she wanted the people gone. Other people at the funeral expressed their condolences to the Hanleys and her parents because Debbie's expression shut them out and now they were going back to her parents' house where a buffet was laid out for them.

Only weeks before it had been a different sort of buffet, then there had been joy and glamour and something to look forward to, now it would be a mockery. People talking in hushed voices, people afraid to smile, and her mother-in-law's distress. Why didn't they all go to their own homes?

The same thoughts were circling Stuart Mansell's mind as he turned to his wife to say, 'I'll be very glad when today's over, we'll get away as soon as it's possible.'

'Oh I really do think, darling, that we should stay as long as Geraldine needs us, she'll want all the support she can get. She says Debbie's still suffering from shock, she's shown no emotion whatsoever.'

'I suppose that is understandable.'

'The Brewster girl is showing too much.'

'Perhaps she's the one he should have married.'

He looked round the room. People were filling up their plates from an amply laid out buffet. Waiters were filling glasses and Mrs Hanley sat near the window, slumped in a large chintz-covered chair with her eyes closed.

Janet Brewster sat with her parents, a glazed expression on her face, but Debbie was holding out her empty glass for a waiter to fill it.

'I suggest we circulate a bit,' Stuart said to his wife. 'There's that new couple who've just come to live in the area, why not introduce yourself?'

He went to the table where Geraldine was helping herself from one of the plates and she turned to see who had joined her.

'I'm glad it's all over,' she said softly. 'Perhaps now we can try to get back to normal.'

He smiled. 'Yes of course. Debbie'll accept it in time, it's been a great shock.'

'Yes. Just think, three weeks ago we had a wedding party in this room and now a funeral. I wish she'd told me she was thinking of going to The Lakes, I would have tried to dissuade her.'

'Why was that?'

'Well, it was never Tod's sort of place. He was never one for scenery and genteel elegance. He would have been happier in Spain, the bars and night clubs, the beaches and the sunshine. She was stupid to think he would ever enjoy himself at The Lakes.'

'Not even on his honeymoon?'

'Not even then. He had to be seen doing something better than anybody else could do it. I should think all his life he's been like that, always the fool-hardiest, always the big man among lesser people.'

Silently Stuart agreed with her. Debbie would never have changed him, and in any case she had tried too soon. He had never really known Tod very well but on the rare occasions when he had seen him Tod had always been surrounded by a crowd of young men and girls, and he had always been the centre of attention.

The girls had revelled in his casual smiles, his hearty friendliness, and the boys had admired his prowess on the tennis courts, the golf course, the

202

cricket field. Then when he took up sailing he had been the one with the largest boat. When his father made money it had meant the best of everything for the son who did it so much justice.

'Are you just here for the weekend?' Geraldine asked.

'Yes, I'm driving back tomorrow afternoon.'

'What are you going to do about your secretary?'

'I'm not with you?'

'Well, isn't she leaving you to work at The Lakes, won't you have to replace her?'

'That won't be a problem, Geraldine. I think she's making a mistake, but there's nothing I can say to persuade her to stay.'

'You've tried then?'

He did not miss the gleam in her dark eyes, and nonchalantly he said, 'I think she'll be bored out of her skin there. Alison's a townie, she enjoys London with its shows and restaurants. Besides, she has a string of young fellows who are going to miss her something rotten.'

'Really?'

'Yes, really. She's a very pretty girl, she has a great many admirers.'

'Single admirers.'

'Of course.'

'Then she'll probably find others at The Lakes. Isn't Anton de Roche a bachelor?'

'I don't know anything about him. Is he French?'

'I think so, but I don't really know. He's rather handsome. The French do have an air, don't they? Elegance, sophistication, it would be amusing if she captured Anton de Roche.'

'Oh, I rather think Alison has other things on her mind than capturing the hotel manager. Josie Martindale is looking very elegant this afternoon, but then she always does.'

He was pleased to see the warm colour in Geraldine's cheeks. He had got his own back.

John Broadhurst was chatting amicably to Josie and her husband, and Geraldine said sharply, 'Perhaps we'll join them, Stuart, she does tend to hog the men and John should be circling among his guests.'

Sybil was chatting to the new couple who had come to live in one of the new houses at the edge of the town and they seemed to be getting on rather well, so that Stuart said hastily, 'If you don't mind, Geraldine, I'll go and have a chat to the couple Sybil is with, they're pretty new in the area, I think I should introduce myself.'

'Oh yes do, they've both joined the party and they're prepared to work for us at the next election. Gracious, it's only eighteen months away, we'll need all the help we can get.'

'You don't think we're in danger of losing surely?'

'Well no, certainly not this seat, but we have to keep vigilant. He's with that new factory producing material for the Forces, rather high up there so I've heard and she's into art. She paints, I believe.'

'You thought they should be invited today?'

'John invited them. They play golf together and they're in the same Lodge.'

He smiled and moved away.

The Broadhursts cultivated people generally in the same walk of life as themselves, moneyed people with similar interests. In the next moment he was being assessed by a pretty blonde woman and shaking hands with her husband, as Sybil introduced them as Mr and Mrs Spendlove. The woman amended the introduction by giving their first names, Roger and Charlotte.

It didn't take Stuart long to ascertain that at the next election they would be willing helpers. For several minutes they chatted amicably together then Stuart said, 'I do think we should think about getting away now, darling. I'm only up here for the one evening and I'm off back to London very early in the morning. I'm sure the Broadhursts will understand.'

'Geraldine was telling us that you've been a tower of strength during this tragedy. We haven't met the Hanleys until today, poor Mrs Hanley is taking it very hard, is the young woman with her his sister?' Charlotte Spendlove asked.

'No, simply a friend. She's rather an emotional girl, but a one-time sweetheart of Tod I believe.'

'Oh I see. Debbie is bearing up very well, rather too well, I think,' she added.

'Yes,' Sybil agreed. 'I hope she doesn't go to pieces later.'

They circled the room to say their farewells and reached the door in time to see Mr Hanley assisting his wife into their car. They went forward quickly to speak to them but Mrs Hanley was in no fit state to speak to anyone and Mr Hanley's few words were strained and short.

They drove the few miles to their home in silence, both immersed in their own thoughts. By the time he had put the car away and returned to the house Sybil had made coffee and they sat down at the kitchen table to drink it.

Her first words surprised him.

'I think I might come up to London for a few days, Stuart, I've been thinking about it for some time.'

'You'll be on your own a lot.'

'I know, but Geraldine said she felt it was very unfair of me not to spend more time with you, after all the children are at university and my parents are well enough. Who are you going to replace Alison with?'

So Geraldine had been putting her oar in. No doubt with the best of motives and with Sybil's welfare in mind, all the same it was really none of her bloody business, he thought irritably.

'I've only been back a short time, I haven't got around to thinking about it yet,' he said shortly.

'Will you have to advertise?'

'We have a pool of would-be secretaries, Alison doesn't think I'll have any trouble in replacing her.'

'Doesn't Alison have a man friend in London?'

'I don't really know what she does in her spare time, she doesn't talk about it.'

'She's a very attractive girl, surely there's somebody.'

'There could well be. If there is he can't be very important or she wouldn't be thinking of moving on.'

'Maybe he's married.'

'Why on earth should you think that? Alison's a sensible girl with her head screwed on. I'm sure she's not got herself entangled with anything sordid.'

'It doesn't have to be sordid, darling, they could be very discreet about it.'

'Has Geraldine suggested that, Sybil? She met Alison for a few minutes at The Lakes and already she's filling your head with all sorts of nonsense.'

'She hasn't. We just wondered why a girl as attractive as Alison isn't married. Surely you must have wondered yourself.'

'No I haven't. There are a lot of girls like her, intelligent, career girls, content to make a life for themselves and think about marriage later. She could well meet somebody at The Lakes, the place was crawling with well-heeled men, the girl she's replacing is leaving to marry some rich American she's met there.'

'Oh well, you'll just have to wish her well then and hope the same thing happens to her.'

Stuart let himself into his London flat in a thoroughly depressed mood. The long evening stretched ahead of him, a long unfamiliar evening. In other days he would have telephoned his wife, then gone to Alison's flat and she would have cooked a meal for them, then they would have settled down in her comfortable living room to listen to music, watch television, perhaps play bezique or some other card game. They would argue often, quarrel a little, but it would all be good-humoured before they retired to the bedroom to spend the night making love.

Now here he was in an empty flat with the sound of rain against the window and the occasional eerie hooter from some steamer on the river.

During the next week he'd think seriously about appointing a replacement for her, some girl in the secretariat with ambition and somebody pretty whom Alison did not like.

It was undoubtedly childish, but he wanted to hurt her. Alison was being unreasonable. Surely she must see that he had to think about his wife and

205

family, it didn't mean he loved her any the less or that it was always going to be like that.

He did not know that at precisely that moment Alison was thinking about him. She was picturing him in his flat, sulking over a whisky and soda, wondering how he could hurt her or how he could make her change her mind.

She'd spent the afternoon showing people around her flat, a girl from Westminster, a friend of Tracie's and a young couple. The first offer had fallen through but she was hopeful about one of the others. Tracie had said her friend had parents who were willing to buy the flat if it was suitable and the girl had drooled over it. She'd been keen to keep most of the furniture and once the flat had been sold, Alison thought, she really would feel that she had burned her boats.

What sort of woman would he find to replace her? Somebody attractive, intelligent, somebody who would admire him for his good looks, his charm and his acumen. Where would it go from there?

She saw little of him during the week. He left notes for her and she complied with them. The smooth running of his everyday life was maintained and it was Friday afternoon when he mentioned her replacement, almost as an after-thought.

'I really must do something about a new secretary,' he said evenly. 'You know most of the girls in the secretariat, anybody spring to mind?'

'You said you would prefer to make your own selection.'

'And I do. I'll ask around and I'm perfectly willing to look at any list you care to give me.'

'I'll see to it next week then. You'll have a list on your desk before Tuesday.'

'They all know you're leaving, I suppose?'

'I think so.'

'Have any of them seemed interested?'

'One or two.'

'Well then, I'll look at your recommendations, think about some names some of my colleagues put forward and I'll be ready to start the interviews the following week.'

She nodded, he smiled briefly, and left the office.

Chapter Twenty-Six

As soon as she opened the front door Mary knew that Mrs Scotson was in a bad mood. There was much clattering of pots and pans from the kitchen and before she could close the front door Mrs Scotson was in the hall, her face a picture of indignation.

'Afore you speak to your mother, Miss Styles, I'd like to 'ave a word with you,' she snapped and retired immediately to the kitchen.

Mary followed with a sinking heart.

She stood with arms akimbo, her back to the kitchen table and Mary waited for whatever had to come.

'It's your sister, Miss Styles,' Mrs Scotson began. 'She's comin' nearly every afternoon now, and there they are sitting whisperin' together and givin' me time off to do shoppin,' as if they think I'm goin' to stand listenin' to them behind the closed door. I don't like it, and what's more I don't 'ave shoppin' to do every day.'

Mary looked at her helplessly.

'She used to come once a week, and then only for a short while, now they make me feel like an eavesdropper. I was that vexed yesterday I went home and told mi 'usband about it. He could tell I was upset.'

'I'm sorry, Mrs Scotson, I'll speak to Millicent, but she's nearly always gone when I get home.'

'That's just it. She comes when you're out and gets rid of me, then this afternoon your sister and her 'usband came. He hardly ever comes, but there they all were shut in together in the room there and I hadn't even dusted.'

'But why? What has Mother to say to them that she can't say to me?'

'Somethin's afoot, and if ye ask me it's somethin' they don't want you to know about. Mi husband says if it goes on I must leave, I 'aven't to be upset like this.'

'Oh please, Mrs Scotson, you can't leave, what will I do without you?'

'I'll be right sorry to leave you, Miss Styles, you've allus been so kind to me and I've liked workin' here even when yer mother was bad-tempered and difficult, but now I'm made to feel that I can't be trusted. It was only one o'clock and they told me to do mi shopping and not get back before four-thirty.'

'Four-thirty! You mean they actually told you not to return until then?'

'That's right, and when I came round the corner there was another car in front of the house so I stood there not knowin' what to do. After a while a man came out carryin' a brief case. He got in his car and drove off then I came back into the house. Yer sister was in the kitchen washin' up the crockery, she'd evidently made tea for them.'

'Did she say anything?'

'No. I slammed mi shopping on the kitchen table and she went on dryin' the saucers. She never once looked at mi, then she went back to the other room where her mother and her husband were sitting. I heard 'em going, but I never went to look and I never went in to see your mother.'

'Maybe it was the doctor, Mrs Scotson.'

'Well of course it wasn't the doctor, I know him well enough. This man was a stranger. A business man, very smart and with a nice car. I thought yer brother-in-law looked a bit sheepish, maybe he had every right to be.'

'It's a mystery, Mrs Scotson. I'm sorry you're upset, but please don't think of leaving. I'll talk to Mother about it.'

'Well I'll say this, if I'm asked to do shoppin' again I'll put mi hat and coat on and go home, and I shan't be comin' back.'

Mrs Scotson departed and Mary began to get the evening meal ready. She took her mother's meal into the sitting room on a tray and placed it on a small table in front of her, but she was aware that her mother was looking at her cautiously. Mary plumped up the cushions behind her and her mother asked, 'Have you had a busy day at the library?'

It was something her mother never asked. Indeed never had Mary known her display any interest either in the library or its members.

'It isn't our busiest day, Mother. Why was Eric here, shouldn't he be working?'

She watched the blood flood into her mother's face and her eyes were filled with confusion before she said, 'He's having a few days off with a very bad cold. Why shouldn't he come to see me?'

'No reason, except that he hardly ever does.'

'Well perhaps he thinks it's about time he did come. We had a nice chat and Milly brought cakes and scones. I suppose Mrs Scotson had something to say about it.'

'Only that she objects to being sent out of the house as though you suspected her of eavesdropping.'

'We gave her time off for shopping, we don't dock her wages.'

'Nevertheless, Mother, you hurt her feelings to such an extent that she's considering leaving.'

'Leaving! What for, for God's sake? We thought she'd appreciate having time off for shopping and getting paid for it.'

'She doesn't need to shop every day, Mother, and it's getting to be every day. Who else was here?'

'Nobody else was here.'

'Mrs Scotson hung about outside waiting for your other visitor to go.'

Her mother screwed up her eyes and appeared to be thinking, then as if the solution had suddenly occurred to her she said, 'Of course, a friend of Eric's called. They had business.'

Why didn't Mary believe her? In the next moment her mother changed the subject.

'Milly says Clive doesn't intend coming back here when he leaves university, he says there's nothing for him around here, and Jayne is thinking the same thing.'

'What do they intend to do then?'

'They're both doing well at their universities and they want a career in some big city and flats or houses of their own.'

'Will they be able to afford them, do you think?'

'Well it's what they want. They'll both get good jobs and Eric will see that they're all right. You were always a clever girl, a lot more so than Milly, but you were content to stay on in this town. Young people are not like that these days.'

'Suppose I'd not elected to stay in this town, Mother, would you have been happy away from here?'

'I'd have had to be, wouldn't I?'

Her mother never ceased to amaze her. Even during her schooldays she'd been conditioned into being the one who would care for her mother and as time went by it became accepted that Mary had a good job and was eminently satisfied with what life was handing her.

As she stared at her mother, the old lady had the grace to look suddenly embarrassed.

'Would you like coffee, Mother?' Mary asked, and, relieved, her mother said 'Yes that will be nice.' And as an after-thought, 'I don't suppose Mrs Scotson means for a moment that she's going to leave. I won't give her time off for shopping again, she can do it in her own time.'

'Don't antagonise her, Mother. We rely an awful lot on Mrs Scotson, she's a very rare treasure.'

'She's well paid, and not just in money. I've seen her going off with food and some of your clothes. You've been very generous with that woman, Mary.'

'And she's repaid me a hundredfold. She would be very difficult to replace, Mother.'

'I never interfere with anything she does and she has a free run of the house.'

'I know that, Mother. I just don't want her to think of leaving.'

Life resumed its pattern. Mary told Mrs Scotson her mother was sorry if she had offended her, she had never meant to, and Millicent reverted to visiting once a week. Eric did not appear again.

All the same she felt considerable unease about the episode. She wished there was somebody she could talk to and she began to realise how isolated her life had become.

Her two assistants at the library would never understand how she lived her life. Once there had been Gerald to lunch with and laugh with, but now whenever she met him in the High Street, he merely favoured her with a swift smile and hurried on. He was embarrassed about his mother's invitation which she had in the end brusquely refused.

It was Dolly Lampeter who accosted her one morning in the chemists who gave her news that troubled her.

'Have you seen Millicent's new house yet, Mary?' she asked with one of her bright smiles.

Mary stared at her in astonishment.

'Why no. I didn't know she was moving.'

'You mean she hasn't told you?'

'Well I really hardly ever see her.'

'Hasn't your mother mentioned it, she goes regularly to see your mother.'

'Mother's awfully forgetful these days.'

She was aware of Dolly's inquisitive bright eyes scanning her face curiously before she said, 'Well you should get round there, they're buying old Mr Chalfont's house at the corner of Merton Road. I must say I'm amazed, they're asking an awful lot for it and it needs a bomb spending on it. I know Eric has a good job, but it would be out of our reach.'

'I didn't know.'

'I never see you in the George these days, but that nice Mr Ralston lunches there most days.'

For the rest of the afternoon Mary pondered on things that were happening in her family from which she had been excluded. She knew nothing of her sister's new house, but why should it be a secret?

When she asked her mother about it that evening she was aware of her mother's sharp intake of breath and her pathetic attempts to explain.

'But I told you about it, Mary. I said they were moving and I told you where.'

'No, Mother, you didn't.'

'Well I intended to. It must have been the evening you were going on about Mrs Scotson leaving. You know I forget things, now you're accusing me of keeping secrets from you.'

'But why are they moving? I thought they were all happy where they are.'

'The house is bigger.'

'I know that, but the children will be leaving them when they find jobs outside the town, and probably only coming home for visits.'

'There's a nice sitting room at the back and Eric's turning it into a granny flat.'

'For you?'

'Well there'll be no stairs, and it's for when you decide to go off on holiday again. Now you won't need to put me into a home.'

For several minutes they stared at each other in silence. Her mother's face was flushed but dominant, and in the next moment she said, 'Don't you go telling Mrs Scotson all our business, I sent her out the afternoon they were here, I don't want it broadcasting all over the town.'

'I had to hear of it from Dolly Lampeter, Mother.'

'She's another one that's full of gossip.'

Why suddenly was Millicent being so concerned about her mother and actually offering her accommodation if Mary decided to go on holiday? Somehow there was more to it than that, this was not the sister she had grown up with.

There were builders working on Millicent's new home, and sold signs outside their present one. Her mother did not mention the matter again and it was left to Mrs Scotson to snap, 'What do you think about yer sister and her husband movin' into that big house on the corner of Merton Road. They were talkin' about it in the butchers, and they were surprised when I knew nothing about it.'

'I don't know very much about it myself,' Mary said gently.

'Don't you think there's something fishy goin' on?'

'Well of course not. People move if they want to, Millicent always liked change.'

Mrs Scotson sniffed.

'I don't know what the builders are doin' but they'll most likely be in until the summer's over. They look to be buildin' an extension at the back, as though the house isn't big enough to start with.'

'I'm really not very interested, Mrs Scotson. If my sister hasn't seen fit to tell me herself then they mustn't think it's any of my business.'

She knew that her attitude exasperated their daily help. Mrs Scotson was of the opinion that something very devious was happening and the outcome would not be beneficial to either of them.

It was the middle of June and the weather was glorious. Gerald had not been into the library for over a week and Mary thought he must be on holiday somewhere. Of course these days he never mentioned holidays either abroad or at home.

She was drinking her morning coffee when the telephone shrilled on her desk and she lifted the receiver to hear a confusion of words, then she recognised Mrs Scotson's voice.

'Miss Styles, it's Mrs Scotson. Can you hear me?'

'Yes, Mrs Scotson, you needn't shout, I can hear you perfectly well.'

Mrs Scotson hated the telephone and tried her level best not to use it, now she sensed in her attitude a strange urgency that alarmed her.

'Is anything wrong, Mrs Scotson?'

'It's your mother, miss, she's had a stroke, just when I was servin' her mornin' cup of tea. I tried the doctor's number but it was engaged so I dialled nine, nine, nine, just like you told me. The ambulance came soon after and they've taken her into St Catherine's Hospital.'

'I'll go there now, Mrs Scotson. Thank you for all you've done, does my sister know?'

'No. I thought you'd want to tell her.'

'Of course. Thank you, I'll see you later.'

It was Market Day in the town and busier than usual. The shoppers were out in summer clothing and there was an air of vitality in the town as they stood in groups chatting, or strolling between the market stalls. The traffic was heavy and Mary had to curb her impatience as she drove behind a stream of cars on the road leading out of the town.

St Catherine's was a new hospital completed in the last few years, a large modern building surrounded by tree-lined gardens and as she drove up to the entrance door she could see that people were sitting out in the gardens to receive their visitors.

A young receptionist informed her that her mother was in a small ward off the main ward in a wing specially reserved for stroke patients, and anxiously Mary made her way to the lift in the main hall. A young nurse greeted her at the entrance to the ward, and then immediately the sister was there, an older sterner woman.

'Your mother's been sedated and is still unconscious,' she informed Mary. 'We don't quite know yet how deep her stroke is, the doctor saw her immediately and he'll be back in a short while. Are you waiting here?'

'Oh yes, as long as you think I should.'

'Then I suggest you get yourself a cup of tea in the canteen along the passage there and I'll let you know as soon as the doctor's examined her again. Don't you work in the library?'

'Yes.'

'I thought I recognised you. I read more when I'm on night duty but I remember seeing you in the library.'

Mary smiled.

'Is it possible to see my mother now?'

'Well I'd rather you didn't. Like I said she's sleeping and I'd like you to speak to the doctor first. He'll give you his opinion on her condition and then you can see her.'

Mary had to be content with that so she obeyed the sister's advice and went in search of her tea.

Her mother's health had given problems for years but her doctor had always made light of her woes, saying that arthritis was not a killing complaint even if it was wearing and painful.

She'd had the usual colds in winter, bouts of influenza and heartburn, but it was her immobility that worried her mostly. Mrs Scotson had always maintained that she was as strong as an ox. Mary's hands shook as she lifted the cup of tea to her lips and a woman sitting opposite smiled at her sympathetically.

'Relative is it, luv?' she asked.

'Yes, my mother.'

'Just been brought in?'

'Yes, she's had a stroke. I don't know how bad it is yet.'

'That's what's wrong with my husband. He keeps on having them, they can do an awful lot for them these days.'

'Yes, I'm sure they can.'

'How old is your mother?'

'In her late seventies.'

'Mi husband's only forty-five and he's been having this trouble for six years now. I reckon strokes are different when you're older.'

Mary smiled.

'Oh well,' said her companion, 'I'd better go in and see him. This last stroke's made him very bad tempered, I hope he's glad to see me.'

Time passed, people came and went and Mary's anxiety increased. She went to stand at the window where she could look out across the gardens, at patients recuperating in the sunlight. There were beds of roses ablaze with colour, and tall beech trees gave shade to the men and women sitting under them. Nurses came and went, some of them carrying trays of cool drinks, others pushed light trolleys filled with medication, yet over it all there was an atmosphere of peace.

She glanced at her wristwatch, surprised that it was only eleven o'clock, she seemed to have been in the hospital for ages. Her mother would not be a good patient, she was often impatient and querulous, finding fault when people were doing their best, now if she had something else to cope with as well as her arthritis she would be difficult.

Mary's thoughts moved on to the worst things that could happen. If her mother was sent home suffering the effects of her stroke she would have to have nursing care. Mary couldn't afford to give up her job, there were bills to pay, a house to maintain, and there would be nurses' fees to add to the load, then suddenly she told herself sharply, time enough to worry about the future when it was clear what the future was likely to be.

Disconsolately she turned away and at that moment the sister came into the canteen and with a brief smile said, 'The doctor will see you now, Miss Styles, I'll take you to his office, just at the end of the corridor.'

The doctor was young, and as she entered his office he rose from his chair to shake her hand, indicating that she should take the chair opposite him.

He smiled reassuringly, and she wondered if all doctors learned this air of reassurance along with their medical degrees.

'I'm sorry we've had to keep you waiting so long, Miss Styles, it's been a particularly busy morning. I suppose you're anxious to see your mother.'

'Well yes.'

'She's awake now, but incoherent. Don't be alarmed, it's largely as a result of the medication.

'The stroke is a mild one and if all goes well she will recover from it. She is paralysed down the right side but already there are signs that this is receding, the danger is that she could suffer from a larger more massive stroke. Unfortunately this is a pattern that often happens to a patient of your mother's age.'

'Is it likely to happen, do you think?'

'Well we hope not. We shall take good care of her, Miss Styles, you can rest assured she will receive the best of attention here. Now I'll take you along to see her, she's in a small side ward for the moment, if she does well she'll be removed into the larger ward.'

Her mother was propped up against her pillows, her eyes were closed and there was a strange colourless pallor in her face, Mary took her hand and pressed it. It was clammy and cold and although she opened her eyes to stare at her there was no sign of recognition.

The doctor said gently, 'Don't worry, Miss Styles, when you come in later you should see a great improvement in her, hopefully an even greater one tomorrow.'

Chapter Twenty-Seven

Gerald brought the car to a halt in a lay-by where they could look down on the sweeping fells and the lake below. Sheep grazed contentedly in the fields laid out like a patchwork quilt within stone walls, and the beautiful lake lay dreaming under a summer sky.

It was a view he never tired of, but today his thoughts were not on the scenery as he watched a solitary horseman riding a chestnut horse down the hillside, jumping the walls with consummate ease so that horse and rider seemed like one entity.

His mother's eyes too were on the horseman, and after a few minutes she said, 'I haven't seen him in the hotel this time, Gerald, I suppose it's because she isn't here.'

It was a conversation Gerald wished to avoid, and changing the subject rapidly he said, 'We're very fortunate that the day's so clear, Mother, you can actually see the Isle of Man and the Mountains of Mourne beyond.'

His mother's eyes remained fixed on the horseman.

Mrs Ralston was not interested in the Isle of Man or the mountains of Ireland, but she was very interested in the stately pile of Alveston Hall and its owner now riding his horse towards the stables at the back of the hall.

'I wonder how often she comes up here?' she said. 'I suppose there's nothing for him at the hotel if she isn't here.'

Patiently Gerald said, 'Mother, you don't know that. I'm sure Miss Styles was merely here for a few days' holiday and they simply happened to meet.'

'Don't be silly, Gerald, people like Lord Alveston don't just happen to meet, they have to be introduced properly, and if there was nothing going on why was she so curt when I mentioned it? It wasn't as though I was going to ask any questions.'

Gerald was tired of the subject which had been referred to over and over since their meeting in the library. He never chatted to Mary now, and the last time he had seen her she seemed very preoccupied.

His mother was like a dog with a bone, and he had the most awful feeling that she would not give up on Mary Styles. One Friday afternoon she would try again to issue an invitation to tea.

He'd heard people talking at the library while he waited for the girls to stamp his books. Mary's mother was in hospital after a stroke, that was evidently the reason for her preoccupation, but she seldom worked at the desk now but preferred to stay in her office seeing to the administrative work in the library.

He was well aware that the two assistants conjectured between themselves as to what had gone wrong between Mary and himself, but they greeted him with bright smiles, occasionally darting glances to where Mary worked behind glass walls.

For the first time since The Lakes had opened he hadn't wanted to come. He recognised among the guests people he had seen there before, but there were no people from the Easter crowd. His mother played bridge and he played snooker in the evenings, during the day they drove to one of the other lakes or sailed on the steamer. His mother enjoyed the food, the ambience and the attention she received from the staff, in that at least there was no cause for complaint.

Anton de Roche stood in the foyer chatting to some guests who had just arrived and his mother hissed softly, 'That's Lord and Lady Rawley, Gerald, she's always on television these days, she writes autobiographies and he's something big in the Foreign Office.'

His mother was well versed in the comings and goings of famous people, and as they moved across the hall she favoured Mr de Roche with a smile. It was his mother's notion that if she talked to the manager she would get to know more than most people.

One of the receptionists informed Anton that there was a telephone call for him, and with the charm he was famous for he made his excuses to leave his guests. This was the telephone call he had been waiting for, it was just after six o'clock.

He smiled as he recognised Alison's voice, faintly hesitant.

'Hello Mr de Roche, I thought I should ring you this afternoon to let you know that I am free to join you in Cumberland. You did say it might be a good idea to move in before the present secretary left.'

'Yes of course. So you have left Westminister, today?'

'Yes. They gave me a farewell party and Mr Mansell has found somebody to replace me.'

'Are you keeping your flat in London?'

'No. I've sold it. I'm leaving everything, Mr de Roche; Mr Mansell, my job, my flat and London.'

'Then we must really make sure that your decision has been a wise one. I shall expect you next week, Tuesday or Wednesday, and please don't worry, if you dealt satisfactorily with the traumas of Westminster, this little corner of England will seem like a haven of peace to you.'

She laughed. 'I do hope so. I'll travel north on Tuesday then. I've kept one or two pieces of furniture and some china, if there isn't room for it I can sell it up there or put it into store. Just one or two things I was particularly fond of.'

'Please don't worry. You will have room for them. Until Tuesday then.'

As he walked back into the foyer he wondered how painful it had been for Alison to say farewell to her past. It took a lot of guts to sever ties with the man she loved, a man she had been close to for a good many years, and not just Mansell, everything that went with him.

He had no doubts about her fitting in. She was efficient, efficient with her job and her life, that much she had shown him, and he did not think she would be in a hurry to replace Mansell with a new love. When he had told Julius Van Hopper that Alison Gray was coming to work for him, the owner had said dryly, 'She could be trouble, Anton, she's beautiful. Could she be a predator?'

Anton had shaken his head sagely. 'No she isn't that, she's hurt and sad. She needs to move on.'

He stood surveying the foyer and the people in it reflectively. From the first moment he had walked into the foyer of that massive hotel in Milan this had been his world. He had been just seventeen, largely brought up by his English grandparents and educated in England he had just spent a year with his mother and her second husband. His stepfather was Italian, rich, handsome and volatile, his mother was a nervous wreck.

For a year he moved with them from one expensive hotel to another, the unhappy recipient of their feuding. Their acrimonious marriage was the talk of every hotel they stayed in and in Milan it came to a head when his mother threw herself from their balcony and his stepfather shot himself. Neither of them died, they separated and Anton walked out of their lives.

The Van Hoppers had been like a family to the lost young English boy but Julius's father had also seen his potential. He offered him his first job in another hotel in Milan and from there he had gone on outwards and always upwards. He had gained a reputation for urbane charm, sensitivity and dependability.

From Singapore to New York, from Hong Kong to London and Berlin to Rome Anton became known and yet he had been surprised when Julius had asked him to manage The Lakes in the English Lake District.

This was a place totally unlike every other hotel the Van Hoppers had owned. It was peaceful and beautiful, it had a select quiet charm that did not rely on gold plating and ornate furnishings. It was something that might have leapt out of the past, out of a more refined and permanent age and Julius had talked to him about the man whose dream it had been.

Fired with the owner's enthusiasm Anton too was determined that The

Lakes should be one to stand out for its good taste and comfort, its style and beauty, and with this in mind he employed only those people who would do it credit. From the first moment he had laid eyes on Alison Gray he had thought she was a girl who could be an asset and it hadn't taken him long to see that she was a sad bewildered girl with too many unhappy memories and little faith in the future. He had hoped that she would take up his offer of employment, yet surprised when she had agreed. Women were not usually so strong.

Anton was forty-five years old and there were many times when he wondered where the years had gone.

He had lived his life in a world within a world. He had seen at first hand all the jealousies and envies, the passions and traumas that were often played out in days instead of lifetimes. Had he been so involved with other people's infidelities and tragedies that he had had no time to look for something outside this little world that had been artificially created?

There were times when Julius Van Hopper looked at him curiously, wondering what went on behind that urbane charm, but he asked no questions.

There had been women in his life, discreet affairs that had not lasted, none of them meaningful, and he told himself that hotel life had made him cynical. Now he told himself that he was too old, too set in his ways to commit himself to loving a woman, he had little doubt that Julius Van Hopper would agree with him.

The traumas of that Easter weekend were still in his mind but to most people they were relegated to the past. Life moved on, but a legacy of that weekend would soon be coming back in the shape of Alison Gray.

He hoped she would come with thoughts on the future and not on the past. She would meet other men here, men who would admire her, either flirt with her or offer something more serious, he wanted no love-sick woman living in the past, however much Alison might tell him it was over and done with.

He smiled at a young girl crossing the foyer to go to the dining room. She was a first-time visitor even if her escort was not. He walked over to the entrance to the dining room and saw that an elderly man had risen from his table to greet her, and now they were chatting together, all smiles and attention. The girl was young enough to be his daughter. He knew for a fact that the man's wife did not like the Lake District and was probably on some cruise liner somewhere else in the world. Was it any wonder that he was steeped in cynicism when this little world went out of its way to provide it?

An elderly lady rising from her table leaned down to collect her Pomeranian dog and leaning heavily on her walking stick she approached him with a delighted smile.

They came back again and again. He chatted to them and knew the sort of questions to ask. He stroked the Pomeranian and his owner smiled at the attention the dog was getting. Bengie was twelve now, she informed Anton, and then followed a list of his accomplishments which he had heard many times before.

Mrs Ralston and her son were here again, this was their fourth visit and as he looked across to where they sat at a table near the wall he was aware that the woman was doing most of the talking while the man appeared to be listening.

What would she do if her son fell in love? Anton asked himself, but he knew the answer already. Gerald Ralston would not fall in love, the outcome would be too traumatic, a halt would be called to his feelings before they had a chance of blossoming.

Mrs Ralston had spoken to him at the reception desk only that morning and surprised him by her questions about Lord Alveston. How often he visited the hotel, had Miss Styles revisited to spend some time in his company? Oh, they knew Miss Styles very well, she was in charge of the local library and looked after the selection of her books. They chatted every Friday and she would be taking tea with them in the near future.

As she prattled on Anton asked himself why she didn't pose the same questions to Mary herself if they were such close friends.

'You do remember her, of course?' she had asked him.

And Anton who never forgot a single one of his guests had answered, 'I remember Miss Styles very well, an extremely nice lady.'

'Oh yes. Unfortunately Gerald tells me she has a rather demanding mother, a semi-invalid, you know. She must find it very difficult when she wants to get away. I'm so grateful that Gerald and I never seem to have problems like that.'

Anton had smiled politely and excused himself on the grounds that he had someone in his office waiting to see him. Mrs Ralston would have been astonished if she could have known how accurately he assessed her.

It was several days later that they were in a shop in the village where Mrs Ralston was searching for a small gift to take home for Aunt Edith, but before she could make her selection she said hurriedly, 'I'll call back later if you don't mind, I've just remembered something I have to do in the post office.'

She almost ran out of the door and Gerald followed nonplussed. She was walking so quickly he had to lengthen his strides to keep up with her, but she did not turn in at the post office, instead she entered the tobacconists next door.

Gerald stared at her in astonishment because neither of them smoked, but he soon realised why she had come into the shop.

Lord Alveston was standing at the counter looking at briar pipes.

The tobacconist turned to speak to them but Mrs Ralston said hurriedly, 'No, please attend to your customer, we're in no hurry.'

Lord Alveston turned and smiled while Mrs Ralston wished him a good afternoon. Gerald stood back, mortified.

At any moment his mother would enter into conversation with him, she would bring Mary into the conservation, and he would die from embarrassment.

Lord Alveston selected the pipe he wished to purchase and while the man wrapped it for him Mrs Ralston said brightly, 'It's a beautiful day, isn't it?'

'Yes, indeed,' Andrew said.

'We were here over Easter, we had quite a bit of rain then, and mist.'

'Yes of course, one expects it at that time.'

'We're staying at The Lakes, such a beautiful place.'

Andrew smiled, and the tobacconist handed over his parcel. He read the signs well, Lord Alveston was often troubled by people who wanted to strike up a conversation with him.

'Good afternoon,' Andrew said courteously, and turned to leave the shop.

For a moment his mother seemed confused, then meeting Gerald's hostile eyes she snapped, 'I thought we'd take cigarettes for your uncle, or tobacco.'

'Hasn't he given up smoking, Mother?'

'Has he? I didn't know.'

'I'm sure he has.'

'Oh well then we'll have to think of something else. I'm sorry,' she said smiling at the tobacconist.

They walked back to the gift shop without speaking. Gerald was annoyed with his mother and she was annoyed with Lord Alveston. He should be pleased that visitors were coming to his village and enjoying themselves. It wouldn't have done him any harm to have stopped to chat, what airs they gave themselves. He'd quite obviously passed some of that lofty behaviour on to Mary Styles. Neither Gerald nor his mother referred to the episode again, and in any case there was something else for her to think about.

When they went down to dinner that evening Anton de Roche was standing at the reception desk with a woman and they appeared to be deep in conversation, so much so that he failed to give her his usual smiling good evening.

There was something vaguely familiar about the woman. She was tall and elegant without being ostentatious. Indeed her attire was more business-like than anything else, and now and again other members of the hotel staff went to speak with them.

Mrs Ralston was curious. All over dinner she was unusually silent and they were halfway through their dessert when she exclaimed, 'I know where I've seen her before, she was here over Easter with Mr Mansell, you know, the Member of Parliament. Wasn't everybody saying she was his secretary and that something was going on?'

Gerald allowed her to prattle on.

'I wonder if he's here, if he is it can't be a coincidence this time. Perhaps you can find out, Gerald.'

'I'm really not interested, Mother.'

His mother looked at him with the utmost exasperation.

'Really, Gerald,' she snapped, 'I don't know what's the matter with you these days, you're interested in nothing at all. It's only natural to be interested in well known people we meet on our travels, we see nobody of note at home. You don't seem to have any enthusiasm for anything.'

'Not for gossip, Mother.'

'It isn't gossip, Gerald. If she's here with Mr Mansell I was merely thinking I might see him at the bridge tables. If you remember that's where I met him at Easter.'

'If you speak to the woman you can't ask her who she is with,' he said stolidly.

'Well of course not, it would come out in the conversation.'

He looked at his mother sternly. 'Mother,' he said adamantly, 'if you ask any leading questions about the man she was with over Easter I promise you we will never come to this hotel again.'

She stared at him dumbfounded. It was not like Gerald to be so stern, normally he was either apathetic or disinterested. He was like his father, content to let her have her own way, taking the line of least resistance. She didn't quite know how to treat this new Gerald.

She was not to know how many times Gerald had blamed his father for the way she was. By giving her all her own way, agreeing with everything she said, idolising her, he had made her what she was. When his father was alive it hadn't mattered quite so much, but now that there was just the two of them it mattered too much.

With a sulky expression on her face she got to her feet saying, 'I don't want coffee, I'm going into the lounge, I feel very hurt by your attitude, Gerald.'

Gerald allowed her to go.

She crossed the foyer with her head held high, there was no sign of Alison Gray or Anton de Roche, but Gerald or no Gerald she'd find out.

Alison surveyed her suite of rooms with pleasure. There was a small bathroom off the bedroom, all decorated in shades of peach and pale green, and a sitting room where she had been able to place the small items of furniture she had brought with her. Her walnut desk and nest of tables. The two pictures she had always loved and several items of expensive glass and china. The room was tasteful without being cluttered.

Anton had introduced her to the staff who had appeared warm and friendly. Tomorrow she would spend with the woman she was replacing and she had been invited to dine with Anton de Roche and the owner of the hotel Mr Van Hopper. The invitation had come from Mr Van Hopper himself who had informed her that he was visiting The Lakes briefly before going on to Paris where he would join his wife. He had been friendly and welcoming, and she opened her wardrobe door to scan the clothes she had brought with her.

Most of them were business-like but she had elected to bring two cocktail dresses even when she hadn't been sure if she would ever need them. Tonight, she decided, she would wear the black which Stuart had liked most.

Along with her colleagues at Westminster, Stuart had given her a good send off. Her replacement was young, attractive and ambitious. She had had no hand in her choosing, nor had Maeve McNamara ever been a personal friend of hers although she had known her for several years. She had the reputation of being pushy and her colleagues at the Treasury had been quick to talk about her.

She had been engaged to a young man who worked at the Treasury but the engagement had come to an end several months ago and he had since married somebody else. Marriage, they told Alison, was not in her mind at the moment, she was more interested in furthering her career.

She had spent several afternoons with Alison to learn her future role, she had met Stuart briefly in the office, but Alison had not missed the speculative look in her blue eyes. She would be working for a man who was handsome, charming, and destined to become a Minister in the not too distant future. Stuart's career was rising, and Maeve had every expectation that hers would rise with him.

Alison had left Westminster with a stream of good wishes and several gifts from friends and colleagues she had known over the years, and with a set of expensive luggage from Stuart. As she covered her typewriter for the last time she had found a small parcel at the side of it, wrapped in gold foil and bearing a gift tab on which Stuart had written, 'Why did you have to go? Something to remember me by. Stuart.'

The parcel contained a brooch in the form of a spray of violets. The flowers were enamelled violet with small diamond centres, the stems and leaves were gold. It was beautiful and expensive, and she had sat and cried over it before impatiently stuffing it in her handbag and telling herself not to be such a fool.

She looked in the mirror. The dress showed off her slender figure and shapely legs, she was a beautiful woman, so why had she been such a sentimental idiot as to bring with her Stuart's Easter bunny? It sat among the cushions on her chair like some tantalising gnome, all pink fur and large coy eyes. With an angry shrug of her shoulders she snapped off the light and stalked out of the room.

Chapter Twenty-Eight

Geraldine Broadhurst stood at the kitchen window watching her daughter riding out from the stables behind the house. The horse was fresh, prancing a little, anxious to be off, and Debbie controlled him with gentle words.

She looked so beautiful in her elegant riding breeches and yellow sweater, her blonde hair covered by her black riding hat, but her mother hazarded a guess that there would be no smiles on that beautiful face.

The last few weeks had not been easy. Debbie was angry, with Tod, with the deal that life had dealt her, with the people she thought of as friends who seemed to have failed her so lamentably.

They left her alone. She was a skeleton at their feasts, a young widow with a chip on her shoulder, despising them for having their perfect memories of Tod, and she felt they blamed her for everything. She was aware of the things they were saying, particularly Janet Brewster and her cronies.

'He wouldn't have been climbing if he'd been on a honeymoon with me. They'd probably had a row and he'd gone off to cool down.' These were the sort of things they were saying, and in Debbie the anger festered and grew.

As she rode down the lane she passed the tennis club where Tod had been such a hero and she'd been welcomed because she was Tod's girl, now she never went there because on the one occasion she had gone silence had suddenly descended on a room alive with conversation minutes before. It was doubtful if the people there could accurately analyse their feelings towards Tod's widow, pity, resentment, hostility. She was the rich girl, the spoilt girl who had everything and had stolen Tod from amongst them and now he was dead. It couldn't have been worse if she'd murdered him, she thought.

Much against her will, her mother had persuaded her to go to the annual Rugger Ball which had been the highlight of Tod's life. She wore black, floating black chiffon that complimented her pale porcelain skin and blonde hair and she knew immediately that her arrival was an embarrassment to the rest of them.

If they felt sorry for her they didn't know how to express it. If they disliked her they showed it openly, if they envied her she was deeply aware of it. She felt she had no right to be there, Tod was dead and she should be keeping a low profile instead of expecting to mingle with his friends as if nothing had happened.

Danny Marsden asked her to dance, and she was immediately aware of his triumphant swagger and the baleful looks of his crowd. Danny had always been Tod's shadow, now he was in line to take over Tod's throne. That he should be dancing with Tod's widow was unacceptable to those people who blamed her for his death.

After the dance was over he grinned at her. 'Nice to see you here, Debbie, I'll be happy to escort you home when the ball's over.'

'Thank you, Danny, but I have my own transport,' she said coolly.

Later in the evening she heard him repeating her answer in posh accents that met with derisive laughter.

She did not wait for the supper dance, she decided to go home.

Her parents looked at her in amazement and then at the clock. It was just eleven and Geraldine said anxiously, 'Why ever have you come home so early, Debbie, haven't you enjoyed yourself?'

'No, Mother, it was terrible. I shall never go to another affair in this town as long as I live.'

'But why, darling?'

'Because I'm not one of them, I never was, and now I've simply got to get on with my life and forget about them.'

'It won't be easy, darling. They were Tod's friends, they ought to be yours.'

'Well they're not. If Tod had married Janet Brewster they'd have gone on their honeymoon to Spain and they'd both have been at the ball tonight surrounded by their crowd. He married me, and nothing turned out the way they expected it to turn out.'

'We don't want you to get bitter about it, love,' her father said anxiously. 'If they can be so unkind to you at this particular time they're not worth bothering about, you don't have to be part of Tod's crowd.'

'I know, Daddy.'

'We'll get off on a cruise, darling,' her mother said stoutly. 'Somewhere nice, the Caribbean, the Far East perhaps. Leave it to your father, we can get away pretty soon, can't we?'

'Not for a while, I'm afraid. There's nothing to stop you and Debbie going off though. I have business interests that will keep me here until the autumn.'

Geraldine pouted, and Debbie cried, 'I don't want a cruise, Mummy, at least not yet. We could go back to the Lake District, just for a few days I mean.'

Her parents looked at her in amazement, and Geraldine said, 'Don't you think that's a bit morbid, darling, you'll have Tod on your mind all the time and what are people going to say?'

'I don't care what people say. I'd like to go back to The Lakes, and it has nothing to do with Tod. Didn't somebody once say we should face our problems not run away from them? I'm going to get out of this dress, Mummy, then I'll make coffee for us.'

Geraldine looked across the hearth at her husband after Debbie had left the room. His newspaper was spread out across his knees but he was not reading, he was staring at the print, his expression as puzzled as her thoughts.

'Surely she can't mean she wants to go back there,' Geraldine said sharply. 'I'd never want to see the place again, it'll bring it all back to her, all that waiting around for Tod to come back, the police, the utter misery of people talking in whispers, having to identify his body. I've never heard of anything so morbid.'

'She could change her mind,' John said hopefully.

'What would the Hanleys be thinking if they knew where she's gone? She has no friends in the town now, she'd have even less if she goes back there. It's like flaunting her tragedy, you must talk to her, John, tell her it's impossible.'

'She'll probably change her mind. Think about the cruise instead.' Geraldine's thoughts were always on cruising, no sooner was she back than she was thinking of the next one, it was her answer to everything but he doubted if it was Debbie's forte. Debbie was more like him. She liked riding her horse across the fells and long country walks. She liked fishing in quiet lakes and sailing in small boats.

His wife's face was pensive and he knew her thoughts were on those disastrous few days when they'd seen the ending of their daughter's girlhood and the sudden propulsion into adult life.

Of course, Geraldine thought suddenly, there was Peter Cavendish. They'd gone around together before she'd really met Tod, and they'd seemed very happy together. He'd been there for her at Easter when her life suddenly went haywire. He liked The Lakes, they could meet up again in happier circumstances and when Debbie was no longer attached to anybody. Peter was all she wanted in a son-in-law, rich, handsome, an established career, that would be the answer to everything and one that would get Debbie away from the people around them.

What did it matter if the Hanleys were affronted, they'd never actually been enthusiastic about Debbie and Tod being together, and they couldn't expect the girl to retreat from life forever.

A little smile played around her lips but John couldn't for the life in him think what had put it there. Nothing in their lives at the moment was worth smiling about.

Debbie surveyed her wardrobe. It was filled with clothes destined for a life with Tod. Ball gowns and cocktail dresses, sun frocks and tennis shorts, clothes for the sun and for the winter snows, and she sat down heavily on the side of her bed and contemplated the empty space that was her life.

She didn't want to feel this consuming hatred for Tod, measured by the depth of love she had felt for him. She couldn't believe how close the two emotions could be. Most people remembered Tod with joy, they mourned him and missed him, but there were so many conflicting emotions buzzing around in Debbie's head that she could only view her future as a bleak and barren waste.

She had given up her job, Tod had insisted on it, now there was nothing for her apart from her horse and she rode alone. At her mother's coffee mornings and bridge parties she was aware of the unspoken sympathy of her mother's friends, or their veiled criticism.

Sybil Mansell had been kind but Debbie could never speak to her without remembering Alison Gray. Her mother probed and questioned her about her presence at The Lakes on that fateful Easter weekend, and invariably Debbie was reticent. She was bored with her mother's questions in the name of her friendship for Sybil, sometimes she felt that her mother would like there to have been an affair, something tangible for her to get her teeth in, something she could titivate up with insinuations.

She made the coffee and took it into the drawing room where her parents suddenly ceased their conversation so that Debbie could only assume they had been discussing her.

She handed the coffee round and her mother said brightly, 'Your father and I have been wondering why you don't spend a week or two with Aunt Muriel in Dorset, the weather forecast is excellent and she'll be very glad to have you.'

'I don't think so, Mummy, I wouldn't be very good company at the moment.'

Her parents looked at one another and decided to drop the subject.

There was a long unnatural silence before Geraldine decided to try again. Unfortunately she chose the wrong subject.

'Have you decided when you're going to see Tod's parents, Debbie? I heard that they were going away for a few weeks.'

'Yes they're going to Majorca.'

'So you called to see them?'

'No. I heard Janet Brewster telling somebody earlier this evening.'

Janet had informed the somebody in a loud voice so that Debbie would hear her. It was her way of saying that she was aware of the Hanleys' movements because she was a constant visitor to their home. Debbie had been several times since Tod's death but not recently. Mrs Hanley was the problem.

She showed Debbie photographs and took her into Tod's bedroom where pictures of his achievements lined the walls. Tod in the centre of an admiring crowd at the Rugger Club. Holding aloft the club's trophy at the Tennis Club, standing at the wicket on the cricket field, his smile triumphant and with every appearance of defeating whatever the bowler threw at him.

Mrs Hanley would chatter on with the tears streaming down her face, and with her tears was the condemnation that Tod might still be alive if he'd gone anywhere but The Lakes for their honeymoon.

Debbie had come away with the utmost conviction that she would never go there again, but in her innermost heart she felt it was her duty. She had been Tod's wife nursing a resentment that had killed love, his mother would love him as long as she lived.

Geraldine looked at her daughter doubtfully, and Debbie said shortly, 'The Brewsters are going with them, and please, Mother, don't look like that, it really doesn't matter, they were friends of the Hanleys before I ever met Tod.'

Geraldine bit her lip and remained silent.

Her father thought it was time to talk of something else and Debbie sat back in her chair listening to them.

'What did Sybil Mansell want when she phoned you this morning?'

'She's decided to go up to London for a few days, she was wondering if I'd like to go with her.'

'Why don't you?'

'Well I don't really want to stay at Stuart's flat where Sybil is staying. I'd much rather stay in some hotel.'

'Well she'll be on her own during the day, you'd be company for each other. I think you might find it very interesting to visit Westminster in the company of an M.P.'s wife, tea on the terrace, the Strangers' gallery. Most people would be keen to take advantage of such a holiday.'

'I don't know. I'm glad Sybil's going, she's not gone to London nearly enough, it would be surprising if he hadn't fooled around.'

'You don't know that he has?'

'Oh I'm pretty sure. Taking that girl to The Lakes over Easter was never to do some work. Sybil was with her parents and leaving him on his own, he wouldn't be the first man to take advantage of it. She was a very attractive girl, and she'd probably known him for years.'

'That hasn't stopped her leaving him for pastures new,' John said shrewdly.

'Well she could have got fed up of hanging on to a man who quite evidently had no wish to leave his wife. Think of the scandal, John, and heaven knows there's been plenty of it. Stuart Mansell's a political animal, his career would always come first.'

'That's a very cynical way of looking at things.'

'It is also a very accurate way of looking at things. You liked her, didn't you, Debbie?'

'I really didn't know Alison very well, Mummy. I thought she was nice, she didn't talk about her job or Mr Mansell.'

'Well she wouldn't, would she?'

'They didn't spend much time together, they didn't always sit down to meals together.'

'I would have expected them to be discreet.'

Debbie was wishing her mother would change the subject, ever since that weekend she had never let the matter drop and it was none of her business what Stuart Mansell chose to do with his time.

Mr Mansell had been kind and Mrs Mansell was very nice, she had been at parties with the Mansell children whom she'd liked, but Alison Gray had become an obession with her mother and remembering that morning she'd spent on the fell with Alison aroused in her some form of loyalty.

Alison had been as troubled as herself. In Alison's beautiful green eyes she had sensed a deep misery even when her conversation had been light-hearted and natural.

'Why don't you come to London with me for a few days, Debbie?' her mother was saying. 'We could stay at the Dorchester, go to shows, do some shopping, that way Mr and Mrs Mansell can be together in the evenings without having to think of entertaining us.'

'Oh I don't know, Mummy.'

'Yes, why don't you?' her father urged.

'Well there's Dancer for one thing. He needs exercising and . . .'

'And nothing,' her father said firmly. 'Why do you think we pay a groom? Dancer'll be well taken care of and the change would do you good, lift your spirits, later we'll think about a longer holiday, a cruise or something.'

She smiled across at him. Her parents were very good to her. Jokingly, Tod had often said she was a spoilt brat with too much money, but he'd liked her to be a rich girl. Her father's affluence had brushed off on Tod.

His father had made money, his mother had never climbed up with him, but Debbie was the sort of girl he liked to be seen with, the sort of girl entirely necessary in his assured future.

Geraldine was looking at her expectantly, and with a smile Debbie said, 'Okay Mother, I'll come. Just for a few days.'

'I'll telephone Sybil in the morning and tell her. We'll have a lovely time, darling and you can stop worrying about Tod's friends. They're quite unimportant, you can rise above them.'

Debbie collected the coffee cups saying, 'I'll get rid of these, Mummy then I'll go to bed.'

She kissed both her parents dutifully and wished them goodnight, then after she'd washed the coffee cups she went up to her room. She pulled back the long drapes from the windows and looked out across the sweep of gardens towards the gates. A full moon shone over the countryside silvering the trees and the roof-tops in the street that wound downhill towards the town.

They would still be dancing in the Town Hall where the Rugger Ball was always held. The last time she had been there Tod had led the dancers in a Conga down the wide ceremonial staircase and up again to the ballroom. She'd worn a white taffeta gown with pink roses at the waist and in her hair, Tod had told her she was beautiful and she'd proudly worn his engagement ring.

They'd all drunk too much, laughed too loudly and the boys had sung their ribald rugger songs while the girls had screamed with merriment.

To Debbie sitting in the window seat staring out into the night it had all happened in another life, in another age, to a different girl, a girl who was in love and light-hearted, a girl who had never known misery and abandonment, not this new Debbie who could feel anger and hatred and so much despair.

It couldn't go on of course. One day she had to face the future and pick up the pieces, live her life, find some degree of forgiveness. It was too soon, but one day she would stop hurting, face the people who had rejected her earlier that night, remember Tod as she had known him and loved him, accept the tragedy that would help her to grow.

Her thoughts turned to Alison Gray. Alison would be living at The Lakes now, settling in to her new job, miles away from Stuart Mansell, and some sudden instinct made her want to telephone her to wish her luck.

She stared at the telephone on her bedside table doubtfully. It was late, but not too late for The Lakes. Perhaps Alison would be in her room, or if she was in the hotel rooms they would tell her there was a telephone call for her, and Debbie hurried to look in the drawer where the hotel telephone number had been entered in her diary.

A man's voice answered the telephone and she could dimly hear music, imagine what the hotel foyer looked like, speculate if it would be crowded with people in evening dress standing around in groups chatting, and always she had been aware of the perfume of carnations from the vast bowls of them in the foyer.

She asked to speak to Miss Alison Gray and the man's voice said pleasantly, 'I'll telephone her room, who shall I say is calling?'

'Mrs Tod Hanley.'

'Just a moment please.'

She could hear the bleeping of the extension line and then Alison's voice saying 'Hello, Alison Gray speaking,' and Debbie cried, 'Alison, it's Debbie Hanley. I'm sorry to call so late but I just want to wish you well in your new job.'

'Debbie, how terribly kind of you. How did you know I was coming to work here?'

'The Mansells told us. Is it very different?'

'Well yes it is, but I'm getting to know things. It's very interesting, everybody's been very kind and I'm sure I'm going to love it. How are things with you, Debbie?'

'Oh they're all right. I'm going up to London for a few days with Mother, we're staying at the Dorchester and going to some shows.'

'That will be nice.'

'Have you missed London very much?'

'Well yes, but I haven't had much time to think about it, there's so much to learn. I'm beginning to recognise the villagers, and the shop-keepers are getting to know me. I love the area, it's so very beautiful, whether I shall enjoy it in the winter is anybody's guess.'

'You will, I'm sure of it. One day I'm going back there, I loved it too.'

'Do you think that would be wise, Debbie, wouldn't it hurt too much?'

'I'd remember things of course, but I can't run away forever, can I?'

Alison admitted that she couldn't, and it was only when she put the receiver down that she thought, no, one couldn't run away. One day Stuart Mansell and his wife would visit The Lakes and she would see him. She'd run away once, she couldn't run away again. Hopefully the next time she looked into Stuart's eyes the past wouldn't matter, there would be nothing left.

Chapter Twenty-Nine

Mary's heart sank as she saw Gerald and his mother come into the library on Friday afternoon promptly at five o'clock and although she responded to their smiles she was determined that it was her assistant who would attend to them. Consequently she was relieved to hear the telephone shrilling from inside her office.

She hurried to answer it, surprised to hear Mrs Scotson's urgent tones at the other end.

'I'm that glad I've caught you in time, Miss Styles, but it's your mother, she's taken a turn for the worse and they want you at the hospital as quickly as possible.'

'But she was so well when I saw her at lunchtime,' Mary cried.

'Well she's had another stroke, it doesn't sound so good. I should get off there, Miss Styles, I'll stay on here as long as I can.'

'No you get off home, Mrs Scotson, there's nothing you can do.'

She grabbed her coat and rushed off through the library with a whispered word to one of the girls that she'd been called to the hospital while Gerald and his mother gazed after her in dismay.

At lunchtime she'd taken her mother a basket of her favourite fruit and a bunch of flowers, and her mother had chatted to her more animatedly than she could remember. She'd discussed the nurses, the doctors and the comings and goings in the large ward where she'd been recuperating, now when Mary arrived at the hospital she found they'd taken her back to the small ward and she'd been told to wait outside until the sister could see her.

She had not been there long when her sister and her husband arrived, and Millicent's face was streaked with tears as she cried, 'I thought you said she was much better when you came in earlier.'

'I thought she was, I was so pleased to see her like that.'

'What's happened then?'

'I don't know, they'll tell us I'm sure.'

Minutes later the doctor came in the room to tell them that their mother had suffered another massive stroke from which she would not recover and they were allowed in to see her.

Mary stared at her mother's still form on the narrow bed thinking that this was not the woman she had chatted to earlier in the day and Millicent sobbed copiously. They were still with her when she died an hour later and as they left the hospital together Eric said, 'I'll make all the arrangements for the funeral, the solicitor is a personal friend of mine, I suggest we invite him up to the house to sort things out.'

Mary didn't answer. It did not seem an appropriate time to think about sorting things out.

She was glad to find that Mrs Scotson was still at the house, making a cup of tea and offering to help in any way she could. Mary was glad of her solid motherly advice.

'When this is all over,' she said stoutly, 'you want to get away on a few weeks' holiday. We can sort the house out together.'

'Sort the house out,' Mary said vaguely.

'Yes. Get rid of your mother's things, her clothes and some of her furniture. You'll be on your own and you've got to get rid of old memories.'

'There are things Millicent will want. Some of Mother's jewellery but she'll have no room for her furniture, she never much liked it anyway.'

'She'll want none of that, and don't you be parting with all your mother's jewellery to her, it's you who's looked after your mother all these years, you should have first choice.'

'We'll see, Mrs Scotson, it's too soon to be thinking of that.'

Mrs Scotson sniffed. 'It's my bet your sister's thought about it,' she snapped.

It was Friday afternoon a week later and they were sitting in the living room waiting for the solicitor to arrive. Mrs Scotson was in the kitchen preparing tea and Mary joined her to escape from the atmosphere where Millicent sat tearful and Eric stared straight ahead without speaking.

When the doorbell rang minutes later Mrs Scotson went to answer it, coming back to the kitchen with her eyes popping with excitement.

'The solicitor's here and it's that man I saw leaving the house the afternoon they sent me out shopping.'

'Are you sure, Mrs Scotson? Why would he be here then?'

'I don't know, but it's him all right. I'd recognise him anywhere. What time will you be wanting tea?'

'I'll let you know, Mrs Scotson. I can't think it will take all that long.'

The solicitor had made himself comfortable in her mother's easy chair. He had opened his briefcase and spread his documents on top of the table her mother had used for her newspapers and magazines. Millicent and Eric sat opposite, so Mary took the easy chair in the window.

They introduced her to the solicitor who smiled toothily saying, 'I suggest we start right away, I have another appointment at four o'clock so if we get on now I can get away.'

'I hope you'll have tea,' Millicent said.

'Well just a cup would be nice. Friday is a busy day for me.'

When Mary went into the kitchen an hour later to tell Mrs Scotson she could serve tea she sat down weakly at the kitchen table, her face a picture of disbelief and Mrs Scotson said sharply, 'You look as if you could do with a glass of whisky instead of a cup of tea. I'll serve them, then I'll come back to look after you.'

Pulling herself together Mary said, 'I'm all right, Mrs Scotson, really, I just need a few minutes to sort myself out.'

She remembered very little about the rest of the afternoon. The solicitor shook hands all round and departed. Millicent said they'd be in touch in a few days' time, and they too left, then she sat staring through the window but she saw nothing of the garden and the road outside, she was concerned with her life and how in the immediate future it was going to change.

The bulk of her mother's money had been left to Millicent and Eric and their children. She had also left them the house so it would have to be sold. Her mother had said that Mary had no dependants, had a good job which would enable her to live comfortably and she had left her five thousand pounds which would go some way to buying a smaller house more adequate for a daughter living alone.

Much of her mother's money had already been donated to Millicent and Eric to enable them to purchase the house in Merton Road where they were providing a granny flat for the use of Mrs Styles.

Mary had sat in stunned silence and neither Millicent nor her husband had looked at her.

Mrs Scotson was loud in her condemnation.

'I told you somethin' was afoot, I could smell it. After Easter your sister was never away and then her husband was coming too. That afternoon they sent me out was so they could make the old lady agree to whatever they wanted. Granny flat indeed! The builders haven't even started on it yet and now they'll have no need to. You've been away once in all the years I've been comin' here and they had to seize on it to get their hands on her money. There's going to be talk, you know, they're not popular round here now, they'll be even less popular when the For Sale signs go up here.'

Mary wished she would shut up, she wanted to be alone, and in some desperation she said, 'Leave the dishes, Mrs Scotson, I'll do them, it will find me something to do. You get off home.'

'But I'm ready to stay, Miss Styles, I told my husband I might be late.'

'No, please, Mrs Scotson, I'd like to be alone just now, I have a lot to think about, I'll see you on Monday morning before I go to work.'

'You're going back so soon?'

'Yes of course, there's nothing else to do.'

She watched Mrs Scotson depart from the front door. It had started to rain, light summer rain that swept across the lawn and clung daintily to the bushes. She watched Mrs Scotson walking briskly along the road, indignation evident in every step, and with her straw hat pulled firmly down over her hair.

She was going to have to move, start looking for a smaller house and her days with Mrs Scotson were probably numbered. She would not want to move away from the area, and a smaller residence might not even need her.

Wearily she returned to the kitchen and started to wash the teacups. Her mind went back to the days before Easter when she'd been happy, looking forward to lunching with Gerald, daring perhaps to think that somewhere somehow there might be something for them, and then the painful let-down when they met at The Lakes.

That was the moment she thought about Andrew, a few wonderful days which seemed like an oasis in the desert that was her life. She would never go back to The Lakes of course, he would not expect it, and she could not encroach on those few brief days and expect them to recur unchanged.

She squared her shoulders. There were worse catastrophes than hers. Her mother had been old and with little quality of life, not like Debbie Hanley's husband who had been full of life and vigour. That had been a far more harrowing tragedy than the one which was happening to her, and what about Alison Gray? She had been desperately in love with the man she was with and he had had a wife. All she had had with Gerald were hopes and illusions, and all he had was his mother and Mary hadn't liked her.

On Monday she returned to her job and the endless visits to estate agents and looking at various properties. Millicent and Eric were quick to extricate themselves from any coercion in an attempt to persuade her mother how she should leave her money, and Dolly Lampeter had a great many snide remarks about them when she met her in the High Street.

Several weeks later Gerald and his mother came into the library on Friday afternoon and Mary could not escape them. One of her assistants was on holiday and the library was busy. Gerald took his books to her assistant, Mrs Ralston headed for Mary.

'We heard about your mother, Miss Styles,' was her opening gambit. 'One of your assistants told us when I asked if you were away. I'm so used to your saving the right sort of books for me.'

Mary smiled.

'Was your mother's death very sudden then?'

'She had a stroke. We thought she was getting better until she had another fatal one.'

'I am sorry, but now, my dear, you must go out more, take some nice holidays, be with people. Gerald and I were at The Lakes a few weeks ago, as always we enjoyed it. Lord Alveston didn't come to the hotel at all but we saw him riding across the fells, I'm sure he'll be looking forward to your visiting very soon.'

By this time Gerald had joined them and looking straight into his eyes Mary surprised an acute misery there.

'I have no plans to visit The Lakes in the immediate future,' Mary said evenly.

'Oh but you should, my dear. The best way to get over a personal grief is to get out and about. Meet up with old friends, visit places you are fond of.'

Mary smiled, and Gerald said quickly, 'I think we should be going, Mother, the car is on a parking meter.'

'Nobody much bothers at this time, Gerald.'

'They bother at all times, Mother,' and to suit his actions with his words he turned and walked towards the door. His mother smiled, 'Gerald is so impatient about his wretched car. Goodnight, my dear, and do think about what I've said, I hope we'll see you very soon at The Lakes.'

Gerald drove home in grim silence but his mother seemed oblivious as she prattled on. 'She'll be up there as soon as possible, just mark my words. I saw her interest when I told her we'd seen his lordship on the fells and now she doesn't have her mother to worry about.'

Mary's thoughts were a long way from The Lakes and Lord Alveston. Her brother-in-law had acted swiftly in advertising the house and people were coming to view. He was suggesting properties she might be interested in, small semi-detached houses nearer to the town, flats in newly erected blocks on derelict sites and Mary found the flats without character of any kind and where she would have to part with furniture that was too big, too out of character, and the semis were not much better.

When she explained about her furniture Eric had been quick to say, 'Well we're moving into a larger house we'll take the furniture off your hands. We'll buy it of course, and give you a fair price for it.'

Mary had been too upset to say that Millicent had already chosen what she wanted from the furniture in their mother's house.

Mrs Scotson was scathing in her criticism and Mary had little doubt that her criticism was continued wherever she shopped.

Millicent and Eric were becoming impatient. They wanted the money. At the beginning of September the house was sold to a local government officer and his teacher wife. They had two children at the local school and were anxious to move in quickly. Mary bought a flat in the town that she hated. It was a first floor flat and she missed her garden. She bought furniture suitable for the size of the rooms, but the furniture was modern and lacked character. She did the best she could with pictures and odd items of porcelain but she found no joy in returning to it in the evening and was happy to part with it in the morning.

Mrs Scotson helped her to settle in. Her expression said it all.

'I'll get used to it, I suppose,' Mary said hopefully. 'The rooms seem so terribly small and the views from the windows are depressing.'

'Why don't you come and eat with us on Sundays?' Mrs Scotson asked. 'I don't like to think of you sitting here all on your own, it won't be so bad during the week when you have the library to go to, but the weekends will be awful.'

'I have to get used to it, Mrs Scotson, but thank you for being so kind. What are you going to do now that you're not coming to me?'

'My husband says I'm to do nothing in a hurry. I've been offered two days a week at the doctor's surgery and Mr Reeves has said he can find me work in the Mayor's Parlour. That might be interesting.'

Mr Reeves was the buyer of Mary's old house and Mrs Scotson was a mine of information about them.

'They couldn't understand why your sister's husband was doing all the negotiating,' she told Mary. 'I told him a thing or two and he thought it was dreadful. Everybody does.'

'It's how Mother wanted it, Mrs Scotson.'

'She was pushed into it. I knew all along there was something afoot and you were oblivious, you couldn't see it.'

'I know. It's over now, Mrs Scotson, we should forget it.'

It was something she found very hard to do. She felt betrayed by her mother, by her sister and in the evenings when she sat alone in her still unfamiliar room she thought about Gerald.

She had met him in the post office in the town and hoped to avoid him, he had smiled and waited for her in the doorway.

'I was sorry about your mother,' he began. 'It takes time to get over a bereavement.'

'Yes it does.'

'Are you staying in the house alone?'

'I've moved. I've bought one of the flats in the town. I can't say I like it, but it's a new start, I'll get used to it.'

'Please don't take exception to anything my mother says about meeting you at The Lakes. She hasn't enough to do with her time and she gets ideas about things and people that are totally wrong.'

Mary smiled, and Gerald went on, 'Are you walking back to the library?'

'No, I have more shopping to do.'

They parted with polite smiles.

All the way back to the bank Gerald was wishing he could turn the clock back, meet Mary for lunch again. They had got along well, found things to laugh and talk about, why had he been so impetuous, so anxious to distance himself from something they were both feeling.

He'd known their friendship was hopeless of course. It was going

236

nowhere, and yet if he hadn't been such a fool they could have gone on seeing each other, being friends.

It wouldn't have worked. Her mother was dead, she'd have been looking for a commitment, something more and he wouldn't have been able to give her one.

Suppose she accepted his mother's invitation to visit them, his mother would like her, see that she was intelligent and charming, suppose their friendship was allowed to grow, but then he pulled himself up sharply, his mother would only tolerate Mary if she thought she was interested in somebody else, any indication that they were interested in each other would be rejected.

Mary's own thoughts were running on similar lines. She must not let herself drift back into meetings with Gerald. For those few days at Easter she had thought she hated him, now she felt sorry for him, sorry for his lifestyle and that he hadn't had the courage to put an end to it years before.

She was so immersed in her thoughts that she did not see her sister until she stopped in front of her.

'Really,' Millicent said sharply. 'You were walking in a dream, I've been waving to you from across the street. Are you settled in yet?'

'Yes thank you. It didn't take long.'

'We'll call round one night to see you. They look awfully small from the outside.'

'They are small.'

'Good job you got rid of the furniture.'

'I suppose so.'

'Jayne's buying a flat with another girl she was at university with, she'll be glad of some of the furniture. She's got a job teaching at a school in Birmingham.'

'How nice.'

'Yes well, we've seen the flats, they look a lot larger than the one you've bought so the furniture will be fine. Of course we didn't go on with the granny flat, we've had a large conservatory and a study for Eric in its place. When are you coming around to see it?'

'Well I have been rather busy.'

'Well you know you can come round anytime. I'm sure you'll like the house, we got the best decorator in town and it really is very tasteful. Dolly Lampeter was green with envy when she looked around, of course quite a lot of people were surprised when we bought it.'

Mary consulted her watch.

'I must go, Millicent, I don't want to be late back.'

'I hear Mrs Scotson's doing some work in the Mayor's Parlour, that'll give her something to talk about.'

'She was always very kind, Millicent, to me and to Mother. I'm glad she's found something.'

'I was going to ask her to work for me two mornings, it would have been a way of keeping her in the family, but she probably won't want to take anything else on.'

'No I'm sure she won't. She is working at the doctor's surgery two afternoons, I believe.'

'Really? Do give us a ring when you're thinking of coming round. We do go out quite a lot, to the golf club and Eric's busy with his Masonic duties.'

Mary smiled without making any promises. She didn't want to go to her sister's house. Why couldn't Millicent have given her a formal invitation? She knew that Mary was free most nights and weekends, why had she suggested a telephone call to see when it was convenient?

Their meeting left a bitter taste in her mouth. Her sister didn't really care where she went, what she did or with whom. Their meeting had emphasised her loneliness, and the tears were not far from falling when she paused in front of a shop window to surreptitiously wipe her eyes.

It was the window of the travel agency. A window filled with holiday brochures of exotic places, places that only weeks before had seemed remote, now they were within her reach. Suddenly her heart lightened, and turning round she stepped out blithely in the direction of the library.

Chapter Thirty

Lord Alveston was giving a dinner party, the first since his return to England. Around the table sat friends of long standing and the table groaned under its cut-glass and silver.

Andrew sat at the head of the table and Grant had been careful to position Lady Carmel at the other end, a lady guaranteed to keep the conversation flowing, she was both witty and amusing. Grant relaxed. They were at the coffee stage and an evening he had dreaded had passed off relatively smoothly.

They had tried too hard. Andrew's smile had not always reached his eyes, and they had all been too careful to talk only of the present and the future, never the past.

Even so they must all have remembered that other evening when Olivia had sat where Lady Carmel was sitting now. Olivia in white chiffon, faintly bored, her green slanting eyes assessing her guests with cynical amusement. They had been Andrew's guests, hers would arrive later, and on that evening too there had been an air of apprehension.

Soon they would wander into the other rooms to sit or stand in groups, and no doubt they would all heave a sigh of relief that normality had reigned at the dinner table.

Lady Carmel was discussing The Lakes.

'Why don't we all go for dinner one evening? I feel like dancing. Oh, I know you don't care for it, Anthony, but it would be fun. I hear you dined there over Easter, Andrew.'

'Yes, on Easter Saturday.'

'Did you enjoy it?'

'Yes, I was agreeably surprised. I couldn't think of some hotel standing on that spot and I was prepared to hate it. I didn't.'

'I wonder who the girl is I've seen riding with Anton de Roche? She's very beautiful, and Anton is such a dark horse, we know so little about him.'

'And because you all know so little about him you're intrigued by him,' her husband said smiling.

'Well you have to admit he's very attractive with those cool saturnine looks. I wonder who the girl is?'

'I can tell you who she is,' said a man sitting further down the table. 'She's his new secretary.'

'Really, he doesn't usually ride with his secretary. He's usually very circumspect.'

'Well, this secretary is making her mark. She's from London, worked as secretary to an M.P. This is a big change for her.'

'Of course,' said Lady Carmel. 'She worked for Stuart Mansell, he's just been made a Minister. Could be she's not made such a good move after all.'

'Oh, I don't know,' said her husband. 'Mansell's a married man, Anton de Roche, I believe, is single.'

Andrew was not interested, and rising from his chair he said, 'I suggest we move into the drawing room, you'll find it more comfortable in there.'

Grant stayed a while to see the staff clear the dining table before going to the kitchen, and there Mrs Stokes said, 'Well, how did it go? Has the ice been broken?'

'Oh yes I think so. Of course it's not been easy, everybody watched the conversation, and they all tried too hard.'

'It'll never be the same until he marries again,' Mrs Stokes said firmly. 'Finding somebody to sit in her place because it's impossible to leave the chair empty, seeing him alone, remembering that awful night.'

'It's early days yet, Mrs Stokes. Things will slowly get back to normal.'

'At least he's made an effort, I wonder what the next step will be?'

'Well, Lady Carmel's suggested dinner at The Lakes and dancing.'

'Not his scene, at least not without a partner.'

Soon after midnight Andrew stood outside the house watching the last car disappearing down the drive. There had been laughter and camaraderie and now he was alone. His guests had assured him that they'd enjoyed the evening, just like old times, but Andrew was not fooling himself.

They were his friends, they would pick up the pieces and he'd play his part, but it could never be like old times, there had to be a new beginning with nothing left of the old days to torment him and bring it all back.

He went back into the drawing room where Grant and one of his assistants were removing glasses and putting the room to rights. The younger man left and Grant asked quietly, 'Will there be anything else, sir?'

'Nothing, thank you, Grant. Please thank the staff for their co-operation, the evening went very well, I think.'

'Yes, sir, very well indeed.'

Neither of them believed it. Grant closed the door quietly and Andrew went to sit in front of the dying fire. It was a cool night at the end of September and as he stared reflectively into the dying embers his mind was going over the conversation at the dinner table.

240

They had said it had been like old times, and yet none of them had felt able to talk about the old times, instead they had talked trivialities, and sudden lulls in the conversation had been hurriedly glossed over in their anxiety to find something new.

In the days to come they would discuss it amongst themselves and then would come the invitations now that he had made the first move. Invitations to play golf and join the hunt, invitations to dinner and concerts, an evening at The Lakes perhaps. Daphne Carmel had suggested it and the next thing was that they would find some woman to make up the party, somebody they thought he would like, some woman who was available. His heart sank at the prospect, and inevitably he thought about Mary.

The few days he had spent with Mary were the happiest he had known for many years. Mary had known nothing of Olivia and even when he had told her about the past nothing had changed. Mary had not known Olivia, she had no memory of the trauma of that last night, unlike his friends who remembered it.

Perhaps Mary would return to The Lakes and they would meet up with each other again, but would things be the same?

They lived different lives. No doubt she had friends where she lived. Perhaps the man who had hurt her would be around apologising for what he had said to her, perhaps like himself she would look back on those few days over Easter and see them for what they were, a charming interlude but nothing more.

He felt restless. Jason the labrador got up from the rug in front of the fire and came to sit besides him, putting his black head on Andrew's knee and looking up at him out of his brown questioning eyes.

'You remember too, don't you, old boy?' Andrew said gently, and the labrador flapped his tail in answer.

That morning they'd walked in the park and Jason had taken the path that led down to the lake. Andrew had called him back but the dog looked back expectantly and carried on so that Andrew had to follow him against all his better judgement.

The dog was sitting outside the boathouse looking across the lake and that New Year's morning came back vividly and instead of seeing the peaceful lake and the stream of wildfowl he was seeing the police cars on the hillside and the stream of policemen standing on the path watching a group of men standing round the still white form of Olivia lying on the grass.

In that last fragment of time it seemed her face was fixed on the retina of his eyes. He transferred it to his mind for eternity.

The old dog had looked up at him making soft plaintive yelps in his throat then Andrew called to him and they walked back through the woodland.

*　*　*

241

When Daphne Carmel had an idea she was not one to let the grass grow under her feet. She loved dancing, and her idea to have dinner at The Lakes and dance later did not go away.

It was several mornings after she had dined at Alveston that she rode into the stables where Andrew was about to mount his horse.

'What an opportue moment to arrive,' she greeted him. 'It was such a lovely morning I decided to ride over to see if you'd ride over to the Stricklands with me.'

Andrew smiled. 'I don't intend to be out very long, Daphne, perhaps some other time.'

'Then we'll ride across the fell in the direction of Thirlmere. I've had an idea but I wanted to ask you before I did anything concrete.'

'And this wonderful idea?' Andrew prompted.

'Well the other evening we talked about dinner and dancing at The Lakes, I thought it was a wonderful idea, I've sounded out the others and they all agree with me.'

'But not for me, Daphne, you're all in pairs. The ladies would feel they had to dance with me and one of the men would be left out.'

'Not a bit of it. I thought I'd ask Stephanie Crawley to make up the party. Stephanie's been so miserable since George died, she hardly ever sets foot outside the house except to visit her mother and go to church, George would have hated it for her, and you know her as well as I do. You're two people in the same boat . . .'

Andrew was looking at her thoughtfully.

'You needn't look at me like that, Andrew, I'm not matchmaking, neither of you is looking for anybody. Stephanie was totally wrapped up in George, and in any case it's too soon, and I know you're not on the market.'

'Have you actually mentioned it to Stephanie?'

'Not in so many words, but I can be very persuasive. I thought perhaps a week on Friday, Andrew.'

'My dancing's a little bit rusty, Daphne.'

'Well of course it isn't. Weren't you at The Lakes over Easter, and dancing with Stella Brampton?'

He stared at her curiously. 'May I ask who told you that story?' he asked stiffly.

'Well, you know what it's like. You're hardly a nonentity in the district, Andrew. We all had bets you wouldn't be seen dead at The Lakes and then we heard you'd gone for dinner on Easter Saturday and were seen dancing with Stella. I knew she was visiting although I didn't actually meet her. She never called to see us.'

Andrew did not enlighten her that he had not danced with Stella, Mary had resembled Stella and he had no wish to tell his companion anything to the contrary.

Her voice was faintly petulant as she said, 'I'm doing this for you, Andrew, and for Steph, too. It would be a wonderful evening, and you have to get back in the swing of things. You were away too long.'

'A week on Friday did you say?'

'Yes. We'll call round for you.'

'There's no need, will you be wanting me to pick Stephanie up?'

'Well that would be nice, darling, and remember, none of us are pushing you into anything, we just think you should both pick up the pieces and rejoin the land of the living.'

That evening he tried to remember what he knew about Stephanie Crawley. He'd known her husband better. They'd played golf together and he'd seemed a nice quiet sort of chap. Stephanie was not a beauty, but she'd seemed like a nice woman, sensible, intelligent. One evening wouldn't do any harm, but he was not looking forward to it.

Somehow or other he had to stop Daphne making arrangements for him. He was prepared to be sociable, to keep friends with them, but he did not want to spend one evening in their company and have them making arrangements for the next one.

They were a party of twelve sitting down to dinner at The Lakes. They sat at a large table bedecked with large bowls of roses, the men wearing dinner jackets, the women elegant evening dress. Andrew and his companion were the last to arrive and were greeted enthusiastically by the others and it did not take Andrew long to realise that Stephanie Crawley had set her stall out.

This was not the Stephanie he remembered in her country tweeds and predictable twin sets, an extension of her somewhat boring spouse.

This Stephanie sparkled in flame-coloured chiffon when Andrew had expected to see her wearing widow's weeds. On the journey to the hotel she had tearfully lamented dear old George, but on arrival at the hotel she had shed her grief as easily as she had shed her wrap.

He did not remember that her hair was quite that colour of deep auburn or that her expertly made-up face had possessed quite that glow. Stephanie Crawley was transformed and as the evening progressed he was more and more aware of her arm possessively through his, her eyes appraising him, her voice cajoling him, and he became increasingly aware of the knowing looks of those around him.

He invited Daphne Carmel to dance, and she asked airily, 'Hasn't this been fun, Andrew, and Stephanie is looking so glamorous tonight, don't you think so?'

He avoided the question and posed one of his own.

'She seems to have recovered from her grief remarkably well, when did you say her husband died?'

'I told her she must make an effort, Andrew, for her own good, and I'm

243

delighted that she seems to have taken my advice. After all George died several months ago.'

'Months!'

'Life has to go on, Andrew, not everybody would want to disappear into the blue for ten years. I'm glad you're both here enjoying yourselves, I hope it's only a beginning, the first of many such evenings.'

Her words confirmed the very thing Andrew was afraid of.

The invitations came thick and fast. Race meetings and cocktail parties, evenings for bridge and more evenings at The Lakes and he would have been a fool not to know what they were about.

Here were two people on their own, a man and a woman united by grief and loneliness and Daphne was on a crusade to see that their days of what she termed loneliness were over.

Andrew turned down an invitation to dinner at Stephanie's house several weeks later.

Her voice was plaintive as she said, 'But all the crowd will be here, Andrew, I desperately want you to come or I shall feel terribly out of things.'

'I'm sorry, Stephi, but I really can't manage that evening,' he'd prevaricated.

'Then I'll change the evening to accommodate you.'

'No, please, I'd much rather you didn't. It's just that I simply can't accept your invitation, but I'm sure we'll meet again very soon.'

'How soon?' she'd asked.

'Well I can't really say, but soon.'

He felt depressed, but she was taking things for granted, thinking of them as a pair. He did not have another engagement but that day he drove into Kendal where he ate an indifferent meal at a new restaurant he wouldn't recommend to anybody.

It rained heavily on his way home and lightning illuminated the sky. He regarded the road ahead with grim amusement, he hadn't enjoyed the evening but it had been preferable to the one he had turned down.

Next day he received a visit from Lady Carmel and her annoyance was evident as he poured the coffee. She accepted the cup he offered with a bleak smile.

'Stephanie was very upset that you declined to join us last night, Andrew, she really had made a great effort and it's so wonderful to see her coping like this.'

'I'm pleased that you enjoyed yourself, Daphne.'

'Andrew, what is the matter with you? Stephanie's making an effort after a few months, it's years since Olivia died, why can't you?'

'I have made an effort, Daphne, I came back here, I've picked up the pieces on the estate and I've done the things I want to do, that I'm not looking for something more doesn't mean that I'm nourishing an old adversity.'

'But it does, Andrew.'

'Daphne, Stephanie is lonely, she had a good marriage and she wants a replacement, I don't. At least I don't want it to be found for me.'

'But grief has to end, Andrew.'

'I'm not grieving, I never grieved for Olivia. I deplored the fact that I hadn't shown more sense, that I'd replaced sanity with tinsel, that I'd loved a woman who proved unworthy of it, but grief, real grief was something else. I ran away, not to forget Olivia, but hopefully to come to terms with the rest of my life, regain some of the values I'd thrown away so lightly.'

'But you were with Stella, don't tell me you're still thinking of her. She's married, for heaven's sake.'

'And very happily married although her husband is an invalid. I'm not thinking of Stella, that is something as deeply buried in my past as all the rest of it.'

For several minutes there was silence while they sat across from one another. He watched the thoughts chasing each other across her face and at last she said, 'I'm sorry, Andrew, I've pushed things too far, haven't I?'

'With the kindest motives I feel sure.'

'But, Andrew, aren't you very lonely in this great big place? Oh, I know you have good servants, your dog and your horses, but can you honestly say it's enough?'

'No, it isn't enough, but moving into marriage with the wrong person isn't the answer.'

'Perhaps you're right. What are we going to do about Stephanie? She liked you, Andrew, she'd begun to hope.'

'I know. But you're a very resourceful woman, Daphne, the county must be heaving with widowers or single men looking for a rich attractive widow. You'll find somebody else for Stephi, I feel sure.'

She grinned. 'I'm a born matchmaker, Andrew, you've disappointed me sorely but I'll keep on looking. Does this mean that we're not going to be seeing much of you from now on?'

'Of course not, but just cool the evenings when Stephanie Crawley is invited as my soul mate.'

'And if and when you do find your soul mate, Andrew, you'll not keep her hidden away?'

'Of course not.'

'Is there someone?'

'You mean to tell me you wouldn't know if there was?'

She laughed.

When Grant came to take away the coffee cups after she had left he favoured Andrew with a wry smile, and when he returned to the kitchen he said evenly, 'I don't think the master will be dining at The Lakes on Friday evening, Mrs Stokes, I rather think he's scotched that idea for the moment.'

Mrs Stokes sniffed.

'I told you they were matchmaking, Mr Grant, I'm glad his lordship's seen for himself what they were about.'

Only ten couples sat down to dinner at The Lakes on Friday evening and Anton de Roche noted with some cynicism that Lord Alveston and Mrs Crawley were the ones who were missing.

He thought of the many times he himself had been the recipient of well-meaning busy-bodies trying to arrange his life. It seldom worked.

He went into his office where Alison was still working on notes she had taken from a guest earlier that day. He was a friend of Julius Van Hopper, an American businessman with interests in Europe and Alison had worked for him on his previous visits.

She looked up with a smile and Anton said, 'I should call it a day if I were you, Alison. It's time you ate dinner.'

'The work's finished, I can let him have it in the morning.'

'Good.'

The staff had their own dining room but there had been times when Alison had been invited to have dinner with some man she had worked for. She liked the variety of her work. Anton did not keep her fully occupied and there was always somebody asking for the services of a competent secretary.

She had settled down well. She was polite to the women guests, and from the men who looked upon her with obvious admiration she maintained a dignified distance. She had made mistakes she was not anxious to repeat and Julius Van Hopper had come to realise that Alison Gray would be an asset rather than a threat to his establishment.

She put the cover on her typewriter and picked up her handbag then, giving Anton a swift smile, moved towards the door. He could not have said what prompted him to issue the invitation, but found himself saying, 'Have dinner with me, Alison, I feel like company this evening.'

Chapter Thirty-One

Debbie Hanley stood at the ship's rail looking across the water to where the smudge that was England was dimly visible. The cruise she'd taken with her mother was almost over.

Her mother was still in their cabin finishing the packing but she'd urged Debbie to go up on deck. 'We'll soon be docking,' she'd said. 'I can finish here and I'll join you presently.'

Debbie was looking better. Some of the colour had returned to her cheeks and Geraldine told herself that her daughter was slowly coming alive again.

For the past two weeks they'd cruised the Mediterranean, calling at ports in Italy and the Greek Islands. Day after day the sun had shone out of a clear blue sky and they had enjoyed the excursions ashore and the entertainment laid on in the evening. A great many young men had invited Debbie to dance, to play deck games, to swim and explore with them but to most of them she had remained an enigma. If they were looking for a shipboard romance they did not find it in Debbie.

Geraldine anxiously wondered what awaited them at home.

Their steward came in to see if she wanted any assistance and Geraldine indicated the luggage and tipped him handsomely before making her way up on deck.

She joined her daughter at the rail and Debbie said with a smile, 'You can see the shoreline, Mummy, we're going to be on time.'

Geraldine smiled. 'You're looking so much better, darling, you'll get out and about I hope when we get home.'

'To go where?'

"Get in touch with the girls you knew at school, ask them to visit and visit them. You're not dependent on the old crowd.'

When her mother said the old crowd she meant Tod's crowd, but her mother never spoke his name, she believed it would be too upsetting.

Debbie knew in her innermost heart that time was working its miracle. The anger was going. She was beginning to appreciate the music and the laughter, the admiration in a young man's eyes as he stared down at her when they danced together, the sheer realisation that she was young and pretty and alive.

If she could stay away forever the improvement would be maintained, but what was there for her in the town that was her home, Tod's home, where his family and his friends were, could the improvement last?

She didn't know that these were the thoughts troubling her mother.

Back in their own environment Debbie would still be Tod's widow. Six months was too soon to have forgotten the ecstasy and the tragedy.

The boat docked soon after lunch in Southampton harbour and then John was greeting them, smiling broadly at them before he piled their luggage onto a trolley and indicating to the porter where he had parked his car.

'We're spending a couple of nights in London,' he informed them. 'I thought we'd take in a show or two and you can look at the shops.'

Debbie thought about something that Tod had once said to her, 'It must have been nice for you growing up in a rich family, everything taken care of, everything running like clockwork,' and she hadn't really known what he was getting at, she'd known nothing else.

'Anything changed at home?' Geraldine asked him in the privacy of their hotel room.

'No, things are much the same. The Hanleys got back from Spain, Mrs Hanley's still obsessed with Tod's death. I haven't seen them, but I've heard from some source or another.'

'What about Mr Hanley?'

'Making money hand over fist. People meet tragedy in different ways, he's looking for more money, and finding it.'

'Have you seen the Mansells?'

'Sybil's in London for a few days. I asked her if she'd met the new secretary and she said she had. She's a bit of a glamour puss, Sybil's taking no chances.'

'Didn't I tell you that she must have had her suspicions about the other one?'

'Not until you put them there, old girl.'

'I didn't put them there. Sybil's not a fool. I'm glad she's keeping an eye on him.

'We should get away for Christmas this year,' Geraldine said. 'Christmas is always a time when one remembers people and the tragedies that happen to us. Debbie won't go to the parties she went to with Tod, and she's going to sit around looking miserable.'

'Oh I don't know,' John demurred. He liked Christmas at home. He liked the Christmas tree in the corner of the lounge and the holly wreath on the door. He liked friends dropping in for drinks and carol singers in the snow, they couldn't run away forever.

Seeing his doubtful face Geraldine said quickly, 'Christmas is for children,

John, we've outgrown it. We should find some comfortable hotel and spend Christmas there. You'll still have your Christmas lunch and the usual trimmings.'

'The weather can be awful for travelling in December, besides there's nothing nicer than home for Christmas.' He looked at her sharply, 'And I hope you're not thinking of The Lakes. That would be disastrous.'

'I wasn't but I do hope it's not barred from us forever. I simply love the place, and staying away from it won't bring Tod back.'

People's thoughts were turning to the Christmas festivities. Mary Styles found that the travel agents in the High Street were busy that Friday lunchtime. She should have chosen a quieter day, and as she turned towards the door she stared at Gerald Ralston and his mother just entering the shop. Quickly she turned away, but not quickly enough, Mrs Ralston had seen her.

'Why, Miss Styles,' she gushed, 'are you on the same errand as us, some sunny place to get away from the winter cold?'

'Well I was just wasting a little time,' Mary said quietly.

'We usually book long before this but Gerald dillied and dallied and couldn't make up his mind. I've made it up for him. I came into town this morning to make sure we did something about our winter holiday.'

'Have you anywhere in mind?'

'Well I'm very fond of Madeira. Have you ever been there?'

'No.'

'It's a beautiful little island and they make quite a thing about Christmas and New Year. We always stay at Reids, couldn't think of staying anywhere else.'

Mary smiled.

'Well, now that you no longer have your mother to worry about the world is your oyster. Are you just getting some ideas to pass on?'

To pass on to whom? Mary was tempted to ask. Instead she shook her head saying, 'Like I said, I just came in out of curiosity. I'll take a few brochures home and think about it quietly.'

'Well of course. It's nice to decide together, I wish Gerald would show a little enthusiasm he's so apathetic at the moment.'

Gerald meanwhile was busy leafing through one of the brochures and his mother said sharply, 'I've just been telling Miss Styles that we're particularly fond of Madeira, Gerald. What do you say?'

'Madeira's very nice. Have you come to a decision?'

'No. I'll look at the brochures.'

'Have you settled in your new flat then?'

'Yes, just about.' She smiled at both of them and made her escape.

Talk of the flat had made her realise that she'd spent an awful amount of money. She'd bought new carpets and some furniture, the flat had needed decorating and she'd spent most of her savings on the flat and the five thousand her mother had left her had dwindled considerably. She had a good job, but perhaps a foreign holiday was something she had to think twice about.

She was expecting to be alone at Christmas, Millicent had already informed her that they were going to Minorca and she thought of herself sitting in her tiny flat with a small Christmas tree on the hall table, cooking her own Christmas dinner.

She listened to her assistants talking about what they were hoping to do. The parties they would go to, the boys they would dance with, and she'd been touched when Helen had said, 'Gosh, Miss Styles, what will you be doing this year without your mother?'

Mary had to admit that she had nothing planned, and Helen had continued, 'Won't you be going to your sister's then?'

'No, they're away.'

'I'm sure my mother'd like you to come to us. We have a big family party, with my grandparents and some of my aunts and uncles. One more won't make any difference.'

'Thank you, Helen, that really is very kind but I may be going away.'

'Well if you decide not to, you will think about coming to us, won't you?'

'Yes of course, thank you again.'

Later that afternoon she made a decision. She'd look for some nice hotel on the south coast. Many of the hotels catered for singles, she'd take the clothes she'd bought for The Lakes, get some bridge lessons and the girl in the travel agents would be able to advise her on the right sort of hotel.

She spared a thought for Gerald and his mother and wondered what they'd decided upon, she was not even concerned that his mother had said he was apathetic. She'd moved on.

Several days later she received a brochure from The Lakes setting out a list of activities to cover the Christmas period. It was evidently a brochure they would send out to every guest who had stayed there, but all the same it brought back to Mary the memories of those days she had spent with Andrew.

What would Andrew be doing for Christmas? There would be parties in country houses, perhaps some exotic holiday planned in some fashionable place.

In the magazines the library bought she'd seen photographs of people like Andrew at hunt balls and hunt meetings. Beautifully dressed women and men wearing hunting pink dinner jackets. She'd read their names, most of them members of the aristocracy, another world, another life.

She didn't know quite what possessed her to put in a call to The Lakes and ask for Alison Gray. Dimly she could hear laughter and the sound of music, and then Alison's voice saying politely, 'Hello, Alison Gray speaking, who is that?'

'Hello, Alison, it's Mary Styles speaking, I was just wondering how you'd settled in?'

'Mary, how nice to hear from you. I love it. Of course it's totally different, perhaps that's what I like best about it. Are you coming to spend Christmas with us?'

'I don't think so. I got your brochure, it would be lovely, but I've half-promised to spend it on the South Coast instead.'

'What a shame. How is your mother?'

'My mother died. I've moved house and there's so much to do.'

'I know. I got rid of most of my things, but even so moving into an apartment here was a little traumatic. I'm sorry about your mother.'

'You're living in the hotel?'

'Yes. I have a set of rooms, they're very nice, I'm so lucky.'

'Do you see or hear from any of the other people who were there over Easter?'

'Debbie Hanley telephoned me. She's been cruising in the Med with her mother, she'll be home now. The Ralstons were here for a few days, you probably don't remember them. I haven't seen the Harveys. Oh and I saw Lord Alveston dining here with some friends once or twice.'

'I'm sure he has a wide circle of friends in the area.'

'I expect so. He hasn't been with them recently.'

'Perhaps he's away.'

'No, I don't think so, I've seen him riding in the village, I saw him at church the other Sunday.'

'You really have entered into the life of the village. You go to church?'

'Yes. This is my home now, I thought I should really get to know people and church is a good place to start from.'

'And are you enjoying working for Mr de Roche?'

'Yes very much. Like I said, the work is different, but enjoyable.'

'Well I must let you go, I expect you're very busy.'

'Do change your mind about Christmas, Mary, it would be so nice to see you again.'

She knew that she would not. She had gone to The Lakes thinking Gerald would be pleased to see her, she couldn't go back there and expect Andrew to take up their friendship. He had his own friends, friends he was evidently dining out with, and there was probably some woman of his own class, some woman he had known a great many years.

By the time Mary decided to book her holiday on the South Coast most of the hotels were fully booked and the ones that weren't were not recommended.

Thinking about Alison, Mary's thoughts turned to Stuart Mansell. He wouldn't have second thoughts about visiting The Lakes, he was a man of the world, he would be very curious to see how Alison was coping in her new environment, a man who had juggled his life between a wife and a mistress would have few qualms about meeting her again, not even if he was accompanied by his wife.

She received an invitation to visit her sister when their new house was completed to their entire satisfaction. She noticed immediately that her mother's furniture was conspicuous by its absence, and on asking why she was told that it had been given to their children for the new flats they were occupying.

'Of course,' Millicent said, 'it's really rather too big for such small rooms but it was better stuff than they could hope to buy. They spend whatever money they have on things we wouldn't dream of buying.'

Millicent's taste had always differed widely from her own. Her dining room was set out with yew furniture while Mary's taste inclined to burr walnut or medium oak. She had chosen chintz covers for her chairs and sofas and patterned curtains for her windows while Mary preferred velvet and soft leather or dralon. She was quick to say however that the house looked charming.

Eric pompously escorted her round the garden which they'd had expertly landscaped.

'We're more for shrubs than roses,' he said, 'and we needed a larger drive and garage for the cars, particularly when the children come to visit.'

'They both drive then?'

'Well, your mother left them some money, you know what they want these days, a car first, a home second.'

Just before tea a man and a woman arrived, evidently friends of long standing and Millicent said, 'We're going to Minorca with Tom and Beryl at Christmas, they have a property there, they're going with us in the spring.'

Beryl and Millicent spent a great deal of time discussing what they would need to take with them to wear, and the men were more interested in their golf clubs.

Beryl asked Mary over tea if she lived alone.

'Yes. I've just moved into a new flat.'

'You work at the library, don't you?'

'Yes.'

'I thought I'd seen you in there. I don't read books, but I do go in to look at the magazines if the weather's not too good and I'm waiting for Tom to pick me up.'

Mary was not surprised when an invitation to take tea with Beryl did not materialise. Millicent chose her friends from the same mould.

She met Dolly Lampeter in the High Street the following Tuesday. Dolly had greeted her enthusiastically.

'Mary, I'm so glad to see you. It's my birthday, I was looking for some-body to have lunch with. Are you free?'

'Well yes, it's our half-day closing.'

'Then how about the George? I was hoping Derek would lunch with me but he's had to go somewhere on business and won't be back until later.'

Mary's expression was doubtful, but Dolly persisted.

'I know you used to lunch with Mr Ralston from the bank, and I'm not asking you to tell me why it all fell through. My table is in the window and nowhere near his.'

'It doesn't matter anyway, Dolly.'

'Well then if it doesn't matter you can afford to be civilised about it. Do come. My treat.'

So for the first time for months Mary followed Dolly into the restaurant at the George. Behind Dolly's back her eyes scanned the room and found Gerald in his usual place. She smiled and received an answering smile in return.

Dolly's conversation was entirely predictable. She talked of Millicent's new house, their foreign holidays, she wondered how they were so affluent. Mary was bored.

Gerald had to pass their table on his way out, and he paused with a smile to say good morning and Dolly said quickly, 'I saw you in the travel agents, Mr Ralston, did you find something nice?'

'We're going to Madeira, we've been many times before but we like it.'

'Oh yes, Madeira is pretty. I take it you'll be there over Christmas.'

'Yes.'

Turning to Mary he asked, 'Did you manage to find something?'

'I'm still thinking about it. Perhaps for the spring.'

'Well yes. Christmas would be a little short notice I think. It's surprising how many people go away at Christmas.'

He smiled again and left them.

'Who's the "we" he talks about?' Dolly asked curiously.

'His mother.'

'Really. So there was no hope in that direction?'

'Of course not. I told you we were simply acquaintances.'

'Oh dear, I did get it wrong, didn't I, but you looked so comfortable together. What a waste. He's good-looking and rather nice, I think, have you met his mother?'

'Yes. They were at The Lakes over Easter.'

'What's she like?'

'Small, well-dressed, talkative.'

'Possessive with her one chick too, I should think.'

'Well yes, perhaps.'

'Well surely he wasn't the only pebble on the beach. There must have been other men at The Lakes, without a wife or mother I mean.'

'I met some very nice people, Dolly.'

'You're not a bit like your sister, Mary. If she'd spent Easter at The Lakes she'd have been going on about all the landed gentry she'd met, the captains of industry, the loaded, but I have to drag it out of you.'

Mary laughed. 'Millicent and I have always been different, but really, Dolly, there's nothing to tell.'

'There was that awful climbing accident, and wasn't that soap actress there, Gloria Weston?'

'Yes. The climbing accident was terrible, the young man had only been married a few days, they were such a handsome young couple, the girl was lovely.'

'Young enough to get over it?'

'In time. I hope so.'

'And Gloria Weston?'

'Yes. She was there. Older than she appeared on the screen, but quite glamorous.'

'Was she alone?'

'No, there was a man with her but we didn't see much of him. I don't know who he was.'

'Is she married at the moment, or between husbands?'

'I really don't know, Dolly, I wasn't particularly interested.'

'Nobody else of note?'

'I don't think so.'

Dolly was thinking that she preferred Mary to her sister, but Millicent would have been more forthcoming about everything in general. Her eyes strayed to the doorway where Gerald Ralston was chatting to the manager. What a waste, she thought, such a nice man and destined to dance attention on his mother as long as she lived.

Surely he must mind. He'd seemed so happy chatting to Mary Styles, they'd looked a pair. Something had gone wrong there or why had Mary suddenly stopped lunching at the George? Had she not known about his mother then, and met her for the first time at The Lakes?

Chapter Thirty-Two

Stuart Mansell wasn't quite sure how to take his new secretary. She was efficient, attractive and ambitious. She'd worked for another M.P. he hadn't particularly liked so he'd had no compunction in taking her away from him, and Alison hadn't liked her. That he supposed had been the main reason he'd appointed her.

His attitude was cool and distant, hers obliging but disinterested, and yet there were times when her dark eyes appraised him, when her smile was warm, when he was acutely aware that she added some sort of allure to the functional atmosphere of his office.

Alison Gray had been beautiful, with a cool English beauty that had inflamed his senses. Maeve McNamara was more flamboyant with her blue-black hair and pale porcelain skin. Her eyes were blue and she spoke with a faint Irish lilt in her voice. She intrigued him.

His wife was spending more and more time in London yet strangely enough it was Sybil who suggested they might spend the next few days off he had at The Lakes.

'Why there?' he'd asked surprised.

'Why not? You liked it, I liked it, everybody thinks it's wonderful and it would be a good well-earned rest for you, darling.'

He'd said nothing more, surprised when moments later she'd said, 'You could see how Alison Gray is settling in with Anton de Roche.'

'I'm not really very interested, Sybil, she went off on her own accord. I tried to get her to change her mind, now I have a new secretary who is equally as efficient, why should I concern myself about Alison?'

'Well it's only natural that you should. She was with you a long time, she worked well for you, Stuart. It would be a kind gesture on your part.'

He asked Maeve to make the reservations for a long weekend at the end of November, and he couldn't be sure if he read a certain surprise in her eyes.

November in the Lake District wasn't exactly his idea of the perfect place to be. It was misty, the mountain tops were obscured and the mist lay across the lakes in floating wraiths. The weather apparently did not detract from the popularity of The Lakes however, because when they arrived there in the late afternoon the car park was practically full.

Lights streamed out from every window of the hotel into the encroaching dusk and Sybil shivered, drawing the collar of her coat closer round her neck.

'I hate this fine drizzle,' she said, 'everything feels so damp.'

'I told you November wasn't the month to be coming here,' he said testily.

'Well we're not likely to be out much in it, are we? Are we taking the luggage up?'

'No. I'll give the porter the key, he can bring it up for us.'

Her high-heeled shoes slithered on the wet drive so that he gave her his arm after telling her to walk carefully.

They blinked in the bright lights that met them in the hotel foyer, and as always it was a place of activity when Anton de Roche came forward to meet them.

'I'll see about your luggage, but you could go straight into the lounge and have tea,' he said with his usual charming smile. 'When you've finished in there your luggage will be waiting for you in your room. I've given you the room you had before, Mr Mansell, on the first floor.'

'Thank you, that will be fine. Does Alison know we're expected?' he asked.

'Yes of course. She'll no doubt see you sometime this evening.'

'Has she settled in all right then?'

'Yes of course. She will tell you herself.'

He should have known that Anton de Roche would not discuss Alison. They were two men in different walks of life, and yet he recognised in Anton an adversary he needed to be wary of. His own little world was Westminster, Anton's world was more personal, less predictable.

Anton watched them walking across the foyer, his arm under his wife's elbow. Alison had shown no emotion when she knew they were visiting the hotel, but that meant nothing. When they actually met face to face would the old enchantment still be there? Would there be that old agonising feeling of remembered pain?

He had invited Alison to have dinner with him that evening, she should not be asked to meet her past alone, and gratefully she had accepted his invitation.

It was too soon, she thought bitterly. Why did he have to come to The Lakes so soon, five months wasn't long enough to forget all they'd meant to each other, and his wife would be with him. Had Sybil any inkling of their affair?

During those five months she had met a great many men who had admired her, some married, some single, but she had kept herself aloof. She would not

256

let Anton de Roche or Julius Van Hopper think she had come to The Lakes to meet men. She had loved one, that did not make her an available woman.

She liked Anton de Roche, he fascinated her with his calm handsome face and aloof charm. She had loved Stuart when she hadn't always liked him, she liked Anton but knew precious little about him. Always gracious, and approachable, yet never familiar. She was stern with herself. She must not fall in love with Anton, she must not store up another misery for herself.

Stuart would be charming, his wife would be charming. They would be concerned about her welfare. She would ask about his new secretary and he would be enthusiastic. They would ask her about her new life and she would be enthusiastic. She knew exactly the way things would go, and she realised with something like shock that she wasn't concerned about the evening ahead. Surely three months hadn't been long enough to forget? When Anton had told her that Stuart was coming to the hotel she'd been afraid, now it had lost some of its trauma.

All the same she was careful to choose the gown she felt most glamorous in for dinner that evening, the same black chiffon gown Stuart had always liked her in.

She surveyed herself in the long mirror in her bedroom and had to agree that from the top of her dark blonde head to the tip of her high-heeled black court shoes she looked elegant.

People standing about in the foyer eyed the beautiful girl as she stepped out of the lift. She was aware of their admiration, and speculation as Anton stepped forward to escort her into the dining room.

Minutes before he had declined to eat dinner with Julius Van Hopper on the grounds that he was dining with Alison Gray, Julius had raised his eyebrows maddeningly and Anton had smiled.

'Stuart Mansell and his wife are in the hotel. She will meet him of course, it's better that she isn't alone.'

'Did she have to meet him this evening?' Julius asked astutely.

'No, but I thought it was better for her to meet him like this than by chance.'

'Are you always so concerned about all our employees?' Julius asked.

'I would like to think so,' Anton had answered with a brief smile, and then Alison was stepping out of the lift and excusing himself he went forward to meet her.

All eyes were upon them when they were escorted to Anton's table in the dining room, but none more speculative than Stuart Mansell's.

She was as beautiful as he remembered her with that cool English beauty that looked its best in a deceptively simple black dress. He'd never liked Sybil in black, she was too dark, it did nothing for her, but black made Alison's complexion glow, brought out the dark gold lights in her hair, showed up her unusual green eyes. Anton de Roche and Alison made a very elegant couple, they complemented each other, with his severe profile and dark sculptured hair, peppered with silver.

From the interest their appearance had created, other people were evidently of the same opinion.

'She's looking very well,' Sybil commented.

'Yes,' he agreed. 'What do you fancy? I thought the lobster myself, either that or the venison.'

'I always think venison is over-rated,' Sybil said scanning the menu. 'I'll have the lobster. Do you suppose her meals are included in her salary or will she have to pay for them?'

'She'll not have to pay for the one she's having tonight, he's probably invited her.'

'Do you think there could be something going on?'

'I shouldn't think so. There's always talk about a man who reaches his age without getting married, either he's homosexual, he's been hurt, or he's got some woman tucked away somewhere and nobody knows anything about her.'

'Where could he tuck her away up here? If you twist your ankle all the neighbours limp,' his wife said cynically.

'I'm only telling you what people say.'

'I think he's fascinating.'

He stared at her in disbelief. 'Why, for heaven's sake? I can't imagine what women see in him. All right he's charming, that's his stock in trade, in his job he has to be charming, but he's also aloof, a trifle condescending and where most women are concerned, unapproachable.'

'He doesn't seem too unapproachable tonight, they're evidently getting along together.'

Stuart looked at them. They were chatting amicably together, occasionally Anton would say something that made her laugh, and when she laughed her eyes lit up and her face became enchantingly alive.

He knew that look, had heard that laughter, seen the sparkle in her green eyes, and had felt pleased himself that he had the power to make her laugh. Now he felt the pain that it was some other man who was bringing that sparkle into her eyes, the warm colour into her cheeks.

Sybil was watching him. 'Don't stare at them, Stuart,' she admonished him.

Later in the evening Alison faced Stuart and Sybil in the hotel ballroom. The music had stopped and they found themselves next to Stuart and his wife on the dance-floor. Never had Alison felt so relieved that Anton was beside her.

The two women smiled at each other in the friendliest way, and Stuart said, 'Well, here you are, Alison, and looking very well I must say. Have you settled down to country living?'

'Very much so, and enjoying the job,' she answered him.

'Well I must say I had my doubts. I always believed you were a townie at heart. Of course Westminster couldn't offer you anything as glamorous as this.'

She smiled, and Anton said evenly, 'Your loss has been our gain, Mr Mansell.'

'Yes of course.'

'How is Maeve McNamara coping, Mr Mansell?' Alison asked.

'Admirably. She's a very competent secretary, charming girl.'

'Yes, I thought you'd find her so.'

He looked at her sharply but Sybil was saying, 'Are you actually living in the hotel, Alison?'

'Yes, I have a suite of rooms on the top floor with a view of the mountains and the gardens.'

'So you wouldn't be able to bring all your furniture?'

'No, most of it went with the flat. But I had room for some of it and several ornaments and other things I was particularly fond of.'

'That's nice.'

'Do you work a five-day week, or are you called upon most days?'

'I work mainly for Mr de Roche and any businessman who needs secretarial work. I get plenty of variety, and I have been known to work Saturday and Sunday. I really don't mind.'

'But what do you do for relaxation?'

'I have the use of the gym, the swimming pool and the tennis courts, anything else I want, and there is life in the village.'

'But what a change from London,' Sybil went on feelingly. 'Don't you miss the shows, the night life and the hub of Westminster?'

Alison smiled. 'Perhaps I've been too busy to miss them,' she said. At the same time she could have said she missed Stuart making himself at home in her flat, she missed making a meal for him, and the nights of love that followed. She missed being a wife and not a wife, and looking into Sybil's pretty bland face she thought, 'To be so sure, that come hell or high water this marriage is safe.'

It was Anton who changed the subject by asking if they saw anything of young Mrs Hanley, with a request to know how she was coping.

'I really think she's recovering,' Sybil said. 'She's been on a Med cruise with her mother and the last time I spoke to her she did seem rather more outgoing than of late.'

'It was a great tragedy, and a foolish one,' Anton said. 'The man who was in hospital recovered and came into the hotel to collect his things when they let him out of hospital. He said it had been madness to carry on with the climb, but from all accounts it was Mr Hanley who pushed things.'

'Yes, he would,' Stuart said. 'He was a nice enough lad, always the centre of a crowd of young people who thought he was marvellous. His father had made a lot of money, he denied Tod nothing and his mother idolised him. I'm afraid she's taken it harder than anybody.'

'I know John and Geraldine are anxious to come here again,' Sybil said. 'I rather think Debbie's the problem.'

'People forget, Mrs Mansell, either that or they don't wish to remember. By the time next Easter comes along it will all be a nine days' wonder and some other excitement will have taken its place. I rather think that we shall find young Mrs Hanley is a survivor.'

With brief smiles they moved on to talk to another group standing nearby. Stuart's eyes followed them, but Sybil turned to speak to Julius Van Hopper and his wife. From the sidelines Julius had watched with interest. He admired Alison's poise, it could not have been easy meeting a man she'd had a long-standing love affair with, in the company of his wife. He disapproved of affairs, they upset the equilibrium of life and he thought them totally un-necessary to a man with a stable marriage. Men like Stuart Mansell wanted the best of both worlds, and he'd been in the hotel business long enough to appreciate what disasters affairs caused. Suicides and bitter emnities, law suits and murderous threats from cuckolded husbands, deserted wives and jealous lovers.

This affair was evidently being conducted on civilised lines, but he had not missed Alison's pallor, Mansell's tight-lipped smile, or Anton de Roche's need to steer them apart. It would seem only Mrs Mansell was oblivious to undercurrents of any kind.

Stuart Mansell was happy talking about politics even to an American, and his wife and Mrs Van Hopper discussed the hotel and the gowns the women were wearing.

Alison and Anton were nowhere to be seen and he guessed that by this time they were sitting in the comfort of his office with a drink.

'It wasn't so bad, Alison?' Anton said gently.

'No.'

'The next time will be better still, and one day you'll say to yourself, "I don't feel anything, I'm really free".'

'You seem very sure.'

'Well of course. It only continues to hurt if one or another of the parties refuses to let go, that way lies stupidity. Far better to call it a day and move on.'

He was sitting on the corner of his desk looking at her quizzically and she asked herself how many times Anton had moved on from something that was over. She liked him enormously, but did she really know him? Had he been so badly hurt that he could be kind to a woman without going further, or was there some woman denied to him? They were questions she could never ask him, but at that moment she wanted him to make love to her, and she felt that he knew it.

She felt strangely unsure of herself, bewildered even. There were days and nights when she agonised over Stuart, so how could she suddenly feel this blinding attraction for somebody else? Anton de Roche had given her no reason to think that he admired her, and yet for a brief moment when she looked into his eyes she had surprised a fleeting affinity, an attraction that went as quickly as it had come, and in some confusion she said, 'If you don't mind I think I shall go to bed now, I have promised to work for Mr Rosenfeldt in the morning and he is very exacting. Thank you so much for inviting me to have dinner, I had a lovely evening.'

He bowed his head graciously and smiled before escorting her to the lift.

From across the room Stuart watched her departure with interest, and then with relief when Anton returned immediately to the foyer.

Watching with the same interest was Mrs Van Hopper, neither did she miss Stuart Mansell's curiosity.

'He's still very interested in that girl,' she said to her husband. 'Is there anything going on between her and Anton de Roche?'

'I wouldn't think so,' he replied evenly.

'She's very beautiful.'

'Anton has had the opportunity to meet a great many beautiful women.'

'But there must have been someone.'

'Possibly.'

'Well, don't you know who it was?'

'There has probably been more than one, discretion is his second name. I doubt if he'll get involved with a girl who is still carrying a torch for somebody else.'

Mrs Van Hopper remained curious. 'But is she, Julius? She was evidently determined to make the break, she won't be content to stay on the sidelines forever.'

'Perhaps not, but Anton de Roche won't be an easy fish to land.'

'He's a man, and he's only human,' his wife retorted. Then sharply she said, 'You don't think it's men that attract him, do you?'

'I don't talk to Anton about his love life, and I don't make suppositions. I have no reason to suspect that he's homosexual simply because I don't know of any woman in his life.'

'Most men of his age are married, people are bound to wonder. He's a very handsome man, women admire him. Surely you must know why he's never married, you've known him long enough.'

'And I don't pry into something that's none of my business. I know he suffered a great deal of trauma with his mother's second marriage, maybe enough to put him off, and he's seen more than his share of scandal in our line of business. If you don't want to dance again this evening I suggest we circulate among the guests once more before we retire.'

She would get nothing more out of Julius, but the next few months might be very interesting.

Julius loved The Lakes. He loved England, even the rain and low hanging clouds. This year he wanted the family to join them at The Lakes for Christmas even when he knew his wife would prefer to spend it at home. The family would come of course, he'd talked about the place long and often and they were all eager to see his 'castle' as he called it.

As they crossed the foyer to the lifts they saw Anton locking his office door so they waited for him.

'I reckon we've done our duty,' Julius said with a smile. 'We're for bed, I don't know about you?'

'I think so. The evening went rather well, I think.'

'It always does. Miss Gray enjoy herself?'

'I'm sure she did.'

'What a very beautiful girl she is,' Mrs Van Hopper said with a smile. 'I expect Mr Mansell was very sorry to lose her.'

Julius looked at his wife sharply, but Anton merely replied casually, 'Secretaries come and go, I believe he's happy enough with her replacement.'

Up in their bedroom Julius permitted himself a small smile.

'You got nothing there, honey, I should give up on it if I were you.'

Mrs Van Hopper had no intentions of doing any such thing.

Chapter Thirty-Three

Christmas came and went. Mary spent it in a very nice hotel in Torquay where the guests were mostly elderly with no families and where she enjoyed the food and precious little else. She resolved that next Christmas she would think of something different.

Debbie and her parents partied. Geraldine enjoyed giving dinner parties but they were conspicuous by the absence of people her daughter's age. The Mansell children attended one of them with their parents but for the rest of the holiday they were visiting friends. Stuart and Sybil attended several functions in the town and spent the rest of the holiday entertaining Sybil's parents.

Gerald and his mother went off to Madeira, and Mrs Ralston dined out on the experience for weeks after they arrived back home. Gerald was rather less forthcoming, he had had a surfeit of Madeira.

The Lakes was at its busiest. Every night entertainment was laid on for the guests. Julius and his wife welcomed their family who immediately endorsed the fact that they thought the hotel was lovely, certainly one of the very best, and Julius, gratified, entered into the true spirit of Christmas.

Alison's feet never touched the ground. She was kept busy on so many duties she never had a minute to herself, but she enjoyed the experience, and memories of Westminster and Stuart became rather hazy until they seemed like an experience that had happened to someone else. The healing had begun.

Andrew accepted one invitation to dine with his friends at The Lakes and was pleased to see that Stephanie Crawley had transferred her attention to a guest of Lady Carmel, a man recently divorced, and not averse to entertaining her.

He felt singularly alone however, and his thoughts constantly moved on to Easter and the possibility that Mary would return to the hotel.

After the New Year festivities were over The Lakes closed its doors so that rooms could be decorated, carpets cleaned, the entire hotel could be got ready for the start of the new season and the staff could think about taking holidays.

Most of the foreign staff returned to their homes in Italy, Spain or wherever they had come from. The Van Hoppers went home to Boston and Alison thought about what she would do with herself for a month in the depths of winter.

Obviously it had to be somewhere abroad and with this in mind she armed herself with a host of holiday brochures and seeing them spread out across her desk one morning Anton asked, 'Have you anything in mind, Alison?'

'Not really. I've spent time abroad before, mostly in Europe, but a month is a long time, most of these holidays are for two weeks, and I'm not sure I can afford to go further afield.'

'Your salary will be paid into the bank as usual,' he said with a smile.

'I know, I shall have to think of something very quickly. Are you going abroad?'

'Yes. To Sicily and Italy. I spent much of my youth there.'

'How wonderful. I love Italy, but you're not Italian, Anton, at least your name isn't.'

'No. My mother was English and my father was French.'

'But you love Italy?'

'I have both happy and bitter memories of it.'

She sighed. 'Oh well, I shall have to think of something very soon. The Italian lakes are tempting, I love Como but I've never been to Garda.'

'Then you should, it's handy for Verona and Venice. I can give you the name of a very nice hotel in Gardone that might appeal to you but then we're talking about February, hardly a prestigious time for visiting the Italian Lakes.'

She had to agree with him, and seeing her disconsolate face Anton said, 'Why not Venice? At all times Venice is enchanting, but in the winter it comes into its own. That is when the Venetians love their city best, when the tourists have gone home and Venice becomes theirs again.'

Her eyes lit up.

'I've never been to Venice, that's where I'll go.'

He smiled and left her, and several days later Alison flew out to Venice and Anton flew to Rome. In Rome the memories crowded in upon him thick and fast, his mother's passion for her new husband and his loneliness, then the quarrels and tantrums that suffocated him, the endless tirades and the forever moving on, but always followed by his stepfather, the ecstatic reconciliations and the final tragedy.

He had seen his mother only once after that in a nursing home in London. She had not known him, and he had left with sadness tinged with relief. Months later he learned that she had bequeathed him all her money which was considerable and he wished he could turn back the clock, understand her better, love her more, but the memories of that sad lost boy he had been were too potent.

264

From Rome Anton drove to the south and sailed over to Sicily, but here there were also too many memories. There had been several years when he had been able to push them to the back of his mind and enjoy the scenes of his childhood, but somehow this time he could find no joy in the streets of Palermo and the thin trail of smoke ascending from distant Etna. He had thought he would never tire of the island, now he felt restless and lonely, when he had never felt lonely before.

In Venice Alison was discovering the enchantment of a city washed with rain, the lagoon a heaving grey mass under leaden skies, and yet there was still magic in the empty squares where even the pigeons had a dejected air. Occasionally the clouds would lift and shafts of sunlight would fall on fairy-tale towers and campaniles, turning the façade of San Marco into a sheet of molten gold, soothing the waters of the Grand Canal, calming the Lagoon dotted with islands.

She had been in Venice two weeks and was wondering if she should move on, but to where? Venice was expensive, and outside the rain was still falling, creating great puddles across the deserted terrace. She sat on a seat in the window looking out disconsolately at the late afternoon gloom unaware that a man had entered the room and was walking towards her. He paused, taking in her dejection, her special loneliness, before speaking to her softly, 'Alison.'

She turned quickly, amazement in her eyes, then they lit up with sudden joy and she rose to greet him.

'Anton, how wonderful. I didn't know you were coming to Venice.'

'Nor I, until yesterday.'

'But why Venice, I thought you were driving south?'

'I did. All the places I intended to visit, but strangely none of them meant the same this year.'

Her eyes wavered and the rich warm colour rose up into her cheeks.

She must not read too much in his words. Life had made her afraid, of words that were not meant, of emotions that were untrue. He took her hand and led her back to her seat.

'Tell me about Venice,' he said gently. What there was between them had to be no instant thing, he had to go gently, susceptible to her hurts and her needs and he had to be sure that there was nothing left in her heart of those years with Stuart Mansell.

Alison told him all the things she had seen in Venice, her delight in its architecture, her enthusiasm for its history, the overpowering magic of its incomparable scenery, and he listened without speaking until she said, 'How long are you here for, Anton, you've seen all this before?'

'I thought a few days, a reintroduction, if you like.'

'And then where will you go?'

'We'll think about that later.'

Her green eyes deepened with unspoken surprise. He'd said 'we', oh surely that meant both of them.

Andrew walked from the stables towards the house. There was a sad air about the dog's drooping head and dripping coat and Andrew too viewed the grey leaden skies and the glassy grey lake below them. It was predictable Lakeland weather and was likely to last for days.

The village street was deserted, the hotel closed until the beginning of March, too dismal even for weekend fell walkers.

He'd been thinking about it for days; a few days in London, to take in some shows, discover civilisation.

Inside the house the dog shook himself, shedding water on the floor of the hall, then running as fast as his legs could carry him towards the kitchens where no doubt a bright fire burned in the grate and the cook would fill his bowl.

Andrew went into the small morning room and now that the dog had advertised their arrival home tea was quickly served to him.

Grant came in with some letters which he placed on the table beside his chair, 'It's a dreadful day, sir,' he said. 'The housekeeper has suggested that she'd like to spend a couple of weeks with her sister in Lancaster, would that be agreeable, sir?'

'Yes of course. Tell Mrs Stokes to get off as soon as she feels like it.'

'Thank you, sir.'

'Actually, Grant, I've been thinking of taking a few days away myself. London perhaps, stay at a decent hotel, visit the theatre.'

'A very good idea, sir, will you be driving down or taking the train?'

'Oh I'll drive there. I might even spend a few days in the Cotswolds or Bath.'

Now that he had made up his mind all he had to do was pack. He saw Mrs Stokes depart by taxi the following morning, and by early afternoon he was packed and ready to leave the next morning.

'Friday isn't a particularly good day for travelling,' Grant remarked.

'Oh, why is that, Grant?'

'Everybody rushing to get home for the weekend, lorries and such like.'

'Oh I'll stay clear of the main roads, I'll meander down the B-roads and the country lanes, I'm in no hurry.'

'Of course not, sir, that would be wise I think.'

For the first time in days it was fine when he left the house. He decided he would keep to the west side of the country until he hit the south, wander into Wales perhaps, find some decent country hotel for his first night.

The big car ate up the miles effortlessly and the country roads were quiet. He drove on through north Lancashire and Cheshire, and after eating lunch at a country pub drove on into Shropshire. It was the sight of Shrewsbury on one of the signposts that halted him in his tracks.

He stopped the car in a lay-by and took out his road map. For some un-
accountable reason he was remembering Mary telling him that she lived in a
small West Midland town, a market town, small and unpretentious but that
they were not too far from Shrewsbury and Shrewsbury was nice.

He found the town without any difficulty, roughly about fifteen miles east
of Shrewsbury and without hesitation he drove on.

It was months since they'd met, perhaps she might not want to see him,
perhaps it wouldn't be convenient, but he knew she worked at the library and
if she wasn't on holiday she would surely be there.

He recognised the town from her description of it. The High Street and the
market stalls in a street leading off it. The tall white clock tower in the midst
of a small green park and the rather imposing civic buildings near by. He
drove slowly, looking for a place to park, asking the parking attendant where
he might find the library.

'Right over there, sir, in the corner, the one with the steps up to it. They
close at six o'clock, it's nearly a quarter to now.'

'Thank you, I'll just about make it.'

The library was busy. Two young girls were moving chairs round the large
reference table and there were people waiting at the desk where Mary stood
stamping their books.

One by one they moved away and now only a small talkative woman
remained and a man. Andrew didn't know if they were together, but he didn't
think so in view of the impatient look on the man's face.

The woman chattered away and Mary looked up anxiously at her two
assistants waiting with their outdoor clothing on, then she saw Andrew and
her eyes opened in amazement.

He smiled, and the woman spun round, then before he could say a word
she said, 'Why, Lord Alveston, we do meet in the most curious places. We
met in the summer if you remember, in the tobacconists in the village.'

He had no recollection of ever having seen the woman before but he
smiled politely and the man standing with her took hold of her arm and
literally dragged her towards the door.

The two girls were giggling, and now showed no urgency whatsoever to
get away. Mary said, 'Goodnight, girls, I'll see you in the morning,' and with
that they had to leave, but not before eyeing him over with swift smiles.

He joined Mary at the counter and took hold of her outstretched hand.

'How are you, Mary?' he asked gently.

'I'm very well, Andrew, what are you doing here?'

'I'm driving to London. I saw the signs for Shrewsbury and decided to
look you up.'

'You've come a long way off your route.'

He smiled. 'Perhaps. I wanted to see you again. Is there somewhere decent
to stay in this town?'

'You want to stay here?'

'For tonight, it's too late to move on. I thought you might join me for dinner, would that inconvenience you too much?'

'Of course not. There's the George, it's the best hotel in the town. I've dined there but never actually stayed there. It's at the top of the High Street, we can walk there.'

'Are you ready to leave now?'

'Yes. I just have to collect my shopping. I can leave it in the car, it's just outside.'

She waited while he booked a room at the George. She felt bemused. She had only lunched at the George and felt too dowdy in her working clothes to eat dinner there, but Andrew appeared unconcerned with her appearance.

She knew that the hotel got busy on Friday evenings but it was early and the waiter ushered them to a table near the wall and in one of the alcoves.

Andrew smiled. 'Are you wanting to telephone home to say you'll be late?' he enquired.

'My mother died several months ago,' she explained. 'I have a small flat in the town and there's nobody waiting for me.'

'I'm sorry about your mother. Was it sudden?'

'In the end, yes.'

'I know very little about Shropshire, would you be willing to be my guide over the next few days?'

'Have you forgotten that I'm a working girl?'

'Surely you have holidays.'

'I do, but I have to ask for them. I work Saturday morning until noon, I'm free then until Monday morning.'

'Can't you ask for a few days off?'

'I thought you were going to London.'

'That was the idea, but I can go there later, I haven't booked in anywhere. I can stay at my club anyway.'

'I can't promise, Andrew, but I'll try.'

'Good. Now what would you like to eat?' he said, picking up his menu.

She had often asked herself what they would talk about if they ever met again, now talk was coming easily to her. She told him about her mother, having to leave her house, finding the flat, and the not very successful holiday she had spent over Christmas.

'Why didn't you go to The Lakes?'

She stared at him helplessly and he smiled. 'I know, you thought if we met I'd think you were hoping to see me. Yes, I would have thought that, and I'd have been very flattered.'

'How could I assume that?'

'Well you can take my word for it, Mary. I can't for the life of me remember that woman who was in the library. Was she at The Lakes over Easter?'

'Yes, she was with her son today.'

'She embarrassed him.'

'Yes, she does it all the time.'

'Why don't we give her something to talk about. Take a few days off and show me Shropshire.

'I'll try.'

He had to be content with that, but they chatted easily together, it had been months since they'd met but it might have been yesterday and as he walked back after escorting her to her car he felt a rare contentment, Mary was uncomplicated, a thoroughly nice woman, a woman he could relate to. He had never felt contented with Olivia, indeed there were times when he thought she was mad with her tears and tantrums over nothing at all.

He had yearned for this calm serenity, for smiles without cynicism, for honesty without subterfuge, meeting Mary on that country lane was something the angels had planned, he had no intentions of letting her go.

He had said he would pick her up outside the library in the morning and they'd drive out somewhere to eat lunch. As he watched her running lightly down the library steps his eyes lit up with pleasure. She was wearing the camel coat he remembered. There was a pure silk scarf knotted round her throat and the sunlight found red-gold lights in her hair.

'I'm lost around here, Mary, you'll have to tell me where we should go,' he greeted her.

'It's a nice day,' she said. 'We could drive into Wales, those are the Welsh hills we can see over there, Llangollen perhaps.'

'Did you manage a few days off?'

'Yes, until Thursday. The early part of the week isn't too busy. Does that upset your plans at all?'

'My plans were very haphazard. We have this afternoon and four more days. Then you have to tell me how long you can stay at The Lakes for Easter.'

'Oh, Andrew, I'm not sure.'

'Why? You no longer have your mother to think about, you're a free agent, or don't you relish the prospect of spending more time with me?'

'It isn't that.'

'Then what is it?'

For several moments she sat deep in thought, then steadily she explained, 'It's the difference between us, Andrew, your life and mine. We get along together, but your lifestyle and mine are so far apart it's impossible. I don't want to become too involved with a man who is so out of reach, I don't want a relationship that can only end in heartache.'

'Does it have to end in heartache, Mary?'

'You must know women in your own walk of life, I don't see myself as a substitute.'

'Are you telling me I am so insensitive that I would treat you as a substitute?'

She looked at him anxiously, and with a little smile he covered her hand with his. 'Mary, we have to enjoy these days together, and you're right I do know women in what you call my own walk of life, but none of them interest me in the slightest.'

Even the grey leaden skies of an English February couldn't take away the enjoyment of those few days. Together they enjoyed the dramatic beauty of Wales and the gentler scenery of Shropshire. They followed the winding Severn on its long meandering journey south but it was the dusk coming down early that sent them back to eat dinner in the early evening.

On their last evening together Mary invited Andrew to eat dinner at her flat. She believed that this would convince him how different their lives were, the splendour of Alveston Hall and the tiny flat she called home.

While she cooked dinner he sat in the tiny living room and looked around him. An electric fire burned in the grate, impersonal after the log fires that burned in the grates of Alveston. There was Mary's good taste in odd items of china and her pictures, but there was no character in the flat and Mary had warned him of that.

The meal was excellent as he had known it would be, but he sensed in her a reticence, an invisible barrier born of class, and he felt helpless to deal with it. Their parting was amicable if unromantic and at the door when he turned to say goodbye, he added, 'You will think about Easter, Mary?'

'Of course.'

'I mean it, Mary. You say of course, as if you will think about it and then discard the idea. You've made me very happy these last few days, I want to look forward to seeing you again.'

'It's some time off, Easter, Andrew, a lot can happen before then.'

'I will telephone you. Easter is only just over a month off. Let me book in for you.'

'No, I'll do it if I'm able to go.'

He felt it was useless to press her further. He held her hand and raised it to his lips, then he was gone.

The living room seemed suddenly alien and lonely.

Chapter Thirty-Four

Mrs Ralston never lost an opportunity to discuss Mary and her Belted Earl as she called Andrew. Gerald had it for breakfast and his evening meal, he had it before he went to the golf club and on his return and he grew increasingly frustrated.

He tried changing the subject but it was futile, and her conversation followed the same time-worn paths. 'I told you, didn't I, Gerald, that there was something going on but you wouldn't have it. A man of his standing doesn't take the trouble to look up an ordinary librarian unless there's something more. That Miss Styles is more than she seems.'

Gerald had ceased to answer her and now allowed her to go on without interruption and he had become an adept at turning her off.

'Do you suppose he's staying in her flat? He won't find it too comfortable after what he's accustomed to.'

'He's staying at the George, Mother.'

'How do you know?'

'His car is parked there.'

'So he's still in the area? That means he's seeing a lot of her. She won't be in the library on Friday that's for sure.'

Gerald sat with the evening paper spread across his knees, and in some exasperation his mother snapped, 'Really, Gerald, you might at least show some interest. This is somebody we know.'

'You don't know her, Mother, and you don't know him at all.'

'You know her,' she snapped.

He was tempted to say, not well enough, thanks to you, but remained silent.

'She'll be at The Lakes over Easter I'm sure, unless she stays at The Hall. That's probably why he's here, to make arrangements for Easter. We are staying there over Easter, I hope.'

'We should have a change, Mother, I haven't booked.'

She stared at him in some anger.

'But you know I want to go. You mean you've actually booked in some-where else without telling me?'

'It's time we had a change.'

'I don't want a change. I want to go to The Lakes. I want a room overlook-ing the gardens and by this time they'll all have gone. Really, Gerald, I was sure you'd booked us in weeks ago. I accommodate you by spending a week at a country club so that you can play some golf, surely it's not too much to ask you to think about my wishes. I'm going to telephone The Lakes tonight and book us in for the whole of Easter.'

'Why not invite Aunt Edith and Uncle Maurice to spend a few days with you at The Lakes. Isn't it their Golden Wedding? They'd be delighted.'

She stared at him in astonishment.

'Your uncle doesn't drive and their minds don't stretch beyond that cottage they rent. Besides they'd be terribly out of their depth in a place like The Lakes and I want my own escort.'

'Doesn't it bother you that I might not want to go this year, Mother?'

'No, Gerald. For fifty-two weeks out of the year I cook for you, wash for you and clean for you, so I expect you to do a little thing for me. Besides it's not a little thing. I'm asking you to spend a few days in the most beautiful place imaginable. You loved the place.'

Gerald didn't argue. His mother had omitted to say that she had two daily women who cleaned the house, did the laundry and some of the cooking. His mother went to the shops, de-headed the flowers in the garden and supervised the gardener who did the heavy work. She liked to do fancy cooking for her bridge friends and she liked dining out, so all in all what she did for him needed some thinking about.

He sat seething in front of the fire while he heard his mother putting in a call to The Lakes. Her voice was querulous so it was obvious things were not to her liking.

When she returned to the room her colour was heightened, her voice fretful.

'Did you hear any of that?' she demanded. 'I spoke to some man who said the hotel was closed for refurbishing but when I asked for two rooms over Easter he said he doubted if there would be any, most of the rooms had been booked months ago. I told him we were regular visitors and demanded to speak to Mr de Roche. He said he was on holiday, somewhere in Europe. I ask you, is that any way to run a place like The Lakes?'

'They have to have holidays some time, Mother, when the hotel is closed for refurbishment seems the best possible time to me.'

'Mr de Roche won't be back until the end of the month so I asked to speak to that girl, Alison her name was, he said she was also travelling abroad. I wouldn't be surprised if they weren't together, last Easter it was Stuart Mansell, this Easter it'll be de Roche.'

'So, how did you leave it?'

'He's made a note that we want two rooms, he didn't promise anything, we'll be lucky if we get two rooms at the back, we'll feel like everybody's poor relations.'

'Mother, we needn't go. I've booked two of the best rooms at the Country Club, it won't do any harm to miss The Lakes for once.'

'Well I'm not missing it. I don't feel that Miss Styles has been very nice to me, I've invited her here and she's never once said she'd like to come. I want her to see that she may be at The Lakes on Lord Alveston's invitation, but we are in the position of getting there without outside intervention.'

Gerald gave up.

They would go to The Lakes whether they were put in back rooms or not, and his mother would be like a little inquisitive bird bobbing this way and that in an endeavour not to miss anything. If Mary Styles wasn't such a nice woman she would be laughing at his predicament.

He was not to know that Mary too was harbouring doubts about Easter. Andrew had said he would telephone her when he arrived home and there was nothing more she could do. When Mrs Ralston informed her that they had booked in for Easter but had had great difficulty in finding accommodation at such short notice, Mary thought that that was probably that. The hotel would be fully booked.

Andrew kept his promise to telephone but when Mary said she doubted if she could get a room so near to Easter, he said not to worry, he'd see what he could do. Two days later a letter arrived from Andrew with the confirmation that a room at the front of the hotel had been reserved for her for the entire Easter holiday.

She might have known that Lord Alveston could open doors denied to lesser individuals and she felt a sudden feeling of annoyance before she saw the comedy of the situation.

When her sister went into the library several days later she prattled on about their Easter holiday abroad and Mary felt obliged to tell her that she was going back to The Lakes.

'What is it about that place that everybody finds so attractive?' Millicent snapped. 'The weather over Easter can be dire up there, why didn't you think of going abroad? There are quite a lot of tourist firms who cater for singles.'

Mary didn't answer, and Millicent went on, 'The clothes you had last year won't do, you know, people will remember seeing you in them, you'll have to shop around for new. Perhaps I can lend you something.'

'We're not the same size, Millicent, I'm taller than you.'

'Oh well clothes are shorter this year. I was hoping to borrow that beige silk dress of yours but I suppose you'll be wanting it yourself now.'

'When did you see it?'

'Oh, Mother said you'd got some new clothes so I took a look in your wardrobe, I didn't think you'd mind.'

"I shall need the dress, Millicent, I'm sorry.'

'Oh well it was just a thought, it probably isn't my colour anyway.'

Easter was very much on Geraldine Broadhurst's mind. Stuart Mansell had brought the matter up over dinner where they were being entertained along with Sybil's parents.

'Have you got anything in mind?' she asked him.

'The Lakes is always a possibility. I booked in when we were there for Christmas, it's a popular venue.'

'Well we haven't thought much about it,' Geraldine said, 'There's Debbie. Easter is bound to be a difficult time for her, but I wouldn't think The Lakes is a possibility, not yet at any rate.'

'And you won't want to leave her on her own,' Sybil put in gently.

'Hardly.'

'I should have thought you'd got shares in the place by the time you spend there,' Sybil's father put in testily. 'We thought you'd want to spend Easter with us in the Dales.'

'The cottage is too small,' Stuart said sharply.

'Not if the children aren't with you.'

'It's a change from cooking and cleaning house for Sybil.'

'Well there's not much of that at the cottage.'

'I do like The Lakes, Father,' Sybil said quietly. 'I feel it's so relaxing. Why don't you and John come with us, Geraldine, I'm sure Debbie will find something else to do?'

'Where is Debbie?' Stuart asked. 'Why isn't she eating dinner with us?'

'She went off early this morning saying she had to meet somebody, she didn't say who.'

'She's evidently making a day of it,' John said shortly.

Debbie was eating out in the company of Peter Cavendish. She had received a Christmas card from him in which he stated he would be in Buxton on business in the New Year and would like her to eat luncheon or dinner with him.

Debbie had eaten both luncheon and dinner with Peter. They had driven along the winding roads over the Pennine Hills and Easter was very much on their minds.

'Easter will bring it all back to you, Debbie,' Peter was saying sympathetically. 'What are your parents saying?'

'We don't talk about it. They don't talk about it because they think it upsets me, I don't talk about it because there's not much point. Tod's gone, Peter, and he isn't coming back. The longer I stay near the people who knew us both the harder it is. I have to get away.'

'Where will you go?'

She shrugged her shoulders.

Suddenly she smiled. 'My parents are dining with the Mansells tonight, they'll be talking about holidays, I know, they'll be saying they can't leave me, that I'd be miserable. I'll be more miserable if I think they're staying at home for my sake.

'The Lakes is out, of course.'

'Can you possibly imagine what everybody would say if I went back there, and yet how many times have I heard it said that you should face your disasters head on? When I was being taught to ride, I was told if I fell off I had to get right back on and ride or otherwise I might never want to ride again.'

'Could you do it, Debbie?'

She stared down at the table reflectively and he waited for her answer, watching the doubts crossing her pretty face, the uncertainty and the assurance.

'Why not? I didn't make Tod go out to climb that mountain, I begged him not to go. All right, it will bring it all back to me but I can't run away forever. I didn't enjoy it with Tod for the simple reason that he was hating it. I did enjoy it for myself and the time I was with you.'

'Then why don't you go?'

'I'll see what my parents are doing. They'll think it's a terrible mistake.'

Peter did not tell her that he had reserved a room months ago.

When she told her parents she thought she might like to go to The Lakes with them for Easter they were horrified.

'How can you go?' her mother cried. 'It's insensitive, think what the Hanleys will say, think what the town will say.'

'The Hanleys are going to Spain, Mother, the Brewsters are going with them. They haven't thought to invite me, I'm the daughter-in-law that never was.'

'They've always been friends with the Brewsters, Debbie.'

'I know, and they would have preferred Tod to marry Janet, he didn't, and they blame me for much that happened. Mother, I have to face the past, not hide from it. Going to The Lakes has nothing to do with Tod, it has to do with being somewhere I like with my parents.'

The Mansells too didn't think it was a good idea either.

'If Debbie's going to go up there bemoaning what happened last Easter it's going to spoil everything for us,' Stuart said sharply.

'Some people might think it's pretty brave of her,' Sybil demurred.

'And more people will think she's forgotten him already.'

Debbie no longer mixed with the old crowd so she didn't hear their comments on the matter. She only knew that they avoided her and there were no more invitations to take tea with her mother-in-law.

On the weekend before Easter Stuart stayed on in London on the grounds that there was urgent business to attend to. He asked his secretary to work late and then he took her out to dinner.

He chose a restaurant he had never been to with Alison, and he set out to be charming and entertaining. Maeve McNamara looked more than attractive as she sat listening to his anecdotes and she told him about herself.

He learned that she was the daughter of an Irish doctor in Dublin and a Scottish mother. She was the youngest of five children, and her one ambition in life had been to work in London, preferably for a Member of Parliament, hopefully for a Junior Minister.

She shared a flat with two other girls, both of whom were civil servants and it was her ambition one day to have a flat of her own. She was looking around.

'If I'd known Alison Gray was selling her flat I'd have been interested,' she confided. 'I'd have asked my father for a loan, I'm sure he'd have said yes.'

'Were you very friendly with Alison?' he asked, knowing full well that she was not.

'I didn't really know her very well. I admired her, she was very beautiful.'

'Yes, I suppose she was.'

'She didn't really have many friends amongst the girls, I always thought Alison was a man's girl.'

He stared at her curiously. He'd said that to Alison many times. The girl a man liked to be seen with, a girl who could be funny but feminine too.

'I hope you're finding me efficient, Mr Mansell,' she said. 'I know you thought a lot of Alison, that she'd be a hard act to follow. I really am trying very hard.'

'My dear girl, you're doing splendidly, I've hardly missed Alison at all. My wife and I are going to The Lakes for Easter, we'll probably see her there.'

With the mention of his wife her expression changed from coy sweetness to businesslike practicality.

She had to know about his wife, he would talk about Sybil and his children, then it was up to her. In his early days with Alison he had never talked about his wife, she'd always thought he was lonely and not too happily married. With this girl he would make his position plain.

He dropped her off at her flat just before midnight, thanked her for a delightful evening, and wished her a very happy Easter.

Tomorrow he would leave for the North.

Lord Alveston's butler was delighted that his master seemed more like his old self since his return from London. It was amazing what a few weeks at his Club and a few girlie shows could do to cheer him up.

Daphne Carmel also noted his obvious good humour and she decided to try again.

'We really ought to think of attending the dinner dance at The Lakes on Easter Saturday,' she began. 'Andrew, I don't want you to think that I'm trying to organise your life for you, but I would ask a favour of you.' She looked at him expectantly.

'What sort of favour?' he enquired.

'My sister's coming to stay with us for Easter, would you be her escort? Jeffrey isn't coming, they've been at loggerheads for years I don't know why they don't call it a day but there's obviously too much at stake. You know Janice, you're old friends so will you come to her rescue and join our party for the dance?'

'I would have thought the hotel would have enough of their own guests without outside participants,' he said doubtfully.

'We've livened up the dances in the winter, they can't tell us they don't want our patronage now. Will you join us?'

'I'm sorry, Daphne, but I have a guest for Easter, you'll find somebody else I'm sure, what about Beresford?'

'He's as dull as dish water. Is your guest staying at The Hall?'

'No. At The Lakes.'

'Well he can join us too.'

'My guest is a lady, Daphne.'

He was aware of the round-eyed curiosity from around the table but particularly from his hostess.

'A woman, Andrew! How long have you been keeping her under wraps?'

Andrew permitted himself a small smile.

'But why The Lakes, Andrew, why not The Hall?'

'I thought the hotel would be more entertaining and she knows people there.'

His explanation should be good enough for them, after all he doubted if Mary would have accepted his invitation to stay at the Hall, she was too obsessed with their different lifestyles.

'What is she like, Andrew, do we know her?'

'No, none of you know her.'

'How long have you known her?'

'About a year.'

'Is she pretty?'

'I think so.'

'You must bring her to dinner one evening, and we must think up lots of things for you to do. Does she hunt?'

'I doubt it.'

'Don't be so tiresome, darling, do tell us a little bit about her. Is she one of us? Where does she live?'

'In the West Midlands, and I'm not sure what you mean by one of us?'

'Of course you know what I mean. You know I'm not a snob, Andrew, I just want to know if I can be a friend to her.'

'That would be up to you, Daphne, but she isn't coming up here to party with a crowd of my friends, we want to spend some time together, perhaps get to know each other a little better.'

'So it could be serious?'

'I rather think I've answered enough questions for one evening, Daphne, if there's any more to tell you'll hear all about it in due course.'

Chapter Thirty-Five

Cornelius Harvey was helping himself to a second helping of scrambled eggs when his wife passed an embossed important-looking card to him across the breakfast table.

He stared at it curiously, then at his wife. Clarissa was wearing a self-satisfied smile and, putting down his knife and fork, he opened the folded card and read the contents. He frowned.

'You're not suggesting we go, I hope?' he said dourly.

'Why not?'

'We went last year, why should he want to ask us again?'

'I think it's very kind of him. He's enclosed a letter, says he's bringing his family over and wants us to meet them, particularly as we were responsible for him buying the place in the first instance.'

'Totally unnecessary.'

'Well I don't think so. You can call to see your brothers and some of the people you knew when you lived in the area. I like to get away at Easter, we've endured all the awful weather the winter's thrown at us, it will be nice to be pampered for a few days.'

He scowled. Clarissa didn't change. She'd been spoiled by both her parents, too much money, they'd been too doting.

She knew exactly what he was thinking, it was a theory he'd trotted out whenever they'd had a difference of opinion. He would give in to her on this issue, he'd argue about it, but in the end she'd have her way.

'The weather's unpredictable at Easter,' he snapped.

'The weather can be unpredictable in July. If we waited for the weather we'd never go anywhere. I'll go into Chester on Tuesday and look at the shops.'

'You've enough clothes in the wardrobe to sink a ship.'

'I took those clothes last year, the same people may be there so I have to have some new ones. That dinner jacket of yours is looking a bit grey, you've had it as long as I can remember.'

'It'll do for the places we go to.'

'You can come into Chester with me and get measured for a new one.'

'I've no time to go into Chester, I told Ted Greenacre I'd give him a hand with his new garage.'

'There's the rest of the week. One day won't make a difference either one way or the other.'

'It's sheer extravagance. When am I likely to wear the thing again?'

'There'll be other holidays. We might be getting on a bit but we're not in our dotage yet.'

He put aside the card and stared down at his scrambled eggs, now cold and congealing on his plate. His wife said evenly, 'Give those to the dog next door and have some more coffee. I'll write to Mr Van Hopper and tell him we'll arrive on Thursday morning and stay until Wednesday like we did last year. I wonder if that nice young lady will be there this year, you know, the one Lord Alveston took a shine to.'

Cornelius scowled.

'It wasn't all wine and roses,' he said dourly, 'that young fellow was killed on Scafell Pike, and that actress woman was posing everywhere in front of those reporters.'

'Of course, I wonder if she'll be there this year. I rather like that new thing she's in. She's taking a much older part but she's very good, she's getting too old anyway to take the romantic roles.'

'It's rubbish. I never watch it.'

'Well if you don't watch it how can you say it's rubbish?' she said adamantly.

Clarissa was thinking of the luxury of their room overlooking the lake, the excellent food and the women's gowns. If he decided not to go she'd go without him.

Geraldine Broadhurst was worried about Debbie's insistence that she would spend Easter at The Lakes. The Hanleys now had considerable prestige in the town since Daniel Hanley had acquired money, been successful in his business ventures and employed a great many people in his various enterprises.

It didn't really matter that the Broadhursts were considered landed gentry, times were changing and Geraldine was aware of the talk going on around them. When she went into her hairdressers the welcome was warm enough, but underneath there were the long silences and the exchanged glances.

John was experiencing similar treatment at his Lodge meetings. In some exasperation she said to Debbie, 'Really, Debbie, I don't think you should go, it's too soon. Next year perhaps, but this year you should be content to go somewhere else.'

'I've done nothing wrong, Mummy. I didn't push Tod off that mountain, I didn't encourage him to go climbing at all, they already ignore me. I don't go to the parties, I'm never invited. I don't go to the tennis club or the gym, in fact they wouldn't care if I was dead so why should I care that a holiday at The Lakes would make things worse? They couldn't be worse.'

'They'll get better, darling, it's all still pretty recent and Tod was their idol after all. They do blame you for going there, and you have to admit Tod didn't have much of a say in the matter.'

'I know. I was wrong about that, I thought he'd love it, I made a terrible mistake and he hated it, but if he'd done it to me I'd have tried, Mother, Tod didn't try.'

'Look, Debbie, your father'll pay for a holiday anywhere you want to go. Telephone one of your old school friends to go with you, I'm sure they would and he'll pay for her as well.'

'No, Mother. I'm not being pushed into going somewhere to please them. I don't need them, and I can please myself. I'm too young to be a widow, but it is my life, I have to run it the way that's best for me.'

Geraldine telephoned the Hanleys to say she hoped they would have a nice holiday in Spain, but her reception was unfriendly, even hostile. When she told her husband he merely said, 'You should have known better than to ring them, obviously they've condemned Debbie, they've cast us in the same mould.'

'But it's so unfair, John. The poor child has suffered enough.'

'I'm not so sure that she's suffered at all. She was angry not grieving.'

'How can you say that?'

'She never talks about him, she never looks at his photograph, at least when I'm there she doesn't. It's not our fault, even when there are some people who are blaming us. But Debbie has to work things out for herself and none of them have helped her, why should she care about them now?'

As they drove up to the Lake District the Thursday before Easter Sybil Mansell was saying much the same thing to her husband.

'I do think Debbie shouldn't come, Stuart, but I can see her point. None of Tod's friends have been nice to her, it's almost as if they blamed her for the tragedy.'

'She should have known that he wouldn't like The Lakes, it wasn't his scene. They blame her for taking him there.'

'Is that what you've heard?'

'Well in my position I listen to all sides. Tod was a Jack the Lad, The Lakes was never for him, he hadn't that sort of intelligence.'

'I feel very sorry for his mother.'

'Naturally. He was the apple of her eye.'

'Debbie's been so withdrawn, bottling things up all the time.'

'And angry, very angry.'

'Angry!'

'Naturally. Too young to be a widow, no friends, no parties, and it's all Tod's fault.'

Sybil regarded her husband with some admiration. He really had become a student of human nature and it had been that special acumen that had made him a Junior Minister.

He was a good M.P. and his majority was climbing when others were falling. She had no doubt that Stuart would go up and up, become one of the inner circle. There had been Prime Ministers who hadn't started out with the same advantages as Stuart.

Stuart's mind was a long way from Debbie Broadhurst and her decision to visit The Lakes. He was thinking that just twelve months ago he was driving along this same road on his way to meet Alison. He had been concerned about how she would greet him, and he was remembering her stepping off the train with a smile on her face.

She had looked so beautiful, people were looking at her, tall and elegant, her hands reaching out to clasp his.

What a fool she'd been to burn her boats the way she had. To leave London and a job most girls would die for. If she'd been patient it would have worked out one day, but she hadn't been patient, she'd pushed him beyond his limits and he'd jolly well see that it didn't happen again.

Maeve McNamara was a different sort of girl. She was more ambitious than Alison, a girl with her eye on the main chance, he'd be a stepping stone, they'd use each other.

'Are we stopping somewhere to eat?' Sybil was asking him.

'If you like. Where are you thinking of?'

'I don't really know.'

'Actually I thought we'd crash on and get a snack at The Lakes after we've seen our room. Are you hungry?'

'Not particularly. We'll do that then. The Broadhursts will be here later so we'll be able to have dinner together.'

'I've no doubt there'll be guests who were here last year, I expect they'll be pretty surprised to see the young Mrs Hanley.'

'Oh, Stuart, I really do wish she wasn't coming.'

Mary Styles was also driving north on that Thursday afternoon but she was worried about something entirely different.

She was looking forward to seeing Andrew even when she regarded the forthcoming weekend as a leap in the dark. She did not think it was going anywhere, there were too many things against it.

Mrs Ralston had informed her the previous Friday that she and her son were going away for about ten days, first to a country club so that Gerald could play golf, and then to The Lakes as last year. She had looked at Mary questioningly, 'I'm telling you, my dear, so that you won't reserve the books for me next week. Of course it will be Good Friday, won't it, how silly of me, the library will be closed.'

Across her head she had looked directly into Gerald's eyes and as so many times recently she saw a deep misery in them. His mother made him embarrassed, and Mary understood and pitied him.

'Will you be at The Lakes over Easter, Miss Styles?' Mrs Ralston had asked brightly.

'Yes,' Mary had answered her and gave her full attention to the books in front of her.

'Well of course, Lord Alveston will have booked in for you. Wouldn't you rather stay at The Hall, my dear?'

Mary passed the books over and Gerald said sharply, 'Do hurry, Mother, we are on a meter.'

'Oh I do think it will be nice to see the same people there this year, it's like meeting old friends,' she trilled. 'Of course that young girl who lost her husband won't be there, but there are sure to be a great many people we met last year. Will you be driving up, Miss Styles or will Lord Alveston be coming down for you?'

'I shall be driving there, Mrs Ralston, and now if you will excuse me the girls are anxious to get away.'

Behind the shelves the girls were giggling. They were well aware that Gerald's mother embarrassed him and Miss Styles.

Mrs Ralston was a difficult woman to shake off. She would not miss an opportunity to chat to her as if she was an old friend, Gerald would squirm with mortification and she was quite capable of approaching Andrew with her questions.

Andrew had said he would join Mary on Thursday evening for dinner but she was wishing it could be anywhere but The Lakes.

The Ralstons would be arriving on Good Friday and Mary hoped Andrew would suggest they spent some time away from the hotel.

It was just after lunch when she drove into the hotel car park but she had seen that already the village street was setting itself out for visitors. Window boxes were gay with spring bulbs, doors and windows had been newly painted and there was a new sign hanging outside the village inn.

Across the lake she could see that the steamer was at her moorings and in the gardens by the lakeside daffodils bloomed profusely. When she passed the great wrought iron gates at the entrance to the parkland of Alveston Hall she had slowed down to gaze momentarily along the drive towards the house sheltered behind its grove of trees.

She was remembering the afternoon Andrew had said he would like to show her the gardens and the lake, but a shower of rain had sent them running back to the house, perhaps this year she would be able to see them.

What a momentous year it had been. Her mother's death and the loss of her home. The new flat which never felt like home, even the loss of Mrs Scotson and her constant chatter about nothing in particular. The only thing that remained of the old life was her job and as she handed over her luggage to the car park attendant and walked through the gardens to the hotel she found it hard to believe that she was actually back at The Lakes when she had been so very sure she would never go there again.

As she stepped into the foyer it seemed that suddenly the curtain had risen to reveal a new world, a world of glamour and richness, even when the future was shrouded in mystery. What, she asked herself, was she really doing here?

The large beautiful bedroom the porter showed her into was twice the size of the one she had occupied last year, and the curtains were drawn back to reveal the expanse of the lake and the sweep of the gardens.

She intended to tell Andrew that although he had asked her to come she would pay for the holiday herself, now she viewed the room with some trepidation. The Lakes was expensive, a room like this would cost the earth.

She started to unpack, putting her clothes away in the wardrobe and the drawers, then she looked into the bathroom, exquisite with pale peach tiling, peach rugs and an abundance of pale peach towels. She started nervously at the shrill ringing of the telephone in the bedroom and went to answer it expecting that it would be Andrew ringing to see if she had arrived. It was a woman's voice that spoke to her however saying, 'Mary, this is Alison Gray, I heard that you had arrived. Lord Alveston telephoned early this morning to say he had to go up to Penrith but he'll meet you in the hotel for dinner this evening.'

'Thank you, Alison. I shall look forward to seeing him, and you too.'

'Have you had lunch?'

'No. I thought I'd wait until I got here.'

'Well I'm about to go into the dining room, would you care to join me?'

'Oh yes, that will be lovely.'

'Good. I'll wait for you in the foyer.'

The two women greeted one another and Mary's first reaction was that Alison seemed different. There was a softness about her, a contentment that had not been there before. The old Alison had been unsure, too brittle, but the new Alison's smile was frank and open, there were no hidden secrets, no anxieties disturbing the flawless beauty of her face.

Over lunch they chatted about things in general until Alison got round to telling Mary who they might expect to meet from the year before.

'The Harveys will be here. Mr Van Hopper has invited them to meet his family. You got along with them rather well, didn't you?'

'Yes, I was hoping they'd be here.'

'The Ralstons will be here. They live in Shropshire, you probably know them.'

'Yes.'

'And I should tell you that Stuart Mansell and his wife are here for the weekend and Debbie is coming with her parents.'

Mary's eyes opened in wide-eyed surprise, and Alison said, 'I know, I'm not at all sure that it's a good idea for Debbie to come after the tragedy of last year, but she must feel she has to come.'

'I'm rather surprised that her parents want to be here,' Mary said gently.

'They booked in with the Mansells, they are Stuart's constituents and they see quite a lot of one another during the year. They haven't arrived yet, no doubt Debbie will weather the storm of criticism. People will be surprised, seeing her here will bring the tragedy back, I'm sure, but everybody will be sympathetic.'

'Yes of course. I suppose we can look forward to the Dinner Dance on Easter Saturday? I had a wonderful evening last year.'

Alison smiled. 'I saw that you did. Perhaps I should warn you that a crowd of Andrew's friends are having dinner on Saturday, he's been here with them once or twice, but he's asked for a table for two which means you won't be joining them for dinner.'

Mary looked at her in some dismay. Andrew's friends would be here but they were not joining them! Was this because she wasn't exactly in their league, or for some other reason? Seeing the anxiety in her eyes Alison said quickly, 'They're the crowd he was friendly with years ago, and Lady Carmel's done her best to get him back in the fold. I must say he's done his best to avoid it.'

'What are they like?'

'Oh they're known as the hunting crowd. They're all into horses and field sports. Lady Carmel is a known matchmaker, she's around Andrew's age, pretty, sits on this committee and that, as well as the Bench, and she'll be curious to meet you. She has tried very hard to include Andrew as an escort for one widow, but nothing materialised, and this weekend she has her younger sister staying with her, however it won't be Lord Alveston who escorts her for the evening.'

'I suppose you get to know everybody, Alison. Are you happy here?'

'Yes very.'

'Did you get away when the hotel was closed for refurbishing?'

'Yes I went to Venice. It rained and rained but the enchantment was still there, and then we toured around Italy until it was time to come home.'

'We?'

Alison blushed. 'I went to Venice on my own, and then Anton came.'

'Mr de Roche?'

'Yes.'

For a few moments Mary stared at her without speaking. She knew nothing about Anton de Roche, but Alison had been hurt once, surely she'd had the good sense to stay out of a similar situation, and Alison smiled. 'It's all right,

Mary, Anton isn't married, this butterfly isn't about to get her wings scorched a second time.

'I didn't come here to find love, I liked him and I respected him first, now I'm falling in love with him. We're two mature people and we are not rushing into anything in a hurry. For now I'm happy to work for him, to dine with him, dance with him, and make love with him.'

'And the future?'

'I think we have a future together, or I hope so. At least he doesn't have a wife and family waiting in the wings.'

'And Stuart?'

'If anybody had told me that in twelve months I'd be in love with somebody else I wouldn't have believed them.

'Stuart was always there, all those years when I told myself I loved him and that one day it would work out. I had no right to believe that, he's got a wife who idolises him, of course he was never going to leave her but why did I have to go on believing that he would, and why couldn't he have been honest with me?'

For a brief second Mary thought about Gerald. She'd thought she was falling in love with Gerald but he hadn't been able to be honest either, but for a very different reason.

Falling out of love had been easier than either of them had dreamed it would be.

Chapter Thirty-Six

For dinner that evening Mary wore the beige dress Millicent had been eager to borrow. The neutral colour was unexciting but the dress had a certain elegance and the colour suited her.

Millicent would probably have suited it better with her blonde hair and hazel eyes. As she surveyed herself in the long mirror her thoughts went back to end of term musical concerts at the school they had both attended. Millicent had been among the fairies on the front row, angelic-looking and winsome, Mary had more often than not been somewhere at the back with the other girls who had no special talents. She had never forgotten the evening Miss Madely had said to their mother, 'It always seems to be Millicent on the front row, I hope Mary doesn't mind.'

'Well, of course not,' her mother had said sharply. 'Millicent is the pretty one, Mary will always be the plain one.'

Miss Madely had looked at her doubtfully before saying, 'A great many children develop later, like the ugly duckling and Mary is undoubtedly the clever one.'

She smiled wryly at her reflection. This evening the ugly duckling hadn't done too badly.

As she entered the foyer she saw Andrew in conversation with Anton de Roche and for a moment she paused to look at them. They were two men cut from a similar mould. Tall and elegant, conversing easily together, occasionally laughing. She could well understand how Alison had begun to fall in love with Anton, but she didn't have Alison's beauty. It was a beauty that would captivate most men, she wasn't too sure what Andrew had found in herself.

He turned his head and saw her, they both smiled and Andrew came forward to greet her.

Anton de Roche said easily, 'I hope your room is to your liking, Miss Styles.'

'Yes thank you, it's lovely.'

'I also hope that we have better weather than last year. Easter is a little later this year, perhaps those few extra days will bring more sunshine.'

He smiled and walked with them across the foyer to the dining room.

'Many of the guests will be arriving tomorrow so the dining room isn't full this evening, your table is in the alcove near the window.'

They followed the head waiter to their table and Mary was immediately aware of a stir among the guests. Even in a company of rich people Lord Alveston would be noticed.

She felt momentarily self-conscious but Andrew was chatting easily, about his trip up to Penrith to purchase a horse he had admired, and then consulting her about the menu, long before the first course arrived she felt at ease, that she never wanted to dine with anybody else.

A pianist played while they ate, light classical music that was easy to listen to and Mary glanced around the room for the first time.

A woman sitting several tables away smiled at her and Mary smiled back as she recognised Mrs Harvey. The Mansells were sitting in the centre of the room and they were dining alone, apparently the Broadhursts had not yet arrived. Mrs Mansell looked nice, a dark pretty woman in a sage green dress and only minutes later there was another stir in the dining room when the Broadhursts accompanied by Debbie sat at their table.

The older people looked self-conscious for a few moments, but Debbie stared straight ahead before devoting her full attention to the menu. Throughout the meal she neither looked at those sitting with her or at those sitting at other tables. There was a tinge of defiance in her attitude and Mary guessed that she must be feeling uneasy.

Meeting Andrew's eyes she said, 'Poor girl, surely this weekend will bring everything back to her.'

'Yes. It is a strange thing that brings her here, what particular demon do you suppose she's chasing?'

'That's a strange thing to say, Andrew.'

'I know, but then I know an awful lot about demons, Mary.'

After dinner people drifted into the bars and lounges, some went into the card rooms, others played snooker, but Andrew suggested that they sit in the room they called the Rose Room where yet another pianist played background music for the conversation that went on in there.

'The place will really come alive tomorrow,' he said. 'You know there is a dinner dance on Saturday evening?'

'Yes, like last year.'

He smiled. 'I booked a table for us, I thought perhaps you would like to come.'

'Yes I would. I expect the hotel will be full and there will be people coming from outside.'

There, she had said it. Andrew's friends would be coming and she had to know if he intended her to meet them.

He did not say anything immediately, he was not aware how desperately she waited for him to mention them. At last he said almost indifferently, 'There are a party of my friends dining here on Saturday, I preferred not to join them on this occasion.'

'Why was that, Andrew?'

'They have been trying very hard to bring back the old days, run with the old crowd and it's the last thing I want. It's not that I don't like them, some of the old times were good times, but I really am not the person they remember, I've had to reshape my life and there can be no turning back, Mary.'

'But you can't ignore them.'

'I don't intend to ignore them, I simply don't want us to be part of their evening.'

'I see.'

He stared at her doubtfully. 'Mary, this has nothing to do with you, it has everything to do with a past I am desperately trying to forget. They have tried too hard when I've been with them, but it was always patently obvious that they were treating me like a man who had come back from oblivion.'

They chatted amicably, and the silences were harmonious. Later in the evening they chatted to the Harveys and the Van Hoppers, and Julius was quick to express his pleasure that Lord Alveston found the hotel much to his liking.

Before Andrew departed for home Mary walked with him to the doorway. Outside the gardens were bathed in the light of a full moon, silvering the lake, vying with the lights of the village across the water, and Andrew looking down at her said softly, 'What would you like to do tomorrow, Mary?'

'Anything you like, Andrew. You don't really have to spend every day with me, I'm sure you have other things you need to do.'

'Would you prefer some time to yourself?'

She looked up at him nonplussed, and he said quickly, 'Tomorrow I'll take you to The Hall for lunch. We can take that walk in the gardens we never did manage the last time, and I'll introduce you to Hassan.'

'Hassan?'

'My new horse. A pure bred Arab and very beautiful. Do you like dogs?'

'Yes I love them but when Sally died we never had another.'

'How long ago was that?'

'She was my father's golden cocker. My mother never really liked dogs, she had heart trouble, I went out to work so she said there would be nobody around to exercise a dog.'

'I see. Well I've got an old labrador and there are some puppies at the stables, I'm bringing one of them into the house. You can select the one you like best.'

She was aware of her blushing face as he wished her goodnight. Why had he said she could select one? It would be Andrew's dog. She had to stop reading more into his words than he intended.

As she crossed the foyer to the lifts she saw that Anton de Roche stood chatting to the Mansells, then they were joined by the Broadhursts. There was no sign of Debbie.

Debbie was in her room, her face sunk in a magazine although she was not reading. She was wishing she hadn't come, she was a skeleton at the feast and her mother'd been right. People were curious, even if they were polite.

The room overlooked the fells at the side of the hotel, a far cry from the bridal suite she had occupied with Tod. There would be four more days of it and there was a dance on Saturday evening. Her father and Stuart Mansell would ask her to dance out of a sense of duty, but it would pretty soon get around among the younger men that she was a recent widow, insensitive enough to return to the scene of the crime so to speak, and they'd think there was very little fun in an association with her.

She was wishing she'd brought her own car, that way she would have been able to go home if the place got too much for her.

There was a light tap on the door and she hesitated in opening it. She really didn't want her mother flapping about like an old hen, but when the tap was repeated she rose with a resigned air and went to open the door. Alison Gray greeted her with a warm smile saying, 'Hello, Debbie, I saw you get into the lift, I thought you'd be on your own. I've brought a bottle of very light white wine, shall we have a drink?'

Debbie's face had lit up with pleasure and she opened the door wider to allow Alison in.

'Are you quite comfortable in here?' Alison asked. 'I chose the room myself, I thought it was modern and cheerful.'

'Yes it's lovely. I didn't expect the bridal suite.'

Alison shook her head sadly. 'Of course not, Debbie, I've brought two wine glasses, I'll perch on the end of the bed.'

'Were you surprised when you knew I was coming?' Debbie asked.

'I thought you might be hurting yourself unnecessarily.'

To her consternation Debbie dissolved into a flood of tears and she watched helplessly until she composed herself, then Debbie looked straight at her with tear-filled eyes. 'Alison, I want to hurt about Tod, I want to think about him and grieve for him, I want to miss him, but I must be an absolutely awful person, all I can feel is anger at what his death has done to me.'

'I think that's pretty natural, Debbie.'

'Do you? Do you really?'

'Yes of course. You're little more than a child and here you are a widow. It wasn't just Tod you lost, it was all the good times you'd promised yourself that went with him.'

'Nobody at home seems to understand. Oh they're kind and considerate but they think I should want to shut myself away until I'm over it, they don't understand the anger I feel. Why are you so understanding?'

'I know all about anger, Debbie. I know all about sitting at home alone waiting for the telephone to ring, knowing it wouldn't be some nice young man who thought he liked me, but knew I was too much involved with somebody else. You think nobody will ever want to know you because of Tod, but one day they will, Debbie, believe me.'

'Were you in love with Stuart Mansell?'

'I believed so. I was younger than you when I met him, when I fell in love with him, and you know how long it lasted. I thought I'd never forgive him for the empty years, the years when I should have been going out with a host of young men, having fun, being young, not even searching for something permanent.'

'Will you ever find anybody else?'

Alison smiled, and Debbie said quickly, 'You have, haven't you, Alison? Somebody nice, somebody you like better than Stuart?'

Alison nodded.

'Who? where did you meet him?'

'Here, in the hotel.'

Debbie stared at her, then suddenly gave a little cry, 'Alison, not Mr de Roche? Oh I think he's gorgeous. He's so good-looking in that severe touch-me-not manner. Does he feel the same way about you?'

'If he doesn't I'm back where I started, but at least he'll have helped me over Stuart.'

'I hope he isn't married.'

'No, at least I don't have a wife to contend with.'

'I should think he's a wonderful lover. He reminds me of one of those knights in shining armour, charming, dignified and a little aloof. Is he able to unbend, Alison?'

Alison laughed. 'Now you're fishing,' she said. 'We spent some time in Venice together and then we made our way back very slowly through Italy, he made Italy come alive for me, I saw it through Anton's eyes and I'll love it forever, we arrived back here and started to think about where we will go next.'

'Where do you want to go?'

'Whenever I went abroad in the past I was itching to get back to Stuart, I never really enjoyed myself. I only ever went to Paris with Stuart and half way through a three-day holiday he received a telephone call that he was wanted urgently in London so we came back. Now I feel that the world is my oyster, I can see Leningrad and Moscow, Warsaw and Prague, all the beautiful exciting cities that Anton knows, all the cities where we don't have to think about politics and who we would meet around the next corner.'

For a few minutes there was silence while they sipped their wine, and then in a small voice Debbie said, 'Mrs Mansell's awfully nice, did you never think of her?'

There was raw pain in Alison's eyes. 'I didn't know her, I hated her without reason except that she kept Stuart away from me. My love was entirely selfish, I was prepared to break up a marriage, regardless of his children, I deserved to be unhappy. But he was the one who had the best of both worlds, his comfortable home with his wife and children, and me to smooth his life at Westminster and give him love when she wasn't around. I had no right to expect anything, Debbie, but Stuart gave me cause to think that one day we would have something together, I believed him.'

Debbie's words about Mrs Mansell troubled Alison strangely after she returned to her room on the top floor. It was true she'd never really thought about Stuart's wife except as a shadowy being who lived at the other end of England and to whom he returned whenever he visited his constituency.

Debbie had said she was nice and no doubt she was. She was a pretty woman with a ready smile and whenever she looked at Stuart there was deep and steady devotion in her eyes. She was the mother of his children, Stuart and those children were her world.

Sybil Mansell had trusted her husband implicitly. Never in a thousand years would she have thought him capable of deceiving her with another woman and yet in her moments of fury Alison had believed herself capable of shattering that complacency and telling her about their affair. She knew now she couldn't have done it.

Stuart had no right to promise her marriage, and she had no right to believe it was possible.

She curled up on the settee and dissolved into tears. She was still sobbing a little later when Anton came to her room so that he stood looking down at her with some concern before sitting down besides her.

'What brought this on?' he enquired softly.

The words tumbled over one another as she reviled herself about Stuart, and in the end he took hold of her hands saying sternly, 'Stop this, Alison, it's over, it no longer means anything, unless seeing him again has raised too many ghosts.'

She stared at him. 'Anton, it isn't that, it's just something Debbie said that made me realise how wrong I've always been. I don't love Stuart at all, I'm over him.'

'Then why are you distressing yourself needlessly?'

'I'm thinking about all the waste and my stupidity in thinking it would all work out. Never in my life will I be so stupid again.'

'About loving some married man, do you mean?'

'About loving any man who doesn't love me enough.'

'Enough for what?'

He was looking at her very intently and she suddenly realised that she had asked for some sort of commitment and it seemed that in the next few minutes the rest of her life would be resolved one way or another.

She was staring at him helplessly, her mind awash with doubts and uncertainties. They were involved in a love affair that had started in Italy and continued since they arrived back. Nobody knew better than Alison that passion and love were not essentially the same thing, now she was asking Anton to make a decision that would establish their future. She was not sure if he was ready for such a commitment.

In those first few minutes his calm handsome face gave nothing away. It was a face she loved, but it was a face that could be equally charming to people he liked and utterly disliked, behind that calm imperturbable mask was there another man who could love unreservedly, surrender the rest of his life to loving one woman who loved him?

He was holding her hands in his, but she could not tell from his expression if he was surprised or even annoyed by her words, then suddenly he smiled and his voice was almost teasing as he said, 'Alison, there really is no reason for you to look so uneasy. If you are asking me if I love you the answer is yes I do. If you want me to ask you to marry me, then yes I will, hopefully sometime at the end of January so that we can spend a few blissful weeks in some desert oasis or some more populated place, I'll leave that to you.'

She stared at him incredulously, then with a little moan she threw herself into his arms and in a strangled voice said, 'Oh, Anton, I'll love you forever, nothing and nobody will ever mean as much to me as you.'

He laughed. 'Well, you can start by drying those tears. I have a surprise for you.'

'A surprise, a present do you mean?'

'Why do women's minds always evolve around presents,' he laughed. 'No actually this surprise involves the arrival of another guest at the hotel, a certain Miss McNamara. Mr Mansell was a little more than surprised when he saw her registering at the desk.'

'Maeve McNamara, Stuart's new secretary!'

'Really?'

'Did she know he was to be here?'

'That I can't tell you.'

'Is she here alone?'

'Yes. She booked in several months ago, she knows you're here of course.'

'Well yes. She knew where I was coming when I left Westminster.'

'Well I would say she's either here to see what you've tumbled into or she knew he was coming here.'

'You say Stuart was surprised?'

'A little shocked, I think. He introduced her to his wife and the Broadhursts. Mrs Mansell was predictably charming, Mrs Broadhurst rather less so I thought.'

'I never particularly liked her.'

'I have no idea if there is anything going on between Mr Mansell and his new secretary, Alison. If there is, I doubt he'll find her as accommodating as you obviously were, my dear.'

'Why do you say that?'

'From long years of mixing with the human race in small worlds called hotels. I would say Miss McNamara is something of a predator, and Mr Mansell had better watch his step if he wants to escape unscathed.'

'Surely he'll have the sense to see it.'

Anton shrugged his shoulders. 'He's not your problem anymore, darling. We're surely not going to spend the night concerning ourselves with Stuart Mansell and his problems, I can think of better things to do.'

It was Good Friday morning and people were going to church. Alison walked down through the gardens to the jetty where the boat was moored and where people had congregated to sail in her across the lake.

She went to stand alone at the prow of the vessel and she stepped back into the shadow when she saw Maeve McNamara hurrying to board the boat. She was alone, and when they reached the jetty for the village Alison hung back until she saw which way the other girl intended to walk. When she dawdled along the village street Alison set off at a brisk walk towards the church. She would not be able to escape, sooner or later she would come face to face with the girl who had taken her place at Westminster, whether she had taken her place in Stuart Mansell's affections or his life was no longer her concern.

Chapter Thirty-Seven

Driving up to Alveston Hall Andrew and Mary met a steady stream of traffic, some of them out for a leisurely drive on Good Friday, others heading for the hotel, and in the village High Street shop-keepers were doing a lively trade.

Even though Easter was a religious festival, they were making hay while the sun shone, but above the activity along the road the sonorous sound of a church bell could be heard tolling.

It was one of those golden days in early April that Browning must have had in mind when he wrote his poem 'Oh to be in England now that April's there'. The sun shone out of a clear blue sky, the lake sparkled, primroses peeped from under the hedgerows and daffodils bloomed profusely in the parkland.

She exclaimed with delight as she saw a herd of deer sheltering under distant trees and as Andrew brought the car to a halt on the terrace a black labrador that had been sitting on the steps above bounded down to meet them with obvious delight.

He leapt up at Andrew with a waving tail and wide grin, then turned his attention on Mary with ecstatic yelps of welcome.

'This is Jason,' Andrew said smiling down to where Mary stooped with her arms around the dog. 'He's a very old gentleman, I'm afraid, but extremely fit.'

'Will he like another dog in the house?' she asked him.

'I'm sure he'll tolerate the puppy. He's met the spaniels down at the stables and he's been very tolerant of Shaney and her brood.'

'A spaniel, Andrew. Oh I love spaniels, Sally was a spaniel.'

'A black one, I'm afraid, Mary.'

'It doesn't matter.'

Grant welcomed her with warm smiles and informed his master that lunch had been laid out for them in the small dining room, and Andrew explained, 'The large dining room is very formal, I keep that for those rare times when I entertain a large group of friends.'

It must be wonderful to live in a place like this, Mary thought, but she kept her opinion to herself. The lunch was excellently cooked and served and she was constantly aware of Grant's benign presence and the smiling face of the young maidservant who waited on them.

In the afternoon they strolled through the parkland towards the stables where Mary was introduced to the old horse who greeted Andrew with soft neighs and some anticipation.

'Not today, old boy,' Andrew said gently, indicating that they should walk on to where another horse stood with his head overlooking his stable door. He was pale cream and beautiful and he allowed Mary to pat his soft satiny neck and gentle face.

'He's beautiful,' she exclaimed. 'I've read about pure bred Arabs, I've never seen one before.'

'Do you know anything about horses, Mary?' Andrew asked.

'Nothing at all. I had a disastrous ride on a donkey on the sands at Bognor Regis one summer. I disgraced myself by falling off.'

He laughed. This was why he liked her, she was so completely unpretentious. There were women who would have claimed to be familiar with horses because he expected them to be, but Mary would never be anything except Mary.

That she loved dogs was evident minutes later when she was introduced to Shaney's puppies, four of them. All identical black bundles of mischief who leapt all over her and she laughed with delight.

'Oh they're adorable, Andrew, how can you possibly choose?'

'I'll let you choose.'

'But how can I? I love them all.'

'There are three bitches and one dog. Perhaps a replacement for Sally.'

'Sally died a long time ago but there could never really be a replacement. I'll choose the dog, but he'll be your dog, Andrew so perhaps you would really rather have one of the others.'

'No, I'll bow to your judgment. What would you like to call him?'

'Let's call him Jet, because he's so very black and shiny, like some old beads my grandmother once had.'

'Then Jet it shall be. We'll take a walk now and call for him on our way back.'

The groom who had the puppies touched his cap and with a smile said, ''E'll be waitin' for ye, sir.'

'Are the others going to good homes?'

'That they are, sir. I'm 'avin one of them miself, the other two are goin' to a gamekeeper and a gardener.'

'That's good then.'

They set off to walk through the parkland. The deer had vanished and Andrew explained that they were shy creatures and invariably did a disappearing trick when he had visitors in the parkland. They walked through the formal Italian gardens at the side of the house, along the long beech groves and across the stone bridges that spanned the gurgling stream where Andrew explained there was excellent fishing.

The labrador bounded ahead of them, and it was only when he shot off towards the lake that Andrew called him back sharply.

'No, Jason, not that way, come back.'

The dog turned to stare at them suddenly deflated, and Mary said, 'Oh do let us go that way, Andrew, the lake looks lovely and there are swans on it,' and to suit her actions to her words she set off after the dog who waited for her wagging his tail.

Andrew hesitated suddenly angry, with the dog, with Mary, with himself. He hated the lake and its memories. He lived in a district famous for its lakes so why should this one small tarn tempt visitors to its shores? He followed Mary and his dog very slowly.

By the time he reached the boathouse they were walking along the path that edged the lake, the swans and other waterfowl approached them hopefully but by this time Andrew's thoughts were no longer in the present, they were on that bleak January morning when the park lay frozen under fallen snow and the lake stretched before them like a thin glaze of icing on a cake.

He was seeing again the dark-coated hordes of policemen, the white ambulance and the police cars, seeing them look down on the shrouded figure of Olivia lying on the frozen ground.

He did not see Mary walking back to him and she paused on the path. He was staring out across the lake but the expression on his face chilled her to the bone. He was miles away, that bleak brooding expression was something new to her, something sad and alien and totally remote from the Andrew she had come to know with his gentle charm and composure.

The dog ran to his side, nuzzling his hand, making soft squeaking noises in his throat, and suddenly Andrew came to life. He looked at her across the grass and she was unhappily aware of the raw pain in his eyes and that the joy in their day had suddenly gone.

They walked back to the stables in silence. She could have wept with despair. He hadn't forgotten Olivia, he probably would never forget her even though she was dead and his life had moved on. That look across the lake had said it all, that beautiful ghost of Olivia had stretched out her long white fingers and dragged him into the past, she would never let him go.

By the time they reached the stables some sort of normality had returned and they greeted the puppy with smiles at his antics while the labrador stood beside Andrew eyeing the young dog with canine patience.

They ate afternoon tea in front of a log fire and Mary racked her brains for an excuse to avoid them spending the evening together. Andrew could not believe that he was grateful when she said, 'Would you mind very much,

Andrew, if I spent the evening with Mr and Mrs Harvey, they were so very good to me last year and I've hardly spoken a word to them this year.'

'Of course not, Mary, I'll run you back and I'll probably have an early night. There's the dinner dance tomorrow evening.'

'Yes of course.'

'I'll be over around seven-thirty, we'll meet in the foyer.'

He hadn't suggested that they met during the day and she sat miserably besides him as they drove back to The Lakes. She didn't want dinner, she wasn't hungry but she supposed she had to make some semblance of ordering something.

Her heart sank when the first people she saw in the foyer were Mrs Ralston and Gerald. They were standing with the Mansells, and she couldn't help hearing Mrs Ralston saying effusively, 'I thought you might be here, Mr Mansell, we were bridge partners last year. Do you play bridge, Mrs Mansell?'

Mary didn't wait to hear her reply but went quickly towards the lifts. What would Mrs Ralston make of her dining alone, she'd have something to say no doubt?

She was more than relieved to find Mr and Mrs Harvey waiting for the lift up to their rooms and Mrs Harvey said, 'Will you be listening to the local choir this evening, Alison? I believe they're really very good, they've been asked because it's Good Friday.'

'I didn't know anything about it, Mrs Harvey.'

'Oh well no doubt Lord Alveston will have something else in mind.'

'I'm not seeing him this evening, Mrs Harvey, he had something else on, so I'll probably listen to the choir.'

'Then you must join us. I don't think it's Cornelius's scene, he'll probably make an excuse halfway through the evening and go to the bar, we'll be better off without him.'

She smiled at Mrs Harvey with some degree of gratitude. This was normality, this nice ordinary woman asking her to join them for a concert in the music room, the gentle taunts about her husband's fidgets. Not that bleak haunted expression in Andrew's eyes as he looked across the lake.

Grant was puzzled that his lordship had not gone out but sat slumped in his chair in front of the fire with the expression of an old sadness on his face.

He had declined dinner, said he wasn't hungry and if he wanted something later he'd ring for it. Grant couldn't think that Miss Styles had put it there, she was too nice, too intrinsically decent. No, it was the other one, but he'd been so sure his lordship had put her out of his mind.

Andrew viewed the past few hours with disbelief. That he'd allowed Mary to spend an evening without his company when he'd been the one to insist that she came here, that something he rarely ever thought about had suddenly reappeared to torment him now.

It was later that evening and the gardens were bathed in moonlight when he called to his dog and they set out together across the parkland. He deliberately took the narrow path leading downhill to the lake and the dog ran on ahead of him, only pausing when he reached the boathouse.

Andrew stood in the same spot he had stood at that afternoon. A small breeze ruffled the surface of the lake and the waterfowl had gone to their nests. Only an eerie cry of an owl came to disturb the peace and he deliberately faced his ghosts.

The dark-blue figures had gone, the shrouded form on the ground was there no more, gone too were the police cars and the white ambulance, it was just a lake. He made himself remember Olivia as she had looked that last night with her black hair gleaming under the lamplight, her unusual slanting eyes faintly mocking as she had danced in his arms. She had been beautiful but he had not loved her for a very long time and he did not love her now. Her body lay entombed in the Alveston vault in the old churchyard, he never laid flowers on her grave, there would be no more memories in his heart.

He turned away, calling to his dog, and they walked quickly back to the house. Grant met him in the hall and Andrew said, 'I think I'll eat dinner now, Grant, something light, I'm not very hungry.'

Mary hadn't particularly enjoyed the concert. The choir had been excellent but memories of the day she had spent with Andrew still rankled. Besides, Mrs Ralston and Gerald sat close by and she was aware of Mrs Ralston's interest. Every time the door opened to admit somebody both mother and son looked up expectantly and Mary had no doubt that questions would be posed at a future time. Mrs Ralston would already have made up her mind that they had either quarrelled or he had lost interest.

As Mrs Harvey predicted, Cornelius left them for the bar during the interval and did not return, but they stayed on to listen to the singing and Mrs Harvey said they had been invited to join in the buffet supper laid on for the choir.

Mary declined on the grounds that she had eaten more than enough for that day, saying she would go to her room and read a little. Seeing Mrs Ralston bearing down upon them she beat a hasty retreat much to that lady's annoyance.

'There's evidently something amiss,' she confided to Gerald, 'she didn't want to speak to us. She's gone to her room and it's only just after ten, what do you make of that?'

'That she's probably tired, Mother.'

She made it her business to speak to Alison Gray later and as she prattled on Alison lost no time in summing her up.

'I was hoping to have a chat to Miss Styles,' Mrs Ralston said. 'She lives near us you know, we meet every Friday afternoon. I was wondering if she was not too well, she went to bed very early.'

'Oh I'm sure she's perfectly all right, Mrs Ralston.'

'I was surprised that Lord Alveston was not with her?'

'They were together during the day, Mrs Ralston, and they will be at the Dinner Dance tomorrow evening.'

Alison smiled briefly and moved on.

Mrs Ralston passed this information on to her son who received it without comment.

Mary wasn't sleepy, on the other hand she couldn't get interested in the book she had brought with her. It was a new novel by an up-and-coming author but she found the story pithy. No doubt it would gather momentum but she didn't have the patience to find out.

She lay back among her pillows and thought about the afternoon she had just spent. All evening while she'd listened to the singers or chattered to Mrs Harvey she'd been remembering Andrew's stricken face and she reached the conclusion that he must still love Olivia even when he denied it.

The shrilling of the telephone on her bedside table startled her and she lifted the receiver, surprised to hear Andrew's voice.

His first words surprised her even more. 'Mary, I'm so sorry, can you forgive me?'

'Why do I have to forgive you?'

'Because I should not have let you spend the evening alone, I asked you to come up here, and then like a coward I ran away.'

'I wasn't alone, Andrew, I went to the concert and I sat with Mrs Harvey. What did you do?'

'I went out with the dog and walked to the lake. I made myself go there, it's only the third time since I arrived home that I found the courage.'

'But you can't forget her, Andrew?'

'I can't forget the scene that morning when they found her dead. I have few good memories of Olivia, and love for her is not one of them. Did you enjoy the concert?'

'Yes. It was the choir from the church, apparently they asked them to sing at the hotel because it's Good Friday.'

'Are you in your room?'

'Yes. There was a buffet but I didn't want anything.'

'And tomorrow there's the dance. I'm looking forward to that.'

'I'm glad. So am I.'

'Goodnight, Mary, and once again, I am sorry about today.'

Sitting in the lounge over their drinks, two couples were looking faintly out of countenance. The Broadhursts were concerned about their daughter whom they hadn't seen since lunchtime. Mrs Mansell was concerned for her friends, while Mr Mansell was irritated by the sight of his current secretary sitting in the corner of the lounge with two foreign-looking men who were apparently finding her company riveting. While at a table in the window his former secretary sat in the company of Anton de Roche and the owner of the hotel and his wife.

They were chatting amicably together and occasionally there was laughter. Alison looked radiant and de Roche was too damned attentive. At the other table a fresh lot of drinks had arrived and catching his eye Maeve raised her glass provocatively.

'I can't think why she didn't come to the concert,' Geraldine was saying. 'I know it's hardly her scene but where else can she be?'

'Wasn't she going across to the village in the boat?' John asked.

'She hadn't made her mind up, and if she did it was early this afternoon. It was dark at five o'clock, how will she get back?'

'By taxi, I suppose.'

'Have you seen taxis in this village? I haven't. The boat has done its last trip.'

'I'm sure she's perfectly all right,' Sybil said softly, 'if there were any problems we'd have heard about them.'

Geraldine consulted her watch. 'It's going on for eleven. Do you think I should ask Mr de Roche if he knows anything?'

'No I don't. We don't want a repetition of last year when one of our party goes missing. Debbie isn't into climbing mountains and I'll telephone her room, she's probably in there.'

He came back several minutes later shaking his head.

'No reply,' he said shortly.

'Then we should speak to Mr de Roche,' Geraldine said adamantly.

Anton got to his feet as Geraldine approached their table, but catching sight of her anxiety he said quickly, 'Is anything wrong, Mrs Broadhurst?'

'Yes, it's Debbie, we haven't seen her since lunchtime. I wondered if she'd rung in with a message for us.'

'I haven't heard anything but I'll make enquiries. Please go back to your table, I'll be back in a few minutes.'

He came back shaking his head with a brief smile. 'There have been no messages, Mrs Broadhurst, but your daughter was seen boarding the steamer shortly after lunch with a gentleman.'

'A gentleman! Oh surely not. It can only have been one of the guests she was chatting to, Debbie doesn't know anybody in the hotel.'

'Well I'm sure she'll be back presently and all will be revealed.' He smiled again and moved back to his table.

'Of course she wasn't with a man,' Geraldine said adamantly.

'But you don't know that, Geraldine,' Sybil prompted.

Geraldine bit her lip angrily and consulted her watch again.

'I'm going to the desk,' she snapped, 'Perhaps somebody there can tell me who she was with.'

Stuart was furious. Why on earth had Debbie come with them? The holiday would be ruined and there'd be another scandal he was involved in. He met his wife's eyes across the table and she shook her head gently. She was aware of his frustration and cautioned him to keep calm.

Maeve McNamara and the two men had risen from their table and were moving towards the door. One of them had an arm thrown carelessly round her shoulder and she was laughing up at him with obvious pleasure. In the other corner the conversation was still going on with four people evidently enjoying the others' company.

Geraldine was receiving no help from the staff behind the desk. The girl who had seen Debbie earlier had gone off duty, none of them had seen her that day at all. They had no means of knowing whom she had boarded the steamer with.

In some exasperation she turned away, then from the doorway she heard laughter and she spun round to see Debbie entering the foyer with a young man.

She stood staring at them in amazement. It had been months since she'd heard Debbie's laughter. The man was looking down at her so she couldn't see his face, and in some annoyance she stormed across the room to confront them.

Debbie looked up as her mother paused in front of them, anger in every line on her face, and her eyes opened in startled surprise.

'Debbie, where have you been?' Geraldine demanded. 'You missed dinner, you left no messages, your father and I have been worried sick.'

'But I did leave a message, Mother, I pushed a note under your bedroom door before we went out.'

'What time was that?'

'I'm not sure, around eight o'clock, I think.'

'We were having dinner at that time. Why couldn't you let us know earlier if you didn't intend to join us for dinner?'

She looked at her mother nonplussed, then up at the young man standing beside her and for the first time Geraldine looked at him. After several moments the anger slowly left her face and the young man smiled apologetically.

'I'm sorry, Mrs Broadhurst, I'm sure it's my fault. I met Debbie on the steamer this morning and the concert wasn't our scene. I asked her if she'd like to drive into Keswick with me to eat dinner there.'

Geraldine had thought since their first meeting that Peter Cavendish was an extremely nice young man. She extended her hand with a warm smile and said, 'If I'd known she was with you, Peter, I wouldn't have worried, it's so very nice to meet you again.'

Chapter Thirty-Eight

Easter Saturday and the hotel was in festive mood. Fresh flowers were arriving, extra staff and vans came carrying musical instruments and musicians. The hairdressing salon was open and doing great business and Anton de Roche presided over it all with his usual panache.

Mrs Ralston encountered Mary Styles as she called for her morning paper and immediately her face beamed with pleasure, 'I suppose you're looking forward to the dance this evening, my dear,' she asked. 'I might just take a look in the ballroom but I haven't danced for years, not since my Horace died in fact.'

'Isn't Gerald a dancer?' Mary enquired.

'Well, he did go dancing years ago when his father was alive, he had a crowd of men friends who used to go off on cruises or on the continent. They all got married, and when Horace died Gerald devoted all his attention to looking after me.'

She said it so complacently Mary didn't think she had any idea how selfish she sounded.

'Are you off with Lord Alveston this morning?' Mrs Ralston enquired.

'No, I have a hairdressing appointment and if I don't hurry I'm going to be late.'

Mary smiled at her and made her escape.

Alison met her in the salon and grinned sympathetically. 'I saw you chatting to Mrs Ralston, was she asking you about the dance?'

'Yes. She comes into the library every Friday where I work and there are days when I actually dread meeting her. She's a very curious woman.'

'I know. It's such a shame, her son is very nice, why didn't he cut and run years ago?'

'I think it has something to do with the generation we belong to. Our parents gave us life and we had to repay them. I doubt if Gerald will ever get away.'

* * *

Eyeing herself in the mirror Geraldine Broadhurst was wishing she'd chosen a different colour. John liked her in beige, he said it was restrained and classy, and it did suit her dark auburn hair. That woman she'd seen dining with Lord Alveston wore beige and she had to admit it had given her a sort of quiet elegance, but then the jade-green chiffon had been striking.

John was irritable.

'I think it's a mistake for Debbie to be dolling herself up tonight to attend this dance,' he snapped. 'People will remember and they'll talk.'

'Well we can't expect the poor child to sit in her bedroom listening to the music from the ballroom. This is what this last twelve months has been about, they didn't just bury Tod, they buried Debbie as well.'

'There's time for her to pick up the pieces, but not so soon,' he argued.

'Well I think she's being very brave to come to the dance and Peter Cavendish will look after her.'

'Another reason for them to talk.'

'Look, John, I like Peter, he's charming, good-looking and he's got a very good job. It's obvious he likes Debbie, we shouldn't interfere and it's nobody else's business what she does and where she goes.'

'Has Mansell said anything about it?'

'No, neither of them have. He's got his hands full watching that girl who used to work for him, and the new one that's turned up out of the blue.'

'Now you're at it again, putting two and two together and making five.'

'That first one's an opportunist. She came here to be a secretary but she's dining with de Roche and the owners. Exactly the same thing went on with Stuart, she worked for him and she came here with him.'

When John didn't answer her, she snapped, 'And what brings the new girl here? I thought he looked a bit startled when she showed up.'

There was a soft tap on the door and Geraldine said, 'Answer it, dear, it's probably Debbie. I told her to call in, I want to see what she's wearing.'

Debbie was wearing a gown she'd brought on her honeymoon and had not had an opportunity to wear. It was pale pink silk taffeta and it swept in long folds to the floor. She looked very pretty, Geraldine admired the gown and said so. John thought she should have worn something less bridal.

'Is Peter meeting you downstairs?' her mother asked.

'In the bar, Mummy.'

'Oh well, it's not as though he doesn't know exactly what you've been through, darling. Just go downstairs and enjoy yourself. Does this dress look all right for the occasion?'

'Yes, Mummy, you look lovely. Is it new?'

'Yes, quite new.'

'And expensive,' her husband put in.

'Don't be such a grouch, Daddy,' Debbie said with a smile. 'You'd be horrified if Mummy didn't do you justice. Are you meeting the Mansells downstairs?'

'Yes. I'll bet Sybil is wearing that blue silk dress she's had for ages. She's spending more time in London now, wouldn't you just think she'd shop around for something a little more elegant.'

John stood at the door looking back at them impatiently. 'We don't want to make a grand entrance in the dining room,' he said sharply. 'I suggest you don't spend too long in the bar, Debbie. Is Peter dining with us?'

'I asked him if he'd like to.'

'Well I suggest we get in there pretty quickly. There are a few parties from outside arriving this evening so it'll be first come first served.'

'It's hardly a cafeteria,' Geraldine said. 'The service will be impeccable.'

The dress was the most beautiful Mary had ever worn in her life, it was also the most expensive. When she had handed over her cheque in payment for it she could almost hear her mother saying she'd been guilty of the utmost extravagance, unnecessary extravagance.

She had a good figure. She was tall and slender and the cornflower-blue chiffon moulded it to perfection. She wore gold kid shoes which barely peeped from beneath the swirling skirt and the one piece of jewellery she possessed, a slender gold chain and locket her father had bought her when she went to university.

She was pleased with the way the girl had done her hair and as she picked up her evening bag and looked once more into the mirror she could hardly believe that the woman who stared back at her was Mary the librarian, and she smiled, thinking that her two assistants would hardly have recognised her.

She dawdled a little, she did not want to arrive in the foyer before Andrew in case Mrs Ralston was around but she need not have worried. Andrew was already there in the company of a crowd of others. When he saw her he went forward to greet her, and she was aware at once of the admiration in his eyes.

'I'll introduce you to my friends, Mary, and then we'll go in to dinner. We're not sitting with them.'

There seemed so many of them. Beautifully dressed women adorned with jewels and expensive furs, the men, like Andrew, in faultless evening dress. They greeted her with warmth tinged with curiosity, and one of them said, 'Now I see why somebody thought you were with Stella Brampton last Easter, you really do resemble her. Have you met Stella, Miss Styles?'

'Yes. But I don't know her very well.'

'Well we must get to know you after dinner, it really is too bad of Andrew to keep you hidden for so long.'

As Andrew escorted her to their table he said, 'Trust Daphne Carmel to see that you resemble Stella. They're not a bad crowd, Mary, no doubt we'll meet up with them again later in the evening.'

Meet up with them later they certainly did since Lady Carmel was determined to get to know Lord Alveston's companion and find out all she could about her.

There was no escape, particularly when Lord Carmel invited Mary to dance, and it was left to Andrew to dance with Daphne.

'She's quite charming, Andrew, and so very much like Stella, is that what drew you to her?'

'I don't think that question is quite worthy of you,' Andrew replied evenly.

'Well we're not going to eat her, so why hide her away?'

'I met her twelve months ago, she does not live in the area and I am with her now, does that answer your questions?'

'Darling Andrew, we're all very happy that you've found a charming woman to keep you company and we hope the happiness continues. Don't be so tetchy.'

The evening progressed and Mary was faced with other aspects of their curiosity.

'Where exactly do you live, my dear?' Daphne asked, smiling sweetly. 'Andrew says you're not a native of these parts.'

'No, I live in the West Midlands.'

'I knew some Styles who lived in Ludlow, in fact I was at school with Angela Styles. Her father bred Herefords and they lived in a very old country house. She told us Henry the Eighth had been a guest there at one time.'

'Do you hunt?' another woman asked her. 'But you ride, of course?'

Mary was tempted to tell them the story she'd told Andrew about the unfortunate episode with the donkey at Bognor, and catching Andrew's amused expression she knew that he was thinking about it also.

They were pleasant, she danced with the men and chatted with the women but they knew no more about her when they said goodnight than at the beginning of the evening.

Mrs Ralston did not enjoy her evening at the bridge table, there was too much going on on the dance floor and she was missing it all. She was glad when her partner rose to his feet at ten thirty to say, 'I'd better find my wife, she's not very pleased that I elected to play bridge at all tonight.'

She wasn't sorry. She'd had rotten cards all evening and she hadn't concentrated too well. The music coming from the ballroom was disturbing and she was anxious to know how Gerald was passing his time. She need not have worried. He had found a man who hated dancing, loved snooker, and preferred the bar to the ballroom.

When his mother appeared in the bar he excused himself to his new friend and went forward to meet her.

'We'll take a look in the ballroom, Gerald,' she said with a smile. 'I didn't play well tonight and the cards were terrible. We can find a seat in there and watch the dancing.'

From the doorway her bright eyes scanned the room and Gerald groaned inwardly. Mary and her escort sat with a party of other people in the far corner of the room, and she looked enchanting. He had never thought that she was strictly beautiful, though nice-looking and refined, but tonight she looked wonderful as she looked up at Lord Alveston with a tender gaze.

His mother said, 'Well, your Miss Styles is looking very charming, Gerald, she obviously knows all Lord Alveston's friends. I told you there was more to that than met the eye.

'That girl who was here with Mr Mansell is dancing with Mr de Roche. There's a lot more to that than calling herself his secretary, too.'

In the next breath there was an expression of amazement in her voice, 'Well really, Gerald, it's only twelve months since that girl's husband was killed and there she is with that young man who was here last year too, and quite obviously enjoying herself.'

Indeed for the first time in twelve months Debbie was coming alive.

Her parents were aware of the polite curiosity of many of the guests who had witnessed the trauma of twelve months ago, and the obvious interest of several young men who had studiously ignored the new young widow earlier in the holiday.

John Broadhurst thought his daughter rather foolish to be so obviously enjoying her evening in the company of a handsome young man who quite evidently was smitten with her. Her mother on the other hand was delighted. What had gone had gone forever, and here was Peter Cavendish, handsome, charming and well-heeled, he was also obviously adoring.

Dancing with his wife, Stuart witnessed the metamorphosis with a certain cynicism and reflection that he need not have worried. Debbie hadn't spoiled the holiday for them but there were other undercurrents not entirely to his liking.

Almost as if she read his thoughts his wife said evenly, 'Don't you think you should ask your secretary to dance, Stuart?'

'Which one, the old one or the new one?'

'The new one of course, the old one looks as though she can look after herself.'

'I rather think the new one won't be left behind in that respect,' he snapped tartly.

Maeve was standing near the doorway looking rather forlorn, he thought. She was wearing a long black skirt and a crimson silk blouse which suited her black hair and pretty face, which at that moment looked slightly bored.

She accepted his invitation to dance, responding to his questions on how she was enjoying herself with a distant smile.

'It was a surprise to see you here,' he said. 'You knew we would be here, of course?'

'Actually no, why should I, Mr Mansell?'

'Didn't you book the accommodation for me?'

'No. I would have remembered if I had.'

She had disclaimed all knowledge of it and he wasn't sure. Perhaps he should give her the benefit of the doubt.

'I suppose you've had a word with Alison?'

'I met her this morning in the village. She's obviously enjoying her work here. Actually I never knew her terribly well.'

'I never knew who Alison's cronies were.'

'Perhaps she never really had much time to mingle with the pool.' He stared at her sharply and with a sweet smile she said, 'She always seemed such a busy person, I expect I shall find out just how busy Alison was in the very near future.'

Was he supposed to read more into those words than was intended? He didn't know. All he was aware of was that this girl might be prepared to be available, on her terms.

'Are you alone, Maeve?' he asked her.

'Yes. The friend I was coming with couldn't make it and I had nothing else to do.'

'There are a few of us but you're very welcome to join us.'

'Thank you, Mr Mansell. If you don't mind I'll take a look around the ballroom for some friends of mine.'

The conversation going on at his table ceased abruptly on his arrival, and his wife turned towards him with a bright smile. 'I've got a surprise for you, Stuart, Alison Gray is engaged to be married to Mr de Roche.'

He stared at her in amazement. 'Who told you that?' he demanded.

'Geraldine heard it being discussed at the owner's table. They're drinking champagne over there and the good wishes were flying around. Look at them, they all look delighted.'

Anton de Roche sat with his arm round Alison's shoulders and the entire table seemed to have erupted into smiles and much laughter, at that moment Mr Van Hopper rose to his feet and walked to the centre of the room. The band struck up a chord to ask for silence so that the owner could address the assembly and Mr Van Hopper beaming said he was delighted to announce the engagement of Mr Anton de Roche to Miss Alison Gray, and holding out both his hands he called them into the centre of the room to receive the applause and congratulations of the guests.

He then invited the band to play a waltz and Alison and Anton danced the length of the ballroom before the other guests joined in.

Stuart was unable to analyse his feelings. He had loved Alison a very long time. At the back of his mind there had always been the idea that one day they would be together as man and wife, but somehow or other time had caught up with them.

The children, their education and the constituency. He still loved his wife, but being in love with her lay in the past. Alison had never understood that he loved her desperately but there were other things he needed to think about. She'd been self-centred.

Watching her dancing with Anton, the way he smiled down at her, the tenderness in her smile, the sheer joy of two people who had found each other at an age when they could be sure of their feelings riled him.

He was dancing with Geraldine and she was well aware of his pre-occupation. There had been something between Stuart and Alison Gray however much John told her she was imagining it. A woman's intuition about something like that was never wrong.

Stuart was reacting badly. Alison was an adventuress, she had played her cards well, and in any case what did she know about de Roche?

What was he, French, Spanish? Who were his family? Foreign men in the hotel industry were automatically suspect, besides he looked too suave by half. She was probably at the end of a very long line of women, and now he was courting respectability.

So Stuart's thoughts were running, but later in the evening when he congratulated the engaged couple his smile was entirely urbane, only Alison was aware of the tightness about his lips, Anton was unconcerned.

Mary Styles greeted them warmly, wishing them happiness and Alison whispered to her, 'I can't really believe it, Mary, I'm so happy.'

'And I'm happy for you,' Mary whispered. 'It seems like a hundred years since I drove you into Kendal to catch your train. Such an awful lot has happened in one year for both of us.'

'Heavens yes,' Alison agreed. 'Look at Debbie with stars in her eyes. I can't think that she's forgotten Tod so soon, look at me, and what about you, Mary, where exactly are you going?'

Mary smiled without answering, and at that moment Lady Carmel and Andrew danced by.

'He's awfully nice,' Alison murmured. 'How are you getting along with his friends?'

'They're being very kind.'

'Lady Carmel is a bit overpowering. Anton handles her beautifully but she does have a reputation for getting what she wants.'

'Are you trying to warn me about something, Alison?'

'I'm sure she doesn't want Lord Alveston, Mary, but she does keep a quite proprietory eye on all the men in what she thinks of as her crowd. I've seen her in action, Mary.'

Mary smiled. 'Then I'd better get back to them before she spirits him away.'

Daphne Carmel hadn't quite made up her mind about Mary. She was not the sort of woman she thought Andrew should be involved with, too much like Stella Brampton and nothing at all like Olivia. She considered her nice-looking, elegant and intelligent, but Andrew'd been fun in the old days.

They'd been a gay crowd and Olivia had fitted in beautifully at first. Of course she ran off the rails and caused an awful lot of problems, so many problems that Andrew'd gone off into the blue for years. When she'd heard he was back she had to see for herself if he was over Olivia. Obviously he was, but was Mary Styles capable of filling the gap she'd left?

He must have deliberately gone about selecting a woman totally opposite to Olivia with her strangely Eastern beauty and thirst for living.

Mary was invited to dance with all the men so that she seldom got the opportunity to dance with Andrew. When their eyes met he smiled at her before he was whisked away with yet another woman, and she began to wonder if Lady Carmel was engineering things to her own liking.

In the end it was Andrew who said adamantly, 'Look, I invited Mary to the dance and I've hardly spent a moment with her since we came into the ballroom. They're playing a waltz and I intend to dance this with her.'

'I'm sorry about this,' he whispered in her ear, 'now you know why I didn't want to eat dinner with them. We should have gone off on our own somewhere. Are you enjoying it, Mary?'

'Yes of course and they'll be your friends when I've gone off home,' she said.

'We'll think about that tomorrow, at any rate we won't let them intrude into the rest of Easter.'

Chapter Thirty-Nine

Andrew sat in the family pew with some members of his staff on Easter Sunday. The church was crowded and the sun shone through the stained glass windows on an array of spring flowers that the ladies of the village had spent all the day before in arranging.

He had asked Mary if she would like to join him there but she had said Mrs Harvey had asked her to join the service which was being held at the hotel. He thought he knew why she had declined.

Also in the church were several of his friends. Lady Carmel and her sister sat in the Carmel family pew and as they left the church they waited for him on the path.

'I'm so glad you're here,' Daphne said, smiling brightly. 'I'm giving a dinner party tomorrow evening and I do want to invite you and Mary. Not a very large party, Andrew,' she hastened to add when his face wore a doubtful expression.

'Well I'm not sure, Daphne, if the day is fine we promised ourselves a day in the Dales.'

'Andrew, it's dark early and the roads will be chock-a-block, you'll be glad to get back to unwind.'

When he still seemed doubtful she urged, 'My sister's going home on Tuesday morning. She's loved being with us and she's no idea when she'll be able to get back here. You know she's not very happy in her marriage, I thought of this as a nice little treat for her.'

'I'll speak to Mary this afternoon and telephone you, Daphne.'

'I've invited the Charlesworths and the Bairds, they both accepted immediately, honestly, Andrew, you do make it difficult for us.'

'I'll telephone you early this afternoon, Daphne,' he said with a smile, and she had to be content with that.

Mary would have preferred to spend the time alone with Andrew, but these were his friends, would be his friends after she had gone home, so she said she would be delighted to go.

She didn't mean it and he didn't believe her. They spent a lovely day driving through the rolling Yorkshire dales, wandering through ancient stone abbeys, eating hot buttered scones in a tiny cafe they found in a village in Wensleydale.

He deposited her at her hotel so that she could change for the dinner party, promising to pick her up at seven-thirty.

She chose the beige dress which she wore under her camel coat. The other women would be wearing furs but since she didn't possess any the camel coat would have to suffice.

The Carmels received them charmingly and they were ushered into the drawing room where Lord Carmel was busy handing round drinks. She had met Janice, Lady Carmel's sister and the other two couples at the dance so introductions were not necessary.

She thought about her tiny flat as she sat looking round the large beautiful room with its ornate ceiling and glass chandeliers and once again she asked herself what she was doing here. Andrew was in conversation with the Bairds, and sitting down beside her Lady Carmel's sister said, 'I believe you've been driving in the Dales?'

'Yes, we had a lovely afternoon.'

'My husband comes from Yorkshire, Richmond to be precise.'

Mary smiled.

'I was very much into horses as a girl and I met him at a hunt ball. His father was the hunt master and they were big in hunting circles in Yorkshire. We were married four months later.'

'It was quite a whirlwind romance then?'

'Too whirlwind, I'm afraid, four months later I was regretting it.'

'I'm sorry.'

'We go our own ways. We had nothing in common beyond horses, now we don't possess one, if I want to ride I have to borrow one.'

'Why is that?'

'Money, my dear. My father-in-law left us loads but my husband speculated unwisely and lost most of it.'

Mary looked at her companion who was wearing an expression of bitter resentment. She was surprised that an almost perfect stranger should be confiding in her and as if she guessed her thoughts Janice said sharply, 'It's a sort of bondage to be married to somebody you've fallen out of love with. Andrew knows what it's all about, you'll know all about that of course.'

'Only the little Andrew's told me.'

'Everybody was so enchanted with Olivia they couldn't see wood for trees. She was beautiful. I have to say that she lit up the party scene like nobody else. She was witty and charming and the men fell like ninepins for her. I thought she was a trollop.'

Mary stared at her in stunned surprise.

'I knew she was having affairs, she had a pretty long-standing one with my husband, but she covered her tracks pretty well, in those days nobody would have had a wrong word said about Olivia.'

'Did Andrew know?'

'I'd say he was the last person to find out. The entire county was stunned by her death, I got drunk to celebrate it. Here we are I think, dinner is served.'

She felt bemused by her conversation with Janice, but over dinner she was to receive a rather different version of Olivia from Janice's sister.

'I'm so glad Andrew is getting over the tragedy,' she confided. 'They seemed so right for each other, they were both such beautiful people, and they had so much in common, horses and country pursuits. She looked so right in that beautiful house, nobody could believe what happened at the end.'

Mary was sure the meal was beautifully cooked and served but it tasted of nothing at all. Lady Carmel was telling her in the nicest possible way that she was wrong for Andrew. They had nothing in common and in all probability he was still under the spell of Olivia.

She had little to contribute to the conversation but the other women more than made up for her. They were all old friends, they'd gone to parties together, hunt balls and wedding receptions, they'd hunted together and shown their dogs at the same shows, they lived in the same kind of houses and bought their clothes from the same salons. Halfway through the evening she had a sudden longing for her little flat and the normality of her job at the local library.

Andrew was puzzled by her air of detachment, and her silence on the way back to The Lakes.

'Tired?' he asked her gently.

'A little.'

'Didn't you enjoy the dinner party, Mary?'

'Yes of course, it was nice of them to invite me.'

'But you didn't really enjoy it, did you, Mary?'

'Well it's just that I don't know them very well. They talk about things and people I've never heard of. I can't expect them to talk about things and people I know, but it's difficult to take part in their conversation.'

'I know. I would have preferred not to go.'

'But they're your friends, Andrew, you should go.'

There was one full day left and she was worried about them. She wanted to be with him, she didn't want to love him, but it was too late for that, she did love him, and it was doomed just as her feelings for Gerald had been doomed.

He was saying, 'We must decide how we're going to spend the next two days, Mary, fortunately we shall be on our own, I prefer it that way.'

Of course he did. She wasn't their sort, it was only with them that he faced the difference in their lifestyles.

At the hotel doorway he held her hand in his as he looked down at her. She looked tired, the evening had been a strain, and he bent forward and gently kissed her.

'Sleep well Mary, tomorrow we'll drive over to Wastwater, you'll love its grandeur, it's a lake totally unlike any of the others.'

The first person she met when she crossed the foyer was Gerald Ralston and he paused to speak to her.

'Enjoy your evening?' he asked.

'Yes thank you, we've been out to dinner with some of Andrew's friends.'

'Very nice.'

'Is your mother playing bridge?'

'No, she had a bit of a headache and went to bed early. When are you leaving?'

'Wednesday morning.'

'We're off early tomorrow. Will you come back, do you think?'

'I really don't know, Gerald, will you?'

'Yes if my mother has anything to do with it, I'm not so sure about myself.'

'But this is the hotel you raved about, Gerald, the most beautiful hotel you'd ever stayed in. Has it suddenly lost its enchantment?'

'Not really. Perhaps it's just lost it for me. Would you like a drink? I was just going to have one myself.'

'Thank you, Gerald, a medium sherry please.'

Over their drinks they discovered some of their old camaraderie. They talked about books, their jobs, even his evenings at his golf club. He did not speak to her about his mother and she did not mention Andrew.

Gerald Ralston lived in her world but now she liked him, she could never love him again. Never for a moment did she think her times with Andrew would last, but she was grateful to him for releasing her from her feelings for Gerald that had been going nowhere.

He wanted to ask her questions, intimate questions about Andrew Alveston, if she would see him again, if there was a future for them but they were questions he could never ask. So he talked about trivialities and all Mary heard was his voice, not his words, and she looked at his face thinking, this is the man I thought I was in love with. He was responsible for my being here and he let me down very badly. It is because of Gerald that I met Andrew, and now I'm to be hurt a second time.

He was staring at her strangely, then he said, 'Mary, you haven't heard a single word I've been saying.'

'No. I'm sorry, I was thinking of something else. What did you say?'

'It doesn't matter, it isn't important. It's late, we're the only two people in the bar.'

She looked around her. The bar tenders had dimmed the lights and two waiters were moving the glasses from nearby tables.

314

She smiled. 'I think they're telling us they want to close up for the night. Heavens, it's after two o'clock, I'd no idea it was so late.'

They walked together to the lifts and Mary asked, 'Which floor are you on?'

'The top one, I'm afraid. My mother was late booking, it was all they had left.'

They got into the lift and Gerald asked, 'The first floor, Mary?'

'Yes please.'

She turned to smile and bid him goodnight as she stepped out of the lift.

She switched on the bedside lights and went to draw back the curtains. A light mist covered the lake shrouding the gardens, through which the moonlight came fitfully. She shivered a little, then drawing the curtains she went into the bathroom.

It seemed that all around her there was a strange eerie stillness, the stillness of a silent world, a world filled with people who came and went into their separate lives. Some would arrange to meet again, some would pass like ships in the night, some would leave memories that would last forever, others would pass into limbo.

She switched off the light and lay staring up into the darkness. There was one more day before she returned to her home and her job, one day to acquire memories that would illuminate more mundane days.

Further along the corridor another guest lay wakeful before with a muttered curse he got out of bed and padded over to the window.

He was longing for a cigarette but Sybil could smell tobacco smoke a mile off. He didn't want to wake her by putting the light on so he pulled back the curtains a few inches to let in the moonlight.

Stuart Mansell reflected that in other years when he had holidayed with his wife and family he had never given Alison much thought. She'd be with friends, visiting her parents, at home in her flat, and longing for his holiday to be over so that she would see him again. Now she was asleep somewhere in this hotel, and probably in the arms of the man she expected to marry.

Of course they'd be in the middle of an affair, he never doubted it, but whereas de Roche was a free agent, he himself had had encumbrances. No, that wasn't quite right, that was unfair. He'd had other things to think about.

Women were the very devil. How long did it take them to get over somebody they'd professed to love? Alison had been over him in less than a year, and there was that young Debbie starry-eyed about a chap in the same hotel where her husband of a few days had gone out to his death. It didn't make sense.

His wife stirred. The moonlight fell across the bed and she sat up saying, 'Stuart, are you awake? I thought you'd drawn the curtains.'

She switched on the bedside light and stared across the room to where he sat in the chair. 'Can't you sleep?' she asked him.

'No. I shouldn't have had that lobster for dinner.'

'It was beautiful, I had it and it hasn't had any effect on me.'

'Go back to sleep, I'll be fine if I just sit here for a few minutes.'

'Shall I make you a cup of tea?'

'No. Don't fuss, Sybil.'

With a resigned sigh she switched off the light and settled down among the pillows.

His thoughts turned to Maeve McNamara. He felt pretty sure she'd known he was coming to The Lakes for Easter and he realised he was going to have to be very careful where she was concerned. Alison hadn't liked her, she'd gone as far as to warn him against her but he'd thought it was simply jealousy because she was pretty and taking her place, now he thought he should have taken notice of her warning.

Other M.P.s had put their career on the line for women they'd become involved with, Alison had been more than patient but even Alison had been getting restless. Perhaps Sybil should spend more time in London, the children were off her hands and her parents had been encouraging her for years not to leave him alone too long.

He felt his way to the tea trolley, poured some water into a glass and added a stiff supply of whisky. Perhaps he'd sleep now.

In the room next door Geraldine Broadhurst lay on her back staring up at the ceiling. In the other bed her husband slept peacefully. She was thinking about Debbie.

Their daughter had spent a wonderful evening in the company of Peter Cavendish, she had not looked so alive for months. Of course it was natural that she should have grieved over Tod, but it hadn't been a normal sort of grieving, there'd been few tears, only a deep resentment on her pretty face.

Tonight she'd witnessed the old Debbie emerging, the beautiful girl they'd always been so proud of, with shining eyes and laughter on her lips. Peter Cavendish had been responsible for that, but it was too soon.

Debbie would want them to invite him to their home, she'd read the signs well when Debbie'd talked about her horse and that he'd have no difficulty in borrowing one from the pony club so that they could ride together.

How could they possibly invite him when the Hanleys lived in the same town and they would be furious that their beloved son had been replaced so quickly in his wife's affections.

If she wanted to spend time with Peter let her go to his home, let her go anywhere with him but not in the town where Tod had been some sort of idol among the younger element, and particularly since they'd given Debbie such a hard time since his death.

She'd liked Tod in spite of his brashness, his exaggerated confidence, and how Debbie had wanted him. Peter was different, gentler, more considerate, but it was still too soon.

In her room on the floor above Debbie slept like a baby, a smile on her lips, her heart untroubled.

By morning the early mist had lifted and a pale sun shone out of a clear blue sky. Andrew picked Mary up soon after breakfast and they drove west towards Wastwater.

'You'll be amazed at the difference,' Andrew said. 'One gets accustomed to gentle beautiful lakes and lush green islands. You'll find Wastwater lonely and grand. There is only one road along the lake because across it the screes come right down to the water, and often the lake is dark because of the mountains surrounding it. Today you'll be seeing it at its best.'

'Isn't it near Wastwater where Debbie Hanley's husband died?'

'Sadly yes. They were attempting to climb Scafell Pike in very unsuitable weather. One should have great respect for the mountains, I think.'

Later that morning they sat on a stone wall overlooking the long emerald lake which seemed to turn dark indigo under the sloping screes. Occasionally a gleam of veiled sunlight lit up the fells and Mary looked at the high fells and the mountains at the head of the lake.

'Which one is Scafell Pike?' she asked.

Andrew pointed to the range saying, 'That is Gable, that Pillar, that is Scafell. They look very benign on a morning like this one but on that wretched day with the mist swirling across the lake and the rain pelting down they must have seemed too formidable to ever think they could be climbed.'

'Have you ever climbed, Andrew?'

'Yes. I've climbed most of them, and Helvellyn, but I did some climbing in Switzerland and in the Himalayas.'

His face was reflective and she thought it wise not to ask any more questions.

Andrew himself supplied the answers. 'When I was young we climbed because it was adventurous and I loved it, in the Himalayas I climbed because it was another way of forgetting, it helped, I think.'

Across the great pyramid of Yewbarrow the sunlight shone in sharp contrast to the dark grey screes and the deep-green water into which they seemed to plunge and suddenly the entire valley was filled with a powerful presence.

Mary thought about the other lakes she had seen, more beautiful lakes dotted with lush wooded islands, where stately trees dipped their branches into the water, and stolid lakeland cattle stood dreaming in the shallows. Today on those lakes pleasure craft of all kinds would be bobbing upon the water, but not here, not this lake possessed of a weird primeval beauty.

Andrew pulled her to her feet saying, 'Shall we drive on, Mary? We'll drive north towards the firth and get something to eat at a very nice hotel I know there.'

As they drove back in the early evening Mary knew she would remember this day for the rest of her life. The easy camaraderie they had shared, the sunshine, and the memory of that dark beautiful lake and the mountains towering above it.

The hotel dining room was half empty that evening. Most of the guests had left and this was her last evening with Andrew, as if he read her thoughts he said, 'What time are you leaving in the morning, Mary?'

'After breakfast I think.'

'Then please drive up to The Hall and have lunch with me, take another look at the puppy, he'll give you an ecstatic welcome I'm sure.'

'Thank you, Andrew, I should like that.'

How impersonal it all seemed. She looked around the room. The Ralstons had already left and the Mansells were dining alone. The Harveys were leaving in the morning and she had not seen anything of Alison.

It was over, she was ready to leave.

'I wonder how many of the guests will keep their friendships alive when they have left here,' she murmured, then wished immediately that she hadn't said it.

He didn't answer and she stared at him doubtfully.

She loved him, his smile, the charm of his voice, his dark hair silvered at his temples and the way his grey eyes darkened with laughter. She didn't want to love him. It had been charming, but all they had really had was seven days, three last Easter and four this. It was not enough to encourage her to expect more.

She was glad she was going home. To her poky little flat and her job at the library. To the old man who came in out of the rain to read the morning newspapers, the old ladies who grumbled when they couldn't find their favourite books, and the constant chatter of her two assistants. That was normality, this was fairytale.

Chapter Forty

Gerald locked the garage door behind him and walked towards the house. The long evening stretched ahead of him and throughout the journey his mother had not been in a good mood. For one thing the holiday had not come up to expectations. Her bedroom at the back of the hotel on the second floor, her bridge partners who had been nondescript, not really the types she could dine out on.

The questions had started as soon as they left the hotel.

'When is Miss Styles leaving?'

'I believe in the morning, Mother.'

'We didn't see her at all yesterday. I expect she was up at The Hall and I do think it's very silly to stay at a place like The Lakes and spend all one's time dining out. Such a waste of money, although I don't suppose that bothers Lord Alveston.'

When he entered the house he heard her pottering around the kitchen and the luggage lay where he had left it in the hall.

'I'm making tea,' she called to him. 'Do you want anything to eat?'

'No thank you, if I'm hungry I'll have something later.'

He went into the living room and turned on the gas fire, when his mother appeared several minutes later pushing a tea trolley he quickly realised that there was more to come.

'I do think it was quite disgusting of that young Mrs Hanley to flaunt her new boyfriend so soon after her husband's death, and in the same hotel where they spent their honeymoon. Don't you think so, Gerald?'

'That young man was staying in the hotel last year, I rather think she's known him for some time.'

'Even so. A little more discretion wouldn't have come amiss. Wasn't that the Broadhursts' car that passed us on the road?'

'I don't know. I was concentrating on my driving.'

'I'm sure it was, I'm not sure if the girl was with them or not.'

She handed him his cup of tea and sat down near the fire.

'I suppose Mr de Roche and that girl will be married in the summer. That should make a difference to his popularity.'

'What do you mean by that?'

'Well he's very handsome and the women do seem to find him fascinating, particularly women like that actress who was there last Easter. When they know he's married some of the glamour will go, I'm sure.'

'I doubt it, Mother. He will have a very beautiful wife and I've never seen him show any interest in any of the women guests beyond politeness.'

'Well of course you wouldn't notice, men never do. I suppose Miss Styles will be back at her desk on Friday, I would really like to know if that friendship is going anywhere.'

Gerald picked up the evening paper and started to read.

Mrs Ralston would have been gratified to hear the conversation taking place at the Broadhursts' house, since the gist of it mirrored her own feelings.

Geraldine was going on about Peter.

'I don't mind you going to his parents' house in the summer, Debbie, but I really don't think we can invite him to visit us just yet. What do you think, John?'

'I'll admit it's a bit too soon.'

'I haven't asked him here, Mummy. His parents are going to Bermuda in a week or two, but I've told Peter I'll go there for a visit when they return home.'

'Well that does seem more sensible, darling, and nobody in this town will know anything about it.

'Mother, I'm sure the Hanleys are not expecting me to be on my own forever.'

Her father's tone was more adamant. 'I'm sure they're not, Debbie, but if the boot had been on the other foot and it had been you and not Tod, I'd have felt a bit aggrieved if he'd brought another girl into the neighbourhood twelve months later.'

'I wonder why the Mansells didn't leave with us,' Geraldine said. 'Did you know they were staying another night?'

'He did mention it. We must have got our wires crossed somewhere, he thought we were leaving in the morning too.'

'Well I told Sybil. That new secretary of his left when we did.'

'What has that got to do with it?'

'Well nothing, but you have to admit he was none too comfortable with the situation.'

Stuart Mansell was waiting for the lift that Alison stepped out of and there was no way they could avoid each other.

Alison smiled. 'You're off in the morning, Stuart,' she said.

'Yes. Our friends have already left, we'll get off immediately after breakfast.'

'Have you enjoyed your stay?'

'Very much. Sybil likes the place but I'm ready for a change.'

'I may not see you before you leave, have a good journey.'

He nodded and turned away, then he seemed to recollect something and turned back. 'Alison, I do wish you and de Roche every happiness you know.'

'Thank you, Stuart.'

'You don't think it's a bit too soon?'

'After what?'

'Well you haven't really known him that long.'

'No that's true, but I'm a big girl, Stuart, I've had a lot of growing up to do and some of it has been difficult. Not everybody gets a second chance of happiness. I love Anton, there is no way I can let my second chance pass me by.'

She smiled at him again and walked into the foyer.

She had meant every word of it but even so their encounter had unnerved her. She was glad he was leaving in the morning, he belonged to the past, only the future was important.

It was almost midnight and Mary had finished her packing. She looked round the lofty beautiful room and wished she felt sleepy. She had a good three hours' drive in front of her the next day and thought that perhaps she should not have agreed to lunch with Andrew.

I'm simply prolonging the agony, she told herself with a bitter smile, but this would be another memory she could live with when everything else was over.

She pulled the drapes back from the window and stood looking through the glass. There was no moonlight and few lights from the village across the water. She could dimly see the white shape of the boat through the trees and she started back as a faint rumble of thunder echoed in the stillness.

The weather was changing.

She had packed her book so she put on the radio and sat in the easy chair to listen to it. It was several hours later when she awoke feeling stiff and cold and she was glad to get into bed where she fell asleep almost immediately.

Alison made a point of walking to her car with her the next morning.

'When shall we see you again?' she asked.

'I really don't know. Will you please say goodbye to the Harveys for me, tell them I had to leave early.'

'Are you going straight home?'

'I'm having lunch with Andrew which might be a mistake. I do need to get off fairly early, I have quite a long drive.'

Alison was looking at her too intently and she could feel the warm colour rising into her face. 'You like him very much, don't you, Mary?' Alison said.

Mary nodded, unable to trust her voice, and Alison said gently, 'He likes you too, Mary, I know he does. I don't think either of you should wait too long.'

Mary smiled and got into her car. There was no answer.

It was dark when Mary let herself into her flat and she was immediately aware of the difference between her humble abode and Andrew's ancestral home.

Lunch with him had been a pleasant affair and yet underneath their conversation and its normality there had been an undercurrent she couldn't define. As she drove home she realised they had talked banalities, the banality of two people who were going their separate ways with no strings and no come-backs.

Andrew had kissed her briefly and held her close. The puppy had been decidedly more affectionate. He had presented her with a huge box of chocolates and an equally impressive bunch of carnations and she had thanked him nicely for his generosity, then she had been driving through the gates of Alveston Hall in something of a daze.

That was it then. Waiting for her was the rest of her life.

Andrew spent the rest of the afternoon walking with his labrador across the fell. The mist had come down and it had started to rain, the first shower since before Easter, and it matched exactly the strange melancholy of his mood.

'Has the young lady gone home?' Mrs Stokes asked Grant after he had served Andrew with dinner.

'Yes, after luncheon.'

'Will he miss her, do you think?'

'He doesn't seem too happy this evening, it's too soon to tell.'

Later that evening Andrew accepted an invitation to dinner from Daphne Carmel.

'I thought you'd be feeling a little lonely now that Mary's left,' she said. 'There'll be eight of us, seven-thirty, darling.'

It was the first evening of many and there was usually a spare woman invited to sit next to him. They were all of a pattern these women. He'd known them for many years, they were either unmarried, experiencing matrimonial problems or married to men who for one reason or another were absent from the matrimonial home.

The Lakes was a constant venue for them, and from the sidelines Alison watched with interest.

Daphne Carmel was making sure that Andrew was on a merry-go-round that never stopped. He'd been on his own long enough, it was up to her to look around and find him a suitable second wife. He was proving very difficult.

She only invited attractive women, worldly women from his own walk of life, women that rode and hunted, knew the people he knew, and enjoyed the pursuits he enjoyed. Of course they had liked Mary, but she hadn't exactly been one of them, a woman like Mary could be guaranteed to take Andrew away from their circle.

Andrew had to admit to himself that he was bored.

The women talked about their horses and their husbands if they had any. Most of them complained bitterly that their husbands neglected them, that if they had their time to come over again they would never ever marry a man who was in the services, a politician or a man too involved with managing his estate.

They never spoke of Olivia and for that he was grateful.

It was one evening when they were dining at The Lakes that Daphne Carmel informed them that Anton de Roche was marrying his fiance in the autumn and another woman expressed her surprise.

'I understood they would be getting married in January so that they could spend all February overseas,' she said.

'I shouldn't think there'll be any problem,' Daphne said, 'they must be able to find a stand-in for him from all the hotels the Van Hoppers own in the world.'

On Sunday morning Andrew met Alison leaving the church and he paused to speak to her. There was such an air of happiness about her he felt forced to say, 'I believe you have decided to get married in the autumn instead of the winter.'

She nodded. 'Yes. My family want me to get married from our home in the south and in January the weather could be unpredictable.'

'Particularly in these parts,' Andrew agreed.

'I haven't really been close to my family for a good few years, I have an awful lot to make up to them for and they're so happy for us.'

'But you're both staying on here at The Lakes?'

'Yes of course. We love it here and I don't think the place would be the same without Anton.'

Andrew smiled. 'No, he does afford The Lakes a certain ambience. He would be sorely missed.'

'We're seeing you there quite often, Lord Alveston.'

'Yes. Lady Carmel has taken me under her wing. She deplores my solitary state.'

'I've been very lucky. We don't all get a second chance, Anton is mine. I wasn't looking for anybody when I came here, and honestly I don't think friends can find anybody for you. I don't think they should try.'

He smiled, and Alison said quickly, 'Oh dear, I shouldn't have said that, please forgive me.'

'No, you were right. Watching them try affords me a certain wry amusement, but I have to confess the amusement is wearing a little thin.'

He smiled again and left her.

She could never have asked him about Mary, it was none of her business, but they'd looked so right together. What a pity if he let the substance go for the shadow.

Anton and Alison departed for the home of Alison's family in late September with everybody's good wishes ringing in their ears and Andrew decided to visit his mother.

They'd been apart so long he found it difficult to pick up their old closeness. She was concerned about his solitary state in that great big house, but Andrew was quick to say that he was surrounded by good and faithful servants and had a bevy of friends he could rely on.

'Which friends?' she asked curiously.

'The old crowd, you know them all, Mother.'

'And I suppose they're trotting out every woman who happens to be on her own for your inspection.'

He laughed. 'Something like that.'

'And has there been anyone?'

'You know the old crowd, Mother. We're a generation older, most of the women I meet are either looking for a second husband or have problems with their first one.'

'Daphne Carmel is a flibbertygibbet, I've always thought so. Has there been anyone, Andrew?'

'You'll be the first to know, Mother, when there is.'

She had to be content with that, and wisely asked no more questions during the rest of their time together.

He had been home several days when Lady Carmel telephoned, her voice was plaintive.

'Andrew, you didn't tell me you were going away, where have you been?'

He smiled to himself thinking that Grant had been discreet in not telling her where he was.

'I've been to see my mother.'

'How nice. How is Lady Alveston?'

'Very well.'

'And now that you're home when are you coming for dinner? I thought next Saturday?'

'Actually, Daphne, I'm thinking of going away again for a few days, London perhaps.'

'London! Why for heaven's sake, the hunting season will soon be starting and London can be so dreary at this time of the year.'

'Oh I don't know. I can stay at my club, take in a few shows. I enjoyed it the last time I was there.'

'Really, Andrew, I thought I could rely on you. My sister has finally thrown in her lot and left him, she's staying with me, I thought we might be able to cheer her up a little.'

'Sorry, Daphne, I'll be in touch when I get back.'

He hadn't even thought of going away again until he heard her voice on the telephone, now he'd have to go. He stood staring out of the window that looked out over the fells and the deer grazing quietly under the trees.

Jet the spaniel brought him a soft ball which he picked up absent-mindedly and tossed across the room. The dog rushed to find it and he patted his head reflecting that he was now fully grown. Mary would see the difference when she saw him again . . .

Mary! He'd thought of her over the passing months since she'd returned home and there had been many times when he'd been part of his crowd when her gentle presence had seemed very near. He would see her smile, hear the soft tone of her voice, sense the calm uncluttered serenity of her presence before somebody dragged him out onto the dance floor.

He made up his mind suddenly. He would leave the house in the morning but he wouldn't go to London. He'd drive into Shropshire.

The traffic was light on that cold early November day and it had started to rain soon after he left the house. Strong gusts of wind swept through the trees and the lake seemed like a heaving mass of grey as he drove along its shores.

It was late afternoon when he drove into the square in front of the library and other civic buildings, with the lights from office windows shining eerily through the gloom. Occasionally a bus lumbered through the rain its head-lights lighting up the puddles that stretched across the square.

He sat for several minutes looking up at the façade of the library. Suppose she wasn't there, suppose she'd left, moved away, made it up with that chap who'd hurt her. He had to know. The rain met him with its full force when he stepped outside the car and his feet splashed through the puddles in the square as he ran to the library steps.

Through the glass windows in the outer hall he could see into the library. One of the assistants was stacking books onto a shelf, there was no sign of the other one but a little queue stood at the desk waiting to have their books stamped.

The other assistant came from behind one of the shelves and took her place at the desk but he couldn't see Mary and his heart sank. An old man seemed to be arguing with the girl, then pointing to a seat she indicated that he should sit down and she went away, returning in a few moments with Mary and his heart lifted.

She was speaking to the old man while the girl attended to the rest of them. He appeared to be distressed about something and she was talking to him gently.

She hadn't changed. Her soft brown hair framed her face, an unremarkable face really, but there was a sweetness about it, marked with the lines of

325

brows, the dark smudges of lashes, the gently smiling mouth and the sheer normality of one human being endeavouring to pacify another. He could not disturb her at the library, she wouldn't know what to say, they wouldn't know how to act so he turned away and went down the steps into the rain.

The library would be closing in a few minutes so he decided quickly to drive the short distance to her flat and wait for her there. On such a night surely she would be glad to go home.

The small garden outside the flats had a dejected air but there were lights in some of the windows and he had no difficulty in finding somewhere to park. A woman parking nearby stared at him curiously before she hurried away towards the flats.

It could only have been a very short time but it felt like hours. Every car that came along the road he felt must be hers and when it passed the gate his heart sank yet again. From somewhere nearby he heard the chiming of a church bell, six o'clock. The library would have closed, she must be on her way.

Waiting for her gave him time to think about his life. His self-indulgence in running away, in thinking that it would erase every sordid memory and the knowledge that in the end he had to come back and face it.

And the last few months with the old crowd. His mother had been predictably scathing in her views of them. They had been the ones who had taken Olivia to their hearts, even when they had expressed horror at the way her life had ended. His mother would like Mary. She would compare her to Stella whom she had always been fond of.

Daphne Carmel and her friends had said they liked Mary, but she hadn't been one of them, could never be one of them, and although he had listened to them with some amusement their views had never counted with him. He didn't want Mary to be one of them, he wanted her sanity and her intrinsic decency.

It was strange that it had been Alison Gray's words that had brought him to his senses. A second chance she had said. A new world to build on and he had been content to let it slip through his fingers. He'd allowed her to leave Alveston with a swift embrace and smiling farewell and then had followed the merry-go-round that never stopped.

A man knew when a woman liked him, more than liked him, and he'd been well aware that Mary felt something for him, the gentle blushes, the tender smiles, the eagerness to please him. With Mary he had discovered realities and some of the old values he had thought he'd lost forever. He thought about the loneliness of those years when he had seemed to be suspended between heaven and earth in a cold grey world from which there was no escape.

There had been nothing left of the world he had known. Everything he had known and loved had retreated into the outer distances beyond regaining, and

326

he had been lost and wandering, adrift in a strange outer fringe of dark swirling mists that would never lift. And now it seemed there was another chance to recapture life in all its poignant clarity.

His heart raced at the sight of the small familiar car coming through the gateway and he watched while she brought it to rest in what must be her parking space. She left the car and locked it, and she appeared to be carrying a shopping bag so that she seemed to be having difficulty in opening her umbrella as she hurried towards the front door.

He left his car and ran towards her calling, 'Mary, Mary,' and his voice was lost on the wind, it was only when she reached down for her shopping bag that he took it from her and she looked up in amazement.

'Come inside,' he said quickly. 'You're getting wet through out here.'

He pushed the door open and gently guided her through it, then he put her bag down on the floor and reached out for her.

The feel of her damp body in his arms, the top of her damp hair against his cheek was an enchantment he could never have believed, and he could feel her heart pounding deep beneath her clothes, then he was kissing her eyes, her mouth, her temples and Mary could hardly believe that it was Andrew's voice saying, 'Mary, I've found you, I love you, I'll never let you leave me again.'

After a while she looked up at him with wide questioning eyes, 'Andrew, I don't understand, I thought I'd never see you again.'

'I know, I'm sorry I've been such a fool, I should never have let you go out of my life, I think I must have hurt you terribly.'

His words brought back to her the misery of her journey home after their last meeting for the mark of the hours she had spent since she had left him had cut deeply, the wounds were raw and the memory of pain came through her happiness and she did not think she could bear to be hurt again, so that once again she murmured, 'Andrew, I don't understand.'

'Mary, I love you, I'm sorry it's taken me so long to realise it, I want you to marry me, please say you will.'

'But we've had so little time together, why me, there must be other women more suitable?'

He shook his head impatiently, 'Mary, please you must stop thinking about the differences, think only of how we are together, our joy at being together, the good things we have in common. There are no other women I want to marry, there are no other women in my life. Will you marry me, Mary?'

'Marry you! When?'

'As soon as possible.'

She couldn't think straight. There was her home, her job, her way of life but the deep tenderness of his kiss reawakened her heart, dispelling all clouds and hurts and fears. She belonged to Andrew now and for ever and the singing within her was so loud and joyous that it all but quelled the little unease that was left.